I0577165

Luise Mühlbach, Chapman Coleman

Frederick the Great and his Court

An historical romance - Vol. 1

Luise Mühlbach, Chapman Coleman

Frederick the Great and his Court
An historical romance - Vol. 1

ISBN/EAN: 9783337351045

Printed in Europe, USA, Canada, Australia, Japan

Cover: Foto ©Andreas Hilbeck / pixelio.de

More available books at **www.hansebooks.com**

FREDERICK THE GREAT AND HIS COURT.

AN HISTORICAL ROMANCE.

BY

L. MÜHLBACH,

AUTHOR OF "JOSEPH II. AND HIS COURT."

TRANSLATED FROM THE GERMAN, BY

MRS. CHAPMAN COLEMAN AND HER DAUGHTERS.

NEW YORK:

D. APPLETON AND COMPANY,

443 & 445 BROADWAY.

1867.

ENTERED, according to Act of Congress, in the year 1866, by

D. APPLETON & CO.,

In the Clerk's Office of the District Court of the United States for the
Southern District of New York.

CONTENTS.

BOOK I.

BOOK II.

BOOK III.

FREDERICK THE GREAT AND HIS COURT.

BOOK I.

CHAPTER I.

THE QUEEN SOPHIA DOROTHEA.

THE palace glittered with light and splendor; the servants ran here and there, arranging the sofas and chairs; the court gardener cast a searching glance at the groups of flowers which he had placed in the saloons; and the major domo superintended the tables in the picture gallery. The guests of the queen will enjoy to-night a rich and costly feast. Every thing wore the gay and festive appearance which, in the good old times, the king's palace in Berlin had been wont to exhibit. Jesting and merry-making were the order of the day, and even the busy servants were good-humored and smiling, knowing that this evening there was no danger of blows and kicks, of fierce threats and trembling terror. Happily the king could not appear at this ball, which he had commanded Sophia to give to the court and nobility of Berlin.

The king was ill, the gout chained him to his chamber, and, during the last few sleepless nights a presentiment weighed upon the spirit of the ruler of Prussia. He felt that the reign of Frederick the First would soon be at an end;

1

that the doors of his royal vault would soon open to receive a kingly corpse, and a new king would mount the throne of Prussia.

This last thought filled the heart of the king with rage and bitterness. Frederick William would not die! he would not that his son should reign in his stead; that this weak, riotous youth, this dreamer, surrounded in Rheinsberg with poets and musicians, sowing flowers and composing ballads, should take the place which Frederick the First had filled so many years with glory and great results.

Prussia had no need of this sentimental boy, this hero of fashion, who adorned himself like a French fop, and preferred the life of a sybarite, in his romantic castle, to the battle-field and the night-parade; who found the tones of his flute sweeter than the sounds of trumpets and drums; who declared that there were not only kings by "the grace of God, but kings by the power of genius and intellect, and that Voltaire was as great a king—yes, greater than all the kings anointed by the Pope!" What use has Prussia for such a sovereign? No, Frederick William would not, could not die! His son should not reign in Prussia, destroying what his father had built up! Never should Prussia fall into the hands of a dreaming poet! The king was resolved, therefore, that no one should know he was ill; no one should believe that he had any disease but gout; this was insignificant, never fatal. A man can live to be eighty years old with the gout; it is like a faithful wife, who lives with us even to old age, and with whom we can celebrate a golden wedding. The king confessed to himself that he was once more clasped in her tender embraces, but the people and the prince should not hope that his life was threatened.

For this reason should Sophia give a ball, and the world should see that the queen and her daughters were gay and happy.

The queen was indeed really gay to-day; she was free. It seemed as if the chains which bound her had fallen apart, and the yoke to which she had bowed her royal neck was removed. To-day she was at liberty to raise her head proudly, like a queen, to adorn herself with royal apparel. Away, for to-day at least, with sober robes and simple coiffure. The king was fastened to his arm-chair, and Sophia dared once more to make a glittering and queenly toilet. With a smile of proud satisfaction, she arrayed herself in a silken robe, embroidered in silver, which she had secretly ordered for the ball from her native Hanover. Her eyes beamed with joy, as she at last opened the silver-bound casket, and released from their imprisonment for a few hours these costly brilliants, which for many years had not seen the light. With a smiling glance her eyes rested upon the glittering stones, which sparkled and flamed like falling stars, and her heart beat high with delight. For a queen is still a woman, and Sophia Dorothea had so often suffered the pains and sorrows of woman, that she longed once more to experience the proud happiness of a queen. She resolved to wear all her jewels; fastened, herself, the sparkling diadem upon her brow, clasped upon her neck and arms the splendid brilliants, and adorned her ears with the long pendants; then stepping to the Venetian mirror, she examined herself critically. Yes, Sophia had reason to be pleased; hers was a queenly toilet. She looked in the glass, and thought on bygone days, on buried hopes and vanished dreams. These diamonds her exalted father had given when she was betrothed to Frederick William. This diadem had adorned her brow when she married. The necklace her brother had sent at the birth of her first child; the bracelet her husband had clasped upon her arm when at last, after long waiting, and many prayers, Prince Frederick was born. Each of these jewels was a proud memento of the past, a star of her youth. Alas, the diamonds had retained their brilliancy; they were still stars, but all else was vanished or dead—her youth and her dreams, her hopes and her love! Sophia had so often trembled before her husband, that she no longer loved him. With her, " perfect love had not cast out fear." Fear had extinguished love. How could she love a man who had been only a tyrant and a despot to her and to her children? who had broken their wills, cut off their hopes, and trodden under foot, not only the queen, but the mother. As Sophia looked at the superb bracelet, the same age of her darling, she thought how unlike the glitter and splendor of these gems his life had been; how dark and sad his youth; how colorless and full of tears. She kissed the bracelet, and wafted her greeting to her absent son. Suddenly the door opened, and the Princesses Ulrica and Amelia entered.

The queen turned to them, and the sad expression vanished from her features as her eyes rested upon the lovely and loving faces of her daughters.

" Oh, how splendid you look, gracious mamma!" exclaimed the Princess Amelia, as she danced gayly around her mother. " Heaven with all its stars has fallen around you, but your sweet face shines out amongst them like the sun in his glory."

" Flatterer," said the queen, " if your father heard you, he would scold fearfully. If you compare me to the sun, how can you describe him?"

" Well, he is Phœbus, who harnesses the sun and points out his path."

" True, indeed," said the queen, " he appoints his path. Poor sun!—poor queen!—she has not the right to send one ray where she will!"

" Who, notwithstanding, assumes the right, gracious mamma," said Amelia, smiling, and pointing to the diadem, "for I imagine that our most royal king and father has not commanded you to appear in those splendid jewels."

"Commanded," said the queen, trembling; "if he could see me he would expire with rage and scorn. You know he despises expense and ornament."

"He would immediately calculate," said Amelia, "that he could build an entire street with this diadem, and that at least ten giants could be purchased for the Guard with this necklace." She turned to her sister, who had withdrawn, and said:

"Ulrica, you say nothing. Has the splendor of our mother bewildered you? Have you lost your speech, or are you thinking whom you will command to dance with you at the ball this evening?"

"Not so," replied the little Ulrica, "I was thinking that when I am to be a queen, I will make it a condition with my husband that I shall be entirely free to choose my toilet, and I will never be forbidden to wear diamonds! When I am a queen I will wear diamonds every day; they belong to majesty, and our royal mother was never more a queen than to-day!"

"Listen," said Amelia, "to this proud and all-conquering little princess, who speaks of being a queen, as if it were all arranged, and not a doubt remained; know you that the king, our father, intends you for a queen? Perhaps he has already selected for you a little margrave, or some unknown and salaried prince, such as our poor sister of Bairout has wedded."

"I would not give my hand to such a one!" said the princess, hastily.

"You would be forced to yield, if your father commanded it," said the queen.

"No," said Ulrica, "I would rather die!"

"*Die!*" said Sophia; "man sighs often for Death, but he comes not; our sighs have not the power to bring him, and our hands are too weak to clasp him to our hearts! No,

Ulrica, you must bow your will to your father, as we have all done—as even the prince, your brother, was forced to do."

"Poor brother," said Amelia, "bound to a wife whom he loves not—how wretched he must be!"

Ulrica shrugged her shoulders. "Is not that the fate of all princes and princesses; are we not all born to be handled like a piece of goods, and knocked down to the highest bidder? I, for my part, will sell myself as dearly as possible; and, as I cannot be a happy shepherdess, I will be a powerful queen."

"And I," said Amelia, "would rather wed the poorest and most obscure man, if I loved him, than the richest and greatest king's son, to whom I was indifferent."

"Foolish children," said the queen, "it is well for you that your father does not hear you; he would crush you in his rage, and even to-day he would choose a king for you, Amelia; and for you, little Ulrica, he would seek a small margrave! Hark, ladies! I. hear the voice of the major domo; he comes to announce that the guests are assembled. Put on a cheerful countenance. The king commands us to be joyous and merry! but remember that Frederick has his spies everywhere. When you speak with Pöllnitz, never forget that he repeats every word to your father; be friendly with him; and above all things when he leads the conversation to the prince royal, speak of him with the most unembarrassed indifference; show as little interest and love for him as possible, and rather ridicule his romantic life in Rheinsberg. That is the way to the heart of the king; and now, my daughters, come."

At this moment the grand chamberlain, Pöllnitz, threw open the doors and announced that the company was assembled. The queen and princesses followed the master of ceremonies through the room, giving here and there a smile or a gracious word, which seemed a shower of gold to the obsequious, admiring crowd of courtiers. Pride swelled the heart of Sophia, as she stepped, to the sound of soft music, into the throne saloon, and saw all those cavaliers, covered with stars and orders—all those beautiful and richly-dressed women bowing humbly before her. She knew that her will was more powerful than the will of all assembled there ; that her smiles were more dearly prized than those of the most-beloved bride; that her glance gave warmth and gladness like the sun. While all bowed before her, there was no one to whom she must bend the knee. The king was not near to-night; she was not bound by his presence and his rude violence. To-night she was no trembling, subjected wife, but a proud queen; while Frederick was a poor, gouty, trembling, teeth-gnashing man—nothing more.

CHAPTER II.

FREDERICK WILLIAM I.

Mirth and gayety reigned in one wing of the palace, while in the other, and that occupied by the king himself, all was silent and solitary ; in one might be heard joyous strains of music, in the other no sound reached the ear but a monotonous hammering, which seemed to come immediately from the room of the king.

Frederick William, when in health, had accustomed himself to use his crutch as a rod of correction ; he would shower down his blows, careless whether they fell on the backs of his lacqueys, his ministers of State, or his wife. When ill, he was contented to vent his wrath upon more senseless objects, and to flourish a hammer instead of his crutch. Under the influence of the gout, this proud and haughty monarch became an humble carpenter ; when chained to one spot by his disease, and unable to direct the affairs of State, he attempted to banish thought and suffering, by working with his tools. Often in passing near the palace at a late hour of the night, you might hear the heavy blows of a hammer, and consider them a bulletin of the king's health. If he worked at night, the good people of Berlin knew their king to be sleepless and suffering, and that it would be dangerous to meet him in his walk on the following day, for some thoughtless word, or careless look, or even the cut of a coat, would bring down on the offender a stinging blow or a severe reprimand. Only a few days had passed since the king had caused the arrest of two young ladies, and sent them to the fortress of Spandau, because, in walking through the park at Schönhausen, he overheard them declare the royal garden to be "charmant! charmant!" One French word was sufficient to condemn these young girls in the eyes of the king; and it was only after long pleading that they were released from confinement. The men were fearful of being seized by the king, and held as recruits for some regiment; and the youths trembled if they were caught lounging about the streets. As soon, therefore, as the king left the proud castle of his ancestors, all who could fled from the streets into some house or by-way, that they might avoid him.

But now they had nothing to fear. His queen dared to wear her jewels; his subjects walked unmolested through the streets, for the king was suffering, chained to his chair, and occupying himself with his tools. This employment had a beneficial effect: it not only caused the king to forget his sufferings, but was often the means of relief. The constant and rapid motion of his hands and arms imparted a salutary warmth to his whole body, excited a gentle perspiration, which quieted his nervous system, and soothed him in some of his most fearful attacks.

To-day the king was once more freed from his enemy,

the gout; this evil spirit had been exorcised by honest labor, and its victim could hope for a few painless hours.

The king raised himself from his chair, and with a loud cry of delight extended his arms, as if he would gladly embrace the universe. He commanded the servant, who was waiting in the adjoining room, to call together the gentlemen who composed the Tobacco Club, and to arrange every thing for a meeting of that august body.

"But those gentlemen are at the queen's ball," said the astonished servant.

"Go there for them, then," said the king; "happily there are no dancers among them; their limbs are stiff, and the ladies would be alarmed at their capers if they attempted to dance. Bring them quickly. Pöllnitz must come, and Eckert, and Baron von Goltz, and Hacke, the Duke of Holstein, and General Schwerin. Quick, quick! In ten minutes they must all be here, but let no one know why he is sent for. Whisper to each one that he must come to me, and that he must tell no one where he is going. I will not have the queen's ball disturbed. Quick, now, and if these gentlemen are not all here in ten minutes, I will give a ball upon your back, and your own howls will be the most appropriate music."

This was a threat which lent wings to the feet of the servant, who flew like a whirlwind through the halls, ordered, with breathless haste, two servants to carry the tobacco, the pipes, and the beer-mugs into the king's chamber, and then hurried to the other wing of the palace, where the ball of the queen was held.

Fortune favored the poor servant. In ten minutes the six gentlemen stood in the king's ante-room, asking each other, with pale faces, what could be the occasion of this singular and unexpected summons.

The servant shrugged his shoulders, and silently entered the king's room. His majesty, dressed in the full uniform

1*

of his beloved Guard, sat at the round table, on which the pipes, and the mugs, filled with foaming beer, were already placed. He had condescended to fill a pipe with his own hands, and was on the point of lighting it at the smoking tallow candle which stood near him.

"Sire," said the servant, "the gentlemen are waiting in the next room."

"Do they know why I have sent for them?" said the king, blowing a cloud of smoke from his mouth.

"Your majesty forbade me to tell them."

"Well, go now, and tell them I am more furiously angry to-day than you have ever seen me; that I am standing by the door with my crutch, and I command them to come singly into my presence."

The servant hurried out to the gentlemen, who, as the door was opened, perceived the king standing in a threatening attitude near the door, with his crutch raised in his hand.

"What is the matter? Why is the king so furious? What orders do you bring us from his majesty?" asked the gentlemen anxiously and hurriedly.

The servant assumed a terrified expression, and said:

"His majesty is outrageous to-day. Woe unto him over whom the cloud bursts. He commanded me to say that each of you must enter the room alone. Go now, for Heaven's sake, and do not keep the king waiting!"

The gentlemen glanced into each other's pale and hesitating countenances. They had all seen the threatening appearance of the king, as he stood by the door with his raised crutch, and no one wished to be the first to pass under the yoke.

"Your grace has the precedence," said the grand chamberlain, bowing to the Duke of Holstein.

"No," he replied, "you are well aware his majesty does not regard etiquette, and would be most indignant if we paid any attention to it. Go first yourself, my dear friend."

" Not I, your grace, I would not dare to take precedence of you all. If you decline the honor, it is due to General Schwerin. He should lead on the battle."

"There is no question of a battle," said General Schwerin, " but a most probable beating, and Baron von Pöllnitz understands that better than I do."

"Gentlemen," said the servant, "his majesty will become impatient, and then woe unto all of us."

"But, my God," said Count von Goltz, " who will dare go forward?"

" I will," said Councillor Eckert; "I owe every thing to his majesty, therefore I will place my back or even my life at his service."

He approached the door with a firm step, and opened it quickly.

The others saw the flashing eyes of the king, as he raised his stick still higher. They saw Eckert enter, with his head bowed down, and then the door was closed, and nothing more was heard.

" Against which of us is the anger of the king directed?" faltered Pöllnitz.

" Against one and all," said the servant, with a most malicious expression.

" Who will go now?" the gentlemen asked each other, and, after a long struggle, the grand chamberlain, Von Pöllnitz, concluded to take the bitter step. Once more, as the door opened, the king was seen waiting, crutch in hand, but the door closed, and nothing more was seen. Four times was this scene repeated; four times was the king seen in this threatening attitude. But as General Schwerin, the last of the six gentlemen, entered the room, the king no longer stood near the door, but lay in his arm-chair, laughing until the tears stood in his eyes, and Baron von Pöllnitz stood before him, giving a most humorous account of the scene which had just taken place in the ante-room, imitating the voices of the different gentlemen, and relating their conversation.

"You all believed in my rage," said the king, almost breathless with laughing. "The joke succeeded to perfection. Yours also, Schwerin. Do you at last know what it is to be afraid, you who never experienced the feeling on the field of battle ? "

"Yes, sire, a shot is a small thing in comparison with the flashing of your eye. When the cannon thunders my heart is joyful, but it is very heavy under the thunder of your voice. I do not fear death, but I do fear the anger and displeasure of my sovereign."

"Oh, you are a brave fellow," said the king, warmly giving the general his hand. "And now, gentlemen, away with all constraint and etiquette. We will suppose the king to be at the ball. I am only your companion, Frederick William, and will now proceed to the opening of the Tobacco Club."

He once more lighted his pipe, and threw himself into one of the chairs, which were placed round the table; the other gentlemen followed his example, and the Tobacco Club was now in session.

CHAPTER III.

THE TOBACCO CLUB.

THERE was a short interval of silence. Each one busied himself with pipe and tobacco. The dense clouds of smoke which rolled from the lips of all had soon enveloped the room with a veil of bluish vapor, from the midst of which the tallow candle emitted a faint, sickly light.

The king ordered the man in waiting to light several additional candles. "To-day our Tobacco Club must also present a festive appearance, that the contrast between it and the ball may not be too great. Tell me, Pöllnitz, how are matters progressing over there? Is the assemblage a handsome one? Are they enjoying themselves? Is the queen gay? and the princesses, are they dancing merrily?"

"Sire," said Pöllnitz, "a more magnificent festival than to-day's I have never witnessed. Her majesty was never more beautiful, more radiant, or gayer than to-day. She shone like a sun in the midst of the handsomely dressed and adorned ladies of the court."

"Indeed! she was then magnificently attired?" said the king, and his countenance darkened.

"Sire, I had no idea the queen possessed so princely a treasure in jewels."

"She has put on her jewels then, has she? It seems they are taking advantage of my absence. They are merry and of good cheer, while I am writhing on a bed of pain," exclaimed the king, who, in his easily excited irritibility, never once remembered that he himself had appointed this festival, and had demanded of his wife that she should lay aside care, and be cheerful and happy.

"Happily, however, your majesty is not ill, and not on a bed of pain. The queen has, therefore, good reason to be happy."

The king made no reply, but raised his mug to his lips, and took a long draught of beer, and let fall its lid with an angry movement.

"I should not be surprised if Frederick had clandestinely come over to this ball," murmured the king. "They dare any thing when not apprehensive of my taking them by surprise."

"But taking by surprise is your majesty's *forte*," ex-claimed Count Hacke, endeavoring to give the conversation another direction. "Never before in my life did I feel my heart beat as it did when I crossed the threshold of this chamber to-day."

The king, who was easily soothed, laughed heartily. "And never before did I see such pale faces as yours. Really, if the gout had not made my fingers so stiff and un-wieldy, I would paint you a picture of this scene that would make a magnificent counterpart to my representation of the Tobacco Club, and I would call it 'The Six Tailor Apprentices who are afraid of Blue Monday.' See! we will now devote ourselves to poetry and the arts, and our learned and fantas-tic son will soon have no advantage over us whatever. If he plays the flute, we paint. While he writes sentimental, we will write satirical poems; and while he sings to sun, moon, and stars, we will do as the gods, and, like Jupiter, envelop ourselves in a cloud. Let it be well understood, however, not for the purpose of deluding a Semele or any other wo-man, at all times, and in all circumstances, we have been true to our wives, and in this particular the prince royal might well take his father as an example.''

"Sire, he could do that in all things," exclaimed Count von Goltz, blowing a cloud of smoke from his lips.

"He thinks at some future day to govern the kingdom with his book-learning and his poems," said the king, laugh-ing. "Instead of occupying himself with useful things, drill-ing recruits, drawing plans, and studying the art of war, he devotes his time to the acquirement of useless and superficial knowledge, which benefits no one, and is most injurious to himself. A dreaming scholar can never be a good king; and he who, instead of sword and sceptre, wields the pen and fiddle-bow, will never be a good general."

"Nevertheless, no regiment made a finer appearance, or

was better drilled, at the last review, than that of the prince royal," said the Duke of Holstein.

The king cast a distrustful look at him, and muttered a few words which no one understood. He was never pleased to hear any defence of the prince royal, and suspected every one who praised him.

"Your majesty forgets that this is a sitting of the Tobacco Club and not of the State Council," said Pöllnitz, in a fawning voice. "If your majesty designed to be angry, it was not necessary to light the pipes and fill the beer-mugs; for while you are neither smoking nor drinking, the pipe goes out, and the beer becomes stale."

"True," replied the king, and raising his glass he continued: "I drink this to the health of him who first overcame his timid heart and dared to enter my chamber. Who was it? I have forgotten."

"It was the privy councillor Von Eckert, sire," said Count Hacke, with an ironical smile. Eckert bowed.

"He entered the chamber as if going to battle," exclaimed Von Pöllnitz, laughing. "In the spirit he took leave of all the fine breweries, and artfully constructed never-smoking chimneys which he had built; he also took leave of the city exchanges, which he had not yet provided with royal commissioners, destined to despoil them of their riches; he bade adieu to his decoration and to his money-bags, and exclaiming, 'To the king I owe all that I am, it is therefore but proper that my back as well as my life should be at his service,' marched courageously into the royal presence."

"Did he really do that? Did he say that?" exclaimed the king. "Eckert, I am pleased with you for that, and will reward you. It is true that I have elevated you from a lowly condition; that I have made a gentleman of the chimney-sweep; but gratitude is a rare virtue, men seldom remember the benefits they have received; your doing so, is an evidence that you have a noble heart, one which I know how to appreciate. The new house which I am building in Jager Street shall be yours; and I will not present you with the naked walls, but it shall be handsomely furnished and fitted up at my expense."

"Your majesty is the most gracious, the best of monarchs!" exclaimed Eckert, hastening to the king and pressing his hand to his lips. "Yes, your majesty is right in saying that you have elevated me from the dust, but my heart, at least, was always pure, and I will endeavor to preserve it so. You have rescued me from the scum of the people. As the ancient Romans gave freedom to those slaves who had rendered themselves worthy of it by good and noble deeds, so has my king also delivered me from the bondage of poverty and lowliness, and given me freedom, and I also will strive to render myself worthy of this great boon by good and noble actions."

"And Berlin offers you the best opportunities of doing so. There are still many smoking chimneys and indifferent beer breweries. Privy Councillor Von Eckert can, therefore, still execute many glorious deeds before he is gathered to his forefathers," exclaimed Von Pöllnitz.

All were amused at this, and the king himself could not refrain from smiling. Von Eckert's countenance had become pale and lowering, and casting an angry look at Von Pöllnitz, he said, with a forced laugh :

"Really your wit to-day is dazzling, and I am so charmed with your pleasantries, that should your wine merchant refuse to supply you with any more wine until your old accounts have been settled, I shall be perfectly willing to send you a few bottles from my own cellar, that your Grace may be able to drink my health."

"That I will gladly do," said Pöllnitz, affably. "Yes, I will drink to your long and lasting health, for the longer you live the more time your ancestors will have to increase and

to multiply themselves. And, as it seems that you are not
destined to become the father of a coming generation, you
should, at least, endeavor to become the progenitor of your
ancestors and the father of your fathers. Ancestors are born
to you as children are to others, and, if I am not mistaken,
you are already the possessor of three. For a gentleman of
wealth and quality, this is, however, too few. I will, therefore, drink to your health, that you may still be able to create
many ancestors. And I propose to your majesty to give him
an ancestor for every chimney which he frees from smoke."

"Silence, Pöllnitz!" exclaimed the king, laughing. "No
more of this raillery. Listen to what I have to say. I have
given Eckert the new house, and as I have invested him with
a title of nobility, it is but proper that a noble coat-of-arms
should be placed over his door. Gentlemen, let us consider
what the escutcheon of Eckert shall be. Each of you, in
his turn, shall give me his opinion. You, duke, commence."

With grave and sober mien the gentlemen began to con-
fer with each other in regard to Von Eckert's escutcheon;
and each one considering the favor in which the former stood
with the king, took pains to propose the most magnificent
coat-of-arms imaginable. But the king was not pleased with
the grave and learned devices which were proposed. He
disliked giving the newly-made baron a coat-of-arms worthy
of any house of old and established nobility, which would
have placed him on an equality with the oldest counts and
barons of the kingdom.

"When I build a house," said the king, "I wish every
one to see that it is a new one; I therefore give it a nice
white coat of paint, and not an old graystone color to make
it look like a robber castle. Eckert should, therefore, have
a fresh touch of paint for his new dignity, a spick and span
new coat-of-arms."

"I am entirely of your majesty's opinion," exclaimed

Von Pöllnitz, solemnly; "and as every noble family bears on its coat-of-arms some emblem and reminiscence of the deeds and events through which it became great, so should also the escutcheon of the noble house of Eckert contain some such reminiscence. I propose to quarter this shield. The first field shall show on a silver ground a black chimney, in which we will also have indicated the Prussian colors. The second field is blue, with a golden vat in the centre, having reference to Eckert's great ability as a beer-brewer. The third field is green, with a golden pheasant in the middle, suggestive of Eckert's earlier occupation as gamekeeper in Brunswick; and the fourth field shows on a red ground a cock and a knife, a reminiscence of the good old times when Privy Councillor Von Eckert fed and dressed fowls in Bairout."

A peal of laughter from the entire club rewarded Von Pöllnitz for his proposition. The king was also so well pleased, that he, in all gravity, determined to accept it, and to have a coat-of-arms with the above designated emblems adjusted over the door of the new house in Jager Street.

The merriment of the gentlemen of the Tobacco Club was now becoming energetic, and jests and jokes were contributed by all. The grand chamberlain, Von Pöllnitz, was, however, the gayest of the gay. And if the pleasantries which bubbled from his lips like water from a fountain at any time threatened to flag, a glance at the pale face of Von Eckert, who fairly trembled with suppressed rage, was sufficient to renew his merriment.

While the king was conversing with Von Eckert on the subject of his new house, Pöllnitz turned to his neighbor and asked if he had not made ample amends for his awkwardness in the first instance.

"By my thoughtless repetition of that hypocritical man's words, I procured him the new house, but I have also given him a coat-of-arms; and I wager the privy councillor would willingly relinquish the former, if he could thereby get rid of the latter."

"Pöllnitz, why are you looking so grave?" asked the king at this moment. "I wager you are in a bad humor, because the handsome house in Jager Street was not given to you."

"By no means, your majesty; as handsome as the house is, it would not suit me at all."

"Ah, yes, you are right; it would be much too large a one for you!" said Frederick William, laughing.

"No, your majesty, it would be much too small for me. When a cavalier of my quality once determines to build a house, it should be arranged in accordance with his rank and standing, and that costs a great deal of money, much more than I ever possessed. It is true that my father left me a fortune of about two hundred thousand dollars, but what is such a trifle to a nobleman? It was not enough for a decent support, and it was too much to go begging on. I calculated how long this sum might be made to last, and finding that, with considerable economy, it would perhaps do for four years, I lived like a noble and generous cavalier for that time; and during that period I was fortunate enough to have the most devoted friends and the truest sweethearts, who never deserted me until the last dollar of my fortune was expended!"

"Do I understand you to say that you expended two hundred thousand dollars in four years?" asked the king.

"Yes, your majesty; and I assure you that I was obliged to practise the most rigorous economy."

Frederick William regarded him with surprise, almost with admiration. To the king there was something in this man's nature which was imposing. It was perhaps the great contrast between the unlimited extravagance of the baron and his own frugality, which exerted so great an influence on the king, excited his astonishment, and enlisted his admira tion in behalf of this ready, witty, and ever-merry courtier.

"An income of fifty thousand dollars is, therefore, not sufficient for a decent support?" asked the king.

"Your majesty, if one attempted to live in a style befitting a nobleman, on that sum, he might die of hunger."

"Ah, explain that. What sum would you consider necessary to enable you to live in a style befitting a nobleman?"

Pöllnitz remained lost in thought for a moment, and then replied:

"Your majesty, in order to live somewhat respectably, I should require four hundred thousand dollars yearly."

"That is not true, not possible!" exclaimed the king.

"That is so very possible, sire, that I hardly know whether it would suffice or not."

"Gentlemen, do you believe that?" asked the king.

"I, for my part, have not the fourth part of this income," said the Duke of Holstein, smiling.

"I not the tenth!" said Count Von der Goltz.

"And I not the twentieth!" exclaimed General Von Schwerin and Count Hacke at the same time.

"And yet," said the king, "you all live as respected cavaliers, as esteemed gentlemen of my court. Let us hear how Pöllnitz would manage to spend so much money. Quick, Jochen, quick, give us a sheet of paper and a pencil."

The valet hastily executed this commission, and handed the king paper and pencil.

"Fill the glasses, Jochen," ordered the king, "and then seat yourself at the foot of the table, and pay attention to what Von Pöllnitz is about to explain. It is worth the trouble to learn how an income of four hundred thousand dollars can be spent in a respectable manner. You shall dictate, and I will be your secretary. Woe to you, however, if you do not keep your word, if you expend less! For every thousand which you fail to account for, you shall drink ten glasses of beer, and smoke a pipe of the strong Havana tobacco recently sent me by the stadtholder of Holland."

" But what shall I receive for every thousand which I expend over and above that sum?" asked Von Pöllnitz, laughing.

" Oh, it is impossible that a nobleman should need more, that is, provided he does not expend it in a foolish manner, like a madman."

" And if, in order to live in a style befitting a nobleman, I should nevertheless need more, what am I to receive for every thousand?"

" Well, then, for every thousand, I will pay a hundred of your oldest debts," said the king. " But commence. And you, gentlemen, drink and smoke, and pay attention to what he has to say."

CHAPTER IV.

AIR-CASTLES.

" I WILL begin." said Pöllnitz. " First of all, I shall need a respectable house, to receive my guests in, to exhibit my collections, and entertain my friends; to pursue my studies, without being disturbed by the slighest noise; a house, in which my wife must have her separate apartments, and as I shall wish to have my friends with me, every now and then, to smoke, my wife's reception-rooms must be entirely separated from mine."

" But," exclaimed the king, " your wife will certainly allow you to smoke in her rooms!"

" And if she permitted it, your majesty, I would not do so; it becomes not a cavalier to smoke in a lady's room."

The king reddened a little, and carried the mug to his lips, to hide his embarrassment; he remembered how often he had smoked in the queen's rooms, notwithstanding her sighs.

Pöllnitz continued quietly: "I must then have several different reception-rooms, and as my wife and myself will frequently be at variance with each other, two different and widely-separated staircases will be necessary, that we may not meet, unless we wish it!"

"Oh! you mean to lead a wretched life with your wife; to quarrel with her every now and then, do you?"

"No, sire, we will never quarrel; it ill becomes a cavalier to have a contest with his wife."

The king reddened again, this time from anger. This exposition of a cavalier began to offend him; it seemed to be a satire upon himself; for unhappily the king not only smoked in the queen's rooms, but the world knew that his wife and children were often the objects of his violent temper, and that the queen had more than once been terribly frightened by his thundering reproaches and unbearable threats.

"Your highness sees that my house must be large, and as it is so, a host of servants and a large income will be necessary. But of this hereafter. Let us speak of my houses, for it is easily understood that I must have a country residence."

"Yes, that is a reasonable demand," said the king, in adding the country house to his list.

"But, as I do not go to the country to live as I do in the city, but to enjoy the beauties of nature and scenery, I must have a garden, with vineyards, and beautiful walks, and, for their cultivation, many servants. And, as I cannot ask my friends to visit me simply to pluck my flowers, and eat my fruits, I must procure for them other and rarer pleasures. I must have a park for hunting, and a lake for fishing."

"Yes, that is well argued and true," said the king, noting the park and lake on his paper.

"Now we are coming to the most important points— the kitchen and wine-cellar. On these two I must bestow most particular care. It would be most unworthy a cavalier to present such dishes to his friends as they can enjoy every day at home. No, if I invite my friends, they must be certain of having such luxuries as they cannot procure elsewhere—such rare and costly viands as will recall the wonders of fairy land!"

"I am quite of your opinion," cried the king, and his face brightened at the thought of the delightful and costly dishes that the rich Pöllnitz would set before his friends. "Listen: from time to time you can prepare for me the delightful bacon-pie that I once tasted at Grumbkou's. Oh, that was really splendid, and reminded one, as you say, of the wonders of fairy land! My cook obtained the receipt immediately; but what do you think? three bottles of champagne and three bottles of burgundy were necessary to stew the meat. I had to give up the intention of having such a pie, but I told Grumbkou that when I felt like eating such an expensive dish, I would be his guest."

"I will obey your commands, your highness," said Pöllnitz, earnestly, and bowing low to the king. "Let us continue to furnish my house ; after that we will speak of the pie. As hunting is decided upon, we must now consider the horses, for I cannot ask my friends to hunt on foot, or walk to the lake. I must have beautiful and noble steeds, and as horses and carriages do not take care of themselves, I must have a number of servants to attend to them."

"That is true," said the king, adding the carriages and horses to his list. "That is true ; but I find that you think a great deal of your friends and very little of yourself. Your whole demand, so far, is for the benefit of your friends."

"Sire, hospitality is one of the noblest virtues of a cavalier, for which one can never do too much, but easily too little."

The king frowned and looked threateningly before him; the rest of the club looked at Pöllnitz with increasing astonishment, surprised at his daring to show the king in this manner his faults and weaknesses.

Pöllnitz alone remained gay and unembarrassed. "Now, as I have attended sufficiently to the pleasure and comfort of my friends, it is time I should think a little of myself. I therefore beg your highness to name the sum you deem necessary for my yearly expenses for charities and presents for my sweetheart."

"Your wife is your sweetheart. You intend to be a very tender husband, notwithstanding the two staircases."

"Sire, it would not become a cavalier to possess a wife and sweetheart in the same person. Your wife represents your family, your sweetheart amuses you. You give your wife name and rank, your sweetheart your love and whole heart. A true cavalier does not love his wife, but he demands that the world shall honor her as the lady that bears his name."

"Pöllnitz, Pöllnitz," said the king, shaking his hand threateningly at him, "take care that I never see your cavalier in my house, and no one that is like him; I would have no pity with him, but crush him with my kingly anger!"

Pöllnitz was frightened, and covered himself in a cloud of smoke, that the king might not see his perplexity.

"Continue," said Frederick William, after a short pause. "I have set aside a certain amount for every single article you have mentioned, but I truly hope you have concluded; and that the demon that dwells in you, and masters you, will make no further suggestions to your luxurious and insane fancies."

" Yes, your highness ; and I beg you will calculate the sum total necessary for these different articles."

The king calculated, his guests smoked and drank in silence, and Pöllnitz listened attentively to the sound of voices, and noise of horses in the court.

The king suddenly uttered an oath, and brought his fist heavily down on the paper. " As truly as God lives, Pöllnitz is right! Four hundred thousand dollars are not sufficient to support a cavalier of his pretensions. The sum here amounts to four hundred and fifty thousand dollars."

" Your highness confesses that I have demanded nothing superfluous or exaggerated ? "

" Yes, I confess it."

" Consequently, your highness will be kind enough to pay me five thousand dollars."

" The devil! How can I understand that ? "

" Your majesty forgets that you promised me one hundred dollars for every thousand over and above the sum of four hundred thousand."

" Did I say that ? " said the king; and as all present confirmed it, he laughed aloud, saying, " I see that none of you understand Pöllnitz. That was not my meaning. I did not say I would pay Pöllnitz the gold; but for every thousand above his four hundred thousand I would pay a hundred of his oldest debts, and that is quite a different affair. You know well, if I gave him the gold, his creditors would never receive a cent of it. But what I have promised I will do ; bring me, to-morrow, a list of your oldest debts, and I will pay five thousand dollars upon them."

" Your highness, my account is not yet finished. I have only mentioned the most pressing and necessary articles, and much has been forgotten. I must have a forester to chase the poachers from my park, and a night watch to guard my country house, to feed the fish in my pond, to strike upon the water in order to silence the frogs, that my sleep and that of my friends may not be disturbed."

"Enough, enough of your castles in the air, fool that you are!" cried the king, half angry, half amused. "Seek another sovereign, who is rich enough to provide for your follies."

"Sire," said Pöllnitz, "I will seek nothing elsewhere. I am too happy to have found so noble and gracious a monarch. I only wished to prove to your majesty, and these gentlemen that do me the honor to consider me a spendthrift, that a great fortune can be easily spent without extravagance and folly, and you will now understand that I have given a worthy proof of economy in fixing my yearly income at four hundred thousand dollars, when I could easily dispose of that sum in six months."

The king laughed, and, raising the beer-pot aloft, commanded the gentlemen to drink to the health of the miser Pöllnitz.

The beer-pots were raised, and were jingling merrily, when suddenly it seemed as if an electric shock had struck them all simultaneously—all with the exception of the king. The six cavaliers placed their beer-pots upon the table, and, rising with breathless haste from their chairs, bowed lowly and humbly.

———

CHAPTER V.

FATHER AND SON.

THE king, in speechless amazement, sank back in his chair. He could not yet conceive what spell had taken hold of these gentlemen, that made them rise from their seats in

spite of the rules of the Tobacco Club. The king did not
see that, behind him, the door had opened, and, in the midst
of the smoke that filled the whole room, a young man was
visible, whose appearance had produced this astounding impression upon the six cavaliers. And, certainly, there was
something exalted and imposing in this youth. A wondrous
combination of beauty, nobility of soul, youth, royalty, and
melancholy was expressed in this face, whose sharp and
marked lines spoke of severe pain and bitter experience,
while so fresh and youthful a smile played upon the soft red
lip, you could but suppose the heart young, confiding, and
impressible. But the eyes were in wonderful contrast to
these beautiful lips; they shone like great, mysterious, un-
fathomable stars—one moment sparkling with youthful su-
perciliousness, the next with the firm, steady, piercing glance
of an observing sage. The lofty, somewhat retreating forehead, and the straight, finely-pointed nose, formed a profile
indicating commanding elevation of character. And the soul
imprisoned behind these temples was powerfully agitated,
seeking ever for freedom of thought and expression. It was
the eye, the head of a hero; and, had his form corresponded
with the giant strength of his glance, he would have been a
Titan, and might have crushed the world like a toy in his
hand. But his slender, symmetrical, and graceful form was
more weak than powerful, more maidenly than heroic.

You felt, however, that this head might lend strength to
the body, and if the Titan could not overcome by physical
strength, he could rule and conquer by the commanding
power of his genius.*

---

* A French traveller, by the name of Birré, who went from Paris
to Berlin to see Frederick, describes him in this manner: "Buste ad-
mirable et vraiment royal, mais pauvre et miserable piédestal. Sa tête
et sa poitrine sont au dessus des éloges, le train d'en bas au dessous de
la critique."—(See *Thiébalt.*)

This was the unexpected apparition that shocked the gentlemen of the Tobacco Club, and forced them hastily from their seats! The king sat speechless and amazed in his chair, while the youth stood close behind him.

"Allow me to wish your majesty good-evening," said the prince, with his full, clear-ringing voice.

The king was greatly agitated, and the blood rushed to his face. "Fritz!" said he, in a light tone. "Fritz!" repeated he more sternly, and already the sound of a coming storm was perceptible in his voice.

"I come from Ruppin," said the prince, in a quiet, kindly voice, "where I was reviewing my regiment, and I beg pardon for my unexpected appearance."

The king made no reply; his mistrust was scornfully exhibited. He thought that the queen believed him to be suffering and confined to his room. He did not doubt for a moment that she had sent for the prince, and Frederick was there to see if the life of the king was not in danger; if the throne of Prussia would not soon be empty, and ready for its successor.

These dark suspicions excited the king's ire, and filled his heart with bitter distrust. With a hasty movement he dashed back the hand of the prince royal, and arose from his chair. His scornful eye took in at a glance the whole circle, still standing in awe-struck silence around the table.

"Why have you arisen from your chairs?" cried the king, with trembling voice. "How dare you arise contrary to my command, and thus set yourselves in opposition to my kingly power? Do you no longer know the laws of the Tobacco Club? Do you not know that these laws positively forbid you to arise from your seats to greet any one? You are all silent, miserable cowards that you are, who do not attempt to defend yourselves, who go always with wind and tide, and deceive and flatter in every direction. Answer me,

Pöllnitz, did you not know the law of the Tobacco Club, forbidding you to arise from your seat?"

"I know it, sire, but thought I might be allowed to make an exception of the prince royal."

"So thought we all," said General Schwerin, in a steady voice.

The king struck with doubled fist on the table, and the pitchers and beer-mugs trembled.

"You thought that," said the king, "and yet knew that no exception was ever made for me! But certainly the prince royal is of more consequence than the king. The prince royal is the future sovereign, the rising sun! What the king was not able to give, the prince royal may bestow. From the king there is nothing left to hope, nothing to fear; for this reason you turn to the prince royal; for this reason you ridicule the laws of the father to flatter the son. The son is a fine French cavalier, who loves ornament and courtesy, to whom the question of etiquette is important. You stand up also when the prince royal enters, although you know in this room all are equal, and here you have often forgotten that I am king. Yes, the king can be forgotten—the prince royal never; he may soon be king!"

"God grant you majesty a long and happy life," said the prince royal.

During this passionate speech of the king, he had stood silent and immovable behind his chair.

"Who spoke to you? Who told you to speak until you were questioned?" said the king, whose whole form trembled with rage. "You, the slave of etiquette, should know that no man speaks to the king until he is spoken to. Truly you think the king does not understand etiquette. He is an old-fashioned man, and knows not how a true cavalier should conduct himself. Now, Pöllnitz, you see there a cavalier after your own heart, a veritable model. Ah, you thought

perhaps I did not see the face lurking behind your picture
you suppose I did not recognize the cavalier you painted in
such glowing colors, in order to prove that he must have
four hundred thousand dollars yearly or be forced to make
debts. Patience! patience! My eyes are at last opened!
Woe, woe to you all when I see that you dare brave me, in
order to please the prince royal! I will prove to you that I
yet live, and am your master. The Tobacco Club is closed,
and you may all go to the devil!"

"As I don't know the way there, will your majesty allow
me to return to Rheinsberg? I now take my leave," said
the prince royal, bowing respectfully to the king.

Frederick William turned his head, and said but one
word—"Go!"

The prince bowed again; then, turning to the cavaliers,
he said:

"Good-evening, gentlemen. I sincerely regret to have
been the cause of the king's anger. Against you this displeasure is however just, for a command of the king should
never be disobeyed, not even with a kind and magnanimous
intent."

The prince had with these words put himself beyond the
reach of the king's rage, and at the same time done justice
to all: to the king in acknowledging the justice of his anger;
to the cavaliers in praising their good intentions. He was
evidently master of the situation.

With a firm, steady tread he left the room, while the
king, in spite of his anger, could not help feeling that he had
again failed in kindness to the prince royal. But this consciousness only made him the more passionate. He muttered
a deep curse, and looked threateningly at the pale, trembling
cavaliers.

"Hypocrites and eye-servants are you all," muttered he,
as he slowly passed by them. "Give me your arm, Hacke,

and lead me into the other room. I cannot look at these men any longer."

Count Hacke rushed forward, and, leaning on his arm, the king tottered into the adjoining room.

When the door closed behind them, the cavaliers seemed to awaken from their torpidity. They raised their heads, and looked at one another with a half-confused, half-angry gaze. They had been scolded like children, and felt that they were men. Their honor had received a sensitive wound, but their awe of the king kept them from demanding satisfaction.

When the count returned to order the gentlemen in the king's name to leave the palace, they did not have the courage to obey this command, but sent the count as their ambassador to the king to ask in the humblest manner for forgiveness and pardon, and to assure him that their behavior to the prince royal was but the consequence of involuntary thoughtlessness.

The count, after much trembling, left the room to deliver this message to the king; the cavaliers waited in anxious silence for his return. At length the door opened, and the count appeared.

"Well, what says the king? Has he forgiven us? Will he take us into his favor again? Is he convinced that we are his true, humble, and obedient servants?"

All these questions the count answered by a slight motion of the hand. It was a moment of anxious expectation; all were eagerly looking at the count, who was to pronounce for them the words of forgiveness or condemnation.

"Gentlemen," at length said the count, and his voice sounded to the trembling courtiers hollow and awful as that of an angel of death, "gentlemen, the king says if you do not leave here at once, he will easily find means to compel you to do so!"

This was a menace that gave strength to the trembling limbs of the courtiers. Silently, with sad, troubled looks, they hastened away, and not until the great portals of the palace had closed upon them did they feel safe from the fear of imprisonment, and the king's crutch.

The king had not yet subdued his anger. He thirsted for another victim. The servants wisely remained at a distance beyond the reach of the royal crutch; the king's ungovernable anger had even banished Count Hacke from the room.

The king was alone, entirely alone in this dark, empty room, and its comfortless silence filled him with anxiety. He sank into his arm-chair, and looked with a sad glance around this large room, which, because of his parsimony, was but badly lighted with four tallow candles. Nothing broke the silence but from time to time the gay music of the dance, which was heard from the other wing of the castle. Mirth still reigned in the saloons of the queen. The king sighed; his heart was filled with melancholy and rage. The queen was gay, while her husband suffered. The court was joyful, while he sat alone and neglected, gnashing his teeth in this dark and joyless room. And yet he was the king, the all-powerful ruler of millions of subjects, who trembled before him, and yet not one of them loved him.

All eyes were fixed upon the rising sun, upon Frederick, so unlike his father, and so little the son of his father's heart. As the king thought of this, deep grief and a foreboding melancholy overcame him. In the anguish of his heart he turned to God and prayed. He silenced the voice of self-accusation and remorse, now whispering in his breast, by prayer.

The king prayed. Exhausted with rage, he fancied that he had given himself up to pious contrition and world-despising godliness.

As the tones of the music were again heard, he experienced a pious exasperation over this unholy levity, a peaceful self-content; he belonged not to the ungodly, who gave themselves up to worldliness and vanity, but alone and deserted he prayed to his Father in heaven. How small, how pitiful, how contemptible did the gay dancers appear to him! how pleased he was with himself, his holy walk and conversation! At this moment the anxious face of his valet appeared at the door.

"Your majesty commanded me to tell you so soon as the coffins which came yesterday were unpacked and placed in the white saloon : this is done, and the coffins can be seen."

"Ah! My coffin is ready!" said the king, involuntarily shuddering. "My coffin, and that of the queen! And Sophia gives a ball, and perhaps dances, in place of bowing her soul in contrition before God. I will awaken her from these soul-destroying vanities; the arrival of the coffins now was an especial providence of God. The queen shall see them!"

He called his two valets, commanded one to lead him to the ball-room, the other to illuminate the white saloon in which the coffins were placed.

<hr />

CHAPTER VI.

THE WHITE SALOON.

THE queen had no suspicion of all that had happened in the chambers of the king; she had not observed the absence of the Tobacco Club, and after having made the grand tour of the saloons, she seated herself at the card-table.

Her majesty had no idea that her husband was free from

2*

pain, and had left his arm-chair; she was, therefore, gay and careless, filled with a sense of freedom and power. The cruel eye of Frederick William was not bent upon her to look her down, and cast a veil of humility over the sparkling diamonds which adorned her brow; no, she was to-night entirely herself—every inch a queen! proud and happy, smiling and majestic. Rejoicing in her own greatness and glory, she was still amiable and obliging to this great crowd of devoted, submissive, flattering, smiling men, who surrounded her; never had she been so gracious, never so queenly. As we have said, she had seated herself at the card-table, and the margrafin Maria Dorothea and the English and French ambassadors were her partners; behind her chair stood her two maids of honor, to whom she now and then addressed a word, or sent them to look after the young princesses, who were dancing in the adjoining room, and giving themselves up merrily to the pleasures of the evening. Suddenly the music ceased, and a strange, unaccustomed silence reigned throughout the rooms.

The queen was arranging her cards, and turned smilingly to one of her maids of honor, commanding her as soon as the dance was ended to lead the princesses to her side; she then gave her attention to the game, when suddenly the Princess Amelia, pale and terrified, rushed hastily to her mother, and whispered a few words in her ear.

Sophia Dorothea uttered a low cry of terror, and exclaimed: "The king! my God, the king! he seems very angry!" said the princess; "do not let him see your diamonds." The partners of the queen sat in respectful silence, waiting for her play; she dashed her cards upon the table, removed her necklace and bracelets hastily, and thrust the glittering heap into her dress pocket.*

* See Thiébault.

"Remove my long ear-rings," she whispered to Amelia, and while the princess obeyed the command, the queen took her cards from the table. The glory was departed; the diamonds were hiding timidly in her pocket, and the fire of her eye was quenched.

The king was there; Sophia Dorothea was no longer a royal queen, but a trembling, dependent woman, cowering before the rage of her husband. The partners of the queen sat quietly with downcast eyes, and did not appear to see the rash change in the toilet of her majesty, still seemingly waiting for the play of the queen. Sophia played a queen, Lord Hastings played the king.

"Lost!" said her majesty, "so must the queen ever lose when the king comes; but it is always a comfort," she said, with a bitter smile, "to be overcome *only* by a king." She played on quietly, though she knew that the king was already in the door of the room and watching her closely.

As the king stepped forward and called her name, she rose and advanced toward him with an expression of joyful surprise.

"Ah, my husband, what a great pleasure you have prepared for us!" she said, smiling; "it is most amiable of your majesty to glorify this feast with your presence."

"I come, however," said the king, in a rude, harsh voice, and thrusting the queen's arm in his own, "to cast gloom upon this *fête;* it is good and necessary in the midst of tumultuous earthly pleasures to be reminded of the fleeting vanity of all sublunary things; and to still the voluptuous music with prayer, I am come to administer this medicine to your vain and sin-sick soul. Come with me, you there!" said the king, turning his head backwards to the courtiers, who were gathered in silent and frightened groups. "You there, follow us!" He dragged the queen forward; silently the procession of richly-adorned guests followed the royal pair, no one knew where.

The queen had in vain implored the king to make known his purpose. This long procession, adorned with flowers, diamonds, uniforms, and orders, had a gay and festal appearance; you might well suppose them wedding guests on their way to church. The principal actors on this occasion, however, did not promise to be a happy pair.

The king looked steadily, with a frowning brow and tightly-compressed lips, right before him ; the queen, wan and trembling, turned her eyes anxiously from side to side, seeking everywhere some new danger, some new terror prepared for her. The procession stepped silently and earnestly through the dressing-rooms, odorous with flowers; through the illuminated antechamber; further on through the corridors and up the wide stair steps ; onward still through long passages till they reached the great doors of the White Saloon, which Frederick had built and adorned.

" We have arrived," said the king, opening the door and leading in the queen. Suddenly Sophia Dorothea uttered a cry of horror, and fell backwards; behind her stood the curious, astonished, and shocked courtiers, pressing themselves hastily through the door of the saloon.

"Two coffins!" murmured the queen, with horror; her timid glance rested first upon the solemn coffins, then wandered anxiously to the lofty, imposing marble statues of the prince electors, who, in solemn rest, in this chamber of the dead, seemed to hold a watch over the coffins of the living.

" Yes, two coffins," said the king—" our coffins, Sophia ; and I resolved in this hour to show them to you and the assembled court, that this solemn warning might arouse you all from your unholy and sinful lusts. Death must strike at your heart to awaken it from voluptuous sleep and cause you to look within. In these coffins we will soon rest, and all earthly vanity and glory will be at an end. No one will fear my glance or my crutch ; no one will compliment the beautiful toilet of the queen, or admire her diamonds ; dust will return to dust, and the king and the queen be nothing more than food for worms ! "

" Not so," said Sophia, whose noble and proud heart felt humbled by this pious grovelling of her husband ; " not so, we will be more than dust and food for worms. The dust of common mortals will be scattered in every direction by the hand of Time, and over their graves will History walk with destroying feet ; but she will remain with us and will gather our dust, and build therewith a monument to our memory ; when our bodies of flesh and blood are placed in the vault of our ancestors, our forms will arise again with limbs of marble and bosoms without hearts. Look, my husband, at these statues of your exalted ancestors ; they have also gone down into the vaults, but their marble forms have the best places in our splendid rooms ; perhaps they listen to our words and behold our deeds."

Whilst the queen spoke, her countenance was illuminated with royal energy and beauty ; she was now, indeed, truly imperial, without the aid of diamond coronets. The queen was herself again ; she had conquered her womanish fears ; she felt herself not only the wife of Frederick, but the sister of the king of England, the mother of the future king.

But Frederick, in what he considered his holy penitential mood, was made angry by her self-possession, her proudly-erected head ; he felt that this soul had made itself free from his heavy yoke, and claimed and enjoyed a separate existence ; but she should acknowledge him again as her lord, and be bowed down with humble penitence. The queen should become the woman, the obedient wife ; had not the Bible said, and " he shall rule over thee " ?

" So, then, let our ancestors behold how we try our

coffins before them," said the king, placing his hand heavily on the shoulder of the queen; "the world knows that diamonds become you, and that I, in my uniform, am a fine-looking fellow; let us see now how our coffins will clothe us!"

"What do you mean, my king?" said Sophia, fixing her trembling glance upon her husband.

"I mean that we will see if we can take our places with dignity and worthily in our coffins; that we will do to-day in sport what we must hereafter do in solemn earnest."

"This is indeed a cruel jest," said the queen.

"Oh, yes, to the children of this world every thing seems cruel which reminds them of death and the fleeting nature of all earthly joys," said the king, "but such a warning is good and healthy to the soul, and if we would accustom ourselves from time to time to leave the ball-room and rest awhile in our coffins, we would, without doubt, lead more holy and earnest lives. Lay yourself, therefore, in your coffin, Sophia; it will be to your soul's advantage, and my eyes will see a picture which, praised be God, you can never behold. I shall see you in your coffin."

"Oh, you are younger than I, my husband; you will surely see me buried; it is not therefore necessary to put me to this trial."

"Conquer thy soul, and make it quiet and humble," said the king; "we have come hither to try our coffins, and we will try them!"

"The king had a feverish attack of piety to-day. I would not have come if I had known the intentions of your majesty," said the queen.

"You would have come as I willed it," murmured the king, while his cheeks glowed with anger and his eyes flashed fire.

Sophia saw these symptoms of a rising storm, and she

knew that all restraints would be removed if she resisted longer. She called with a commanding tone to one of her maids of honor, and said proudly:

"Reach me your hand, duchess; I am weary, and will for awhile rest upon this bed, of a new and uncommon form."

With the appearance and nobility of a truly royal soul, she raised her robe a little, lifted her foot over the edge of the coffin, and placed it firmly in the bottom. She stood in the coffin proudly erect, commanding and majestic to behold; then, with inimitable grace, she stooped and lay down slowly. The coffin creaked and groaned, and amongst the crowd of courtiers a murmur of horror and disgust was heard. The king stood near the coffin, and Sophia Dorothea looked at him so steadily, so piercingly, that he had not the courage to meet her glance, and fixed his eyes upon the ground. The queen stood up quietly. The Countess Hacke held out her hand to assist her, but she waved her proudly back.

"No," she said, "kings and queens leave their coffins by their own strength and greatness, and sustained by the hand of History alone. Sophia then stepped over the edge of the coffin, and, bowing profoundly to the king, she said—

"Your majesty, it is now your turn."

The king was confused. He cast a dark, distrustful glance upon the queen. Her simple words had for him a prophetic meaning, and he shuddered as he drew near the coffin. With a powerful effort he overcame himself, stepped into the coffin, and nodded to some of his courtiers to assist him in lying down.

"Ah, I rest well upon this couch," said Frederick. "Here will I soon sleep till it shall please God to wake me at the resurrection!"

"May that time be far removed, my king!" said Sophia earnestly. "Allow me to assist you."

She reached her hand to the king; he seized it with alacrity, and was in the act of rising, when a wild and unaccustomed sound was heard without—a loud, piercing cry, which was many times repeated, then the sound of hasty steps approaching the room! The pallid and awe-struck courtiers whispered to each other.

"What is it?" cried the king, who was still sitting in his coffin.

No one answered. The courtiers whispered confused and wild words, but no one dared to answer.

"I demand to know what has happened," said the king, as with much difficulty he sought to raise himself up.

The major domo stepped forward. "Your majesty, two soldiers are without who held watch in the corridor; they declare that a long, white figure, with a veiled face and black gloves, passed slowly by them the whole length of the corridor, and entered this room; they, believing that some unseemly mask wished to approach your majesty, followed the figure, and saw it enter this room. They ran hither to seize the maskers, but your majesty knows no such person is here."

"The white lady!" cried the king, and sank powerless and as if broken to pieces in the coffin. "The white lady! veiled and with black gloves! That signifies my death!"

"The white lady!" murmured the courtiers, withdrawing involuntarily from the door through which the evil-omened white lady should enter.

The queen alone was silent. She looked around with a searching glance upon the marble statues of the prince electors, and her soul was far away with her beloved son Frederick.

CHAPTER VII.

THE MAID OF HONOR, AND THE GARDENER.

I⊤ was a lovely day in May. The lilacs were in bloom; the birds were singing their sweetest songs; the swans floating upon the tranquil lake, which, bordered with water lilies and other fragrant plants, was one of the chief ornaments in the garden of the prince royal at Rheinsberg. It was still early; the residents of the palace, which was surrounded by this beautiful garden, were sleeping; the windows were closed and curtained, and you heard none of the sounds which usually arose from this gay and charming palace. No music fell on the ear but the melting tones of the nightingale and the morning song of the lark.

The prince royal himself was still asleep, for his flute was silent, and that was a sure sign to all who lived in the palace, that the lord of the house was not awake, or at least that he had not yet begun the day.

The music of his flute was the morning sacrifice with which the young prince greeted the day; it, like the pillar of Memnon, which gave forth a sound when touched by the rays of the sun, announced to his flattering courtiers that *their* sun had arisen.

But the flute was silent; the sun had therefore not arisen, although its beams had long been flooding the park in golden light, and drinking from every flower the dew that had fallen during the past sultry night.

Fritz Wendel, the gardener, was already busy with his watering-pot, and was at the same time anxiously selecting and gathering the most beautiful flowers, and concealing them carefully under the various plants and bushes; perhaps to protect them from the heat of the sun, perhaps to secure them from the curious eyes of some observer. Such eyes were already observing him, and resting upon him with an expression so tender and smiling, that you could see that the young girl to whom they belonged had a special interest in the tall, handsome gardener, who, in his modest, simple dress, and his great and imposing beauty, appeared to realize the truth of the old fables, of the gods who visited the earth in disguise. He might have been Apollo charmed by some Daphne, and taking this rude dress to approach the shepherdess he loved. Perhaps this charming young girl thought thus, and on that account looked at him so smilingly from behind the lilacs, or perhaps she believed him to be a prince, and waited anxiously for the moment when he would throw off his disguise and declare himself her equal. For she was, although not a princess, maid of honor to one, and of noble birth.

But youth is indifferent to such things as a genealogical tree, or a coat-of-arms, and what cared this child of thirteen summers whether Fritz Wendel was the son of a prince or a peasant? He pleased her because he was young and handsome, and he had one other great charm, he was her first lover. Every one else called Mademoiselle von Schwerin a child, and jested with little Louise. The princess royal had begged her from her mother, as a sort of plaything with which to amuse her lonely hours, and the title "maid of honor" was only a jest, which served merely to secure the entrance of the young lady to her royal mistress at any time.

But Louise was only a child in years; she possessed already the heart, the feelings, and the desires of a woman; nothing, therefore, hurt her pride so much as being called a child, and she was never happier than when her beauty and talent caused her youth to be forgotten.

Fritz Wendel, the young gardener, knew nothing of her age. For him she was Mademoiselle von Schwerin, a young lady, the goddess at whose shrine he worshipped, the fairy under whose glance his flowers bloomed, and his heart beat high. For her alone he tended the flowers and the fruits; for her alone had God created the earth; was she not its queen, and was it not natural that Fritz Wendel lay at her feet, and called her the star of his existence?

The young lady having watched her silent, dreaming "first lover" long enough, and tired of this unnatural silence, walked forward from her place of concealment, and bade Fritz Wendel good-morning, just as he was gathering a beautiful narcissus.

Poor Fritz trembled, and a deep blush overspread his face; he was so embarrassed that he forgot to return the young girl's greeting, and only bent still lower over the flower which he held in his hand.

"For whom are your flowers intended?" said Louise, "and why have you hidden the most beautiful ones? Will you not place them in the bouquet which you arrange every morning for the princess?"

"I have never been ordered to gather the most beautiful flowers for the princess," said Fritz Wendel, who had not yet dared to glance at the young lady. "The prince royal commanded me to place fresh flowers in the vases every morning; that is all."

"But it seems to me that is not all," said Louise, laughing, "for you were gathering other flowers; for whom are they intended, if not for the princess royal?"

Fritz Wendel at length dared to raise his eyes, and glance timidly at the smiling face of the young girl who stood near him.

"They are also intended for a princess," he said, in a low voice—"for my princess."

"Oh! then you have a special princess for whom you gather flowers?"

"Yes, I have my princess, whom I serve, and for whom I

would willingly sacrifice my life," cried the impetuous young man, with all the energy of his passionate and untamed nature.

Mademoiselle von Schwerin played carelessly with the branch of lilac which she held in her hand. She plucked off the small blossoms, and throwing them in the air, blew them about, as she danced here and there on tiptoe.

"I would like to know how it is that I find a magnificent bouquet in my room every morning, and who it is that dares to gather more beautiful flowers for me than any to be found in the vases of the princess royal?"

"It must be some one who adores you," said the young gardener, with his eyes on the ground, and blushing deeply at his own temerity.

"Then it is a nobleman, perhaps one of the court gentlemen," she said, casting a teasing glance on her embarrassed lover. "Who else would dare to adore me, or to send me flowers?"

"Yes, you are right, who would dare?" murmured Fritz Wendel; "perhaps some poor, deluded mortal, led by a wild insanity to forget his humble condition, and consider himself your equal. There have been maniacs who imagined themselves great among earth's greatest men, and equal even to the very God in heaven."

"How pale you are!" cried Louise, looking at the young man with undissembled tenderness. "Why do you weep, Fritz?"

She took his hand, and gazed into his eyes with a most singular expression, half curious, half questioning.

Fritz Wendel trembled with delight at her touch, but withdrew his hand almost with violence.

"I weep because I am a miserable gardener," he murmured; "I weep because I am not great and noble, like the gentlemen at court."

"Yesterday Baron von Kaiserling gave an account of an Austrian general, who was the son of a peasant, and had been a cowherd. Now he is a general, and is married to the daughter of a count."

The countenance of Fritz Wendel beamed with energy and courage.

"Oh! why is there not a war?" he cried, enthusiastically. "I could not fail to become a general, for I should fight like a lion."

"You would like to become a general, in order to marry the daughter of a count?"

"Not the daughter of a count, but——"

"Fritz Wendel! Fritz Wendel!" called a voice in the distance.

"It is the head gardener," said poor Fritz, sadly. "Farewell, farewell; be kind and gracious, and come again to-morrow to the garden."

He took his basket of flowers, and hurried down the avenue.

Mademoiselle von Schwerin followed him, with an angry glance. "Once more no declaration of love," she murmured, stamping on the ground with the spitefulness of a child. "He shall make me a declaration. Madame von Morien says there is nothing more heavenly than to hear for the first time that you are beloved. She also says it is wisest not to choose your lovers among your equals, but either above or beneath you, for then you may be sure that you will not be betrayed. She told me yesterday that she was never so worshipped as by a young huntsman who served her father when she was just my age, and that no other man had ever adored her as he had done. Now Fritz Wendel loves me also, and he shall make me a declaration, for I must know what this charming sensation is. He shall do it to-morrow. I will be so kind and gentle that he will tell me of his love. But now

I must return to the palace.   I dare not be found here," and the young girl flew away lightly as a gazelle.

––––––––

CHAPTER VIII.

VON MANTEUFFEL, THE DIPLOMAT.

THE garden was again solitary.   Nothing was heard but the chattering of birds, as they flitted from limb to limb, and the whispering of the wind among the trees; all else was tranquil and still.   But this did not last long.   The noise of advancing footsteps gave evidence of the approach of some one, whose figure was soon visible at the entrance of the grand avenue.

This person was again a lady, who, if not so . beautiful as Mademoiselle von Schwerin, was still pretty enough to be called one of the fair sex.   She was dressed in a charming and tasteful morning robe, which was eminently adapted to display to advantage the beautiful contour of her tall and stately figure.

Nor had she come into the garden merely to breathe the fresh morning air, and enjoy the delightful fragrance of flowers; these were scarcely observed, as she hurriedly swept past them.   She stood still for a moment at the end of the long avenue, and looked cautiously around in all directions. Seeing that no one was near, that she was alone and unobserved, she turned aside into the bushes, and, following a narrow, overgrown path, at last arrived at the garden wall, where she remained standing before a small door for a moment, listening with suppressed breathing.   Hearing . nothing, she clapped her hands three times, and listened again.   And now a repetition of her signal could be heard

from the other side, and she cried in clear and silvery tones,
"Good-morning, good-morning!" A deep, manly voice returned her greeting from the other side of the wall.

"It is he!" murmured the lady, and quickly drawing a
key from her pocket, she opened the door.

The man who had been standing outside sprang forward
through the open gate, and, bowing low to the lady, pressed
her proffered hand to his lips.

"Good-morning, Count Manteuffel," said she, smiling.
"Really you are as punctual as if coming to a rendezvous
with your lady love."

"*Tempi passati!*" sighed the count. "I am married."

"So am I," said the lady, laughing; "that is, however,
no reason why——"

"You should not still have ardent and devoted ad-
mirers," said the count, interrupting her. "But you are still
young and beautiful, while I have grown old. Tell me, kind
lady, by what art you have preserved the charming freshness
of youth, and those bright and sparkling eyes by which I
was so completely enslaved when I still had a heart?"

The lady gave him a penetrating, mocking look. "Count
Manteuffel," said she, "you are so friendly, and your adoration is of so profound a nature, that you undoubtedly have
some very particular favor to solicit at my hands. But come,
let us enter that little pavilion; there we will find comfortable seats, and be secure from all interruption."

They passed silently along the wall to the pavilion, to
which the same key gave access which had before opened
the garden door.

"Here we are safe," said the lady, throwing back the
lace veil which had concealed her face. "Come, count, let
us be seated; and now tell me why you desired this meeting, and why it is that your valet was not sent as usual to
deliver your letters and to receive mine?"

"I had an irresistible longing to see you, to behold once more your lovely countenance," said the count, with a deep sigh.

"But just now you said you had no heart," said the lady, laughing.

"You are the enchantress who recalls it to life. Really you do credit to your name, and, thanks to Madame Brandt, my heart is again in flames."

"Count, it is very evident that you are now playing a part to which you are not accustomed," exclaimed Madame Brandt, laughing. "When you attempt to act the lover you become insipid, while you are known and acknowledged to be one of the shrewdest and most ingenious of diplomatists. But no diplomatic subterfuges with me, I pray. Let us waste no time on the shell, but to the kernel at once! What do you require of me? In my last letter I gave you an accurate account of the state of affairs at court, and also of the state of my finances, which is precisely that of the prince royal's; that is, his purse is as empty as mine.

"And both of you have an empress who is only too happy to have the privilege of supplying this deficiency," said Count Manteuffel, drawing forth a well-filled purse, through the silken meshes of which gold glittered, and presenting it to the lady. "I am only sorry to say there are several empresses who have the inestimable privilege of assisting the prince royal and Madame Brandt."

"What do you mean, count? We no longer understand each other, and I beg of you not to speak in riddles, which I am not prepared to solve."

"I mean to say that the prince royal, in his moneyed embarrassments, no longer addresses himself to the Empress of Austria, although she, as his nearest relative, as the aunt of the princess royal, has undoubtedly the first claim to his confidence."

"But perhaps the purse of the Empress of Austria is in-sufficient to meet his demands," said Madame von Brandt.

"He should first have tested the purse of the empress, as he frequently did in former times—in times when not only the prince royal, but also his sister of Bairout, experienced the generosity of their imperial aunt. But the prince royal readily forgets the benefits which he has received."

"That he does," sighed Madame von Brandt. "We poor women are the greatest sufferers. He has loved us all, and forgotten us all."

"All?" asked Count Manteuffel.

"All, count! We are nothing more to him than the plaything of an hour; he then wearies of us, and throws us aside. There is but one whom he loves truly and con-stantly."

"And this lady's name?"

"The flute, count! Ah, you looked sadly crestfallen. True, this lady cannot be bribed, either with Austrian gold or with the flattery of the skilful Count Manteuffel; she is always discreet, always mysterious; she never betrays her lover. Ah, count, we might both learn something from this noble flute. Yes, believe me, I would try to be like her, if, unfortunately, I did not need so many things for which a flute has no use, and if the glitter of Austrian gold were not so alluring. But you, Count Manteuffel, why are you not like the flute? Why have you spies and eavesdroppers at all places? Why are you an Austrian spy at the court of Prussia—you who have wealth, rank, and standing which should place you above such paltry considerations?"

Count Manteuffel's brow darkened, and he compressed his lips angrily. But he quickly subdued this momentary irritation, and was once more the affable, easy, and attentive diplomat.

"I serve the Austrian court from inclination," said he,

"from preference, and certainly with honest intentions. I serve that court, because I am deeply convinced that upon Austria devolves the privilege and duty of dethroning all other German princes, and uniting all Germany under one government, of converting Austria into Germany. Prussia must then cease to exist in Austria, and must bend the knee as a vassal. That is my political conviction, and I act in accordance with it."

"And for this political conviction you receive Austrian gold and Austrian decorations," observed Madame von Brandt, laughing. "For the sake of your political conviction you have spies at all points, at the court of Potsdam, at the court of Dresden, and even here at the little court at Rheinsberg. Not satisfied with having bought over the prince royal's cook, and induced him to keep a diary for your inspection,* you have also succeeded in securing the services of that humble and modest little person, Madame von Brandt, who well knows that all this costs your Grace a considerable amount of money. And now you wish to make me believe that you do these things on account of your political conviction. Softly, my dear count! I, too, am a little diplomat, and have my convictions, and one of these is, that Count Manteuffel has but one passion, and that is, to play a political *rôle*, and to make as much money in that way as he possibly can. And to the good Count Manteuffel it is a matter of perfect indifference whether this money comes from Prussian or from Austrian sources."

"And why these amiable pleasantries?" said the count, with a forced smile.

"They mean, my dear count, that this miserable acting should cease; that we should lay aside our masks, and deal with each other truly and sincerely, when alone, as we are at

---

* "Youth of Frederick the Great," by Preuss, page 132.

present. I serve you, because I am paid for it; you serve Austria, because you are paid for it. If, in time of need, you were not at hand with a well-filled purse, I would cease to serve you; and you would no longer be enthusiastic on the subject of Austrian dominion, if Austria's money should cease to flow into your coffers. And now, my dear count, I believe we understand each other; and, without further circumlocution, what do you require of me—what have you to communicate?"

"I must speak with you on matters of very grave importance."

"I knew it! your flattery betrayed you," said Madame Brandt. "Well, begin."

"First of all, my dear baroness, you must know that the prince royal will in a few days be king."

"Not so, count; a courier arrived yesterday evening with the intelligence that his majesty was much better. The prince royal is so rejoiced that he has determined to give a *fête* in honor of Madame von Morien to-day."

"Does the prince royal still love this lady?"

"I told you before that he loved his flute alone," said Madame Brandt.

"Does he not, then, love the princess royal?"

"No! And perhaps he would not love her even if she were changed into a flute. He would probably say to Quantz, 'It is not made of good wood, and has a bad tone,' and would lay it aside."

"And do you believe he would do that with the princess? although she is no flute, do you believe he would cast her aside?"

"The princess dreads it."

"And so does the empress!"

"But why was a woman, who not only knows nothing about music, but has a hoarse and discordant voice, and who articulates so indistinctly that the prince royal could not understand her were she to say the wittiest things imaginable, why should such a woman have been given as a wife to a prince of such remarkable musical proclivities? One does not marry a woman merely to look at her."

"Then you believe the prince royal will separate himself from his wife as soon as he obtains his freedom, that is, when he becomes king?" observed Count Manteuffel, thoughtfully.

"Of that I know nothing, count. The prince never speaks of his wife, even to his most intimate friends; and in his tenderest moments Madame Morien herself endeavors in vain to obtain some information on this subject."

"The prince is very discreet and very suspicious. Madame Morien must be bought over," murmured the count.

"That will be a difficult task," said Madame Brandt. "She is unfortunately very rich, and attaches but little importance to money. I know of but one means. Procure for her a lover who is handsomer, more ardent, and more passionate than the prince royal, and she can be won! For it is well known that Madame Morien has a very susceptible heart."

"Baroness, no jesting, if you please; the matters under discussion are of the gravest importance, and our time is limited. Madame Morien must be won over. She alone can influence the prince through his heart, and her influence must be exerted to prevent a separation of the prince royal from his wife. You, my dear baroness, must induce Madame Morien to do this; you, with your bewitching eloquence, must make Madame Morien comprehend that this is the only means of doing penance for her sinful life, and that her only chance of reconciliation with Heaven depends upon her restoration of the faithless husband to the arms of his noble wife. She could, perhaps, save the princess royal and the imperial court the disgrace of a separation. The princess must remain the wife of the king. This is the only tie which can bind the king to Austria. The prince is surrounded by the enemies of Austria, of whom Suhm is the most dangerous."

"Well, he, at least, is not near the prince. You know that he is the ambassador of Saxony at the court of Petersburg."

"Therein lies the main difficulty! The prince royal places unlimited confidence in him, they correspond in characters which we have vainly endeavored to decipher; and the result of this correspondence is, that Suhm has already procured the prince royal a loan of ten thousand dollars from the Duke of Courland, and that he has now secured him the annual sum of twenty-four thousand dollars from the Empress Anne. These payments will continue until the prince ascends the throne; the first has just been received." *

"That is a fable," exclaimed Madame Brandt, laughing. "The prince is as poor as Job, and for some time past has been literally besieged by his creditors!"

"And it can be no other than Russia who assists him in these difficulties!" exclaimed Count Manteuffel, in despair. "We must leave nothing undone to lessen the influence of this dangerous enemy, and to win Prussia to Austrian interests. Germany wishes for peace, and Prussia and Austria must be on good terms. If Prussia and Austria were to take up arms against each other, the balance of power in Europe would be destroyed, and a war would be inaugurated which, perhaps, for years would deluge Germany with blood and tears! Austria will do all that lies in her power to avoid this; and we, my dear friend, will be Austria's allies, and will assist her to the best of our ability. Russia has given Prussia money, it is true, but an indebtedness of this kind

---

* Œuvres de Fréderic le Grand, vol. xvi., pp. 340, 356, 360, 384.

ceases the moment the money is returned. When the prince royal ascends the throne, he will pay to Russia what he owes her, and with that all obligations will be at an end. Then another tie must be found to bind Austria more firmly to Prussia. And you must help to weave this tie. The prince royal must never be separated from his wife! The future Queen of Prussia will then be the niece of the empress. The duties of a nephew will consequently devolve on the king. To unite the two houses more closely, another marriage must be brought about. The Prince Augustus William, the presumptive heir of the prince royal, must, like the latter, espouse a princess of the house of Brunswick—a sister of the princess royal."

"That is impossible!" exclaimed Madame Brandt, with vivacity.

"Impossible? Why impossible?"

"Because the heart of the Prince Augustus William is already filled with a deep and passionate love—a love which would even touch you, that is, if you are susceptible to pity."

"My dear madame, we are speaking of affairs of State, and you discourse of love! What have politics to do with love? The prince may love whom he will, provided he marries the Princess of Brunswick."

"But his is a great and noble, a real love, count—a love over which we have no power, in which the devil had no hand; a love as pure as Heaven, and deserving of Heaven's blessing! You must give this plan up, count; the Prince Augustus William will never marry the Princess of Brunswick. He is far too noble to give his hand without his heart, and that is devoted to the beautiful Laura von Pannewitz."

"A prince of the blood who loves a little maid of honor, and wishes to marry her?" exclaimed von Manteuffel, laughing loudly. "How romantic! how sublime! what excellent materials for a sentimental romance! My dear baroness, I congratulate you! This discovery does all honor to your poetical temperament."

"Mock me, if you will, count; but I repeat, nevertheless, Prince Augustus William will not marry the Princess of Brunswick, for he loves the beautiful maid of honor of the queen, and is determined to make her his wife."

"We will know how to break this determination," said Count Manteuffel. "The prince royal will assist us, depend upon it. He is not an enthusiastic lover, like Augustus William, and will never consent to his brother's making a misalliance."

"And I tell you, the prince would rather die than give up the beautiful Laura."

"Well, then she must give him up," said Count Manteuffel, with cruel composure.

"Poor Laura," said Madame Brandt, with a sigh, "she loves him so dearly! it will break her heart to lose him."

"Pshaw! the heart of every woman is broken one or more times, but it always heals again, and when warmed by a new love, the old scars disappear entirely. You, dear baroness, have experienced this in yourself. Have you no recollection of the days of our ardent and passionate love? Did we not expect to die when we were separated? Did we not wring our hands, and pray for death as a relief? And are we not still living, to smile pityingly at the pangs we then endured, and to remember how often we have experienced delight, how often love has since triumphed in our hearts?"

"It is true," sighed Madame Brandt, "we outlive our sorrows; the heart of women resembles the worm—it still lives and quivers, although cut in pieces."

"Well," said Count Manteuffel, laughing, "the heart of Laura von Pannewitz is merely a worm, and we will not hesitate to cut it in pieces, as it will still live merrily on.

You, my dear friend, shall be the knife which performs the operation. Are you willing?"

For a moment Madame Brandt looked down sadly, and seemed lost in thought.

"True," she murmured, "we outlive it, but the best part of our being is destroyed! I should never have become what I am, if I had not been ruthlessly torn from my first dream of love. We will not kill Laura von Pannewitz's body, but her soul will suffer!"

"And as it is not our province to look after souls, that need give us no care; a political necessity demands that Prince Augustus William shall marry the Princess of Brunswick. It demands, moreover, that the prince royal shall not be divorced from his wife, but that the niece of the empress shall be Queen of Prussia. In both of these affairs we need your assistance. You must closely watch the Prince Augustus William and his lady love, and, at the proper time, bring the affair to light. By your eloquence you must convince Madame Morien that it is her duty to exert her influence with the prince royal to prevent his separation from his wife. This is your task, and a noble task it is. Its objects are—to protect the peace of married life; to recall two noble hearts to the duties which they owe to the world; and lastly, to create a new bond of union between two mighty German powers. The wife of the Emperor Charles VI., the noble empress, will not be ungrateful to her ally, Madame Brandt. On the day on which Prince William espouses the Princess Louisa Amelia of Brunswick, Madame Brandt will receive a present of twenty thousand dollars from the empress."

The countenance of Madame Brandt was radiant with pleasure and delight.

"The prince shall and will marry the Princess Louisa Amelia—my word for it. I am then to be the demon who, with his poisonous breath, destroys this romantic, this beautiful love; the evil genius who drives fair Laura to despair. But why should I pity her? She suffers the fate of all women—my fate. Who pitied, who saved me? No one listened to my cry of anguish, and no one shall heed the wailing cry of the fair Laura von Pannewitz. Count, she is condemned! But, hark! Do you not hear faint tones of distant music? The prince royal has arisen, and is playing the flute at his open window. We must now separate; the garden will soon be full of people, and we are no longer safe from intrusion. A boat-ride on the lake is in contemplation for the early morning hours, and then Chazot will read Voltaire's last drama to the assembled court."

CHAPTER IX.

FREDERICK, THE PRINCE ROYAL.

MADAME BRANDT was not mistaken; the prince royal was awake, and was bringing a tribute to beautiful, sunny Nature in return for the sweely-scented air that came through his window. There he stood, with the flute at his lips, and looked out at God's lovely, laughing world with a sparkling eye and joyful countenance. A cheerful quiet, a holy peace radiated from his beautiful face; his whole being seemed bathed in perfect harmony and contentment, and the soft, melting tones of his flute but echoed his thoughts. Suddenly he ceased playing, and slightly bowed his head to catch the sweet, dying notes that were still trembling in the air.

"That was good," said he, smiling, "and I believe I can note it down without exciting the anger of Quantz." **He**

3*

took his flute again, and softly repeated the air he had just finished. " I will write it immediately, and play it this evening before my critical musicians."

While speaking, Frederick left his bedroom, and passed into his library. On entering this room, a beautiful smile flitted over his face, and he bowed his head as if saluting some one. It would be impossible to imagine a more charming and tasteful room. It had been arranged according to the directions of the prince royal, and was in a great degree a true portrait of himself, a temple which he had erected to art, science, and friendship.

This room was in the new tower, and its circular form gave it a peculiar appearance. It was most appropriately compared to a temple. High glass cases around the walls contained the works of Voltaire, Racine, Molière, and Corneille; those of Homer, Cæsar, Cicero, and Ovid; also the Italian poets Dante, Petrarch, and Machiavel. All that had a good name in the literary world found its way into the library of the prince royal—all, excepting the works of German authors.

Between the book-cases, the shelves of which were ornamented here and there with busts of celebrated writers, were alcoves, in which stood small satin damask sofas, over which hung, in heavily-gilt frames, the portraits of Frederick's friends and contemporaries.

The largest and most beautiful was one of Voltaire. He had received the honored place; and when Frederick raised his eyes from his work, while sitting at his escritoire, they rested upon the smiling face of the talented French writer, whom the prince royal had selected as his favorite, and with whom he had for many years corresponded.

The prince went with hasty steps to his table, and, without noticing the sealed letters that were lying there, he took a piece of lined paper, and began to write, humming softly the melody he had just composed. He occasionally threw down his pen, and took the flute that was lying at his side, to try, before noting them, different accords and passages.

"It is finished at last," said the prince, laying aside his pen. "My adagio is finished, and I think Quantz will have no excuse for grumbling to-day; he must be contented with his pupil. This adagio is good; I feel it; I know it; and if the Bendas assume their usual artist airs, I will tell them—; no, I will tell them nothing," said the prince, smiling. "It is useless to show those gentlemen that I care for their approval, or court their applause. Ours is a pitiful race, and I see the time approaching when I shall despise and mistrust the whole world; and still my heart is soft, and gives a warm approval to all that is great and beautiful, and it would make me very happy to love and trust my fellow-men; but they do not desire it—they would not appreciate it. Am I not surrounded by spies, who watch all my movements, listen to every word I utter, and then pour their poison into the ear of the king? But enough of this," said the prince, after a pause. "This May air makes me dreamy. Away with these cobwebs! I have not time to sigh or dream."

He arose, and walked hastily up and down his room, then approached the escritoire, and took the letters. As his eye fell on the first, he smiled proudly.

"From Voltaire," he murmured softly, breaking the seal, and hastily opening the enclosure, which contained two letters and several loose scraps of printed matter. The prince uttered a cry of joyful astonishment, and scarcely noticing the two letters, he gazed with a half-tender, half-curious expression on the printed papers he held in his hand.

"At last! at last!" exclaimed the prince, "my wish will be accomplished. The first step toward fame is taken. I shall no longer be unknown, or only known as the son of a king, the inheritor of a throne. I shall have a name. I shall acquire renown, for I will be a poet, an author, and shall claim a place in the republic of genius. I shall not need a crown to preserve my name in history. The first step is taken. My 'Anti-Machiavel' is in press. I will tread under foot this monster of knavish and diabolic statecraft, and all Europe shall see that a German prince is the first to break a lance against this Machiavel, who is making the people the slaves of princes. By his vile principles, he is moulding princes into such monsters that all mankind must curse them."

And again looking at the paper, the prince read a few lines, his voice trembling with displeasure :

"If it is a crime to destroy the innocence of a private individual who exercises a limited influence, is it not far worse to undermine the moral character of princes who should exhibit to their subjects an example of goodness, greatness, kindness, and love ? The plagues sent by Heaven are but passing, and destroy only in certain localities ; and although most disastrous, their effects pass away in time. But the vices of kings create incurable misery ; yes, misery enduring for generations. How deplorable is the condition of nations who have every evil to fear from their ruler, their property exposed to the covetousness of a prince, their freedom to his humor, and their lives to his cruelty !"

Frederick ceased, and turned over a few pages of his "Anti-Machiavel," and then continued to read :

"Machiavel speaks in his *'Principe'* of miniature sovereigns, who, having but small states, can send no armies to the field. The author advises them to fortify their capitals, and in time of war to confine themselves and their troops to them.

"The Italian princes, of whom Machiavel speaks, only play the part of men before their servants. Most of the

smaller princes, and especially those of Germany, ruin themselves by spending sums far exceeding their revenues, and
thus by vanity are led to want. Even the youngest scion
of the least important salaried prince imagines himself as
great as Louis. He builds his Versailles, and sustains his
army. There is in reality a certain salaried prince of a
noble house, who has in his service all the varieties of
guards that usually form the households of great kings, but
all on so minute a scale that it is necessary to employ
a microscope to distinguish each separate corps, and whose
army is perhaps strong enough to represent a battle on the
stage of Verona."

Prince Frederick laughed aloud. "Well, I think my most
worthy cousin, Ernest Augustus, of Saxe-Weimar, will understand this allusion, and in gratitude for my giving his
name to posterity in my 'Anti-Machiavel,' will unravel the
mystery, and inform the world how it is possible, with the
annual income of four hundred dollars, to keep a retinue
of seven hundred men, a squadron of one hundred and eighty,
and a company of cavalry; if he is capable of accomplishing this, without plunging into debt, he is certainly my
superior, and I could learn a great deal from him. I could
learn of him how to rid myself of this torment that I endure
from day to day, from hour to hour. What could be a
greater degradation to an honorable man than to be compelled to flatter the base pride of these vile usurers to whom
I am forced to resort for the money I need; this money
pressed, perhaps, from widows and orphans. To think that
I, the inheritor of a kingdom, am in this condition—that I
must lower myself to sue and plead before these men, while
millions are lying in the cellars of my father's palace at
Berlin! But what! Have I the right to complain? am I
the only one who suffers from the closeness of the king? are
not the people of Berlin crying for bread, whilst the royal

larder is filled to overflowing? But patience! the day will
come when the keys will be in my hands—on that day I
will give the people what rightly belongs to them, bread. I
will unlock the treasury and set free the imprisoned millions.
But what noise is this?" said the prince, approaching the
door.

Loud and angry noises were heard from without. "I tell
you I must and will speak with the prince royal," cried a
threatening voice; "I have waited in vain for two months,
in vain addressed to him the most modest and respectful
letters; I have not even been deemed worthy to receive an
answer. Now I have come to receive it in person, and I
swear I will not leave this spot without an explanation with
the prince royal."

"It is Ephraim," muttered Frederick, with a deep
frown.

"Well, you can stand here until you become a pillar of
salt, like your great-grandmother of old," cried another voice.

"This is Knobelsdorf," said Frederick.

"The idea is good," said the first voice, "but it is not I
who will become a pillar of salt, but others will from fright
and terror, when I come with my avenging sword; for justice
I will have, and if I do not obtain it here, I shall go and
demand it of the king."

"From the king! you do not know, then, that his majesty
is dying?"

"Not so, not so! if that were so, I would not be here; I
would have waited quietly for that justice from the new king
which I demanded in vain from the prince royal. The
king is recovering; I saw him in his arm-chair in the garden;
for this reason I insist on speaking to the prince."

"But if I tell you his royal highness is still asleep?"

"I would not believe you, for I heard him playing on his
flute."

"That was Quantz."

"Quantz! he is not capable of playing such an adagio; no, no, it could only have been the prince royal."

"Ah! this man wishes to bribe me with his flattery," said the prince, smiling, "and make me believe I am an Orpheus. Orpheus tamed lions and tigers with his music, but my flute is not even capable of taming a creditor."

"But I say it was Quantz," cried the poor frightened Knobelsdorf; "the prince still sleeps, or is in bed, for he is not well, and gave orders to admit no one."

"Ah! I know all about that; noble gentlemen are always ill if they have to breathe the same air with their creditors," said Ephraim, with a mocking smile; "but I tell you I will stay here until I have spoken to the prince, until he returns me four thousand dollars that I lent to him, more than a year ago, without interest or security. I must and will have my money, or I shall be ruined myself. The prince cannot wish that; he will not punish me so severely for the kindness and pity I showed to him in his greatest need."

"This is really too much," cried Knobelsdorf, "you are shameless; do you dare to speak of pity for the prince royal? do you dare to boast of having lent him money, while you only did it knowing he could and would repay you with interest?"

"If Ephraim knows that, he is cleverer than I am," said Frederick, smiling sadly; "although I am a prince, I do not know how to get the miserable sum of four thousand dollars. But I must leave poor Knobelsdorf no longer in this condition; I must quiet this uproar." And he hastened toward the door, as the noise without became louder and louder.

CHAPTER X.

THE PRINCE ROYAL AND THE JEW.

AT this moment, while Knobelsdorf was threatening the Jew and calling the servants to thrust him out, the prince royal opened the door and showed his smiling face to the two combatants.

"Come in," said the prince, "I grant you the audience you so importunately demand."

Frederick stepped back quietly in his room, while Ephraim, confused and humiliated by the calm dignity of the prince, advanced with bowed head and downcast eyes.

"Dear Knobelsdorf," said Frederick, turning to his gasping secretary, who stood amazed behind the Jew, "I pray you to assemble all the ladies and gentlemen in the garden; we are going yachting; I will be with you in five minutes."

"Five minutes," said Ephraim to himself, as Knobelsdorf withdrew, "only one moment's audience for every thousand dollars! This is a proud debtor; I would have done better not to place myself in his power. But I will not be frightened, I will stand up boldly for my rights!"

"And now, what have you to say to me?" said the prince, fixing his angry eyes upon Ephraim.

"What have I to say to your highness!" said Ephraim, astonished. "More than a year ago I lent your highness four thousand dollars! I have as yet received neither principal nor interest."

"Well, what more?"

"What more!" said Ephraim.

"Yes, what more? It is impossible that you have come from Berlin to Rheinsberg to tell me what I have known for a year as well as yourself."

"I thought your highness had forgotten," said the Jew,

fixing his eyes upon the prince, but casting them suddenly to the floor, as he met the flashing glance of Frederick.

"Forgotten," said he, shrugging his shoulders; "I have a good memory for every act of kindness, and also for every offence against the respect and reverence due to the son of the king."

His voice was so harsh and threatening, that Ephraim trembled in his inmost heart, and stammered some words of apology.

"My prince," said he, "I am a Jew, that is to say a despised, reviled, and persecuted man! no—not a man, but a creature—kicked like a dog when poor and suffering, and even when the possessor of gold and treasures, scarcely allowed human rights. It is better for the dogs than for the Jews in Prussia! A dog dare have its young, and rejoice over them, but the Jews dare not rejoice over their children! The law of the land hangs like a sword over them, and it may be that a Jewess may be driven out of Prussia because a child is born to her, only a specified number of Jews being allowed in this enlightened land! Perhaps the father is not rich enough to pay the thousand dollars with which he must buy the right to be a father every time a child is born to him! For this reason is gold, and again gold, the only wall of protection which a Jew can build up between himself and wretchedness! Gold is our honor, our rank, our destiny, our family, our home. We are nothing without gold, and even when we extend a golden hand, there is no hand advanced to meet it that does not feel itself contaminated by the touch of a Jew! Judge, then, your royal highness, how much we love, how highly we prize one to whom we give a part of our happiness, a part of our honor. I have done for you, my prince, what I have done for no other man. I have given you four thousand dollars, without security and without interest. I lent to Knobelsdorf, for the prince royal, upon his mere word, my honest gold, and what have I received? My letters, in which I humbly solicit payment, remain unanswered. I am mocked and reviled—the door contemptuously shut in my face, which door, however, was most graciously opened when I brought my gold. Such conduct is neither right nor wise; and as the worm turns when it is trodden upon, so is there also a limit to the endurance of the Jew. He remembers at last that he is also one of God's creatures, and that God himself has given him the passion of revenge as well as the passion of love. The Jew, when too long mishandled, revenges himself upon his torturers, and that will I also do, if I do not receive justice at your hands. That will I also do, if you refuse me my gold to-day."

"You have made a lengthy and impertinent speech!" said Frederick. "You have threatened me! But I will forgive you, because you are a Jew; because the tongue is the only weapon a Jew has, and knows how to use. I now advise you to put your sword in its sheath, and listen calmly to me. It is true, you have lent me four thousand dollars without security and without interest. You need not extol yourself for this, for you well know it is not the wish or the intention of the prince royal to oppress even the most pitiful of his subjects, or to withhold the smallest of their rights. You knew this; then why were you not satisfied to wait until I sent for you?"

"I can wait no longer, your highness," cried Ephraim, passionately. "My honor and credit are at stake. Count Knobelsdorf gave me his sacred promise that at the end of six months my money with interest should be returned. I believed him, because he spoke in the name of the prince royal. I now need this money for my business. I can no longer do without it. I must have it to-day."

"You must? I say you shall not receive one penny of it to-day, nor to-morrow, nor for weeks!"

"If your highness is in earnest, I must go elsewhere and seek redress."

"That means you will go to the king."

"Yes, your highness, I will!"

"Are you ignorant of the law by which all are forbidden to lend money to the princes of the royal house?"

"I am not ignorant of that law; but I know that the king will make an exception—that he will pay the money I lent to his successor. It is possible I may feel his crutch upon my back, but blows will not degrade me. The Jew is accustomed to blows and kicks—to be daily trodden under foot. Even if the king beats me, he will give me back my honor, for he will give me back my gold."

"Suppose that he also refuses you?"

"Then I will raise my voice until it is heard over the whole earth," cried Ephraim, passionately.

"Well, then, raise your voice and cry out. I can give you no gold to-day."

"No gold!" said Ephraim. "Am I again to be paid with cunning smiles and scornful words? You will withhold my gold from me? Because you are great and powerful, you think you can oppress and mistreat a poor Jew with impunity, but there is a God for the just and unjust, and He——"

He stopped. Before him stood Frederick, blazing with anger. His lips were pallid and trembling, his arm uplifted.

"Strike, your highness!—strike!" cried Ephraim, fiercely. "I deserve to be beaten, for I was a fool, and allowed myself to be dazzled with the glory of lending my gold to an unhappy but noble prince! Strike on, your highness! I see now that this prince is but a man like the rest; he scorns and loathes the poor Jew, but he will borrow his money, and defraud him of his rights."

Frederick's arm had fallen, and a soft smile played about his lips.

"No," said he, "you shall see that Frederick is not a man like other men. This day you shall have your money. I cannot pay you in money, but I will give you jewels, and horses from the stud that the king lately gave me."

"Then your highness has really no money?" said Ephraim, thoughtfully. "It was not then to frighten and torment the poor Jew that my gold was denied me. Can it be possible that the great Prince Frederick, on whom the hopes of the people rest, and who is already dearly loved by his future subjects, can be without money? Is it possible that he suffers like other men? My God! how dare we poor Jews complain when the heir to a throne is harassed for money, and must endure privations?"

The prince was not listening to Ephraim; he had opened a closet, and taken from it a silver-bound casket, and was gazing intently at its contents. He drew forth a large diamond cross and some *solitaires* and approached the Jew.

"Here are some jewels, I think, well worth your four thousand dollars; sell them and pay yourself," said the prince, handing him the sparkling stones.

Ephraim pushed the prince's hand gently back. "I lent gold, and gold only will I accept in payment."

The prince stamped impatiently upon the ground. "I told you I had no gold!"

"Then I cannot receive any," said Ephraim, passively. "The poor Jew will wait still longer; he will give to the prince royal the gold which he needs, and of which the poor Jew still has a little. I humbly ask your highness if you would not like to borrow another thousand, which I will gladly lend upon one condition."

"Well, and this condition?"

"Your highness is to pay me upon the spot the interest

upon the four thousand in ready money? Does your highness understand? Just now you wished to pay my capital
with diamonds and horses. Will you give me as interest a
few costly pearls—pearls which lie hidden in that flute, and
which appear at your magical touch? I will count this as
ready money!"

Frederick came nearer to Ephraim, and eying him
sternly, he said:

"Are you mocking me? Would you make of the prince
royal a travelling musician, who must play before the Jew, in
order to soften his heart?—would you——? Ah, Fredersdorf," said he, interrupting himself, as his valet approached
him in a dusty travelling-suit, "have you just arrived from
Berlin?"

"Yes, your highness; and as I was told who was impor-
tuning your highness, I came in without changing my dress.
The banker gave me this package for you. I believe it is
from Petersburg."

"From Suhm," said the prince, with a happy smile, and
hastily breaking the seal, he drew from the package a letter
and several books. Casting a loving glance at the letter, he
laid it on his writing-table; then turning away, so as not to
be seen by Ephraim, he took up the two books, and looked
carefully at their heavily-gilded covers. Frederick smiled, and,
taking a penknife, he hastily cut off the back of the books,
and took out a number of folded papers. As the prince saw
them, a look of triumph passed over his expressive face.

"Ten thousand dollars!" said he to himself. "The empress and the Duke Biron have fulfilled their promise!"

Frederick took some of the papers in his hand, and
walked toward Ephraim.

"Here are your four thousand dollars, and one hundred
interest. Are you satisfied?"

"No, your royal highness, I am not satisfied! I am not

satisfied with myself.   When I came to Rheinsberg I thought I had been wronged. It now seems to me that I have wronged your highness!"

"Let that pass," said Frederick. "A prince must always be the scapegoat for the sin-offering of the people. They make us answerable for all their sufferings, but have no sympathy for us in our griefs.   I owe you nothing more—you can go."

Ephraim bowed silently, and turned slowly toward the door. The eyes of the prince followed him with a kindly expression. He stepped to the table, and took up his flute. Ephraim had reached the door of the ante-chamber, but when he heard the soft melting tones of the flute, he stopped, and remained listening breathlessly at the outer door. The piercing glance of the prince rested on him; but he continued to play, and drew from his flute such touching and melancholy tones that the poor Jew seemed completely overcome. He folded his hands, as though engaged in fervent prayer; and even Fredersdorf, although a daily hearer of the prince, listened in breathless silence to those sweet sounds.

When the adagio was ended, the prince laid down his flute, and signed to Fredersdorf to close the door; he wished to give Ephraim an opportunity of slipping away unobserved.

"Did your highness know that the Jew was listening?" said Fredersdorf.

"Yes, I knew it; but I owed the poor devil something; he offered to lend me still another thousand dollars! I will remember this. And now, Fredersdorf, tell me quickly how goes it in Berlin? How is the king?"

"Better, your highness. He set out for Potsdam a few days since, and the pure fresh air has done him good. He shows himself, daily upon the balcony, in full uniform. The physicians, it is true, look very thoughtful; but the rest of the world believe the king is rapidly improving."

"God grant that the physicians may be again mistaken!" said the prince. "May the king reign many long and happy years! If he allow me to live as I wish, I would willingly give an arm if I could thereby lengthen his life. Well, now for mirth and song! We will be gay, and thus celebrate the king's improvement. Make, therefore, all liberal arrangements. Give the cook his orders, and tell the ladies and gentlemen assembled in the garden that I will be with them immediately."

The prince was now alone; he opened the letter he had received with the gold; his eye rested lovingly upon the handwriting of his distant friend, and his heart glowed as he read the words of friendship, admiration, and love from Suhm.

"Truly," he said, raising his eyes devoutly to heaven, "a faithful friend is worth more than a king's crown. In spite of all my brilliant prospects in the future, what would have become of me if Suhm had not stood by me for the second time and borrowed this money for me in Russia—this paltry sum, which I have in vain sought to obtain in my own land? My heart tells me to write a few lines at once to Suhm, expressing my unshaken friendship, my enduring love."

Frederick seated himself, and wrote one of those soul-inspiring letters for which he was so celebrated, and which ended thus: "In a short time my fate will be decided! You can well imagine that I am not at ease in my present condition. I have little leisure, but my heart is young and fresh, and I can assure you that I was never more a philosopher than now. I look with absolute indifference upon the future. My heart is not agitated by hope or fear, it is full of pity for those who suffer, of consideration for all honest men, and of tenderness and sympathy for my friends. You, whom I dare proudly count among the latter, may be more and more convinced that you will ever find in me what Orestes was to his Pylades, and that it is not possible for any one to esteem and love you more than your devoted Frederick."

"Now," said the prince, as he arose, "away with the burdens, the gravities and cares of life! Come, now, spirit of love! spirit of bliss! We will celebrate a feast this day in thy honor, thou goddess of youth and hope! Come, lovely Venus, and bring with thee thy son Cupid! We will worship you both. To you belongs this day, this night. You, goddess of love, have sent me the little Morien, that fluttering, light gazelle, that imperious, laughing fairy—that 'Tourbillon' of caprice and passion. Here is the poem I composed for her. Madame Brandt shall hand it to her, and shall lead the 'Tourbillon' into the temple of love. Away with earnest faces, dull eyes, and the wisdom of fools! Come over me, spirit of love, and grant me one hour of blessed forgetfulness."

The prince rang for his valet, and commanded him to lay out his latest French suit; he entered his boudoir, and with a comic earnestness, and the eager haste of a rash, impatient lover, he gave himself to the duties and arts of a royal toilet.

CHAPTER XI.

THE PRINCESS ROYAL ELIZABETH CHRISTINE.

THE princess royal had not yet left her rooms; she still waited for the prince, whose custom it was to give her his arm every morning and lead her to the saloon. On these occasions only did the Princess Elizabeth ever see her husband alone, then only did he address one word to her, touch her

hand, or allow her to lean upon his arm. A sweet and sad
happiness for this young wife, who lived only in the light of
her husband's countenance; who had no other wish, no other
prayer, no other hope than to please him. She felt that the
eye of Frederick never rested upon her with any other expression than that of cold friendship or absolute indifference.
The reason for this she could never fathom. Elizabeth would
have given her heart's blood to be beloved by him for one
single day, yes, for one short, blessed hour; to be clasped to
his heart, not for form or etiquette, but as a loving and beloved wife, to receive in her ear the sweet whispers of his
tenderness and his fondness. She would have given years
of her life to have bought this man, whom she so passionately loved; he was her earthly god, the ideal of her maiden
dreams. This man was her husband; he belonged to her;
he was bound to her by the holiest ties, and yet there was an
impassable gulf between them, which her unbounded love,
her prayers, her sighs, could not bridge over. The prince
loved her not; never had the slightest pulse of his heart belonged to her! He endured her, only endured her by his
side, as the poor prisoner, sighing for fresh air, permits the
presence of the jailer, when he can only thus buy a brief
enjoyment of God's gay and sunny world. The prince royal
was a prisoner, her prisoner. Not love, but *force* had placed
that golden ring upon his hand, that first link in the long, invisible heavy chain, which from that weary hour had bound
his feet, yes, his soul; from which even his thoughts were
were never free. Elizabeth knew that she was an ever-
present, bitter memento of his sad, crushed, tortured, and
humbled youth—a constant reminder of the noble friend of
his early years, whose blood had been shed for him, and to
whose last wild death-cry his tortured heart had been compelled to listen. Her presence must ever recall the scorn, the
hatred, the oposition of his stern father; the hardships, the

4

abuse, the humiliations, yes, even the blows, all of which had at last bowed the noble mind of the prince and led him to take upon himself the slavery of this hated marriage, in order to be free from the scorn and cruelty of his father. To escape from his dreary prison in Ruppin, he rushed into the bonds of wedlock. How could· he ever forgive, how could he ever love this woman forced upon him, like drops of wormwood, and swallowed only with the hope of thereby escaping the torturous pains and last struggle with death?

Elizabeth had been ignorant of all these bitter truths. The prince had been ever considerate and kind, though cold, when they met; she had had one single confidential interview with him, and in that hour he had disclosed to her what had forced them together, and at the same time forever separated them. Never could he love the wife associated in his mind, though innocently, with such cruelties and horrors; he was fully convinced that she, also, could not love a husband thus forced upon her; could entertain no feeling for him but that of respectful consideration and cold indifference.

Frederick did not know with what deadly wounds these words had pierced the princess; she had the strength to veil her passion and her shame with smiles, and in her modest maidenly pride she buried both in her heart. Since that interview years had gone by, and every year the love of the princess royal for her husband became more ardent; his eyes were the sun which warmed and strengthened this flower of love, and her tears were the dew which nourished and gave it vitality.

Elizabeth hoped still to ravish the heart of her husband; she yet believed that her resigned, modest, but proud and great love, might conquer his coldness; and yet, in spite of this hope, in spite of this future trust, Elizabeth trembled and feared more than formerly. She knew that the hour of decision was drawing nigh; she felt with the instinct of true

love that a new storm was rising on the ever-clouded horizon
of her marriage, and that the lightning might soon destroy
her.

Frederick had been forced by the power of the king, his
father, to marry her; how would it be when this power
should cease, when her husband should be king? by no one
held back; by no one controlled; free himself, and free to
give laws to the world; to acknowledge no man as his judge;
to be restrained by nothing but his conscience. Might not
even his conscience counsel him to dissolve this unnatural
marriage, which had within itself no spark of God's truth,
no ray of God's blessing? might not her husband cast her
off and take this English princess for his wife? had she not
been the choice of his heart? had not King George, although too late, declared his willingness for the betrothal?
had they not loved each other with the enthusiasm of youth,
although they had never met? did not Sophia Amelia's
portrait hang in the library of the crown prince? did not
the English princess wear his picture constantly near her
heart? had she not sworn never to be the wife of another
man?

As Elizabeth thought of these things she trembled, and it
seemed to her that her whole life would go out in one great
cry of anguish and horror.

"No," she said, "I cannot live without him! I will never
consent! he can kill me, but he cannot force me to break
the solemn oath I have sworn on God's holy altar. He shall
not cast me out into the wild wilderness, as Abram did
Hagar, and choose another wife!"

He could not force her to leave him, but he could beseech
her, and Elizabeth knew full well there was nothing in the
world she could refuse to her husband, which he would condescend so far as to entreat; for one loving. grateful word
from his lips, she would give him her heart's blood, drop by

drop ; for one tender embrace, one passionate kiss, she would lay down her life joyfully.   But she would not believe in this separation ; she would yet escape this unblessed fate—would find a way to his love, his sympathy, at least to his pity.

It was a struggle for life, for happiness, for her future, yes, even for honor ; for a divorced wife, even a princess, bears ever a stain upon her fair name, and walks lonely, unpitied, ever despised through the world.

For these reasons the poor princess of late redoubled her efforts to please her husband ; she entered more frequently into the gayeties of the court circle, and sometimes even took a part in the frivolous and rather free jests of her husband's evening parties ; sometimes she was rewarded by a smile and a glance of applause from Frederick.   This was for Elizabeth the noblest jewel in her martyr crown of love, more costly, more precious than all her pearls and diamonds.

To-day one of these joyous and unrestrained circles was to meet.   The prince loved these *fêtes ;* he was more charming, witty, talented, and unrestrained, than any of his guests. Princess Elizabeth resolved to be no quiet silent member of this circle to-day ; she would force her husband to look upon her and admire her ; she would be more beautiful than all the other ladies of the court ; more lovely than the gay and talented coquette, Madame Brandt ; more entrancing than the genial 'Tourbillon,' Madame Morien ; yes, even the youthful Schwerin, with her glancing eye and glowing cheek, should not excel her.

She was also young and charming, might be admired, loved—yes, adored, not only as a princess, not only as the wife of the handsome and genial prince royal, but for her own lovely self.   She had dismissed her maid, her toilet was completed, and she waited for the prince royal to lead her into the saloon.   The princess stepped to the glass and examined herself, not admiringly, but curiously, searchingly.

This figure in the mirror should be to her as that of a stranger to be remarked upon, and criticised coldly, even harshly; she must know if this woman might ever hope to enchain the handsome prince royal. "Yes," whispered she to herself, "this form is slender and not without grace; this white satin robe falls in full voluptuous folds from the slender waist over the well-made form; it contrasts well with these shoulders, of which my maids have often said 'they were white as alabaster;' with this throat, of which Madame Morien says 'it is white and graceful as the swan's.' This foot, which peeps out from the silken hem of my robe, is small and slender; this hand is fair and small, and well formed. I was constrained yesterday to promise the painter Pesne to allow him to paint it for his goddess Aurora; and this face! is it ugly to look upon? No, this face is not ugly; here is a high, clear forehead; the eyebrows well formed and well placed, the eyes are large and bright, the nose is small but nobly formed, the mouth good, the lips soft and red: yes, this face is handsome. O my God! why can I not please my husband?—why will he never look upon me with admiration?"

Her head sank upon her breast, and she was lost in sad and melancholy dreams; a few cold tears dropping slowly upon her cheeks aroused her; with a rash movement she raised her head, and shook the tears from her eyes; then looked again in the glass. "Why does not the prince love me?" whispered she again to herself with trembling lips. "I see it, I know it! It is written in unmistakable lines in this poor face. I know why he loves me not. These great blue eyes have no fire, no soul; this mouth has no magical, alluring smile. Yes, alas! yes, that is a lovely form; but the soul fails!—a fine nature, but the power of intellect is wanting. My Father, my heavenly Father, I sleep; my soul lies dead and stiffened in the coffin with my secret sorrows;

the prince could awaken it with his kisses, could breathe a new life into it by a glance."

The princess raised her arms imploringly on high, and her trembling lips whispered, "Pygmalion, why come you not to awaken thy Galatea? Why will you not change this marble statue into a woman of flesh and blood, with heart and soul? These lips are ready to smile, to utter a cry of rapture and delight, and behind the veil of my eyes lies a soul, which one touch of thine will arouse!　O Frederick! Frederick! why do you torture me? Do you not know that your wife worships, loves, adores you; that you are her salvation, her god?　Oh, I know these are unholy, sinful words! what then? I am a sinner! I am ready to give my soul in exchange for thee, Frederick. Why do you not hear me?—why have not my sighs, my tears the power to bring you to my side?"

The poor, young wife sank powerless into her chair, and covering her face with her hands, wept bitterly. Gay voices and loud laughter, sounding from beneath her window, aroused her from this trance of grief.

"That is Madame Brandt and the Duke of Brunswick," said Elizabeth, hastening to the window, and peeping from behind the curtains into the garden.

Yes, there stood the duke in lively conversation with Jordan Kaiserling Chazot, and the newly-arrived Bielfeld; but the ladies were nowhere to be seen, and the princess concluded they were already in the ante-room, and that the prince would soon join her.

"He must not see that I have wept; no one must see that." She breathed upon her handkerchief, and pressed its damp folds upon her eyes. "No, I will smile and be gay, like Madame Brandt and Morien. I will laugh and jest, and no one shall guess that my heart is bleeding and dying with inexplicable grief. Yes, gay will I be, and smiling; so only can I please my husband." She gave a sad, heart-breaking laugh, which was echoed loudly and joyously in the ante-room.

CHAPTER XII.

THE POEM.

THE ladies of the court, and those who were guests at the palace of Rheinsberg, were assembled, and waiting in the ante-room, as the princess royal had supposed. A few of them had withdrawn to one of the windows with Madame von Katch, the first lady of honor, and were conversing in low voices, while Madame von Brandt and Madame von Morien held an earnest but low-toned conversation in another part of the room.

Madame von Morien listened anxiously to her friend, and the varying emotions of her soul were clearly mirrored on her speaking countenance. At one moment a happy smile overspread her lovely features, but the next a cloud lay on that pure, fair brow, and darkened those black and glorious eyes.

" As I told you," whispered Madame von Brandt, " the empress desires you to understand that, if you will assist in carrying out her wishes, you may depend upon her grati-tude. You must employ all your eloquence and influence to induce the prince royal to dismiss from his mind the idea of divorcing his wife at the death of the king."

" I do not blame the empress," said Madame von Morien, with a roguish smile. " It remains to be seen, however, whether the wishes of the prince royal and those of the empress coincide. You are well aware that Prince Frederick is not the man to be led by the will of others."

"Not by the will of the empress, dearest, but by yours."

"Well, how does this good empress expect to bribe me, for I hope she does not think me so silly and childish as to consider her words commands, merely because they fall from the lips of an empress.   No, the little Morien is at this moment a more important person to the empress than the empress is to me, and it is, therefore, very natural that I should make my conditions."

"Only name them, my dear friend, and I assure you in advance that they will be fulfilled, unless you should demand the moon and the stars; these the empress cannot obtain for you."

"Ah, you have divined my condition," said Madame von Morien, smiling.   "I demand a star—one that is brighter and more beautiful than those in the sky—one that the empress can give."

"I do not understand you," said her astonished friend.

"You will soon understand—only listen.   Have you not heard that the Austrian empress intends to establish a new order—an order of virtue and modesty ? "

Madame von Brandt burst into a clear, silvery laugh. " And do you wish to belong to this order ? "

"Yes; and if the empress will not present me with the star of this order, I shall enter into no further arrangements."

Madame von Brandt, still laughing, replied: "This is a most edifying idea.   Le Tourbillon desires to become a member of the 'Order of Virtue.'   The beautiful Morien, whose greatest pride was to despise the prudish, and to snap her fingers at morality, now wishes to be in the train of modesty."

"Dear friend," said Madame von Morien, with a bewitching smile, which displayed two rows of the most exquisitely white teeth, " dear friend, you should always leave open a way of retreat; even as Æsop in descending the mountain was not happy in the easy and delightful path, but already sighed over 'the difficulties of the next ascent, so should women never be contented with the joys of the present moment, but prepare themselves for the sorrows which most probably await them in the future. A day must come when we will be cut off by advancing years from the flowery paths of love and pleasure, and be compelled to follow in the tiresome footsteps of virtue. It is wise, therefore, to be prepared for that which must come as certainly as old age, and, if possible, to smooth away the difficulties from this rough path. To-day I am Le Tourbillon, and will remain so a few years; but when the roses and lilies of my cheek are faded, I will place the cross of the 'Order of Virtue' on my withered bosom, and become the defender of the God-fearing and the virtuous."

The two ladies laughed, and their laughter was as gay and silvery, as clear and innocent as the tones of the lark, or the songs of children. Le Tourbillon, however, quickly assumed an earnest and pathetic expression, and said, in a snuffling, preaching voice: "Do I not deserve to be decorated with the star of the 'Order of Virtue?' Am I not destined to reunite with my weak but beautiful hands two hearts which God himself has joined together? I tell you, therefore, procure this decoration for me, or I refuse the rôle that you offer me."

"I promise that your caprice shall be gratified, and that you will obtain the star," said Madame von Brandt, earnestly.

"Excuse me, my dear, that is not sufficient. I demand the assurance, in the handwriting of the Empress of Austria, the exalted aunt of our princess royal, that this order shall be established, and that I shall become a member. It would do no harm for the empress to add a few words of tenderness and esteem."

4*

"I shall inform the empress of your conditions imme
diately, and she will without doubt fulfil them, for the
danger is pressing, and you are a most powerful ally."

"Good! thus far we are agreed, and nothing fails now
but the most important part," said Madame von Morien.
with a mischievous smile; "that is, to discover whether l
can accomplish your wishes—whether the prince royal considers me any thing more than 'Le Tourbillon,' 'the pretty
Morien,' or the Turkish music to which he listens when he
is gay.   Nothing is wanting but that the prince royal
should really love me.   It is true that he makes love to me ;
he secretly presses my hand ; he occasionally whispers a
few loving, tender words in my ear; and yesterday, when I
met him accidentally in the dark corridor, he embraced me
so passionately, and covered my lips with such glowing,
stormy kisses, that I was almost stifled.   But that is all—
that is the entire history of my love."

"No, that is not all.   This history has a sequel," said
Madame von Brandt, triumphantly, as she drew a sealed
letter from her bosom, and gave it to her companion.
"Take this, it is a new chapter in your romance."

"This letter has no address," returned Madame von Morien, smiling.

"It is intended for you."

"No, it is mine," suddenly cried a voice behind them,
and a small hand darted forward, and tore the sealed paper
from Madame von Morien."

"Mine, this letter is mine!" said Louise von Schwerin,
the little maid of honor, who, without being remarked, had
approached the two ladies, and seized the letter at this decisive moment.   "The letter belongs to me; it is mine,"
repeated the presumptuous young girl, as she danced laughingly before the two pale and terrified ladies.   "Who dares

affirm that this letter, which has no address, is not intended for me ? "

"Louise, give me the letter," implored Madame von Morien, in a trembling voice. But Louise found a pleasure in terrifying her beautiful friend, who invariably laughed at her, and called her a child when she spoke of her heart, and hinted at a secret and unhappy passion. Louise wished to revenge herself by claiming the privileges of a child.

"Take the letter if you can," cried the young girl, as she flew through the room as lightly as a gazelle, waving her prize back and forth like a banner, "take the letter!"

Madame von Morien hurried after her, and now began a merry race through the saloon, accompanied by the laughter of the ladies, who looked on with the liveliest interest. .And in reality it was a charming picture to see these beautiful figures, which flew through the hall like two Atlantas, radiant with eagerness, with glowing cheeks and smiling lips, with fluttering locks and throbbing breasts.

The young girl was still in advance ; she danced on, singing and laughing, far before the beautiful Morien, who began already to be wearied.

"The letter is mine!" sang out this impudent little maiden, "and no one shall take it from me."

But fear lent wings to Madame von Morien, who now made a last despairing effort, and flew like an arrow after Louise. Now she was just behind her ; Louise felt already her hot, panting breath upon her cheek; saw the upraised arm, ready to seize the letter—when suddenly the door opened, before which Louise stood, and the princess royal appeared. The youthful maid of honor sank laughing at her feet, and said breathlessly, "Gracious princess, protect me!"

Madame von Morien remained motionless at the appearance of the princess royal, breathless not only from her rapid race, but also from fear, while Madame von Brandt con-

cealing, with a smile, her own alarm, approached her
friend, that she might not remain without assistance at this
critical moment. The rest of the company stood silent at a
respectful distance, and looked with curious and inquiring
glances at this singular scene.

"Well, and from what shall I protect you, little Louise?"
said the princess royal, as she bent smilingly over the breathless child.

Louise was silent for one instant. She felt that the
princess would reprove her for her naughtiness; she did not
wish to be again treated as a child before the whole court.
She hastily resolved to insist upon the truth of her assertion
that the letter was hers.

"Madame von Morien wished to take my letter from me,"
said Louise, giving the latter a perverse look.

"I hope your royal highness knows this impudent child
well enough not to put any faith in her words," said Madame
von Morien, evasively, not daring to claim the letter as her
property.

"Child! She calls me a child!" murmured Louise, enraged, and now determined to revenge herself by compromising Madame von Morien.

"Then the letter does not belong to Louise?" asked the
princess royal, turning to Madame von Morien.

"Yes, your royal highness, it is mine," declared Louise;
"your royal highness can convince yourself of it. Here is
the letter; will you have the kindness to read the address?"

"But this letter has no address," said the astonished
princess.

"And still Madame von Morien asserts that it is intended
for her," cried Louise, wickedly.

"And Mademoiselle von Schwerin declares it belongs to
her," said Madame von Morien, casting a furious look on Louise.

"I implore your royal highness to be the judge," said Louise.

"How can I decide to whom the letter belongs, as it bears no name?" said the princess, smiling.

"By opening and reading it," said the young girl, with apparent frankness. "The letter is from my mother, and I do not care to conceal its contents from your royal highness."

"Are you willing, Madame von Morien? shall I open this letter?"

But before the amazed and terrified young woman found time for a reply, Madame von Brandt approached the princess with a smiling countenance. She had in this moment of danger conceived a desperate resolution. The prince royal had informed her that this paper contained a poem. Why might not this poem have been intended for the princess as well as for Madame von Morien? It contained, without a doubt, a declaration of love, and such declarations are suitable for any woman, and welcome to all.

"If your royal highness will permit me, I am ready to throw light on this mystery," said Madame von Brandt.

The princess bowed permission.

"This letter belongs neither to Madame von Morien nor to Mademoiselle von Schwerin," said Madame von Brandt.

"You promised to enlighten us," exclaimed the princess, laughing, "and it appears to me you have made the mystery more impenetrable. The letter belongs neither to Madame von Morien nor to little Louise. To whom, then, does it belong?"

"It belongs to your royal highness."

"To me?" asked the astonished princess, while Madame von Morien gazed at her friend with speechless horror, and Mademoiselle von Schwerin laughed aloud.

"Yes, this letter belongs to your royal highness. The prince royal gave it to me, with the command to place it upon your table, before you went to your dressing-room; but I was too late, and understood that your highness was occupied with your toilet. I dared not disturb you, and retained the letter in order to hand it to you now. As I held it in my hand, and said jestingly to Madame von Morien that the prince royal had forgotten to write the address, Mademoiselle von Schwerin came and tore it from me in a most unladylike manner, and declared it was hers. That is the whole history."

" And you say that the letter is mine?" said the princess, thoughtfully.

" It is yours, and it contains a poem from his royal highness."

" Then I can break the seal?" said the princess, tearing open the paper. " Ah!" she cried, with a happy smile, " it is a poem from my husband."

" And here comes his royal highness to confirm the truth of my statement," cried Madame von Brandt, stepping aside.

CHAPTER XIII.

THE BANQUET.

MADAME VON BRANDT was right. The prince royal, surrounded by the cavaliers of his court, entered the saloon just as the princess had commenced reading the poem.

On his entrance a murmur of applause arose, and the countenance of his wife was radiant with pleasure and delight on beholding this handsome and engaging young prince, whom she, emboldened by the love-verses which she held in her hand, joyfully greeted as her husband. On this day the prince did not appear as usual in the uniform of his regiment, but was attired in a French costume of the latest fashion. He wore a snuff-colored coat of heavy moire-antique, ornamented at the shoulders with long bows of lace, the ends of which were bordered with silver fringe. His trousers, of the same color and material, reached to his knees, and were here ornamented with rich lace, which hung far down over his silk stockings. On the buckles of his high, red-heeled shoes, glittered immense diamonds. These gems were, however, eclipsed by the jewelled buttons which confined his long, silver-brocaded waistcoat.*

The costume of the cavaliers who accompanied the prince was of the same style, but less rich.

As this group of handsome and richly-attired gentlemen entered the saloon, the bright eyes of the ladies sparkled, and their cheeks colored with pleasure.

The princess royal's countenance was illumined with delight; never had she seen the prince so handsome, never had he looked so loving. And this was all for her, the chosen one, whom he now blessed with his love. Yes, he loved her! She had only read the commencement of the poem which he had written, but in this she had seen words of tender and passionate love.

While she was gazing on her husband in silent ecstasy, Madame von Brandt approached the prince, and gracefully recounting the scene which had just occurred, requested him to confirm her statement.

The prince's quick glance flitted for a moment from the beautiful Morien, who trembled with consternation and terror, to his wife, and, judging by the pleased expression of her face, he concluded that she believed this poem had been really addressed to herself. She had, therefore, not read it to the end; she had not yet arrived at the verse which con-

* Bielfeld, vol. ii., page 82.

tained a direct appeal to the beautiful Tourbillon, the charming Leontine. She must not be permitted to read the entire poem. That was all!

The prince approached his wife with a smile, to which she was unaccustomed, and which made her heart beat high with delight.

"I crave your indulgence," said he, "for my poor little poem, which reached you in so noisy a manner, and is really scarcely worth reading. Read it in some solitary hour when you are troubled with *ennui*; it may then possibly amuse you for a moment. We will not occupy ourselves with verses and poems to-day, but will laugh and be merry; that is, if it pleases you, madame."

The princess murmured a few low and indistinct words. As usual, she could find no expression for her thoughts, although her heart was full of love and delight. This modest shyness of the lips, this poverty of words, with her rich depth of feeling, was the great misfortune of the princess royal. It was this that made her appear awkward, constrained, and spiritless; it was this that displeased and estranged her husband. Her consciousness of this deficiency made her still more timid and constrained, and deprived her of what little power of expression she possessed.

Had she at this moment found courage to make a ready and witty reply, her husband would have been much pleased. Her silence, however, excited his displeasure, and his brow darkened.

He offered her his arm; and, exchanging glances with Madame Morien, he conducted his wife to the dining-saloon, to the magnificently arranged and glittering table.

"The gardener of Rheinsberg, Frederick of Hohenzollern, invites his friends to partake of what he has provided. For the prince royal is fortunately not at home; we can, therefore, be altogether *sans gêne*, and follow our inclinations, as the mice do when the cat is not at home."

He seated himself between his wife and Madame Morien, whispering to the latter: " Beautiful Tourbillon, my heart is in flames, and I rely upon you to quench them. You must save me ! "

" Oh, this heart of yours is a phœnix, and arises from its ashes renewed and rejuvenated."

" But only to destroy itself again," said the prince. Then taking his glass and surveying his guests with a rapid glance, he exclaimed: " Our first toast shall be youth—youth of which the old are envious !—youth and beauty, which are so brilliantly represented here to-day, that one might well imagine Venus had sent us all her daughters and playmates, as well as all her lovers, the deposed and discarded ones as well as those whom she still favors, and only proposes to discard."

The glasses rang out merrily in answer to this toast, and all betook themselves with evident zest to the costly and savory dishes, prepared by the master-hand of Duvall the French cook, and which the prince seasoned with the Attic salt of his ever-ready wit.

They all gave themselves up to gayety and merriment, and pleasure sparkled in every eye.

The corpulent Knobelsdorf related in a stentorian voice some amusing anecdotes of his travels. Chazot recited portions of Voltaire's latest work. The learned and witty Count Kaiserling recited verses from the " Henriade," and then several of Gellert's fables, which were becoming very popular. He conversed with his neighbor, the artist Pesne, on the subject of the paintings which his masterly hand had executed, and then turning to Mademoiselle von Schwerin, he painted in glowing colors the future of Berlin—the future when they would have a French theatre, an Italian opera, and of all things, an Italian ballet-corps. For the latter the most celebrated dancers would be engaged, and it should eclipse every thing of the kind that had ever been seen or heard of in Germany.

At the lower end of the table sat the two Vendas, the two Grauns, and Quantz, the powerful and much-feared virtuoso of the flute and instructor of the prince royal, whose rudeness was almost imposing, and before whom the prince himself was somewhat shy. But to-day even Quantz was quiet and tractable. His countenance wore the half-pleased, half-grumbling expression of a bull-dog when stroked by a soft and tender hand. He is inclined to be angry, but is so much at his ease that he finds it absolutely impossible to growl.

In their merriment the gentlemen were becoming almost boisterous. The cheeks of the ladies glowed with pleasure, and their lovers were becoming tender.

The princess royal alone was silent; her heart was heavy and sorrowful. She had carefully reconsidered the scene which had occurred, and the result was, she was now convinced that the poem which she had received was not intended for her, but for some other fair lady. She was ashamed of her credulity, and blushed for her own vanity. For how could it be possible that the handsome and brilliant man who sat at her side, who was so witty and spirited, who was as learned as he was intelligent, as noble as he was amiable, how could it be possible that he should love her?— she who was only young and pretty, who was moreover guilty of the great, unpardonable fault of being his wife, and a wife who had been forced upon him.

No, this poem had never been intended for her. But for whom, then? Who was the happy one to whom the prince had given his love? Her heart bled as she thought that another could call this bliss her own. She was too

mild and gentle to be angry. She ardently desired to know
the name of her rival, but not that she might revenge herself.
No, she wished to pray for her whom the prince royal loved,
to whom he perhaps owed a few days of happiness, of bliss.

But who was she? The princess royal's glance rested
searchingly on all the ladies who were present. She saw
many beautiful and pleasing faces. Many of them had intelligence, vivacity, and wit, but none of them were worthy
of his love. Her husband had just turned to his fair neighbor, and, with a fascinating smile, whispered a few words in
her ear. Madame Morien blushed, cast down her eyes, but,
raising them again and looking ardently at the prince royal,
she murmured a few words in so low a tone that no one else
heard them.

How? Could it be this one? But no, that was impossible. This giddy, coquettish, and superficial woman could
by no possibility have captivated the noble and high-toned
prince; she could not be Elizabeth's happy rival.

But who, then? Alas, if this long and weary feast were
only at an end! If she could but retire to her chamber and
read this poem, the riddle would then be solved, and she
would know the name of his lady-love.

It seemed, however, that the prince had divined his
wife's wish, and had determined that it should not be gratified.

They had taken their seats at table at a very late hour
to-day, at six o'clock. It had now become dark, and candelabras with wax candles were brought in and placed on
the table.

"The lights are burning," exclaimed the prince; "we
will not leave the table until these lights are burned out,
and our heads have become illuminated with champagne."*

And amid conversation, laughter, and recitations, all went

* Bielfeld, vol. i., page 84. The prince's own words.

merrily on.   But the heart of the princess royal grew sadder and sadder.

Suddenly the prince turned to her.   " I feel the vanity of an author," said he, " and beg permission to inquire if you have no curiosity to hear the poem which I had the honor of sending you to-day by Madame Brandt ? "

" Indeed I have, my husband," exclaimed the princess, with vivacity.   " I long to become acquainted with its contents."

" Then permit me to satisfy this longing," said the prince, holding out his hand for the poem.   The princess hesitated, but when she looked up and their eyes met, his glance was so cold and imperious, that she felt as if an icy hand were at her heart.   She drew the poem from her bosom and handed it silently to her husband.

" Now, my little maid of honor, Von Schwerin," said the prince royal, smiling, " this sagacious, highly respectable, and worthy company shall judge between you and me, and decide whether this paper is a letter from her dear mother, as this modest and retiring child asserts, or a poem, written by a certain prince, who is sometimes induced by his imaginative fancy to make indifferent verses.   Listen, therefore, ladies and gentlemen, and judge between us.   But that no one may imagine that I am reading any thing else, and substituting the tender thoughts of a lover for the fond words of motherly affection, Madame Morien shall look at the paper I am reading, and bear witness to my truth."

He read off the first verses as they were written, and then improvising, recited a witty and humorous poem, in which he did homage to his wife's charms.   His poem was greeted with rapturous applause.   While he was reciting the improvised verses, Madame Morien had time to read the poem.   When she came to the verses which contained a passionate declaration of love, and in which the prince half-humbly, half-imperiously, solicited a rendezvous, her breast heaved and her heart beat high with delight. After the prince had finished he turned to his wife with a smile, and asked if the poem had pleased her.

" So much so," said she, " that I pray you to return it. I should like to preserve it as a reminiscence of this hour."

" Preserve it? By no means! A poem is like a flower. It is a thing of the present, and is beautiful only when fresh. The moment gave it, and the moment shall take it. We will sacrifice to the gods, what we owe to the gods."

Having thus spoken, the prince tore the paper into small pieces, which he placed in the palm of his hand.

" Go ye in all directions and teach unto all people that nothing is immortal, not even the poem of a prince," said he, and blowing the particles of paper, he sent them fluttering through the air like snowflakes. The ladies and gentlemen amused themselves with blowing the pieces from place to place. Each one made a little bellows of his mouth, and endeavored to give some strip of paper a particular direction or aim—to blow it on to some fair one's white shoulders or into some gentleman's eye or laughing mouth.

This caused a great deal of merriment. The princess was still sad and silent. Now and then a scrap fell before her; these she blew no further, but mechanically collected and gazed at them in a listless and mournful manner. Suddenly she started and colored violently. On one of these strips of paper she had read two words which made her heart tremble with anger and pain. These words were, " Bewitching Leontine ! "

The secret was out. The prince royal's poem had been addressed to Leontine, to a bewitching Leontine, and not to Elizabeth ! But who was this Leontine ? which of the ladies bore that name ? She must, she would know ! She called all her courage to her assistance. Suddenly she took part in the general merriment, commenced to laugh and jest; she entered gayly into a conversation with her husband, with Madame Morien and the young Baron Bielfield, who was her *vis-a-vis.*

The princess had never been so gay, so unconstrained, and so witty. No one suspected that these jests, this laughter, was only assumed; that she veiled the pain which she suffered with a smiling brow.

The candles had burnt half way down, and some of the gentlemen had begun to light the first tapers of the champagne illumination which the prince had prophesied. Chazot no longer recited, but was singing some of the charming little songs which he had learned of the merry peasants of Normandy, his fatherland. Jordan improvised a sermon after the fashion of the fanatical and hypocritical priests who for some time past had collected crowds in the streets of Berlin. Kaiserling had risen from his seat and thrown himself into an attitude, in which he had seen the celebrated Lagière in the ballet of the Syrène at Paris. Knobelsdorf recounted his interesting adventures in Italy; and even Quantz found courage to give the prince's favorite dog, which was snuffling at his feet, and which he hated as a rival, a hearty kick. The prince royal alone had preserved his noble and dignified appearance. Amid the general excitement he remained calm and dignified. The candles were burning low, and the champagne illumination was becoming intense in the heads of all the gentlemen except the prince and the Baron Bielfeld.

"Bielfeld must also take part in this illumination," said the prince, turning to his wife, and calling the former, he proposed to drink with him the health of his *fiancée,* whom he had left in Hamburg.

After Bielfeld had left his seat and was advancing toward the prince royal, the princess hurriedly and noiselessly gave her instructions to a servant. She had observed that Bielfeld had been drinking freely of the cold water which had been placed before him in a decanter. The servant emptied this decanter and filled it with sillery, which was as clear and limpid as water. Bielfeld returning to his seat, heated by the toast he had been drinking, filled his glass to the brim, and drank instead of water the fiery sillery.*

The princess royal, whose aim was to discover which of the ladies was the bewitching Leontine, determined to strike a decisive blow. With an ingratiating smile she turned to Bielfeld and said:

"The prince royal spoke of your *fiancée;* I may, therefore, congratulate you."

Bielfeld, who did not dare to acknowledge that he was on the point of shamefully deserting this lady, bowed in silence.

"May I know the name of your *fiancée?*" asked she.

"Mademoiselle von Randau," murmured Bielfeld, drinking another glass of sillery to hide his confusion.

"Mademoiselle von Randau!" repeated the princess, "how cold, how ceremonious that sounds! To imagine how a lady looks and what she is like, it is necessary to know her Christian name, for a given name is to some extent an index to character. What is your *fiancée's* name?"

"Regina, royal highness." .

"Regina! That is a beautiful name. A prophecy of happiness. Then she will always be queen of your heart. Ah, I understand the meaning of names, and at home in my father's house I was called the Sibyl, because my prophecies were always true. If you will give me your first names, I will prophecy your future, ladies. Let us commence. What is your given name, Madame von Katsch?"

While the princess was speaking, she played carelessly with the beautiful Venetian glass which stood before her.

---

* Bielfeld, vol. i., page 85.

The prince royal alone saw what no one else observed; he saw that the hand which toyed with the glass trembled violently; that while she smiled her lips quivered, and that her breathing was hurried and feverish. He comprehended what these prophecies meant; he was convinced that the princess had become acquainted with the contents of his poem.

"Do not give her your name," he whispered to Madame Morien. He then turned to his wife, who had just prophesied a long life and a happy old age to Madame von Katsch.

"And your name, Mademoiselle von Schwerin?" said the prince royal.

"Louise."

"Ah, Louise! Well, I prophecy that you will be happier than your namesake, the beautiful La Vallière. Your conscience will never reproach you on account of your love affairs, and you will never enter a convent."

"But then I will probably never have the happiness of being loved by a king," said the little maid of honor, with a sigh.

This naïve observation was greeted with a merry peal of laughter.

The princess continued her prophecies; she painted for each one a pleasant and flattering future. She now turned to Madame Morien, still smiling, still playing with the glass.

"Well, and your name, my dear Madame Morien?" said she, looking into the glass which she held clasped in her fingers.

"She is called 'Le Tourbillon,'" exclaimed the prince royal, laughing.

"Antoinette, Louise, Albertine, are my names," said Madame Morien, hesitatingly.

The princess royal breathed free, and raised her eyes from the glass to the beautiful Morien.

" These are too many names to prophesy by," said she.
" By what name are you called ? "

Madame Morien hesitated; the other ladies, better acquainted with the little mysteries of Tourbillon than the
princess, divined that this question of the princess and the
embarrassment of Madame Morien betokened something
extraordinary, and awaited attentively the reply of this
beautiful woman. A momentary pause ensued. Suddenly
Mademoiselle Schwerin broke out in laughter.

" Well," said she, " have you forgotten your name, Madame Morien ? Do you not know that you are called Leontine ? "

" Leontine ! " exclaimed the princess, and her fingers
closed so tightly on the glass which she held in her hand,
that it crushed, and drew from her a sharp cry of pain.

The prince royal saw the astonished and inquiring
glances of all directed to his wife, and felt that he must turn
their attention in some other direction — that he must
make a jest of this accident.

" Elizabeth, you are right ! " said he, laughing. " The
candles have burnt down ; the illumination has begun ; the
festival is at an end. We have already sacrificed a poem to
the gods, we must now do the same with the glasses, out of
which we have quaffed a few hours of happiness, of merriment, and of forgetfulness. I sacrifice this glass to the gods ;
All of you follow my example."

He raised his glass and threw it over his shoulder to the
floor, where it broke with a crash. The others followed the
example of the prince and his wife with shouts of laughter,
and in a few minutes nothing was left of these beautiful
glasses but the glittering fragments which covered the floor.
But the company, now intoxicated with wine and delight,
was not contented with this one offering to the gods, but
thirsted for a continuation of their sport; and not satisfied

with having broken the glasses, subjected the vases and the bowls of crystal to the same treatment. In the midst of this general confusion the door was suddenly opened, and Fredersdorf appeared at the threshold, holding a letter in his hand.

His uncalled-for appearance in this saloon was something so extraordinary, so unprecedented, that it could be only justified on the ground of some great emergency, something of paramount importance. They all felt this, notwithstanding their excitement and hilarity. A profound silence ensued. Every eye was fixed anxiously upon the prince, who had received the letter from Fredersdorf's hands and broken the seal. The prince turned pale, and the paper trembled in his hands. He hastily arose from his seat.

"My friends," said he, solemnly, "the feast is at an end. I must leave for Potsdam immediately. The king is dangerously ill. Farewell!"

And offering his arm to his wife, he hastily left the saloon. The guests, who but now were so merry, silently arose and betook themselves to their chambers, and nothing could be heard save now and then a stolen whisper or a low and anxious inquiry. Soon a deep and ominous silence reigned in the castle of Rheinsberg. All slept, or at least seemed to sleep.

CHAPTER XIV.

LE ROI EST MORT. VIVE LE ROI!

KING FREDERICK WILLIAM's end was approaching. Past was his power and greatness, past all his dreams of glory. Long did the spirit fight against the body; but now, after months of secret pain and torture, he had to acknowledge himself overpowered by death. The stiff uniform is no longer adapted to his fallen figure. Etiquette and ceremony had been banished by the all-powerful ruler—by death. He is no longer a king, but a dying man—nothing more. A father taking leave of his children, a husband embracing his wife for the last time; pressing his last kisses upon her tearful face, and pleading for forgiveness for his harshness and cruelty. Frederick William has made his peace with God and the world; his proud spirit is broken; his hard heart softened. Long he had striven in the haughtiness of his heart before acknowledging his sins, but the brave and pious Roloff approached his couch, and with accusations and reproaches awakened his slumbering conscience. At first he had but one answer to the priest's accusations, and that was proudly given: "I have ever been true to my wife." Roloff continued to speak of his extortions, oppressions, and inhumanity. Frederick William was at last convinced that he must lay down his crown, and approach God with deep repentance, humbly imploring pardon and mercy.

Now that he had made his peace with God, there remained nothing for him to do but to arrange his earthly affairs, and take leave of his wife, and children, and friends. They were all called to his room that he might bid them farewell. By the side of the arm-chair, in which the king was reclining, wrapped in his wide silk mantle, stood his wife and the prince royal. His hands rested in theirs, and when he raised his weary eyes, he always met their tear-stained faces, their looks of unutterable love. Death, that would so soon separate them forever, had at last united in love father and son. Weeping loudly, Frederick William folded the prince royal in his arms, and with a voice full of tears, exclaimed: "Has not God in his great mercy given me a noble son?" Prince Frederick bowed his head upon his father's breast, and prayed deeply and earnestly that his life might be spared.

But the end was approaching; the king knew and felt it. He had the long coffin, the same in which he had laid himself for trial a few months before, brought into his room, and looking at it sadly, said, with a peaceful smile: " In this bed I shall sleep well!" He then called his secretary Eichel, and ordered him to read the programme for his funeral, which he had himself dictated.

It was a strange picture to see this king, lying by the side of the coffin, surrounded by his children and servants, his weary head reclining on the shoulder of his wife, listening attentively to this programme, that spoke of him, a still living and thinking being, as of a cold, dead, senseless mass. Not as for a sad festival, but for a grand parade, had the king arranged it, and it made a fearful, half-comic impression upon the auditors, when was added, at the especial request of the king, that, after his laying out, a splendid table should be set in the great hall for all who had been present at the ceremony, and that none but the best wines from his cellar should be served.

After having provided for his corpse, Frederick William still wished to leave to each of his favorites, the Prince of Dessau and Baron Hacke, a horse. He ordered the horses to be led from their stalls to the court. He then desired his chair to be rolled to an open window, where he could see the entire court, and give a farewell look to each of these animals which had so often borne him to feasts and parades. Oh! what costly, glorious days those were, when he could lightly swing himself upon these proud steeds, and ride out into God's fresh, free air, to be humbly welcomed by his subjects, to be received with the roll of drums and the sound of trumpets, and every moment of his life be made aware of his greatness and power by the devotion and humility of those who surrounded him! And that was all set aside and at an end. Never again could he mount his horse, never again could he ride through the streets of Berlin, and rejoice over the beautiful houses and stately palaces called into life by his royal will. Never again will he receive the humble welcome of his subjects; and when on the morrow drums are beating and cannon thundering, they will not salute the king, but his corpse.

Oh! and life is so beautiful; the air is so fresh and balmy; the heavens of so clear and transparent a blue; and he must leave it all, and descend into the dark and lonely grave.

The king brushed a tear from his eye, and turning his gaze from heaven and God's beautiful earth, looked upon the horses which a servant was leading to and fro in the court. As he did this, his countenance brightened, he forgot for the moment that death was near at hand, and looked with eager attention to see which of the horses the gentlemen would choose. When he saw the selection the Prince of Dessau had made, he smiled, with the pitying look of a *connoisseur*.

"That is a bad horse, my dear prince," he exclaimed; "take the other one, I will vouch for him."

After the prince had chosen the horse shown him by the king, and Baron Hacke the other, he ordered the most magnificent and costly saddles to be placed on them; and while this was being done, he looked on with eager interest. Behind him stood the minister Rodewills, and the secretary of state, whom the king had summoned to his presence to receive his resignation, by which he transferred the kingly authority to his son the prince royal. Behind him stood Frederick and the queen, the generals and the priests. The king was unconscious of their presence; he had forgotten that he was dying; he thought only of his horses, and a

dark cloud settled on his face as the groom buckled a saddle
covered with blue velvet over the yellow silk housing of
Prince Anhalt's horse.

"Oh, if I were only well, how I would beat that stupid
boy!" exclaimed the king, in a loud, menacing voice.
"Hacke, have the kindness to beat him for me."

The horses pointed their ears and neighed loudly, and
the servants trembled at the voice of their master, who was
speaking to them as angrily as ever, but in a deep, sepulchral
voice.

But his anger was of short duration, and he sank back
into his chair, breathing heavily and brokenly. He had not
the strength to sign his resignation, and demanded to be
taken from his chair and placed upon the bed.

There he lay motionless, with half-closed eyes, groaning
and sighing. A fearful stillness reigned in the chamber of
death. All held their breath; all wished to hear the last
death-sigh of the king; all wished to witness the mysterious
and inscrutable moment when the soul, freeing itself from its
earthly tenement, should ascend to the spring of light and
life as an invisible but indestructible atom of divinity. Pale
and trembling the prince leaned over his father; the kneeling
queen prayed in a low voice. With earnest and sorrowful
faces the generals and cavaliers, physicians and priests, looked
at this pale and ghost-like being, who but a few moments before was a king, and was now a clod of the valley. But no,
Frederick William was not yet dead; the breath that had
ceased returned to his breast. He opened his eyes once
more, and they were again full of intelligence. He ordered
a glass to be given him, and looked at himself long and attentively.

"I don't look as badly as I thought," said he, with the
last fluttering emotion of human vanity. "Feel my pulse,
doctor, and tell me how long I have still to live."

" Your majesty insists on knowing ? "

" I command you to tell me."

" Well, then, your majesty is about to die," said Ellert, solemnly.

" How do you know it ? " he asked, composedly.

" By your wavering pulse, sire."

The king held his arm aloft, and moved his hand to and fro.

"Oh, no," said he, " if my pulse were failing I could not move my hand; if——"

Suddenly he ceased speaking, and uttered a loud cry, his uplifted arm sinking heavily to his side.

" Jesus, Jesus ! " murmured the king, " I live and die in Thee. Thou art my trust."

The last fearful prayer died on his lips, the spirit had flown, and Frederick was no longer a living, thinking being, but senseless, powerless clay.

The prince royal conducted the weeping queen from the apartment. The courtiers remained, but their features were no longer sad and sympathetic, but grave and thoughtful. The tragedy here was at an end, and all were anxious to see the drama from which the curtain was now to be drawn in the apartments of the prince royal. Frederick William had breathed his last, and was becoming cold and stiff; he was only a corpse, with which one had nothing more to do.

In unseemly haste they all crowded through the widely-opened folding doors of the death-chamber, and hastened into the ante-room that led to the young king's apartments.

Who will be favored, who receive the first rays of the rising sun ? They all see a sunny future before them. A new period begins, a period of splendor, abundance, and joy ; the king is young, and fond of display and gay festivities ; he is no soldier king, but a cavalier, a writer, and a learned man. Art and science will bloom, gallantry and fashion

reign; the corporal's baton is broken, the flute begins her
soft, melodious reign.

Thus thought all these waiting courtiers who were assembled in the young king's ante-chamber. Thus thought
the grand chamberlain Pöllnitz, who stood next to the door
that led to the chamber within. Yes, a new period must
commence for him; his would be a brilliant future, for the
prince royal had always been loving and gracious to him,
and the young king must remember that it was Pöllnitz who
induced Frederick William to pay the prince's debts. The
king must remember this, and, for the services he had
rendered, raise him to honor and dignity; he must be
the favorite, the envied, feared, and powerful favorite, before
whom all should bend the knee as to the king himself. The
king was young, inexperienced, and easily led; he had a
warm heart, a rich imagination, and an ardent love of pleasure and splendor. These qualities must be cultivated in the
young king; by these reins he would control him; and
while, intoxicated with pleasure and delight, he lay on his
sweet-scented couch, strengthening himself for new follies,
Pöllnitz would reign in his stead, and be the real king.

These were no chimeras, no vain dreams, but a well-con-
sidered plan, in which Pöllnitz had a powerful abettor in the
person of Fredersdorf, chamberlain of the young king, who
had promised that he should be the first that the king should
call for.

For this reason Pöllnitz stood nearest the door; for this
reason he so proudly regarded the courtiers who were breathlessly awaiting the opening of that door.

There, the door opens, and Fredersdorf appears.

"Baron Pöllnitz!"

"Here I am," exclaimed Pöllnitz, casting a triumphant
look at his companions, and following Fredersdorf into the
royal presence.

" Well, have I not kept my promise?" said Fredersdorf, as they passed through the first room.

" You have kept yours, and I will keep mine ; we will reign together."

" Step in, the king is there," said Fredersdorf.

The young king stood at the window, his forehead resting on the sash, sighing and breathing heavily, as if oppressed. As he turned, Pöllnitz noticed that his eyes were red with weeping, and the courtier's heart misgave him.

A young king, just come into power, and not intoxicated by his brilliant fortune, but weeping for his father's death ! It augured ill for the courtier's plans.

" All hail and blessing to your majesty !" exclaimed Pöllnitz, bowing with apparent enthusiasm to kiss the king's robe.

The king stepped aside, motioned him off, and said, with a slight smile, " Leave these ceremonies until the coronation. I need you now for other things. You shall be master of etiquette and ceremonies at my court, and you will commence your duties by making the necessary arrangements for my father's funeral. Unhappily, I must begin my reign by disobeying my father's commands. I cannot allow this simple and modest funeral to take place. The world would not understand it, and would accuse me of irreverence. No, he must be interred with all the honors due to a king. That is my desire ; see that it is accomplished."

The grand chamberlain was dismissed, and passed out of the royal chambers lost in contemplation of his coming greatness, when, suddenly hearing his name, he turned and perceived the king at the door.

" One thing more, Pöllnitz," said the king, his eye resting with a piercing expression on the smiling countenance of the courtier ; one thing more—above all things, no cheating, no bad jokes, no overrating, no accounts written with

5*

double chalk. I will never forgive any thing of this kind, remember that."

Without awaiting an answer, the king turned and re entered his room.

Baron Pöllnitz stared after him with widely-distended eyes ; he felt as if a thunderbolt had destroyed his future.

This was not the extravagant, voluptuous, and confiding monarch that Pöllnitz had thought him, but a sober, earnest, and frugal king, that even mistrusted and saw through him, the wily old courtier.

CHAPTER XV.

WE ARE KING.

Two days and nights had passed, and still no news from the prince royal. King Frederick William still lived, and the little court of Rheinsberg was consumed with impatience and expectation. All means of dissipation were exhausted. Time had laid aside its wing, and put on shoes of lead. She flew no longer, but walked like an aged woman. How long an hour seems, when you count the seconds! How terribly a day stretches out when, with wakeful but wearied eyes, you long for its close !

Kaiserling's wit and Chazot's merry humor, where are they ? Why is Bielfeld's ringing laugh and the flute of Quantz silenced? All is quiet, all are silent and waiting, dreaming of the happiness in store for them, of the day of splendor, power, and magnificence that will dawn for the favorites and friends of the prince royal when he ascends the throne.

Is it not a proud and delightful thing to be the confidant

and companion of a king—to spend with him his treasures and riches, to share with him the devotion and applause of the people ?

Until now they had been forced to disguise their friendship and devotion for the prince royal. They trembled for fear of exciting the king's anger, and were in daily terror of being banished by him from the presence of their prince.

When the prince royal ascends the throne they will be his powerful and influential favorites, and their favor will be courted by all. They will be his co-regents, and through and with him will rule the nation.

It is, therefore, not astonishing that they looked forward to his accession to the throne with longing and impatience; not astonishing that they cursed these sluggish, slowly-passing hours, and would fain have slept, slept on until the great and blessed moment when they should be awakened with the news that their friend Prince Frederick had ascended the throne of his fathers, and was King of Prussia.

In the midst of this excitement the princess royal alone seemed quiet and unconstrained. She was calm and composed; she knew that the events of the next few days would determine her whole life; she feared that her happiness hung on the slender thread which bound the dying king to life.

But Elizabeth Christine had a brave heart and a noble soul; she had passed the night on her knees weeping and praying, and her heart was full of misery. She had at last become quiet and composed, and was prepared for any thing, even for a separation from her husband. If Frederick expressed such a wish, she was determined to go. Where ? Anywhere. Far, far away. Whichever route she took, she was certain to reach her destination, and this destination was the grave. If she could not live with him, she would die! She knew this, and knowing it, she was tranquil, even happy.

"I invite all the ladies and gentlemen of the court to spend the evening in my room," she said, on the second day of this painful expectation; "we will endeavor to imagine that the prince royal is in our midst, and pass the hours in the usual manner; we will first go yachting; afterwards we will all take tea together, and Baron Bielfeld will read us a few chapters from the 'Henriade.' We will then play cards, and finish the evening with a dance. Does this programme meet with your approbation?" All murmured some words of assent and thanks, but their faces were nevertheless slightly clouded. Perceiving this, the princess royal said: "It seems that you are not pleased, that my suggestion does not meet with your approbation. Even the face of my little Louise von Schwerin is clouded, and the countenance of my good Countess Katsch no longer wears its pleasant smile. Well, what is it? I must know. Baron Bielfeld, I appoint you speaker of this discontented community. Speak, sir."

The baron smiled and sighed: "Your highness spoke a few days since of your gift of prophecy, and in fact you are a prophetess, and have seen through us. It is certainly a great happiness and a great honor to spend the evening in the apartments of the princess royal. But if your highness would allow us to ask a favor, it would be that our exalted mistress would condescend to receive us either in the garden saloon or music-room, and not in your private apartments; for these apartments, beautiful and magnificent as they are, have one great, one terrible defect."

"Well," said the princess, as Bielfeld concluded, "I am curious to know what this defect is. I believed my rooms to be beautiful and charming; the prince royal himself regulated their arrangement, and Pesne and Buisson ornamented them with their most beautiful paintings. Qui k, then, tell me of this great defect!"

"Your highness, your apartments are in the right wing of the castle." The princess looked at him inquiringly, astonishment depicted in her countenance, and then laughed.

"Ah, now I see, my apartments are in the right wing of the castle; that is, from there you cannot watch the great bridge, over which all that come from Berlin or Potsdam must pass. You are right, this is a great defect. But the music-room is in the left wing, and from there you can see both the bridge and the road. Let us, then, adjourn to the music-room for our reading, and when it becomes too dark to see, we will play cards in my apartments."

They all followed the princess to the music-room, where by chance or out of mischief the princess chose the seat farthest from the window, and thus compelled the company to assemble around her. As they followed her, they all looked longingly through the window and toward the bridge, over which the messenger of happiness might at any moment pass.

Bielfeld took the book selected by the princess, and commenced reading. But how torturing it was to read, to listen to these pathetic and measured Alexandrines from the "Henriade," while perchance in this same hour a new Alexander was placing the crown upon his young and noble head! In fact, but little was heard of these harmonious verses. All looked stealthily toward the window, and listened breathlessly to every sound that came from the road. Bielfeld suddenly ceased reading, and looked toward the window.

"Why do you not read on?" said the princess.

"Excuse me, I thought I saw a horse's head on the bridge!"

Forthwith, as if upon a given signal, they all flew to the

windows; the princess herself, in the general commotion, hastened to one.

Yes! Between the trees something was seen moving. There it is coming on the bridge now! A peal of laughter resounded through the rooms. An ox! Count Bielfeld's courier had transformed himself into an ox!

They all stole back to their seats in confusion, and the reading was recommenced. But it did not last long; again Bielfeld came to a stop.

"Pardon me, your highness, but now there is positively a horse on the bridge."

Again they all rushed anxiously to the window. It certainly was a horse, but its rider was not a royal messenger, but a common peasant.

"I see," said the princess, laughing, "that we must discontinue our reading. Let us walk in the left wing of the garden, and as near the gate as possible."

"Will the sun never set?" whispered Bielfeld to Count Wartensleben, as they walked up and down. "I fear another Joshua has arrested its course."

But it set at last; it was now evening, and still no courier had passed the bridge. They accepted the princess' invitation, and hastened to her apartments and to the card-tables. And on this occasion, as heretofore, the cards exercised a magic influence over the inhabitants of Rheinsberg, for they were striving to win that, from the want of which, not only the prince but all his courtiers had so often suffered—gold! Count Wartensleben had lately arrived and brought with him a well-filled purse, which Bielfeld, Kaiserling, and Chazot were anxious to lighten.

The princess played with her maids of honor a game called Trisset, in her boudoir, while the rest of the company, seated at several tables in the adjoining room, played their beloved game of quadrille. The door suddenly opened, and a valet appeared. In passing the table at which Count Wartensleben, Bielfeld, and several ladies were playing, he stealthily showed them a letter with a black seal, which he was about to deliver to the princess.

"The king is then dead!" murmured they, hastily throwing their cards on the table; the counters fell together, but they looked at them in disdain. What cared they for a few lost pennies, now that their prince had become king?

Count Wartensleben arose and said in a solemn voice: "I will be the first to greet the princess as queen, and I will exert every effort to utter the word 'majesty' in a full, re sounding tone."

"I will follow you," said Bielfeld, solemnly.

And both advanced to the open door, through which the princess could be seen still occupied in reading her letter. She seemed unusually gay, and a bright smile played upon her lips. Accidentally looking up, she perceived the two cavaliers advancing slowly and solemnly toward her.

"Ah, you know, then, that a courier has at last crossed that fatal bridge, and you come for news of the prince royal?"

"Prince royal?" repeated Wartensleben, in amazement. "Is he still the prince royal?"

"You then thought he was king!" exclaimed the princess, "and came to greet me as your queen?"

"Yes, your highness, and the word 'majesty' was already on my lips."

They all laughed heartily, and jested over this mistake, but were nevertheless thankful when they were at last dismissed and were allowed to retire to their rooms. When entirely alone, the princess drew from her bosom the letter she had received, to read it once more; she cast a loving and tender glance at the characters his hand had traced, and as her eyes rested on his signature, she raised the paper to her lips and kissed it.

"Frederick," whispered she, "my Frederick, I love you so deeply that I envy this paper which has been touched by your hand, and upon which your glorious eyes have rested. No, no," said she, "he will not cast me off. Is it not written here—'In a few days I and the people will greet you as Queen.' No, he could not be so cruel as to set the crown on my head, and then cover it with ashes. If he acknowledges me as his wife and queen before his people, and before Germany, it must be his intention never to disown me, but to let me live on by his side. Oh, he must surely know how truly I love him, although I have never had the courage to tell him so. My tears and my sighs must have whispered to him the secret of my love, and he will have compassion with a poor wife who asks but to be permitted to adore and worship him. And who knows but that he may one day be touched by this great love, that he will one day raise up the poor woman who now lies trembling at his feet, and press her to his bosom. Oh, that this may be so, my God; let it be, and then let me die!"

She sank back on her couch, and, pressing the letter to her lips, whispered softly: "Good-night, Frederick, my Frederick!" She smiled sweetly as she slept. Perhaps she was dreaming of him.

A deep silence soon reigned throughout the castle. All the lights were extinguished. Sleep spread its wings over all these impatient and expectant hearts, and fanned them into forgetfulness and peaceful rest.

All slept, and now the long-expected courier is at last passing over the bridge, which trembled beneath his horse's feet, but none hear him, all are sleeping so soundly. His knocks resound through the entire castle. It is the herald of the new era, which sheds its first bright morning rays over the evening of the dark and gloomy past.

Now all are awake, and running to and fro through the

halls, each one burning with eagerness to proclaim the joyful news: "Frederick is no longer prince royal. Frederick is king and the ruler of Prussia!"

Bielfeld is awakened by a loud knocking; he springs hastily out of bed and opens the door to his friend Knobelsdorf. "Up, up, my friend," exclaims the latter. "Dress quickly. We must go down and congratulate the queen; we must be ready to accompany her immediately to Berlin. Frederick William is dead, and we will now reign in Prussia."

"Ah, another fairy tale," said Bielfeld, dressing hastily; "a fairy tale, by which we have been too often deceived to believe in its truth."

"No, no, this time it is true. The king is dead, quite dead! Jordan has received orders to embalm the corpse, and once in his hands, it will never come to life again."

Bielfeld being now ready, the two friends hurried to the ante-chamber that led to the princess royal's apartments. The entire court of the new queen had assembled in this chamber, and they were endeavoring to suppress their joy and delight, and to look grave and earnest in consideration of the solemnity of the occasion. They conversed in whispers, for the bed-chamber of the princess was next to this room, and she still slept.

"Yes, the princess royal sleeps, but when she awakes she will be a queen! She must be awakened, to receive her husband's letter."

The Countess Katsch, with two of Elizabeth's maids of honor, entered her bed-chamber, well armed with smelling-bottles and salts. Elizabeth Christine still slept. But on so important an occasion the sleep even of a princess was not considered sacred. The countess drew back the curtains, and Elizabeth was awakened by the bright glaring light. She looked inquiringly at the countess, who approached her with a low and solemn courtesy.

"Pardon me for waking your majesty—"

"Majesty, why 'your majesty?'" said the princess, quickly. "Has another ox or horse crossed the fatal bridge?"

"Yes, your majesty, but it was Baron Villich's horse, and he brought the news that King Frederick William expired yesterday at Potsdam. I have a smelling-bottle here, your majesty; allow me to hold—"

The young queen pushed back the smelling-bottle; she did not feel in the least like fainting, and her heart beat higher.

"And has the baron brought no letter for me?" said she, breathlessly.

"Here is a letter, your majesty."

The queen hastily broke the seal. It contained but a few lines, but they were in her husband's handwriting, and were full of significance. To her these few lines indicated a future full of splendor, happiness, and love. The king called her to share with him the homage of his subjects. It is *true* there was not a word of tenderness or love in the letter, but the king called her to his side; he called her his wife.

Away, then, away to Berlin, where her husband was awaiting her; where the people would greet her as their queen; where a new world, a new life would unfold itself before her; a life of proud enjoyment! For Elizabeth will be the queen, the wife of Frederick. Away, then, to Berlin!

The queen received the congratulations of her court in the music-room. And now to Berlin, where a new sun has risen, a King Frederick the Second!

CHAPTER XVI.

ROYAL GRACE AND ROYAL DISPLEASURE.

THE cannon thundered, the bells rang loudly and merrily; the garrison in Berlin took the oath, as the garrison of Potsdam had done the day before.

The young king held his first great court to-day in the White Saloon. From every province, from every State, from every corporation, deputations had arrived to look upon the long-hoped-for king, the liberator from oppression, servitude, and famine. Delight and pure unqualified joy reigned in every heart, and those who looked upon the features of Frederick, illuminated with kindliness and intellect, felt that for Prussia it was the dawning of a new era.

But who was called to assist in organizing this new movement? Whom had the king chosen from amongst his friends and servants? whom had he set aside? upon whom would he revenge himself? Truth to tell, there were many now standing in the White Saloon who had often, perhaps, in obedience to the king's command, brought suffering and bitter sorrow upon the prince royal; many were there who had humbled him, misused his confidence, and often brought down his father's rage and scorn upon him.

Will the king remember these things, now that he has the power to punish and revenge his wrongs? Many had entered the White Saloon trembling with anxiety; timidly keeping in the distance; glad that the eye of the king did not rest upon them; glad to slip unseen into a corner.

But nothing escaped the eye of Frederick; he had remarked the group standing in the far-off window; he understood full well their restless, disturbed, and anxious glances. A pitiful and sweet smile spread over his noble features, an expression of infinite gentleness illumined his face; with head erect he drew near to this group, who, with the instinct of a common danger, pressed more closely together, and awaited their fate silently.

Who had so often and so heavily oppressed the prince as Colonel Derchau? who had mocked at him and persecuted him so bitterly? who had carried out the harsh commands of the king against him so unrelentingly? It was Derchau and Grumbkow who presided at the first cruel trial of "Captain Fritz," and had repeated to him the hard and threatening words of the king. "Captain Fritz" had wept with rage, and sworn to revenge himself upon these cruel men. Will the king remember the oath of the captain? The king stood now near the colonel; his clear eye was fixed upon him. This man, who had prepared for him so many woes, now stood with bowed head and loudly-beating heart, completely in his power. Suddenly, with a rash movement, the king extended his hand, and said, mildly:

"Good-day, Derchau." It was the first time in seven years that Frederick had spoken to him, and this simple greeting touched his heart; he bowed low, and as he kissed the outstretched hand, a hot tear fell upon it. "Colonel Derchau," said the king, "you were a faithful and obedient servant to my royal father; you have punctually followed his wishes and given him unconditional obedience. It becomes me to reward my father's faithful subject. From to-day you are a major-general."

As the king turned, his eye fell upon the privy councillor Von Eckert, and the mild and conciliating expression vanished from his features; he looked hard and stern.

"Has the coat-of-arms been placed upon the house in Jager Street?" said the king.

"No, your majesty."

"Then I counsel you not to have it done; this house is the property of the crown, and it shall not be sacrificed by such home. Go home, and there you will receive my commands."

Pale and heart-broken, Eckert glided from the group; mocking laughter followed his steps through the saloons; no one had a word of regret or pity for him; no one remembered their former friendship and oft-repeated assurances of service and gratitude. He passed tremblingly through the palace; as he reached the outer door, Pöllnitz stepped before him; a mocking smile played upon his lips, and his glance betrayed all the hatred which he had been compelled to veil or conceal during the life of Frederick William.

"Now," said he, slowly, "will you send me the wine which you promised from your cellar? You *understand*, the wine from your house in Jager Street, for which I arranged the coat-of-arms! Ah, those were charming days, my dear privy councillor! You have often broken your word of honor to me, often slandered me, and brought upon me the reproaches of the king. I have, however, reason to be thankful to you; this house which you have built in Jager Street is stately and handsome, and large enough for a cavalier of my pretensions. You have, also, at the cost of the king, furnished it with such princely elegance that it is in all things an appropriate residence for a cavalier. Do you not remember my description of such a house? The king called it then a Spanish air-castle. You, great-hearted man, have made my castle in the air a splendid reality, and now that it is finished and furnished, you will, in your magnanimity, leave that house to me. I shall be your heir! You know, my dear Eckert, that the privy councillor is dead, and only the chimney-builder lives; and even the adroit chimney-builder is banished from Berlin, and must remain twenty miles away from his splendid home. But tell me, Eckert, when one of my chimneys smokes, may I not send a messenger for you, will you not promise me to come and put things in order for me?"

Eckert muttered some confused words, and tried to force Pöllnitz from the door, before which the hard-hearted, spiteful courtier had placed himself, like the angel with the avenging sword.

"You wish to go," said he, with assumed kindliness. "Oh, without doubt you wish to see the royal commands now awaiting you at your house. I can tell you literally the sentence of the king: you have lost your office, your income, your rank, and you are banished from Berlin! that is all. The king, as you see, has been gracious; he could have had you executed, or sent to Spandau for life, but he would not desecrate his new reign with your blood. For this reason was he gracious."

"Let me pass," said Eckert, trembling, and pale as death. "I am choking! let me out!"

Pöllnitz still held him back. "Do you not know, good man, that a thousand men stand below in the court-yard? do you not hear their shouts and rejoicings? Well, these hurrahs will be changed into growls of rage when the people see you, my dear Eckert; in their wild wrath they might mistake you for a good roast, with which to quiet their hunger. You know that the people are hungry; you, who filled the barns of the king with grain, and placed great locks and bars upon the doors, lest the people, in their despairing hunger, might seize upon the corn! You even swore to the king that the people had enough, and did not need his corn or his help! Listen, the people shout again; I will not detain you. Go and look upon this happy people. The king has opened the granaries and scattered bread far and wide, and the tax upon meal is removed for a month.* Go, dear Eckert, go and see how happy the people are!"

With a wild curse Eckert sprung from the door; Pöllnitz

---

* See King's "History of Berlin," vol. v. The king's own words.

followed him with a mocking glance. "Revenge is sweet,'' he said, drawing a long breath; "he has often done me wrong, and now I have paid him back with usury. Eckert is lost. Would that I had his house! I must have it! I will have it! Oh, I will make myself absolutely necessary to the king; I will flatter, I will praise, I will find out and fulfil his most secret, his unspoken wishes. I will force him to give me his confidence—to make me his *maître de plaisir*. Yes, yes, the house in Jager Street shall be mine! I have sworn it, and Fredersdorf has promised me his influence. And now to the king; I must see for myself if this young royal child can, like Hercules in his cradle, destroy serpents on the day of his birth; or, if he is a king, like all other kings, overcome by flattery, idle and vain, knowing or acknowledging no laws over himself, but those of his own conscience and his *bon plaisir*. But hark! that is the king's voice; to whom is he speaking?"

Pöllnitz hastened into the adjoining room; the king was standing in the midst of his ministers, and a deputation of magistrates of Berlin, and was in the act of dismissing them.

"I command you," said the king, in conclusion, turning to his ministers, "as often as you think it necessary to make any changes in my orders and regulations, to make known your opinions to me freely, and not to be weary in so doing; I may, unhappily, sometimes lose sight of the true interests of my subjects; I am resolved that whenever in future my personal interest shall seem to be contrary to the welfare of my people, their happiness shall receive the first consideration."

"Alas, it will be very difficult to tame this youthful Hercules!" murmured Pollnitz, glancing toward the king, who was just leaving the apartment; "the serpents that we will twine about him must be strong and alluring; now happily Fredersdorf and myself are acquainted with some such serpents, and we will take care that he finds them in his path."

In the mean time the king had left the reception-room, and retired to his private apartments, where the friends and confidants from Rheinsberg awaited him with hopeful hearts. They were all ready to receive the showers of gold, which, without doubt, would rain down upon them. They were all convinced that the young king would lay upon them, at least, a corner of the mantle of ermine and purple with which his shoulders should be adorned. They alone would be chosen to aid in bearing the burden of his kingly crown and royal sceptre. They were all dreaming of ambassadorships, presidencies, and major-generals' epaulettes.

As the king entered, they received him with loud cries of joy. The Margrave Henry, who had often borne a part in the gay *fêtes* at Rheinsberg, hastened to greet the king with gay, witty words, and both hands extended. Frederick did not respond to this greeting; he did not smile; looking steadily at the Margrave, he stepped back and said:

"Monsieur, now I am the king; no longer the gardener at Rheinsberg." The king read the pained astonishment in the faces of his friends, who, one moment before, had been so *hopeful*, so assured; he advanced and said, in a kindly tone, "We are no longer in Rheinsberg. The beautiful proverb of Horace belongs to our past—'Folly is sweet in its season.' There I was the gardener and the friend—here I am the king; here all must work, and each one must use his talents and his strength in the service of the State, and thus prove to the people that the prince had reason to choose him for a friend."

"And may I also be a partaker of that grace and be counted amongst the friends of the king?" said the old Prince of Anhalt Dessau, who, with his two sons, had just entered and heard the last words of Frederick; "will your majesty continue to me and my sons the favor which your ever-blessed father granted to us during so many long and happy years? Oh, your majesty, I beseech you to be gracious to us, and grant us the position and influence which we have so long enjoyed." So saying, the old prince bent his knee to his youthful monarch. The king bowed his head thoughtfully, and a smile played upon his lips; he gave his hand to the prince, and commanded him to rise.

"I will gladly leave you your place and income, for I am sure you will serve me as faithfully and zealously as you did my father. As regards the position and influence which you desire, I say to you *all*, no man under my reign will have position but I myself, and not even my best friend will exercise the slightest influence over me."

The friends from Rheinsberg turned pale, and exchanged stolen glances with each other. There was no more jesting; a hand of ice had been laid upon their beating hearts, and the wings of hope were broken. The king did not seem to remark the change; he drew near to his friend Jordan, and taking his arm, walked to the window, and spoke with him long and earnestly.

The courtiers and favorites looked after their happy friend with envious glances, and observed every shade in the countenances of the king and Jordan. The king was calm, but an expression of painful surprise settled like a cloud upon Jordan. Now the king left the window, and called Bielfeld to him; spoke with him also long and gravely, and then dismissed him, and nodded to Chazot to join him; lastly he took the arm of the Duke of Wartensleben, and walked backward and forward, chatting with him. The duke was radiant with joy, but the other courtiers looked suspicious and lowering; with none of them had he spoken so long; no other arm had he so familiarly taken. It was clear that Wartensleben was the declared favorite of the king; he had driven them from the field.

The king observed all this; he had read the envy, malice, rage, and melancholy in the faces of his friends; he knew

6

them all too well; had too long observed them, not to be able to read their thoughts. It had pleased him to sport awhile with these small souls, so filled with selfishness, envy, and every evil passion; he wished to give them a lesson, and bring them down from their dizzy and imaginary heights to the stern realities of life. The king had used Wartensleben as his instrument for this purpose, and now must the poor duke's wings be clipped. The mounting waves of his ambition must be quieted by the oil of truth.

"Yes," said the king, "I am the ruler of a kingdom; I have a great army and a well-filled treasury, you cannot doubt that it is my highest aim to make my country blossom as the rose; to uphold the reputation of my army, and to make the best use of my riches. The gold is there to circulate; it is there to reward those who faithfully serve their fatherland; but above all other things it is there for those who are truly my friends."

The features of the young duke were radiant with expectation; as the king saw this, a mocking smile flashed from his eye.

"I will, however, naturally know how to distinguish between my friends, and those who do not need gold will not receive it. You, for example, my dear duke, are enormously rich; you will content yourself, therefore, with my love, as you will naturally never receive a dollar from me." So speaking, he nodded kindly to the duke, passed into the next room, and closed the door behind him. Grave and dumb, the friends from Rheinsberg gazed upon each other; each one regarded the other as his successful rival, and thought to see in him what he had not become—a powerful favorite, a minister, or general. All felt their love growing cold, and almost hated the friends who stood in their way. Jordan was the first who broke silence. Reaching his hand to Bielfeld, he said:

"It must not be thought that disappointed hopes have hardened our hearts, and that envy blinds us to the advantages of our friends. I love you, Bielfeld, because of your advantages and talents; and I understand full well why the king advances you before me. Receive also my good wishes, and be assured that from the heart I rejoice in your success."

Bielfeld looked amazed. "My success!" said he. "Dear friend, you need not be envious; and as to my advancement, it is so small an affair that I can scarcely find it. The king said he intended me for a diplomatist, but that I needed years of instruction. With this view he had selected me to accompany Duke Trückfess to Hanover. When I returned from there, I would receive further orders. This is my promotion, and you must confess I make a small beginning. But you, dear Jordan, what important position have you received? You are the king's dearest friend, and he has without doubt advanced you above us all. I acknowledge that you merit this. Tell us also what are you?"

"Yes," cried they all eagerly, "what are you? Are you minister of State or minister of Church affairs?"

"What am I?" cried Jordan, laughing. "I will tell you, my friends. I am not minister of Church affairs; I am not minister of State. I am—ah, you will never guess what I am—I belong to the police! I must remove the beggars from the streets of Berlin, and found a workhouse for them. Now, dear friends, am I not enviable?" For a moment all were silent; then every eye was fixed upon Wartensleben.

"And you, dear duke, are you made happy! You have cut open the golden apple; you have the longed-for portfolio."

"I!" cried the duke, half angry, half merry. "I have nothing, and will receive nothing. I will tell you what the king said to me. He assured me earnestly and solemnly that I was rich enough, and would never receive a dollar from him."

At this announcement they all broke out in uproarious laughter. "Let us confess," said Bielfeld, "that we have played to-day a rare comedy—a farce which Molière might have written, and which must bear the title of *La Journée des Dupes*. Now, as we have none of us become distinguished, let us all be joyful and love each other dearly. But listen! the king plays the flute; how soft, how melting is the sound!"

Yes, the king played the flute; he cast out with those melodious strains the evil spirit of *ennui* which the tiresome etiquette of the day had brought upon him. He played the flute to recover himself—to regain his cheerful spirit and a clear brow. Soon he laid it aside, and his eye rested upon the unopened letters and papers with which the table was covered. Yes, he must open all these letters, and answer them himself, he alone. Nobody should do his work; all should work only through him; no one should decree or command in Prussia but the king. Every thing should flow from him. He would be the heart and soul of his country.

Frederick opened and read the letters, and wrote the answer on the margin of the paper, leaving it to the secretary to copy. And now the work was almost done; the paper with the great seal, which he now opened, was the last.

This was a declaration from the Church department, which announced that, through the influence of the Catholic schools in Berlin, many Protestants had become Catholics. Did not his majesty think it best to close these schools? A pitiful smile played upon the lips of Frederick as he read. "And they say they believe in one God, and their priests and ministers preach Christian forbearance and Christian love, while they know nothing of either. They have not God, but the Church, always before their eyes; they are intolerant in their hearts, imperious, and full of cunning. I will bend them, and break down their assumed power. My whole life will be a battle with priests; they will mock at me, and call me a heretic. Let the Church be ever against me, if my own conscience absolves me. Now I will begin the war, and what I now write will be a signal of alarm in the tents of all the pious priests."

He took up the paper again and wrote on the margin, "All religions shall be tolerated. The magistrates must have their eyes open, and see that no sect imposes on another. In Prussia each man shall be saved in his own way." *

* Busching. The king's words.

BOOK II.

CHAPTER I.

THE GARDEN OF MONBIJOU.

The excitement of the first days was quieted. The young king had withdrawn for a short time to the palace in Charlottenburg, while his wife remained in Berlin, anxiously expecting an invitation to follow her husband.

But the young monarch appeared to have no care or thought but for his kingdom. He worked and studied without interruption; even his beloved flute was untouched.

Berlin was, according to etiquette, draped with mourning for a few days; it served in this instance as a veil to the joy with which all looked forward to the coronation of the new king. All appeared earnest and solemn, but every heart was joyful and every eye beaming. The palace of the king was silent and deserted; the king was, as we have said, at Charlottenburg; the young queen was in the palace formerly occupied by the prince royal, and the dowager queen Sophia Dorothea had retired with the two princesses, Ulrica and Amelia, to the palace of Monbijou. All were anxious and expectant; all hoped for influence and honor, power and greatness. The scullion and the maids, as well as the counts and princes, and even the queen herself, dreamed of happy and glorious days in the future.

Sophia Dorothea had been too long a trembling, subjugated woman; she was rejoicing in the thought that she might at length be a queen. Her son would doubtless grant to her all the power which had been denied her by her husband; he would remember the days of tears and bitterness which she had endured for his sake; and now that the power was in his hands she would be repaid a thousand-fold. The young king would hold the sceptre in his hands, but he must allow his mother to aid in keeping it upright; and if he found it too weighty, the queen was ready to bear it for him, and reign in his stead, while her dreamy son wrote poems, or played on the flute, or philosophized with his friends. Frederick was certainly not formed to rule; he was a poet and a philosopher; he dreamed of a Utopia; he imagined an ideal which it was impossible to realize. The act of ruling would be a weary trial to him, and the sounds of the trumpet but ill accord with his harmonious dreams.

But happily his mother was there, and was willing to reign for him, to bear upon her shoulders the heavy burdens and cares of the kingdom, to work with the ministers, while the king wrote poetical epistles to Voltaire.

Why should not Sophia Dorothea reign? Were there not examples in all lands of noble women who governed their people well and honorably? Was not England proud of her Elizabeth, Sweden of her Christina, Spain of Isabella, Russia of Catharine? and even in Prussia the queen Sophia Charlotte had occupied a great and glorious position. Why could not Sophia Dorothea accomplish as much or even more than her predecessor?

These were the thoughts of the queen as she walked up and down the shady paths of the garden of Monbijou, and listened with a proud smile to the flattering words of Count Manteuffel, who had just handed her a letter of condolence from the Empress of Austria.

" Her majesty the empress has sent me a most loving

and tender letter to-day," said the dowager queen, with an ironical smile.

"She has then only given expression to-day, to those sentiments which she has always entertained for your majesty," said the count, respectfully.

The queen bowed her head smilingly, but said, "The houses of Hohenzollern and Hapsburg have never been friendly ; it is not in their nature to love one another."

"The great families of Capulet and Montague said the same," remarked Count Manteuffel, "but the anger of the parents dissolved before the love of the children."

"But we have not arrived at the children," said the queen proudly, as she thought how her husband had been deceived by the house of Austria, and recalled that, on his death-bed he had commanded his son Frederick to revenge those treacheries.

"Pardon me, your majesty, if I dare to contradict you ; we have most surely arrived at the children, and the difficulties of the parents are forgotten in their love. Is not the wife of the young king the deeply-loved niece of the Austrian empress ?

"She was already his wife, count, as my husband visited the emperor in Bohemia, and it was not considered according to etiquette for the emperor to offer his hand to the King of Prussia." *

"She was, however, not his wife when Austria, by her repeated and energetic representations, saved the life of the prince royal. For your majesty knows that at one time that precious life was threatened."

"It was threatened, but it would have been preserved without the assistance of Austria; for the mother of Fred-

* Seckendorf's Leben.

erick was at hand, and that mother was sister to the King of England." And the queen cast on the count so proud and scornful a glance, that his eyes fell involuntarily to the ground, Sophia Dorothea saw this, and smiled. This was her triumph; she would now show herself mild and forgiving. "We will speak no more of the past," she said, in a friendly manner. "The death of my husband has cast a dark cloud over it, and I must think only of the future, that my son, the young king, may not always behold me with tears in my eyes. No, I will look forward, for I have a presentiment that Prussia's future will be great and glorious."

"Would that it might be thus for the whole of Germany!" cried the count. "It must be so, if the houses of Hohenzollern and Hapsburg will forget their ancient quarrels, and live together in love and peace."

"Let Hapsburg extend to us the hand of love and peace; show us her sympathy, her justice, and her gratitude, in deeds, not words."

"Austria is prepared to do so, your majesty; the question is, whether Prussia will grasp her hand and place upon it the ring of love."

The queen glanced up so quickly that she perceived the dark and threatening look of the count. "Austria is again making matrimonial plans," she said, with a bitter smile. "She is not satisfied with one marriage, such as that of her imperial niece, she longs for a repetition of this master-work. But this time, count, there is no dear one to be saved at any cost from a prison, this time the decision can be deferred until the arrival of all the couriers." And the queen, dismissing the count with a slight bow, recalled her ladies of honor, who were lingering at a short distance, and passed into one of the other walks.

Count Manteuffel remained where the queen had left
6*

him, looking after her with an earnest and thoughtful countenance. "She is prouder and more determined than formerly," he murmured ; "that is a proof that she will be influential, and knows her power. What she said of the
courier was without doubt an allusion to the one who
arrived an hour too late, with the consent of England, on the
betrothal day of the prince royal. Ah! there must be other
couriers *en route*, and one of them was most probably sent to
England. We must see that he arrives an hour too late, as
the former one did." At this instant, and in his immediate
vicinity, Manteuffel heard a soft and melodious voice saying,
"No, count, you can never make me believe in your love.
You are much too blond to love deeply."

"Blond!" cried a manly voice, with a tone of horror.
"You do not like fair hair, and until now I have been so
proud of mine. But I will have it dyed black, if you will
promise to believe in my love." The lady replied with a
light laugh, which brought an answering smile to the countenance of Count Manteuffel. "It is my ally, Madame von
Brandt," he said to himself. "I was most anxious to see her,
and must interrupt her tender *tête-à-tête* with Count Voss for
one moment." So speaking, the count hurried to the spot
from which he had heard the voices of Madame von Brandt
and her languishing lover. The count approached the lady
with the most delighted countenance, and expressed his
astonishment at finding his beautiful friend in the garden of
the dowager queen.

"Her majesty did me the honor to invite me to spend a
few weeks here," said Madame von Brandt. "She knew
that my physician had ordered me to the country, as the
only means to restore my health ; and as she knows of my
great intimacy with Mademoiselle von Pannewitz, one of her
ladies of honor, she was so kind as to offer me a few rooms
at Monbijou. Now I have explained to you the reason of

my presence here as minutely as if you were my father confessor, and nothing remains to be done but to present you to my escort. This is Count Voss, a noble cavalier, a *sans peur et sans reproche*, ready to sacrifice for his lady love, if not his life, at least his fair hair."

"Beware, my dear count," said Manteuffel, laughing, "beware that the color of your hair is not changed by this lovely scoffer—that it does not become a venerable gray. She is sufficiently accomplished in the art of enchantment to do that; I assure you that Madame von Brandt plays a most important *rôle* in the history of my gray hairs."

"Ah! it would be delightful to become gray in the service of Madame von Brandt," said the young count, in so pathetic a tone, that his companions both laughed. "As often as I looked at my gray hair I would think of her." And the young count gazed into the distance, like one entranced, and his smiling lips whispered low, unintelligible words.

"This is one of his ecstatic moments," whispered Madame von Brandt. "He has the whim to consider himself an original; he imagines himself a Petrarch enamored of his Laura. We will allow him to dream awhile, and speak of our own affairs. But be brief, I beg of you, for we must not be found together, as you are a suspicious character, my dear count, and my innocence might be doubted if we were seen holding a confidential conversation."

"Ah! it is edifying to hear Madame von Brandt speak like a young girl of sixteen, of her threatened innocence. But we will tranquillize this timidity, and be brief. In the first place, what of the young queen?"

"State of barometer: cold and damp, falling weather, stormy, with unfulfilled hopes, very little sunshine, and very heavy clouds."

"That means that the queen is still fearful of being slighted by her husband."

"She is no longer fearful—he neglects her already. The king is at Charlottenburg, and has not invited the queen to join him. As a husband, he slights his wife; whether as king he will neglect his queen, only time will reveal."

"And what of Madame von Morien?"

"The king seems to have forgotten her entirely since that unhappy *quid pro quo* with the poem at Rheinsberg; his love seems to have cooled, and he converses with her as harmlessly and as indifferently as with any other lady. No more stolen words, secret embraces, or amorous sighs. The miserable Morien is consumed with sorrow, for since she has been neglected she loves passionately."

"And that is unhappily not the means to regain that proud heart," said Count Mantéuffel, shrugging his shoulders. "With tears and languishing she will lose her influence, and only gain contempt. You who are the mistress of love and coquetry should understand that, and instruct your beautiful pupil. Now, however, comes the most important question. What of the marriage of the Prince Augustus William?"

Madame von Brandt sighed. "You are really inexorable. Have you no compassion for the noble, heartfelt love of two children, who are as pure and innocent as the stars in heaven?"

"And have you no compassion for the diamonds which long to repose upon your lovely bosom?" said Count Mantéuffel; "no compassion for the charming villa which you could purchase? You positively refuse to excite the envy of all the ladies at court by possessing the most costly cashmere? You will—"

"Enough, Count Devil! you are in reality more a devil than a man, for you lead my soul into temptation. I must submit. I will become a serpent, reposing on the bosom of my poor Laura, poisoning her love and lacerating her heart. Ah, count, if you knew how my conscience reproaches me when I listen to the pure and holy confession of her love, when trembling and blushing she whispers to me the secrets of her youthful heart, and flies to me, seeking protection against her own weakness! Remember that these two children love each other, without ever having had the courage to acknowledge it. Laura pretends not to understand the deep sighs and the whispered words of the prince, and then passes the long nights in weeping."

"If that is the case, it is most important to prevent an understanding between these singular lovers. You must exert all your influence with the young lady to induce her to close this romance with an heroic act, which will make her appear a holy martyr in the eyes of the prince."

"But, for example, what heroic act?"

"Her marriage."

"But how can we find a man so suddenly to whom this poor lamb can be sacrificed?"

"There is one," said the count, pointing to Count Voss, who appeared to have forgotten the whole world, and was occupied writing verses in his portfolio.

Madame von Brandt laughed aloud. "He marry the beautiful Laura!"

"Yes," said the count, earnestly, "he seeks a Laura."

"Yes, but you forget that he considers me his Laura."

"You can, therefore, easily induce him to make this sacrifice for you; he will be magnified in his own eyes, if, in resigning you, he gives himself to the lady you have selected."

"You are terrible," said Madame von Brandt. "I shudder before you, for I believe you have no human emotions in your heart of iron."

"There are higher and nobler considerations, to which such feelings must yield. But see, the count has finished his

poem. To work now, my beautiful ally; to-day you must
perfect your masterpiece; and now farewell," said the count,
kissing her hand, as he left her side.

Madame von Brandt approached the young count, who
seemed to be again lost in thought. She placed her hand
lightly on his shoulder, and whispered, half tenderly, half
reproachfully, " Dreamer, where are your thoughts?"

" With you," said the count, who trembled and grew
pale at her touch. " Yes, with you, noblest and dearest of
women; and as that tiresome gossip prevented me from
speaking to you, I passed the time he was here in writing."

" But you did not remember," said she, tenderly, " that
you were compromising me before Count Manteuffel, who
will not hesitate to declare in what intimate relationship we
stand to one another. Only think of writing without apology, while a lady and a strange gentleman were at your
side!"

" The world will only exclaim ' What an original!' " said
Count Voss, with a foolish, but well-pleased smile.

" But it will also say that this original shows little consideration for Madame von Brandt; that he must, therefore,
be very intimate with her. The reputation of a woman is
so easily injured; it is like the wing of the butterfly, so soon
as a finger touches it or points at it, it loses its lustre; and
we poor women have nothing but our good name and un-
spotted virtue. It is the only shield—the only weapon—
that we possess against the cruelty of man, and you seek to
tear that from us, and, then dishonored and humiliated, you
tread us under foot!"

" You are weeping!" cried the count, looking at his beloved, in whose eyes the tears really stood—" you are weeping! I am truly a great criminal to cause you to shed tears."

" No, you are a noble but most thoughtless man," said

Madame von Brandt, smiling through her tears. "You betray to the world what only God and we ourselves should know."

"Heavens! what have I betrayed?" cried the poor frightened count.

"You have betrayed our love," whispered Madame von Brandt, as she glanced tenderly at the count.

"What! our love?" he cried, beside himself with delight; "you admit that it is not I alone who love?"

"I admit it, but at the same time declare that we must part."

"Never! no, never! No power on earth shall part us," said he, seizing her hand, and covering it with kisses.

"But there is a power which has the right to separate us—the power of my husband. He already suspects my feelings for you, and he will be inexorable if he discovers that his suspicions are correct."

"Then I will call him out, and he will fall by my hand, and I shall bear you in triumph as my wife to my castle."

"But if you should fall?"

"Ah! I had not thought of that," murmured the count, turning pale. "That would be certainly a most unhappy accident. We will not tempt fate with this trial, but seek another way out of our difficulty. Ah, I know one already. You must elope with me."

She said, with a sad smile, "The arm of the king extends far and wide, and my husband would follow us with his vengeance to the end of the world."

"But what shall we do?" cried the count, despairingly; "we love each other; separated, we must be consumed with grief and sorrow. Ah! ah! shall I really suffer the fate of Petrarch, and pass my life in an eternal dirge? Is there no way to prevent this?"

Madame von Brandt placed her hand with a slight but

tender pressure on his. "There is one way," she whispered, "a way to reassure, not only my husband, but the whole world, which will cast a veil over our love, and protect us from the wickedness and calumny of man."

"Show me this way!" he exclaimed, "and if it should cost half of my fortune I would walk in it, if I could hope to gain your love."

She bent her head nearer to him, and, with a most fascinating and tender glance, whispered, "You must marry, count."

He withdrew a step, and uttered a cry of horror. "I must marry! You desire it—you who profess to love me?"

"Because I love you, dearest, and because your marriage will break the bands of etiquette which divide us. You must marry a lady of my acquaintance, perhaps one of my friends, and then no one, not even my husband, will consider our friendship remarkable.

"Oh! I see it; there is no other way," sighed the count. "If I were only married now!"

"Oh! you ungrateful, faithless man," cried Madame von Brandt, indignantly. "You long already for your marriage with the beautiful young woman, in whose love I shall be forgotten."

"Oh! you are well aware that I only wish to be married because you desire it."

"Prove this by answering that you will not refuse to marry the lady I shall point out to you."

"I swear it."

"You swear that you will marry no other than the one I name? You swear that you will overcome all obstacles, and be withheld by no prayers or reproaches?"

"I swear it."

"On the word of a count?"

"On the word of a count. Show me the lady, and I will marry her against the will of the whole world."

"But if the lady should not love you?"

"Why should I care? Do I love her? Do I not marry her for your sake alone?"

"Ah! my friend," cried Madame von Brandt, "I see that we understand one another. Come, and I will show you your bride."

She placed her arm in his, and drew him away. Her eye gleamed with a wild, menacing light, and she said sneeringly to herself, "I have selected a rich husband for my beautiful Laura, and have bartered my soul for diamonds and cashmeres, and the gratitude of an empress."

CHAPTER II.

THE QUEEN'S MAID OF HONOR.

AFTER her interview with Count Manteuffel, the queen Sophia Dorothea left the garden, and retired to her chamber. She dismissed her maids of honor for a few hours, requesting them to admit no one to her presence. She wished to consider and develop her plans in undisturbed quiet. She felt that Austria was again prepared to throw obstacles in the way of her favorite project—an English marriage for one of her children. She wished to sharpen her weapons, and marshal her forces for the approaching combat.

For a few hours, therefore, the maids of honor were free to follow their own inclinations, to amuse themselves as they thought fit.

Laura von Pannewitz had declined accompanying the

other ladies in their drive. Her heart required solitude and
rest. For her it was a rare and great pleasure to listen in
undisturbed quiet to the sweet voices which whispered ir
her heart, and suffused her whole being with delight.

It was so sweet to dream of him—to recall his words,
his smiles, his sighs; all those little shades and signs which
seem so unimportant to the careless, but which convey so
much to the loving observer?

He had written to her yesterday, and she—she had
had the cruel courage to return his letter unopened. But
she had first pressed it to her lips and to her heart with
streaming eyes, and had then fallen on her knees to pray to
God, and to implore him to give her strength and courage
to overcome her heart, to renounce his love.

Since then an entire day had passed, and she had not
seen him, had heard nothing of him. Oh, he must be sad
and very angry with her; he wished never to see her again.
And because he was angry, and wished to hold himself
aloof from her, he, the loving and attentive son, had even
neglected to pay the accustomed morning visit to his royal
mother, which he had never before omitted.

Her heart beating hurriedly, and weeping with anguish,
Laura had been standing behind her window curtain awaiting him, and had prayed to God that she might see him, or
at least hear his voice in the distance. But the prince did
not arrive, and now the time had passed at which he was
accustomed to come. The queen had already retired to her
study, and would admit no one.

Laura could, therefore, no longer hope to see the prince
Augustus William on this day. As she thought of this, she
felt as if a sword had pierced her bosom, and despair took
possession of her heart. She threw herself on her knees,
wrung her hands, and prayed to God, not for strength and
courage to renounce him as before, but for a little sunshine

on her sad and sorrowful love. Terrified at her own prayer, she had then arisen from her knees, and had hurried to the room of Madame von Brandt, to take refuge from her own thoughts and sorrows in the bosom of a friend.

But her friend was not there, and she was told that Madame von Brandt had gone down into the garden. Laura took her hat and shawl, and sought her. As she walked down the shady avenue, her glowing cheeks and burning eyes were cooled by the gentle breeze wafted over from the river Spree, and she felt soothed; something like peace stole into her heart. Laura had forgotten that she had come to the garden to seek her friend; she felt only that the calm and peace of nature had quieted her heart; that solitude whispered to her soul in a voice of consolation and of hope. Hurriedly she passed on to the denser and more solitary part of the garden, where she could give herself up to dreams of him whose image still filled her heart, although she had vainly endeavored to banish it.

She now entered the conservatory at the foot of the garden, which had been converted into a beautiful and charming saloon, for the exclusive use of the queen and her maids of honor. There were artificial arbors of blooming myrtle and orange, in which luxurious little sofas invited to repose; grottoes of stone had been constructed, in the crevices of which rare mountain plants were growing. There were little fountains which murmured and flashed pleasantly, and diffused an agreeable coolness throughout the atmosphere. Laura seated herself in one of the arbors, which was covered with myrtle, and, in a reclining position, her head resting on the trunk of an aged laurel-tree, which formed part of the framework of the arbor, she closed her eyes that she might see nothing but him.

It was a lovely picture, the beautiful and noble countenance of this young girl, enclosed as it were in a frame of

living myrtle; her delicate but full and maidenly figure reclining against the trunk of the tree, to which the chaste and
timid love of a virgin had once given life. She also was a
Daphne, fleeing from her own desires, fleeing from the sweetly-
alluring voice of her lover, who, to her, was the god of
beauty and of grace, the god of learning and the arts—her
Apollo, whom she adored and believed in, whom she feared,
and from whom she fled like Daphne, because she loved him.
For woman flees only from him whom she loves; she fears
him only who is dangerous, not because his words of tenderness and flattery are alluring, but because her own heart
pleads for him.

Laura was still sitting in the arbor, in a dreamy reverie.
His image filled her thoughts; her love was prayer, her
prayer love. Her hands lay folded in her lap; a sweet,
dreamy smile played about her lips, and from under her
closed eyelids a few tears were slowly rolling down her soft,
rosy cheeks. She had been praying to God to give her
strength to conquer her own heart, and to bear, without murmuring and without betraying herself, the sorrow, the anger,
and even the indifference of the prince. Still she felt that
her heart would break if he should desert and forget her.
An alluring voice whispered that it would be a more blissful
end to die, after an hour of ecstatic and intoxicating happiness, than to renounce his love, and still die.

But the chaste Laura did not wish to hear this voice; she
would drown it with her prayers; and still, even while she
prayed, she thought how great and sublime a happiness it
would be to kiss the lips of her beloved, to whisper in his
ear the long-concealed, long-buried secret of her love. And
then his kiss still on her lips, and in the sunshine of his eyes,
to fall down and die!—exchanging heaven for heaven; re-
deeming bliss with bliss. And sweeter dreams and more
painful phantasies came over her; heavier and heavier sank

b r eyelids; a weight of sorrow rested on her heart, and made it weary unto death; until at the last, like the disciples on the Mount, she slept for very sorrow.

The silence was profound. Suddenly stealthy footsteps could be heard, and the figure of a man appeared at the entrance of the grotto. Cautiously he stepped forward, and cast an inquiring glance through the trailing vines which overhung the grotto, to the young girl who still slumbered, reclining on the trunk of the laurel-tree. It was Fritz Wendel, the gardener of Rheinsberg. Queen Sophia Dorothea had desired to have her green-houses and flower-beds arranged in the style of those at Rheinsberg. And, by command of the young king, several of the most expert gardeners of Rheinsberg had been sent to Berlin to superintend this arrangement in the garden of Monbijou. Fortune had favored the young gardener, and had again brought him near her he loved. For the little maid of honor, Louise von Schwerin, was not only the favorite of Queen Elizabeth, but Queen Sophia Dorothea also loved this saucy and sprightly young girl, who, because she was a child, and as such was excusable, was allowed to break in upon court etiquette with her merry laughter, and to introduce an element of freshness and vivacity into the stiff forms of court life. Moreover, by her thoughtless and presumptuous behavior at Rheinsberg, she had lost favor with the young couple who now reigned in Prussia. Queen Elizabeth could not forget that it was through Louise she had learned the name of her happy rival. And the king was angry with her, because, through her, the secret of his verses to Madame von Morien had been discovered. Louise von Schwerin was rarely with Queen Elizabeth. Sophia Dorothea, however, kept this young girl near her person for whole days. Her childish ways amused the queen, and her merry pranks drove the stiff and formal mistress of ceremonies, and the grave and stately cavaliers and ladies of the court, to despair. And the little maid of honor came to the queen willingly, for Monbijou had for her a great charm since the handsome gardener, Fritz Wendel, had been there. The romance with this young man had not yet come to an end; this secret little love affair had a peculiar charm for the young girl; and as no other admirer had been found for the little Louise, she for the present was very well pleased with the adoration of the young gardener, to whom she was not the "little Louise," but the bewitching fairy, the beautiful goddess. It was Fritz Wendel who appeared at the entrance of the grotto, and looked anxiously toward the sleeping Laura. He had been occupied in arranging the plants and flowers in this conservatory, which had been confided to his especial care. As the queen never entered the garden at this time, this hour had been set apart for his labors.

In the midst of his occupation he was interrupted by the entrance of Laura von Pannewitz, and had hastily retired to the grotto, intending to remain concealed until the lady should have left the conservatory. From his hiding-place, concealed by the dense Indian vines, he could see the myrtle arbor in which the beautiful Laura reposed; and now, seeing that she slept, he advanced slowly and cautiously from the grotto. He listened attentively to her slow and regular breathing—yes, she really slept; he might therefore stealthily leave the saloon.

"Ah, if it were she!" he murmured; "if it were she! I would not leave here so quietly. I would find courage to fall down at her feet and to clasp her to my arms, while pressing my lips to hers, to suppress her cry of terror. But this lady," said he, almost disdainfully, turning to the sleeping Laura, "is so little like her—that she is—"

The words died on his lips, and he hastily retreated to the entrance of the grotto. He thought he heard footsteps approaching the conservatory. The door of the vestibule creaked on its hinges, and again—Fritz Wende. slipped hastily into the grotto, and concealed himself behind the dense vines.

On the threshold of the saloon stood a young man, who looked searchingly around. His tall and graceful figure was clad in the uniform of the guards, which displayed his well-knit form to great advantage. The star on his breast, and the crape which he wore on his arm, announced a prince of the royal house; his beautifully-formed and handsome features wore an expression of almost effeminate tenderness. The glance of his large blue eyes was so soft and mild, that those who observed him long, were involuntarily touched with an inexplicable feeling of pity for this noble-looking youth. His broad brow showed so much spirit and determination, that it was evident he was not always gentle and yielding, but had the courage and strength to follow his own will if necessary.

It was Prince Augustus William, the favorite of the deceased king, on whose account the elder brother Frederick had suffered so much, because the king had endeavored to establish the former as his successor to the throne in the place of his first-born.*

But the prince's inclinations were not in accordance with the wishes of his father; Augustus William desired no throne, no earthly power; in his retiring modesty he disliked all public display; the title of royal highness had no charm for him, and with the indifference of a true philosopher he looked down upon the splendor and magnificence of earthly glory.

In his brother Frederick, the disdain of outward pomp might be attributed to his superior mind and strength of understanding; while Augustus William was actuated by a depth of feeling, a passionate and ardent sensitiveness. He

---

* Dr. Fred. Busching, page 172.

had come to pay the queen, his mother, the customary
morning visit, but when told she had desired that no one
should be admitted to her presence, he was not willing that
an exception should be made in his favor. "He had time
to wait," he said, "and should be announced and called up-
from the garden only when the queen was again at leisure."

After giving this order he had gone down into the garden, where a lover's instinct had conducted him to the conservatory, in which, to him, the most beautiful of all flowers,
the lovely Laura von Pannewitz, reposed. He did not dream
of finding her there, supposing she had accompanied the
other ladies on their drive ; he had sought this building that
he might pass a few moments in undisturbed quiet—that he
might think of her and the unrequited love which he had
vainly endeavored to tear from his heart.

It was therefore not her he sought when, on entering the
conservatory, he looked searchingly around. He only wished
to know that he was alone, that no one observed him. But
suddenly he started, and a deep red suffused his countenance.
He saw the beautiful sleeper in the arbor. In the first ecstasy
of his delight he was on the point of throwing himself at her
feet, and awakening her with his kisses. He started forward
—but then hesitated, and stood still, an expression of deep
melancholy pervading his features.

"She will not welcome me," murmured he, "she will repel me as she did my letter yesterday. She does not love
me, and would never forgive me if I should desecrate her
pure lips with mine." He bowed his head and sighed. "But
I love her," said he, after a long pause, "and will at least look
at and adore her, as the Catholics worship the Virgin Mary."
And with a beaming smile, which illumined his whole countenance, the prince slowly and noiselessly stepped forward.

"Well," murmured Fritz Wendel in his hiding-place, "I
have some curiosity to know what the prince has to say to

this sleeping beauty; but, nevertheless, I would give a year of my life if I could slip away unobserved, for if the prince discovers me here I am lost!"

He retired to that part of the grotto where the foliage was thickest, still however securing a place from which he could observe all that took place in the myrtle arbor

---

CHAPTER III.

PRINCE AUGUSTUS WILLIAM.

THE prince entered the myrtle arbor, and, perceiving the lovely sleeper, he approached her with a joyful countenance.

"Madonna, my Madonna, let me pray to you, let me look at you," he murmured. "Listen to my pleadings, and let a ray of your love sink into my heart." Laura moved in her sleep, and uttered a few indistinct words. The prince kneeled motionless before her, and watched all her movements. The dreams that visited her were not bright; Laura moaned and sighed in her sleep; her countenance assumed an expression so sad and painful that the eyes of the prince filled with tears. "She is suffering," he murmured; "why should she suffer? what is it that causes my beloved to sigh?" Suddenly she opened her eyes, arose, and fastened her astonished and half-dreamy gaze upon the prince, who with folded hands was still kneeling before her, and gazing on her with tender, pleading eyes. A trembling seized her whole being, as the ocean trembles when touched by the first ray of the sun. A sweet, blissful astonishment was painted on every feature. "Am I still dreaming?" she murmured, passing her hand across her brow, and pushing aside her long dark hair—"am I still dreaming?"

7

"Yes, you are dreaming," murmured Prince Augustus, seizing her hands and pressing them to his lips, "you are dreaming, Madonna, let me dream with you, and be forever blessed. Oh! withdraw not your hand, be not angry, let us still dream for one blessed moment." But she hastily set her hands free and arose from her seat; grandly and proudly she stood before him, and her flashing eyes rested with a severe and reproachful expression upon the still kneeling prince.

"Arise, my prince; it is not proper that the brother of the king should kneel before me; arise, and have the kindness to inform me what circumstances procured me the rare and unsolicited favor of being sought by your royal highness. But no, I divine it; you owe me no explanation; the queen has asked for me, and your highness was so gracious as to seek for the tardy servant, who is sleeping while her mistress calls; allow me to hasten to her." Laura, feeling her strength failing, and suppressing with pain the tears that sprang from her heart to her eyes, endeavored to pass the prince.

But he held her back; the timidity that had so often made him appear shy and embarrassed had vanished; he felt that at this moment he faced his destiny, and that his future depended upon the result of this interview. "No," he said earnestly, "the queen did not call you, she does not need you; remain, therefore, mademoiselle, and grant me a few moments of your time." His solemn voice and determined expression made her tremble, but still entranced; her soul bowed in humility and fear before him. She had always seen him humble and pleading, always submissive and obedient; now his glance was commanding, his voice imperious; and she, who had been able to withstand the entreaties of a lover, found no courage to resist the angry and commanding man. "Remain," he repeated; "be seated, and allow me to speak to you honestly and truly."

Laura seated herself obediently and tremblingly; the prince stood before her, and looked at her with a sad smile.

"Yesterday you returned my letter unopened, but now you must hear me, Laura; I wish it, and no woman can withstand the strong will of the man who loves her."

Laura trembled and grew pale; she feared that if at this moment he bade her forsake all, cast away, and trample under foot her honor, her reputation, her innocence and pure conscience, she would obey him as a true and humble slave, and follow and serve him her whole life.

"Yes, you shall hear me; I will know my fate—know if you really despise my great and devoted love, if you are without pity, without sympathy for my suffering, my struggles and despair. I should think that true, genuine love would, like the music of Orpheus, have power to animate stones and flowers, and my love cannot even move the heart of a noble, feeling girl. What is the reason? why do you fly from me? Is it, Laura, because you deem me unworthy of your love? because your heart feels no emotion for me? are you cold and severe because you hold me for a bold beggar, who longs for the treasure belonging to another, whom you despise because he begs for what should be the free gift of your heart? Or has your heart never been touched by love? If this is so, Laura, and my love has not the power to awaken your heart, then do not speak, but let me leave you quietly. I will try to bear my misery or die; I shall have no one but myself to reproach, for God has denied me the power of winning love. But if this is not the reason of your coldness, if we are only separated by the vain prejudices of rank and birth, O Laura, I entreat you, if this is all that separates us, speak one single word of comfort, of

hope, one single low word, and I will conquer the whole world,
break down all prejudices and laws, and cast them from me.
I will be as great and strong as Hercules, to clear the way,
and make it smooth for our love. I will present you to the
world as my betrothed, and before God and my king call
you my wife. Speak, Laura, is it so? Do you fly from me
because of this star upon my breast—because I am called a
royal prince? I implore you, tell me, is it so? if not, if you
cast me from you because you do not love me, say nothing
and I will go away for ever."

A long, painful silence ensued. The prince watched the
pained, frightened countenance of the young girl, who sat
before him with bowed head, pale and motionless.

"It is decided," he sighed, after a long pause; "farewell,
I accept my destiny, you have spoken my sentence; may
your heart never accuse you of cruelty!" He bowed low before her, then turned and walked across the saloon.

Laura had remained motionless; she now raised her head;
she followed him with a glance that, had he seen it, would
have brought him back to her—a look that spoke more than
words or protestations.

The prince had reached the door once more; he turned,
their looks met, and a trembling delight took possession of
her whole being; forgetting all danger, she longingly extended
her arms toward him, and murmured his name.

With a cry of delight he sprang to her side, and folded
her with impassioned tenderness in his arms. Laura concealed her tear-stained face upon his breast, and murmured,
"God sees my heart, He knows how long I have prayed and
struggled; may He be more merciful, more compassionate
than man! I shall be cast off, despised; let it be, I shall
think of this hour, and be happy."

"No one shall dare to insult you," he said proudly;

"from this hour you are my affianced, and some day I shall present you to the world as my wife."

Smiling sadly, she shook her head. "Let us not speak of the future; it may be dark and sorrowful. I will not complain, I will bear my cross joyfully, and thank God for your love."

He kissed the tears from her eyes, and murmured sweet and holy promises of love and faith. It was a moment of blissful joy, but Laura suddenly trembled and raised her head from his breast to listen. The beating of drums and quickly-rolling carriages were heard without. "The king!" cried the young girl. "The king," murmured Prince Augustus, sadly, and he ventured no longer to hold the young girl in his arms. They were both awakened from their short, blessed dream, both were reminded of the world, and the obstacles that lay in their path. In their great happiness they had appeared small, but now were assuming giant-like proportions.

"I must hasten to the queen," said Laura, rising; "her majesty will need me."

"And I must go and meet the king," sighed the prince.

"Go quickly; let us hasten, and take different paths to the castle."

He took her hand and held it to his lips. "Farewell my beloved, my bride; trust me, and be strong in love and hope."

"Farewell," she murmured, and endeavored to pass him.

Once more he detained her. "Shall we meet here again? will you let me enjoy here another hour of your dear presence? Oh, bow not your head; do not blush; your sweet confession has made of this place a temple of love, and here

I will approach you with pure and holy thoughts." **He** looked long into her beautiful, blushing face.

" We will see each other here again," she murmured ; " every day I shall await you here at the same hour; now hasten, hasten."

Both left the saloon; it was again silent and deserted; in a few moments Fritz Wendel stepped out from the grotto with glowing cheeks and sparkling eyes.

" This is a noble secret that I have discovered—a secret that will bring me golden fruits. Louise von Schwerin is not more widely separated from the poor gardener, Fritz Wendel, than Mademoiselle Pannewitz from Prince Augustus William. A gardener can rise and become a nobleman, but Mademoiselle Pannewitz can never become a princess, never be the wife of her lover. Louise von Schwerin shall no longer be ashamed of the love of Fritz Wendel; I will tell her what I have seen, I will take her into the grotto, and let her witness the rendezvous of the prince and his beloved, and whilst he is telling Laura of his love, I will be with my Louise."

CHAPTER IV.

THE KING AND THE SON.

LAURA was not mistaken. It was the king whom the castle guard were saluting with the beat of the drum. It was the king coming to pay his first visit to his mother at Montbijou. He came unannounced, and the perplexed, anxious looks of the cavaliers showed that his appearance had caused more disturbance and terror than joy. With a slight laugh he turned to his grand chamberlain, Pöllnitz.

" Go tell her majesty that her son Frederick awaits her."

And followed by Kaiserling and the cavaliers of the queen, he entered the garden saloon.

Queen Sophia Dorothea received the king's message with a proud, beaming smile. She was not then deceived, her dearest hopes were to be fulfilled; the young king was an obedient, submissive son; she was for him still the reigning queen, the mother entitled to command. The son, not the king, had come, disrobed of all show of royalty, to wait humbly as a suppliant for her appearance. She felt proud, triumphant! A glorious future lay before her. She would be a queen at last—a queen not only in name, but in truth. Her son was King of Prussia, and she would be co-regent. Her entire court should be witness to this meeting; they should see her triumph, and spread the news far and wide.

He came simply, without ceremony, as her son, but she would receive him according to etiquette, as it beseemed a queen. She wore a long, black trailing gown, a velvet ermine-bordered mantle, and caught up the black veil that was fastened in her hair with several brilliants. All preparations were at last finished, and the queen, preceded by Pöllnitz, arrived in the garden saloon.

Frederick, standing by the window, was beating the glass impatiently with his long, thin fingers. He thought his mother showed but little impatience to see her son who had hurried with al' the eagerness of childlike love to greet her. He wondered what could be her motive, and had just surmised it as the door opened and the chamberlain announced in a loud voice—"Her majesty, the widowed queen." A soft, mocking smile played upon his lips for a moment, as the queen entered in her splendid court dress, but it disappeared quickly, and hat in hand he advanced to meet her.

Sophia Dorothea received him with a gracious smile, and gave him her hand to kiss.

"Your majesty is welcome," said she, with a trembling

voice, for it grieved her proud heart to give her son the title of majesty. The king, perceiving something of this, said:

"Continue to call me your son, mother, for when with your majesty I am but an obedient, grateful son."

"Well, then, welcome, welcome my son!" cried the queen, with an undisguised expression of rapture, and throwing her arms around him, she kissed his forehead repeatedly. "Welcome to the modest house of a poor, sorrowful widow."

"My wish, dear mother, is, that you shall not think of yourself as a sad widow, but as the mother of a king. I do not desire you to be continually reminded of the great loss we have all sustained, and that God sent upon us. Your majesty is not only the widowed queen, you belong not to the past, but to the present; and I beg that you will be called from this moment, not the widowed queen, but the queen-mother. Grand chamberlain Pöllnitz, see that this is done."

For a moment the queen lost her proud, stately bearing; she was deeply touched. The king's delicate attentions made her all the mother, and for a moment love silenced all her proud, imperious wishes.

"Oh, my son, you know how to dry my tears, and to change the sorrowing widow into a proud, happy mother," said she, pressing his hand tenderly to her heart.

The king was so overjoyed at his mother's unfeigned tenderness that he was prepared to agree to all her demands, and humor her in every thing

"Ah," said he, "I, not you, ought to render thanks that you are so willing to enter into my views. I will put your magnanimity still further to the test, and state a few more of my wishes."

"Let us hear them, my son," said the queen, "but first let me ask a favor."

"Let us be seated."

The king led her to an arm-chair near a window, from which

there was a beautiful view of the garden. The queen seated herself, and the young king remained standing in front of her, still holding his hat. Sophia Dorothea saw this, and was enraptured at this new triumph. Turning to the king, she said:

"Let us now hear your wishes, and I promise joyfully to fulfil them."

"I wish," said he, "your majesty to surround herself with a larger and more brilliant court. Two maids of honor are not sufficient for the queen-mother, for if by chance one were sick, and the other fretful, there would be no one to divert and amuse your majesty. I therefore propose that you have six instead of two maids of honor."

The queen looked at him in tender astonishment.

"My son," said she, "you are a veritable magician. You divine all my wishes. Thanks—many, many thanks. But your majesty is not seated," said she, as if just perceiving this.

"Madame," said he, laughing, "I awaited your permission." He seated himself, and said, "You agree to my proposal, mother?"

"I agree to it, and beg your majesty to point out to me the ladies you have decided upon as my six maids of honor. Your majesty has free choice, and all I wish is, to be told when you have decided. I only fear," said the queen, "that with my enlarged court there will not be room for the ladies to have their separate apartments at Mont-bijou."

"Your majesty is no longer to live in this house," said the king; "it is large enough for a passing summer visit, but it does not answer for the residence of the queen-mother. I spoke some time since to Knobelsdorf, and already a magnificent palace is being built for you."

The queen blushed with pleasure; all her wishes seemed

7*

to be fulfilled to-day. She must now know whether Sophia Dorothea was to be queen-regent as well as queen-mother. She thanked her son tenderly for this new proof of his love and kindness.

"And still," said she, sighing, " perhaps I ought not to accept of your kindness. My husband's death should remind me of the transitory nature of life, and should lead me to pass the remainder of my days in seclusion, devoting my time to God."

The king looked so anxious, so shocked, that the queen repented having given the conversation this gloomy turn.

"It is cruel, mother," said he, "not to let me enjoy the pleasure of being with you without a drop of wormwood. But I see by your rosy cheeks and bright smile that you only wished to frighten me. Let the architects and masons continue their work : God will be merciful to me, and grant a long life to the noblest and best-beloved of mothers !"

He kissed her hand and rose ; Sophia Dorothea was terrified. The king was leaving, and she still did not know how far her influence was to reach and what were to be its limits.

"You will already leave me, my son ?" said she, lovingly.

"I must, your majesty. For from here I can hear the Government machinery creaking and groaning; I must hasten to supply it with oil, and set it in motion again. Ah! madame, it is no easy task to be a king. To do justice to all his obligations, a king must rise early and retire late ; and I think truly it is much more pleasant to be reigned over than to reign."

The queen could scarcely suppress her delight; the king's words were balm to her ambitious heart.

"I can well see that it is as you say," said she, " but I think that the king has a right to amuse himself; I think that a mother has some claims on her son, even if he is a king. You must not leave now, my son. You must grant me the pleasure of showing you my new conservatory. Give me your arm, and comply with my request."

"Madame, you now see what power you have over me," said he, as she laughingly took his arm. "I forget that I am the servant of my country, because I prefer being the servant of my queen."

The large glass door was opened, and, leaning on the king's arm, the queen entered the garden.

At some distance the princesses with their brother and the rest of the court followed. They were all silent, eagerly listening to the conversation of the royal couple. But the queen did not now care to be heard by her court. They had seen her triumph, but they should not be witness to a possible defeat. She now spoke in a low tone, and hurried her steps, to put a distance between herself and the courtiers. She spoke with the king about the garden, and then asked if he thought of passing the summer at Rheinsberg.

"Alas," said he, "I will not have the time. For a king is but the first officer of his State, and as I receive my salary I must honestly fulfil the duties I have undertaken."

"But I think your majesty does too much," said the queen. "You should allow yourself more relaxation, and not let State matters rest entirely upon your own shoulders. To one who is accustomed to associate with poets, artists, and the sciences, it must be very hard suddenly to bury himself in deeds, documents, and all sorts of dusty papers; you should leave this occasionally to others, and not work the State machinery yourself."

"Madame," said the king, "this machine has secrets and peculiarities that its architect can intrust to no workman, therefore he must lead and govern it himself; and if at times the wheels creak and it is not in perfect order, he has only himself to thank."

"But you have your ministers?"

"They are my clerks—nothing more!"

"Ah, I see, you intend to be a rock and take counsel from no one," said the queen, impatiently.

"Yes, your majesty, from you always; and with your gracious permission I will now consult you."

"Speak, my son, speak," said the queen, in breathless expectation.

"I wish your advice upon theatrical matters. Where must the new opera-house be built?"

The queen's face darkened.

"I am not a suitable adviser for amusements," said she, pointing to her black gown. "My mourning garments do not fit me for such employment, and you well know I do not care for the theatre; for how many cold, dull evenings have I passed there with your father!"

"Ah, madame," said the king, "I was not talking of a German threatre, which I dislike quite as much as yourself. No, we will have a French threatre and an Italian opera. The French alone can act and only the Italians can sing, but we Germans can play; I have therefore charged Graun to compose a new opera for the inauguration of the new opera house."

"And undoubtedly this inauguration will take place on a festive occasion," said the queen, going directly to the point? "Perhaps at the wedding of one of your sisters?"

"Ah," said he, "your majesty is thinking of a wedding?"

"Not I, but others. Yesterday I received from London a letter from my royal brother. And a few moments ago Count Manteuffel brought me letters of condolence from the Empress of Austria. It seems the count was, besides this, commissioned to sound me as to a possible marriage with Prince Augustus."

"It was very unnecessary for the count to burden you

with matters which are happily beyond the reach of your motherly duties. For, alas! the marrying of princes is a political affair, and is not determined by the mother's heart, but by the necessities of the kingdom."

The queen bit her lip until it bled. "Your majesty is, undoubtedly, thinking of performing this political obligation, and have chosen a bride for the prince," said she, sharply.

"Forgive me," said the king laughing, "I am not now thinking of marrying, but of unmarrying."

Sophia Dorothea looked anxiously at the king. "How, my son, are you thinking of a divorce?" said she, tremblingly.

"Not of one, but of many, mother. Does your majesty know that I have abolished the torture?"

"No," said the queen impatiently, "I did not—politics do not concern me."

"That is in conformity with the true womanly character of my mother," said he. "There is nothing so insipid and tiresome as a woman who gives up the graces and muses, to excite herself with politics."

"And still your majesty was just initiating me into politics."

"Ah, yes, I told you I had abolished the torture."

"And I ask, how does that concern me?"

"You ask why I am thinking of divorces? Well, I told you that I had abolished the torture, and in doing this it was but natural that I busied myself about marriage. For your majesty will grant me that there is no severer rack, no more frightful torture, than an unhappy marriage."

"It seems as if with the torture you will also abolish marriage," said the queen, terrified.

The king laughed. "Ah, no, madame, I am not pope, and have not received the right from God to decide over men's consciences, though perhaps the majority would be inclined to call me holy, and to honor me with godlike worship, if I would really abolish the torture of matrimony. But I am not ambitious, and renounce all claim to adoration. But while engaged in abolishing the torture, I could but see that when the marriage chains had ceased to be garlands of roses, and were transformed into heavy links of iron, there should be some means found to break them. I have therefore commanded that if two married people cannot live harmoniously, a divorce shall not be denied them. I hope that my royal mother agrees with me."

"Ah, there will soon be many divorce cases," said the queen, with a contemptuous smile. "All who are not thoroughly happy will hasten to the king for a divorce. Who knows but that the king himself will set the people a good example?"

"With God's help, madame," said the king, gravely. "My noble mother will always wish me to set my people a good example. A king is but the servant of the nation."

"That is, indeed, an humble idea of a king, a king by the grace of God."

"Madame, I do not crave to be called a king by the grace of God. I prefer being king by my own right and strength. But forgive me, mother. You see how these politics mix themselves up with every thing. Let them rest. You were speaking, I think, of the marriage of one of the princes?"

"We were speaking of the marriage of Prince Augustus William," said the queen, who, with the obstinacy of a true woman, always returned to the point from which she had started, and who, in the desire of gaining her point, had lost all consideration and presence of mind. "I was telling you that I received yesterday a letter from my royal brother, and that King George the Second is anxious to form an alliance between our children."

"Another marriage with England!" said the king, dejectedly. "You know there is no good luck in our English marriages. The courier who brings the English consent is always too late."

The queen was enraged. "You mean that you have decided upon a bride for my son, that again my darling wish of intermarrying my children with the royal house of England is not to be realized? Ah, your father's example must have been very satisfactory to you, as you follow so quickly in his footsteps."

"I truly find, madame, that the king acted wisely in not regarding in the marriage of the prince royal the wishes of his heart and his family, but political interests, which he was bound to consider. I will certainly follow his example, and take counsel over the marriage of the prince royal, not with my own heart, not even with the wishes of my royal mother, but with the interests of Prussia."

"But Augustus William is not prince royal," cried the queen, with trembling lips. "The prince is only your brother, and you may have many sons who will dispute with him the succession to the throne."

An expression of deep sorrow lay like a dark veil upon the handsome face of the king. "I will have no children," said he, "and Prince Augustus William will be my successor."

The queen had not the heart to reply. She looked at her son in amazement. Their eyes met, and the sad though sweet expression of the usually clear, sparkling eyes of her son touched her, and awoke the mother's heart. With a hasty movement she took his hands, pressed them to her heart, and said: "Ah, my son, how poor is this life! You are young, handsome, and highly gifted, you are a king, and still you are not happy."

The king's face was brighter, his eye sparkled as before.

"Life," said he, smiling, "is not a pleasure, but a duty, and if we honestly perform this duty we will be happy in the end. It is now time to return to my prison and be king once more."

He embraced his mother tenderly, laughed and jested for a few moments with his sisters Ulrica and Amelia, then left, followed by his cavaliers. Sophia Dorothea remained in the garden, and Ulrica, her favorite daughter, followed her.

"Your majesty looks sad and grave," said she, "and you have every reason to look happy. The king was remarkably kind and amiable. Only think of it, you will have six maids of honor, and a beautiful palace is being built for you!"

"Oh, yes," said the queen, "I will be surrounded with outward glory."

"And how anxious the king seemed for you to forget the past!" said Princess Amelia, who, with Prince Augustus William, had joined her mother and sister, "you are not the widowed queen but the queen-mother."

"Yes," murmured Sophia Dorothea to herself, "I am queen-mother, but I will never be queen-regent. Ah, my children," cried she, passionately, "the king, your brother, was right. Princes are not born to be happy. He is not so, and you will never be!"

CHAPTER V.

THE QUEEN'S TAILOR.

A DREARY silence had reigned for some time in the usually gay and happy family circle of the worthy court tailor. No one dared to speak or laugh aloud. M. Pricker, the crown and head of the house, was sad and anxious, and the storm-cloud upon his brow threw a dark reflection upon the faces of his wife and two children, the beautiful Anna, and the active, merry Wilhelm. Even the assistants in the work-room were affected by the general gloom; the gay songs of the apprentices were silenced, and the pretty house-maids looked discontented and dull.

A tempest lowered over the house, and all appeared to tremble at its approach. When Wilhelm, the son and heir of the house, returned from his work, he hastened to his mother's room, and casting a curious glance upon the old woman, who was seated on a sofa, grim-looking, and supporting her head upon her hand, he said, mysteriously—

"Not yet!"

Mother Pricker shook her head, sighed deeply, and replied:

"Not yet!"

The beautiful Anna was generally in her elegant room, painting or singing, and did not allow herself to be disturbed; but now when the bell rang, or a strange step was heard, she hastened to her mother, and said:

"Well, has it come?"

Again Mother Pricker sighed, shook her head, and answered—

"Not yet!"

M. Pricker asked nothing, demanded nothing; silent and proud he sat in the midst of his family circle; stoically listened to the ringing of the bell, and saw strangers enter his counting-room, too proud to show any excitement. He wrapped himself in an Olympian silence, and barricaded himself from the curious questions of his children by the stern reserve of parental authority.

"I see that he suffers," said his wife to her daughter

Anna; "I see that he looks paler every day, and eats less and less; if this painful anxiety endures much longer, the poor man will become dangerously ill, and the king will be answerable for the death of one of his noblest and best subjects."

"But why does our father attach such importance to this small affair?" said Anna, with a lofty shrug of her shoulders.

Mother Pricker looked at her with astonishment.

" *You* call this a small affair, which concerns not only the honor of your father, but that of your whole family; which affects the position and calling enjoyed by the Pricker family for a hundred years? It is a question whether your father shall be unjustly deprived of his honorable place, or have justice done him, and his great services acknowledged!"

Anna gave a hearty laugh.

" Dear mother, you look at this thing too tragically; you are making a camel of a gnat. The great and exalted things of which you speak have nothing to do with the matter; it is a simple question of title. The great point is, will our father receive the title of 'court tailor' to the reigning queen, or be only the tailor of the queen-dowager. It seems to me the difference is very small, and I cannot imagine why so much importance is attached to it."

"You do not understand," sighed Mother Pricker; "you do not love your family; you care nothing for the honor of your house!"

"Pshaw! to be the daughter of a tailor is a very poor and doubtful honor," said Anna, drearily, " even if he is the tailor of one or even two queens. Our father is rich enough to live without this contemptible business; yes, to live in style. He has given his children such an education as nobles only receive; I have had my governess and my music-teacher; my brother his tutor; my father has not allowed him to walk through the streets, fearing that he might fall into the hands of the recruiting-officers. We have each our private rooms, beautifully furnished, and are the envy of all our friends. Why, notwithstanding all this, will he condemn us to be and to continue to be the children of a tailor? Why does he not tear down the sign from the door; this sign, which will be ever a humiliation, even though 'court tailor' should be written upon it! This title will never enable us to appear at court, and the noble cavaliers will never think of marrying the daughter of a tailor, though many would seek to do so if our father would give up his needle-work, buy a country seat, and live, as rich and distinguished men do, upon his estate."

"Child, child, what are you saying?" cried Mother Pricker, clasping her hands with anguish. "Thy father give up his stand, his honorable stand, which, for more than a hundred years, has been inherited by the family! Thy father demean himself to buy with his honorably-earned gold a son-in-law from amongst the poor nobles, who will be ever thinking of the honor done us in accepting thee and thy sixty thousand dollars! Thy father buy a country seat, and spend in idleness that fortune which his forefathers and himself have been collecting for hundreds of years! That can never be, and never will your father consent to your marriage with any other than an honest burgher; and he will never allow Wilhelm to have any other calling than that of his father, his grandfather, and his great-grandfather, a *court tailor.*

The beautiful Anna stamped involuntarily upon the floor, and a flush of scorn spread itself over her soft cheek. "I will not wed a burgher," said she, tossing her head proudly back, "and my brother Wilhelm will never carry on the business of his father."

"Then your father will disinherit you—cast you out

amongst strangers to beg your bread," said the old woman, wringing her hands.

"God be thanked," said Anna proudly, "there is no necessity for begging our bread; we have learned enough to carry us honorably through the world, and when all else fails, I have a capital in my voice which assures me a glittering future. The king will found an opera-house, and splendid singers are so rare that Prussia will thank God if I allow myself to be prevailed upon to take the place of prima donna."

"Oh! unhappy, wretched child!" sobbed Mother Pricker, "you will dishonor your family, you will make us miserable, and cover us with shame; you will become an actress, and we must live to see our respectable, yes, celebrated name upon a play-bill, and pasted upon every corner."

"You will have the honor of hearing all the world speak of your daughter, of seeing sweet flowers and wreaths thrown before her whenever she appears, and of seeing her praises in every number of every journal in Berlin. I shall be exalted to the skies, and the parents called blessed who have given me life."

"These are the *new* ideas," gasped out her mother—"the new ideas which are now the mode, and which our new king favors. Alas! wailing and sorrow will come over our whole city; honor and principle will disappear, and destruction like that of Sodom and Gomorrah will fall upon Berlin! These are the alluring temptations with which Baron Pöllnitz fills your ear and crushes in your heart the worthy and seemly principles of your family. That,"— suddenly she stopped and listened; it seemed to her the bell rung; truly there was a step upon the stairs, and some one asked for M. and Madame Pricker.

"Pöllnitz," whispered Anna, and a glowing blush overspread her face, throat, and neck.

"The Baron Pöllnitz, the master of ceremonies," said Madame Pricker, with a mixture of joy and alarm.

The door flew open, and with a gay, frolicsome greeting, Pöllnitz danced into the room; Anna had turned to the window, and made no reply to his greeting. Madame Pricker stepped toward him, and greeted him with the most profound reverence, calling him master of ceremonies and master of the bed-chamber.

"Not so," said Pöllnitz; "why so much reverence and so many titles? I am indeed master of ceremonies, but without the title. His majesty, the young king, has no special fondness for renewing the titles lent to us by his blessed father, and every prayer and every representation to that effect has been in vain; he considers titles ridiculous and superfluous."

Madame Pricker turned pale, and murmured some incomprehensible words. Anna, however, who had up to this time been turned toward the window, suddenly looked at the two speakers, and fixed her great eyes questioningly upon the baron.

"Ah, at last I have the honor to see you, fair, beautiful Anna!" said Pöllnitz; "I knew well some magic was necessary to fix those splendid eyes on me. Allow me to kiss your hand, most honored lady, and forgive me if I have disturbed you. He flew with an elegant pirouette to Anna, and took her hand, which she did not extend to him, and, indeed, struggled to withhold; he then turned again to Madame Pricker, and bowing to her, said, with a solemn pathos: "I am not here to-day simply as the friend of the house, but as the ambassador of the king; and I beseech the honored Madame Pricker to announce to her husband that I wish to speak to him, and to deliver a message from the queen."

Madame Pricker uttered a cry of joy, and forgetting

all other considerations, hastened to the counting-room of her husband, to make known to him the important information.

Baron Pöllnitz watched her till the door closed, then turned to Anna, who still leaned immovable in the window. "Anna, dearest Anna," whispered he tenderly, "at last we are alone! How I have pined for you, how happy I am to see you once again!"

He sought to press her fondly to his heart, but the maiden waved him proudly and coldly back. "Have you forgotten our agreement?" said she, earnestly.

"No, I have held your cruelty in good remembrance; only, when I have fulfilled all your commands, will you deign to listen to my glowing wishes; when I have induced your father to employ for you another singing-master, and arranged for your glorious and heavenly voice to be heard by the king and the assembled court?"

"Yes," cried Anna, with glowing eyes and burning cheeks, "that is my aim, my ambition. Yes, I will be a singer; all Europe shall resound with my fame; all men shall lie at my feet; and princes and queens shall seek to draw me into their circles."

"And I will be the happiest of the happy, when the lovely nightingale has reached the goal. From my hand shall she first wing her flight to fame. But, when I have fulfilled my word, when you have sung in the royal palace before the queen and the court, then will *you* fulfil your promise? Then Pöllnitz will be the happiest of mortals."

"I will fulfil my word," she said, as proudly and imperiously as if she were already the celebrated and grace-dispensing prima donna. "On the day in which I sing for the first time before the king—the day in which the tailor's daughter has purified herself from the dishonor of her humble birth, and becomes a free, self-sustaining, distinguished artist—on that day we will have no reason to be ashamed of our love, and we can both, without humiliation, present our hearts to each other. Baron Pöllnitz can take for his wife, without blushing, the woman ennobled by art, and Prima Donna Anna Pricker need not be humbled by the thought that Baron Pöllnitz has forgotten his rank in his choice of a wife."

Baron Pöllnitz, courtier as he was, had not his features so completely under control as to conceal wholly the shock conveyed by the words of his beautiful sweetheart. He stared for a moment, speechless, into that lovely face, glowing with enthusiasm, ambition, and love. A mocking, demoniac smile appeared one moment on his lips, then faded quickly, and Pöllnitz was again the tender, passionate lover of Anna Pricker. "Yes, my dearly-beloved Anna," whispered he, clasping her in his arms, "on that blessed and happy day you will be my wife, and the laurels entwined in your hair will be changed into a myrtle-wreath." He embraced her passionately, and she resisted no longer, but listened ever to his words, which, like sweet opium, poisoned both the ear and heart of the young girl. But Pöllnitz released her suddenly, and stepped back, colder and more self-possessed than Anna. He had heard a light, approaching step. "Some one comes; be composed, dear one; your face betrays too much of your inward emotion." He danced to the open piano and played a merry strain, while Anna hid her blushes in the branches of a geranium placed in the window, and tried to cool her glowing cheeks on the fresh green leaves.

Madame Pricker opened the door, and bade the master of ceremonies enter the adjoining room, where M. Pricker awaited him.

CHAPTER VI.

THE ILLUSTRIOUS ANCESTORS OF A TAILOR.

Pöllnitz offered his arm to the lovely Anna, and followed Madame Pricker, laughing and jesting, into the next room. This was a long hall, which had an appearance of gloom and solemnity in its arrangements and decorations. The high walls, hung with dark tapestry, were poorly lighted by two windows. Several divans, covered with a heavy silken material, the same color as the tapestry, were placed against the sides of the room, and over them hung a few oil paintings in black frames, each representing the figure of a man with a most solemn expression and bearing. The remarkable resemblance which these pictures bore to each other convinced you that they must be the portraits of one family. In each appeared the same countenance, the same short, clumsy figure, and only the costumes served to point out by their various styles the different periods at which they had been painted. A figure, closely resembling the pictures, stood in the centre of the hall; it had the same countenance, the same short, clumsy figure, and even the same dress as that represented in one of the pictures. You might have supposed that some galvanic experiment had given life and motion to the painted form, and that as soon as this power was exhausted it would become lifeless, and return to its place among the other pictures. But this figure was certainly living, for it greeted the grand chamberlain, without, however, leaving the round table which stood in the centre of the room.

"I welcome you to the house of my fathers," it said, with great dignity. Pöllnitz threw a laughing, jesting glance toward Anna, who had left his side on entering the room, and had withdrawn to one of the windows.

"Why are you so earnest and solemn to-day, my dear Pricker?" said he, turning to the old gentleman.

"Are you not here as the ambassador of the royal court?" he replied. "I wished to receive you with all honor, and therefore desired you to come into this hall, that I might hear the royal message in the midst of my ancestors. Tell me now how I can serve the house of my sovereign."

"You can serve it, my dear Pricker," said Pöllnitz, smiling, as he displayed a large sealed paper, "by altering the sign upon your door. In the place of 'court tailor of the queen and princess royal,' it should read—'court tailor of the dowager and of the reigning queen.' Here is the patent, my dear sir."

The old man quietly took the paper; not a feature of his cold, solemn face moved.

Madame Pricker, however, could not conceal her joy. With a cry of delight she hurried to her husband, to embrace and congratulate him on his appointment.

Pricker waved her proudly back.

"Why do you congratulate me?" he said. "The house of Hohenzollern has only done justice to my house, that is all. The title of court tailor to the reigning queen has become an inheritance in my family, and it would be great ingratitude in the house of Hohenzollern to withhold it from me. For more than a century the Hohenzollerns have been dressed by my family; we have prepared their apparel for every ball and wedding, every baptism or burial; and if they were arrayed with elegance, it was entirely owing to our taste and dexterity. The proverb says, 'The tailor makes the man,' and it is true. We made the coronation dresses of both the queens; it follows that they could not have been crowned without our assistance, for which we, of course, deserve their gratitude."

"I assure you, however, my dear friend," said Pöllnitz, "that it was with much difficulty I obtained this appoint-

8

ment for you, and you owe me some acknowledgments.
All of my eloquence was necessary to induce the queen to
grant my prayer."

Pricker grew pale, and his countenance lost its calm dignity.

"Take back your patent," he said, proudly, handing the
baron the sealed paper; "I will not accept this title if it is
not given willingly."

"No, no, keep it," cried Pöllnitz; "you merit it; it is
your right; I only mentioned the difficulty with which I obtained it, that I might win your heart, and incline you to
grant a request which I wish to make."

"I suppose you allude to the five hundred dollars which
I lent you last month," said Pricker, smiling. "Speak of
that no more—the debt is cancelled."

"Thank you," said Pöllnitz, "but I was not thinking of
that small affair; it was quite another request I wished to
make."

"Let me hear it," said the tailor, with a most gracious
inclination of the head.

"It concerns a young artist, who I would like to recommend to your protection," returned the crafty Pöllnitz, with
a side glance at Anna. "He is a young and talented musician, who desires to gain a livelihood by giving instruction,
but unfortunately he is a stranger here, and has found but
few patrons. I thought, therefore, that if you, who are so
well known, would interest yourself in him, and give him
your patronage, it would greatly benefit him, for doubtless
many others would hasten to follow your example. If you
will allow him to give singing-lessons to your daughter Anna,
his fortune is assured."

"I grant your request," said Pricker, solemnly, not for
an instant doubting the motive of the baron. "I will bestow
my protection upon this young artist; he can give my

daughter a daily lesson, that is, if Anna is willing to show this kindness to the poor young man."

Anna could scarcely restrain her laughter, as she replied:

"You have commanded it, and I will obey, as a daughter should do."

"Very well," said her father, majestically; "that matter is arranged. And now, baron, I beg you will inform me at what time the coronation will take place, that I may make my preparations, and not be the cause of any delay on that solemn occasion."

"The day of the coronation has not been decided, but it will certainly not be fixed before the first of August. You will have time to make all your preparations. Later we will hold a consultation with her majesty the queen, and decide the style, color, and material of the costumes. I will only give you a single word of counsel, my dear friend. Accommodate yourself to the new era. Remember that we have a new king, who is the counterpart of his father. The father hated and despised elegance and fashion—the son adores them; the father was the sworn enemy of French manners—the son has a perfect passion for them: and if you would please the son, you must lay aside your old German habits and customs, as we have all done, and walk in the new path. I tell you a new era is approaching, a period of glory and splendor. Every thing will be altered, but, above all, we will have new fashions. In the first place, you must rid yourself of your German apprentices, and replace them as quickly as possible with French workmen from Paris. That is the only means of retaining the court favor."

Pricker listened to all this with horror and astonishment. His cheeks were white, and his voice trembled with anger, as he cried:

"Never shall that happen? Never will I adopt the innovations which are now the fashion. Shall I lay aside my re-

spectable dress, to replace it with a monkey-jacket, and become
a laughing-stock to all honest men? Shall I so far forget my
God, my forefathers, and my native land, as to call French
workmen into my German work-room? Shame on me if I
ever conduct myself in such a godless and unchristian manner! Never shall a French foot cross the threshold of my
dwelling! never shall a French word be spoken there! I
was born a German, and I will die a German. True to my
fathers, and to the commands of my sainted sovereign, who
hated and despised these frivolous French fashions, it shall
be my pride to retain the good old German customs, and
never shall a dress cut in the French style be made in my
work-room."

"If you act in this manner, the time of your good fortune is passed," said Pöllnitz.

Pricker paid no attention to him, but looking at the pictures which hung on the wall, he bowed respectfully before
one of them.

"Look!" he said, pointing to one of the portraits, "that
is my great-great-grandfather. He was a German, and the
best and ablest of men. With him began the connection
between the houses of Hohenzollern and Pricker. For him
the Prince George William created the title of court tailor,
and he would wear no garment that was not made by his
favorite. He remembered him in his will, and from that time
began the importance of the Prickers.

"Then look at the next picture. It is the portrait of his
son, who was the court tailor of Frederick William, the great
elector. He made the suit worn by the elector at the battle
of Fehrbellin; it was, however, the unhappy duty of his son
to make the burial-dress of this great man.

"But with this portrait begins a new era for Prussia; this
was the tailor of Frederick the Third, and he made the robe
and mantle which Frederick wore on the day of his corona-

tion. His son succeeded him, and now began a new era for the Prickers.

"The son did not follow the example of his father; he was of a softer, a more poetical nature. He loved flowers and poetry, and adored beauty; he therefore became a lady's tailor. The princess royal, Sophia Dorothea, appointed him her tailor. He made the coronation robe of the queen, and the wedding-dress of the Margravine of Baireuth.

"When he died he was succeeded by his son, the now living Pricker. I made the wedding-dress of the Duchess of Brunswick, and the mourning of the present dowager-queen. And now, in the very presence of my ancestors, you tempt me to become a traitor to them and to their customs. No, I am a German, and I remain a German, even should it cause my ruin!"

He bowed to the amused and astonished baron, and walked proudly through the hall to his work-room. His wife followed him, with folded hands and heavy sighs.

Pöllnitz and the lovely Anna were again alone.

"What an absurd man!" said Pöllnitz, laughing. "If Molière had known him, he would have worked his character into a charming farce."

"You forget that this absurd man may soon be your father-in-law," said Anna, sternly, as she left his side.

"That is true," said Pöllnitz, smiling; "we will spare him. Come, one last kiss, my beautiful Anna—one kiss as a reward for my successful acting. To-morrow you will have a singing-master, who is no poor wretch, but a celebrated and influential musician, who has undertaken to instruct you out of pure kindness for me, for he is not a teacher but a composer. Graun himself will be your instructor, and it rests with you to crown our love with the happiest results."

CHAPTER VII.

SOFFRI E TACI.

THE most ardent desire of the young queen was about to be accomplished; she was to have a private and unconstrained interview with her husband. The days of resignation, of hope deferred, and of hidden sorrow, were now over. The dearly-beloved and longed-for husband had at last returned to her! She need no longer hide her head in shame from her own servants, who, she imagines, are secretly laughing at and mocking her, because the young king is so cold and indifferent. She need no longer envy the poor woman she saw in the street yesterday, carrying dinner to her laboring husband. She will also have a husband, and will feel the guiding and supporting arm of a strong man at her side. No longer will she be a poor, neglected queen, but a proud and happy wife, envied of all the world.

He had written that he desired to pay her a visit, and had requested her not to lock her door, as important business would prevent his coming until quite late. He would, however, certainly come, as he desired to have a private interview with her on this very evening.

How wearily the hours of this day have passed, how slowly the sun sank to rest! It is at last evening; night is coming on. Elizabeth can now dismiss her attendants, and retire to her private apartments to await her husband. He shall see how joyfully she will receive him, how happy he has made her. She will adorn herself, that he may be pleased; she will be beautiful, that he may smile upon her.

The queen, with the assistance of her astonished maids, attires herself for the first time in one of the charming *negligées* recently sent by the Empress of Austria; for the first time she dons her prettily-worked and coquettish little cap, and encloses her tiny feet in gold-embroidered white satin slippers. This *negligée* is really charming, and the queen's waiting-maids assure her that she never looked better, and was never more becomingly attired. But the queen desires to assure herself of this fact, and stepping forward to the mirror, she examines her dress with the careful eye of a connoisseur; then bending down, she regards her face attentively, and an expression of satisfaction flits over her features. Elizabeth sees that she is young and pretty, and for the first time rejoices in her beauty. The maids regarded with astonishment these unusual preparations. Why was Elizabeth now so much rejoiced at the beauty of which she had never before seemed conscious?

The toilet is at an end; the queen seats herself on the light blue sofa, and dismisses her maids with a mute gesture. But when the first maid approaches the door, and as usual drew the key from the lock in order to secure it from the outside, Elizabeth awakes from her dreamy state and arises from her reclining position; a glowing color suffuses her cheek, and a happy smile plays around her lips.

"Do not lock the door to-day," said she, with emotion; "I await the king."

As if astonished at her new happiness, she sinks back on the cushions, and covers her glowing face with her handkerchief, as if to shut out the dazzling light. The waiting-maids courtesy respectfully, and leave the room. In the ante-chamber this respectful expression vanishes from their features, and they turn to each other with mocking and derisive laughter.

"Poor queen! she wishes to make us believe that the king, while he altogether neglects her in public, sometimes pays her a secret visit. She wishes to make us believe that she is really the wife of the handsome young king; and we all know—yes, we all know—"

And all three shrugged their shoulders derisively, and hurried off to their associates, to gossip with them about the poor, despised, neglected queen.

But what was that? Did they not hear a carriage driving into the inner court, and the guard presenting arms amid the rolling of drums? Could it be as the queen had said? was the king really coming to his wife? The waiting-maids stood and listened; they heard steps on the grand staircase. Yes, it was the king, who, preceded by his pages, carrying silver candelabras with wax candles, walked hastily down the corridor to his chambers, and from thence to those of the queen.

What the queen had said was therefore true. He did not despise her; perhaps he loved her! The astonished waiting-maids hurried off to inform their friends that the king loved his wife passionately, and the royal pair was the happiest couple on earth. Elizabeth Christine also heard the equipages drive into the court. With a cry of delight she sprang from her seat and listened. A fervent glow of happiness shot through her veins. She pressed her hands to her heart to still its rapid beating; her countenance was illumined with joy. But these feelings were so novel they almost terrified her, and filled her heart with tremulous anxiety.

"My God," murmured she, "give me strength to bear this happiness, as I have borne misery!"

But her prayer died on her lips, for she heard the door of the corridor open. She was no longer the queen, no longer the resigned and timid wife; she was now the happy and joyful woman hurrying to meet the husband of her love And with uplifted head and proud satisfaction she might now confess without shame that she loved him; for he loved her also. He had requested a rendezvous, and was coming as a lover—her first love meeting. She will not be shy and silent to-day, now that she knows he loves her; her tongue will no longer be chained; she will have courage to confess

all, to tell him how ardently she loves him, and how long
and vainly she has struggled with her heart; how the flames
had ever broken out anew; how his glances had ever renewed the ardor of her love.

There—he knocked at the door—she could scarcely
breathe; she could scarcely bid him enter; she could not
move, and stood transfixed in the middle of the room; she
could only stretch out her arms longingly, and welcome him
with her smiles and tearful glances.

The door opened; now he entered. The light of the wax
candles fell on his face. It was handsome as ever, but his
eye was cold, and his lips uttered no loving greeting. He
walked forward a few steps, stood still, and bowed in a stiff
and formal manner. A chill of horror crept over Elizabeth;
her arms sank down, and the smile vanished from her pallid
face.

"Madame," said the king, and his voice sounded harsher
and colder than she had ever before heard it—"madame, I
must first beg your pardon for having disturbed you at so
unseemly a time, and for having robbed you of an hour's
sleep. But you see that I am a repentant sinner, and you
will forgive me when I assure you that, as this is my first, it
shall also be my last violation of your retirement!"

The queen uttered a low cry, and pressed her hand to her
heart. She felt as if a sword had pierced her breast, as if
she were dying.

The king raised his large blue eyes with a surprised look
to the pale, trembling face of his wife.

"You are pale, you are ill," said he, "and my presence
is undoubtedly annoying; I will retire and send your waiting-
maids to your assistance."

While he was speaking the queen prayed to God for
courage and strength; she called her womanly pride to her
assistance, and struggled against her tears and her despair.

8*

The king, who in vain had waited for an answer, now hastily approached the door, murmuring a few impatient words.

But Elizabeth's courage had now returned, she had conquered her heart.

"Remain, sire," she said; "I beg you to remain; I feel well again. It was only a passing spasm from which I often suffer, and for which I crave your indulgence."

"If I may then remain," said the king, smiling, "permit me to conduct you to a seat."

She accepted the king's proffered arm and followed him to the sofa on which she had awaited him with such blissful anticipations, and on which he was now about to put her heart to the torture.

The king did not seat himself by her side, but rolling an arm-chair forward, seated himself at some distance in front of her.

"Madame," said he, "is it credible that we two have been married for seven long years, and still have never been as man and wife to each other? Our lips were forced to pronounce vows of which our hearts knew nothing. Having been forced into this marriage, you must have hated me. You can never have forgiven me for having led you to the altar. At the foot of the altar we did not vow eternal love to each other, but eternal coldness and indifference; and to this hour, madame, you, at least, have faithfully kept this vow."

The queen sank back, murmuring a few incomprehensible words, and her head fell wearily upon her breast.

The king continued: "I come to-day to solicit your forgiveness for the involuntary injustice which I committed. I have made you unhappy, for you were forced to give your hand to an unloved man, of whom you knew that he loved you not. Madame, it is unfortunately true, an abyss lies between us, and this abyss is filled with the blood of the dearest friend of my youth. Oh, madame, forgive me this wrong, for the sake of what I have suffered! I then had a soft and tender heart, but it was trodden under foot, and has become hardened. I placed full confidence in the world, and it has deceived me terribly. I have suffered more than the poorest beggar; I was forced to regard my own father as a cruel enemy, who watched me unceasingly, awaiting a favorable moment to give me a death-blow. It was necessary that I should be continually on my guard, for the smallest fault, the slightest thoughtlessness, a trifle, a mere nothing, was sufficient to condemn me. Oh, if you knew with what venom I have been publicly calumniated and accused! After doing their utmost to make me odious to the world, and fearing they might perhaps still fail, they resorted to another expedient to compass my ruin, and endeavored to kill me with their ridicule. *Soffri e taci*, this Italian proverb was then the motto of my life. And believe me, it is hard to obey this seemingly so dry maxim; it has a grand significance." *

The king, oppressed as it were by these reminiscences, leaned back in his chair and breathed heavily. With downcast eyes and in silence the queen still sat before him, charmed by the music of his words, which found an echo in her heart like the dying wail of her youth.

"I do not tell you this," continued the king, after a pause, "in order to play the *rôle* of a martyr in your sight, but because I wish you to understand by what means my spirit was at last broken, and my will made subservient to that of my father. I purchased my freedom, madame, by chaining you to myself. But in doing this, I vowed you should no longer be bound when it should be in my power to release you. This moment has come, and true to my vow, I am here. I know that you do not, cannot love me, madame. The question arises, Is your aversion to me so great that you insist on a separation?"

* The king's own words. See Œuvres, etc., tom. xvi., page 161.

The queen raised her head and looked wonderingly into the mild and sorrowful countenance of her husband. She could no longer restrain the cry which trembled on her lips, no longer stem the tide of tears which gushed in torrents from her eyes.

"My God! my God!" she exclaimed, with a plaintive wail, "he asks me if I hate him!"

There was something in the tone of her voice, in this despairing cry of her soul, which ought to have betrayed the long-hidden secret of her love to the king. But perhaps he knew it already, and did not wish to understand. Perhaps, in the nobility and native delicacy of his soul, he wished to represent the indifference and coldness which he experienced for his wife, as coming from herself. However, the king did not seem to notice her tears.

"No, madame," said he, "I did not ask if you hated me, for I well know that your noble and womanly heart is not capable of this passion. I merely asked if your aversion to me was so great that it demanded a separation. I pray you to give me a short and decisive answer."

But Elizabeth Christine had lost the power of speech; tears rained down her cheeks, and she could only give a mute assent.

"You are, then, willing to be my wife before the world?" asked the king. "You are willing to remain Queen of Prussia, and nominally the wife of the king? You do not demand that my reign shall be inaugurated with the exposure of our domestic misfortunes, and that your chaste and virtuous name shall be bandied about with mine before the calumniating world?"

"No," said the queen, with feverish haste, for she feared her strength might fail her. "No, I do not demand it; I desire no separation!"

"I thank you for this word," said the king, gravely. "It

ʌs worthy of a queen. You then feel with me that we princes
have not even the right to cast off the burden which weighs
us down, but must bear it patiently if it serve to secure the
stability of our throne. Enviable are those who dare complain of their sufferings, and show their scars. But it becomes us to wrap ourselves in silence, and not to show to
the miserable, pitiful, and drivelling world, which envies
and abuses, even while applauding us, that a king can also
suffer. I thank you, madame, and from this hour you will
find in me a true friend, a well-meaning brother, ever ready
to serve you. Give me your hand to this contract, which
shall be more lasting and holier than that blest by priests,
to which our hearts did not say amen."

In his proffered hand Elizabeth laid her own slowly and
solemnly. But when he clasped it in his own with a firm
pressure, Elizabeth started and a cry escaped her lips. She
hastily withdrew her hand, and sinking back on the sofa,
burst into tears. Frederick allowed her tears to flow, regarding her with a look of deep sympathy.

"You weep, madame," said he, after a long and painful
pause. "I honor your tears; you weep for your lost youth;
you weep because you are a queen, and because reason has
conquered your heart and forbids you to make yourself free
as any other woman except a princess might do. Weep on,
madame, I cannot dry your tears, for like yourself I have been
cheated of my happiness; like yourself I am well aware of
the sacrifice which we are both making to our royal standing
Ah, madame, if we were only private individuals, if we were
not the rulers of Prussia, but her subjects, we might now be
happy. Feeling our own unhappiness, and desiring to save
our subjects from a like misfortune, I have made a divorce
more easily attainable."

Elizabeth arose from her reclining position and regarded
the king with a mournful smile.

"I thank your majesty," said she. "It is noble in you to alleviate that misfortune for others, which you have determined to endure."

"Ah, madame," exclaimed the king, smiling, "you forget that I have in you a noble friend and sister at my side, who will help me to bear this evil. And then we are not altogether unhappy; if we do not love, neither do we hate each other. We are brother and sister, not by blood, but united by the word of a priest. But never fear, madame, I will regard you only as a sister, and I promise you never to violate the respect due to your virtue!"

"I believe you," murmured the queen, blushing, and inwardly ashamed of the charming and coquettish *negligée* in which she had received the king.

"Before the world we are still married, but I promise that this chain shall gall you as little as possible. In your private life you will only be reminded that you are still my wife, when it is absolutely unavoidable. At the coronation I must request your presence at my side. When this is over you will be as free and independent as circumstances will admit. You will have a court of your own, a summer and a winter residence, in which I shall never intrude."

"I shall then never see you again!" said the queen, in the sad voice of resignation, which is often produced by an excess of pain.

"Oh, I pray you, madame, to permit me to meet you at times when etiquette demands it; but I shall take care that these meetings take place on official and neutral ground, and not in our private houses. I will never enter your house without your permission, and then only on particular *fête* days—your birthday for instance; and I trust that you will not refuse to receive me on such occasions."

"No, I will not refuse," replied the queen, regarding her husband with a sad and reproachful look. But Frederick did not see this look, or would not see it.

"I beg," said the king, smiling, "that you will permit me to present you with the castle of Schonhausen, as a reminiscence of the hour in which you found a faithful brother, and I a noble sister. Accept this little gift as an earnest of our new bond of friendship. It has been fitted up and prepared as a summer residence for your use, and you can retire to it immediately after the coronation, if you are so inclined."

"I thank you," said the queen in so low a voice that her words could scarcely be distinguished. "I thank you, and I will go there on the day after the coronation;" a sigh, almost a sob, escaped her breast.

The king regarded with a clear and penetrating glance the meek woman who sat before him, who accepted her joyless and gloomy future with such heroic resignation. Her mute anguish excited his compassion. He wished to throw a sunbeam into her dark future, to warm her heart with a ray of happiness.

"Well," said he, "I am on the point of making a little journey *incognito*, in the meanwhile you can go to Schonhausen; but when I return I desire to spend a few weeks in Rheinsberg in my family circle, and, as a matter of course, madame, you are a member of my family. I beg, therefore, that you will accompany me to Rheinsberg."

Elizabeth's countenance was illumined with so beautiful and radiant a smile that even the king saw it and admired her beauty. She held out both her hands and greeted him with a loving glance, but her trembling lips refused to utter the words which her heart prompted.

The king arose. "I must no longer deprive you of your repose, and I also need rest. We must both keep ourselves well and strong for the sake of our country and our subjects, for we both have a grand task to accomplish. You will administer consolation to the miserable and suffering; you will diffuse happiness and reap blessings; you will shine as a model of nobility and feminine virtue before all other women, and through your example will give noble wives and mothers to Prussia's sons! And I," continued the king, a ray of enthusiasm lighting up his handsome face, "I will make my people great; my country shall have a place in the counsels of mighty nations. I will enlarge Prussia and make her strong and powerful. My name shall be engraven in golden letters in the book of history. As fate has destined me to be a king, and will not permit me to spend my days in retirement and philosophic tranquillity like other and happier mortals, I will at least endeavor to accomplish my mission with honor to myself and advantage to my people. You will be a ministering angel to the needy and suffering of our subjects, and I will extend the boundaries of Prussia and diffuse prosperity throughout the land! Farewell, Elizabeth! our paths will seldom meet, but if I were so fortunate as to believe in a hereafter, and your noble and gentle nature would almost persuade me to do so, I would say: 'In heaven we will perhaps meet oftener, and understand each other better.' Pray to God in my behalf. I believe in God and in the efficacy of the prayers of the good and pious. Farewell!"

He bowed deeply. He did not see the deathly pallor and convulsive trembling of the queen. He did not see how she, after he had turned from her and was advancing toward the door, hardly knowing what she did, stretched out her arms after him, and whispered his name in a plaintive and imploring tone. He hurried on, and without once turning left the room. On the outside he stood still for a moment, and drew a long breath of relief.

"Poor woman! unfortunate queen!" he murmured, returning slowly to his chambers. "But why pity her? Is not her lot mine, and that of all princes? A glittering misery— nothing else!"

A few minutes later and the royal equipage again drove through the court yard.

The king was returning to his summer residence at Charlottenburg. The queen, who was on her knees, crying and sobbing, heard the carriage as it drove off. "Gone! he is gone!" she exclaimed, with a cry of anguish; "he has deserted me, and I am a poor discarded woman! He despises me, and I—I love him!" And wringing her hands, she sobbed aloud. For a while she was tranquil, and prayed, and then again burst into tears. Her soul, which had suffered so long in silence, once more rebelled. The voice of her youth made itself heard, and demanded in heart-rending accents a little sunshine, a little of the joy and happiness promised to mankind.

She was at last quieted; she accepted her destiny, and bowed her head in humility and patience. Morning was already dawning when Elizabeth Christina arose from her knees, pale and trembling, but resigned. " *Soffri e taci!* " said she, sadly. "This was the motto of his youth, and this shall be the motto of my whole life! *Soffri e taci!* how sad, and yet how grave are these words." Oh! Frederick, Frederick! why do you condemn me to such torture; why has your heart no pity with me, no pity with my love? But no!" she exclaimed, firmly, "I will weep no more. He shall not despise me. I have accepted my destiny, and will bear it as beseems a queen. Be still, my heart, be still. *Soffri e taci!* "

CHAPTER VIII.

THE CORONATION.

BERLIN was resplendent; the streets were filled with happy faces and gayly-dressed people, and the houses garlanded with flowers. To-day was the young king's coronation festival

The citizens of Berlin were assembled to take the oath
of allegiance, and the nobles and officials to do homage to
Frederick as their king. Crowds were moving toward the
castle ; all were anxious to see the king in his coronation
uniform, to see him step upon the balcony to greet the people with the queen at his side, the young and lovely lady
with the sweet smile and cloudless brow; all wished to see
the rich equipages of the nobility, and, if possible, to collect
some of the coins which, according to an old and time-honored custom, were to be showered amongst the people.
Thousands were standing before the castle, gazing intently
upon the balcony where the king would soon appear. The
windows of the surrounding houses were filled with lovely
women richly dressed, holding wreaths and bouquets of fragrant flowers with which to greet their young and worshipped king. All were gay and joyous, all were eager to
greet the new king with shouts of gladness. The people
were ready to worship him who, during the few weeks of
his reign, had done so much for them ; had showered upon
them so many blessings ; had opened the granaries, diminished the taxes, and abolished the torture ; who had recalled
the religious sect so lately driven with derision from Berlin,
and declared that every man in Prussia should worship God
and seek his salvation in his own way. Yes, all wished to
greet this high-minded, high-souled king, who, being himself
a philosopher and a writer, knew how to reward and appreciate the scholars and poets of his own land. Frederick
had recalled the celebrated philosopher Wolf, punished some
time before by Frederick William. He had organized the
Academy of Science, and filled it with learned and scientific
men of the day. All this had been done in a few weeks.
How much could still be hoped for!

The king loved pomp and splendor; this would pro-
mote the industry of the people. How much money

would be conveyed through him and his gay court to the
working classes! What a costly festal life would now become the fashion in Berlin, and what a rich harvest would
the manufacturers and tradesmen reap! Not only the people
dreamed of a golden era, but the noblemen and high officials, who now crowded the palace, were hopeful and expectant, and saw a rare future of costly feasts and intoxicating
pleasures. The stupid and frugal entertainments of Frederick William would give place to royal *fêtes* worthy of the
Arabian Nights.

Pöllnitz, the Grand Chamberlain, was in his element; he
was commissioned with the arrangements for all the court
balls, was empowered to order every thing according to his
own judgment and taste, and he resolved to lavish money
with a liberal hand. Pöllnitz wished to realize his great
ideal; and he wished to see embodied in Frederick the picture he had drawn, for the benefit of the old king, of a true
cavalier. The king had given him the power, and he was
resolved to use it. He thought and dreamed of nothing,
now that the court mourning was drawing to a close, but
the costly feasts which he would give. Pöllnitz was ever
searching, with an experienced and critical eye, amongst the
ladies`and maids of honor for the fascinating beauty who
should charm the heart of the young king, and draw him into
the golden net of pleasure—the net Pöllnitz was so anxious
to secure for him.

That the king did not love his wife was no longer a
secret at court. Who, then, would win the love of this impassioned young monarch? This was the great question
with Pöllnitz. There was the lovely Madame Wreeckie,
who had shown so much kindness to the prince during his
imprisonment. Madame Wreeckie was still young, still bewitching; perhaps it was only necessary to bring them together in order to rekindle the old flame. There was Mad-

ame Morien, "Le Tourbillon," who had so often charmed
the prince during his minority, and for whom he had manifested a passionate preference. To be sure, since his coronation he had not noticed her, she had not received a single invitation to court. Then Dorris Ritter, the poor innocent young girl who had been flogged through the streets
of Berlin, her only fault being that she was the first love
of the crown prince. Would the king, now that he was free
to act, remember poor Dorris and what she had suffered for
him; her sorrow, her shame, and her despair? Would not
Dorris Ritter now rise to power and influence, be prayed to
as a lovely saint, her shame being covered with a martyr's
crown? Pöllnitz determined to keep an eye on Dorris
Ritter, and if the king showed no special interest in any
other woman, to draw her from her exile and abasement.
But, alas! the coronation threw no light upon this torturing
subject. Pöllnitz had hoped in vain that a round of intoxicating pleasures would begin with this day; in vain did he
suggest to the king that a court ball should crown the
solemnities of the day.

"No," said Frederick, "this shall be no day of thoughtless joy; it brings me sad retrospective thoughts and the consciousness of weighty duties. On this day my father seems
to me to die anew. Dismiss, therefore, your extravagant
fancies to a more fitting time. I cannot trust you, Pöllnitz,
with the decorations of the throne, your taste is too oriental
for this occasion; I will therefore place this affair in the
hands of M. Costellan, who will order the simple decorations which I deem most fitting."

The grand chamberlain could only shrug his shoulders
contemptuously, and rejoice that he was not compromised
by these contemptible arrangements; he grumbled to himself, and said scornfully: "This pitiful saloon, with no
gilded furniture, no paintings, no works of art, with faded,

shabby silk curtains; and that black, uncouth structure,
is that really a throne—the throne of a young king? A
long platform covered with cloth; an old arm-chair, black,
worn, and rusty; a canopy covered with black cloth; faugh!
it looks like a crow with his wings spread. Can this be the
throne of a king who receives for the first time the homage
of his subjects?" A contemptuous mocking smile was on
the lips of Pöllnitz as he saw the king and his three brothers
enter the room.

Pöllnitz could scarcely suppress a cry of horror, as
he looked at the king. What, no embroidered coat,
no ermine mantle, no crown, nothing but the simple
uniform of the guard, no decorations—not even the star
upon his breast, to distinguish him from the generals and
officials who surrounded him! Nevertheless, as Frederick
stood upon that miserable platform with the princes and
generals at his side, there was no one that could be compared
with him; he seemed, indeed, to stand alone, his bearing
was right royal, his countenance beamed with a higher
majesty than was ever lent by a kingly crown; the fire of
genius was seen in the flashes of his piercing eye; proud
and fearless thoughts were engraved upon his brow, and an
indescribable grace played around his finely-formed mouth.
There stood, indeed, "Frederick the Great;" he did not need
the purple mantle, or the star upon his breast. God had
marked him with elevated kingly thoughts, and the star
which was wanting on his breast was replaced by the lustre
of his eye.

The solemn address of the minister of state, and the
reply of President Görner, were scarcely listened to. Frederick, though silent, had said more than these two ministers,
with all their rounded periods; his glance had reached the
heart of every one who looked upon him, and said, "I am
thy king and thy superior;" they bowed reverently before

him, not because chance had made him their sovereign,
they were subdued by the power of intellect and will. The
oath of allegiance was taken with alacrity. The king stood
motionless upon his throne, betraying no emotion, calm, im-
passive, unapproachable, receiving the homage of his subjects, not haughtily but with the composed serenity of a
great spirit accepting the tribute due to him, and not dazzled
by the offering.

The coronation was at an end. Frederick stepped from
the throne, and nodded to his brothers to follow him; the
servants hastily opened the doors which led to the balcony,
and carried out the bags filled with the gold and silver
coins. The air resounded with the shouts of the populace.
The king drew near to the iron railing, and greeted his subjects with a cordial smile. "You are my children," he
said, "you have a right to demand of your father love,
sympathy, and protection, and you shall have them." Then
taking a handful of coin he scattered it amongst the crowd.
Shouts of merriment and a fearful scuffling and scrambling
was seen and heard below; each one wished to secure a coin
thrown by the king himself, and they scarcely noticed the
silver and gold which the young princes were scattering
with liberal hands; all these were worthless, as long as it
was possible to secure one piece which had been touched by
Frederick. The king saw this, and, much flattered by this
disinterested mark of love, he again scattered the coin far
and wide.

While the men were struggling roughly and angrily
for this last treasure, a weak, pallid woman sprang boldly
into the thickest of the surging crowd. Until now she had
been cold and indifferent; the coins thrown by the young
princes, and which had fallen at her feet, she had cast from
her with disdain; now, however, as the king once more cast
the coins in the midst of the gaping crowd, with a power

which passion only gives she forced her way amongst the wild multitude, and with outstretched arms she shrieked out, "Oh! give me one of these small coins, only a silver one, give it to me as a keepsake! Oh! for God's sake, give me one!" Suddenly strange murmurs and whispers were heard from amongst those who now recognized this poor outcast; they looked askance at her, they shrank from her as from a leper; and she who a moment before had sued to them so humbly, now stood in their midst like an enraged lioness.

"It is she!—it is she!" they whispered; "she has come to see the king, for whom she suffered so much; for his sake she has been covered with shame; she has been driven from amongst the poor and innocent, and now she dares to come amongst us!" cried a harsh and pitiless voice.

"We know how cruelly she was insulted and abused," said another, "but we all know that she was innocent; my heart is full of pity for her, and she has a right to a coin touched by the king." The last speaker approached the poor woman, and offered both a gold and silver coin. "Take these coins, I beg you, and may they be to you an earnest of a better and happier future."

She gazed with a hard and tearless eye upon the good-natured, kindly face. "No, there is no happy future for me—nothing but want, and misery, and despair; but I thank you for your pity, and I accept these coins as a memento of this hour." She took them and laid them in her tattered dress, walked erect through the circle which gathered around, and was soon lost in the crowd.

She was soon forgotten. The king with his brilliant suite was still upon the balcony, they had not noticed the scene passing amongst the people below; none of them remarked this poor creature, who, having made her way through the crowd, now leaned against one of the pillars of the spire, and gazed earnestly upon the king. The money was exhausted, the king had shown himself to the people sufficiently, and now, according to etiquette, he must leave the balcony and make the grand tour of the saloons, greeting with kind and gracious words the assembled nobles. He motioned, however, to his followers to leave him, he wished. to remain a few moments alone, and look thoughtfully upon this sea of upturned faces. Frederick gazed eagerly below. That was no inanimate and pulseless creation moved to and fro by the wind, which he now looked upon, but a living, thinking, immortal people ; with hearts to hate or love, with lips to bless or curse, their verdict would one day decide the great question as to his fame and glory as a monarch, or his neglect of holy duty, and the eternal shame which follows. They seemed to Frederick to be pleading with him ; they demanded but little—a little shade to rest in when weary with their daily labor ; prompt justice and kindly protection, the right to live in peace, bearing the burden and sorrow of their lives patiently ; pity for their necessities, forbearance for their weakness and folly. What did he, their king, demand of them ? That alone, which a million of people, his people, could bestow, immortal fame !—they must give him the laurel of the hero, and crown him with the civic wreath ; he would make his subjects strong, healthy, and happy— they must make his greatness known to all the world, and future ages.

Such were the thoughts of the king as he stood alone upon the balcony. His eye often wandered across to the spire, and as often as it did the wretched woman who was leaning against the pillar trembled fearfully, and her lips and cheeks became deadly pale. The king did not see her; he saw nothing of the outer world, his eye was turned within, reading the secrets of his own heart.

In the grand saloons the nobles stood waiting in grim and angry silence the return of Frederick ; a cloud rested upon every brow; even Pöllnitz could no longer retain his gracious and sterotyped smile; he felt it to be a bitter grievance that the king should keep the nobility waiting while he stood gazing at a dirty mass of insignificant creatures called human beings! Looking around the circle, Pöllnitz saw displeasure marked upon every face but three. "Ah," said he to himself, "there are the three Wreeckies, no doubt they have come to be rewarded for services rendered the crown prince; they were doubtless dangerous rivals for us all; they suffered much for the prince, and were banished seven years from court on his account. The king must indemnify them for all this, and who knows, perhaps he may give them the house in Jäger Street, the house I am in the habit of calling mine! Well, I must draw near them and hear all the king promises." So saying, Pöllnitz drew quietly near the Messieurs Wreeckie. At this moment there was a movement in the vast assembly, and all bowed low; as the king stepped into the saloon he commenced the grand tour of the room; he had a kind and friendly word for all; at last he reached the Messieurs Wreeckie, and remained standing before them. All glances were now directed to this group; all held their breath, not wishing to lose a word which Frederick should say to these formidable rivals.

The king stood before them, his eye was severe, and his brow clouded. "Gentlemen," he said, "it has been a long time since I have seen you at the court of the King of Prussia. I suppose you seek the prince royal; I do not think you will find him here. At this court you will only find a king who demands, above all things, that his majesty should be respected; that you subjugate yourselves to him in silent obedience; even when his orders appear harsh and cruel they must not be questioned for a moment; he who opposes the will of the king deserves punishment; I will not bear opposition at my court. There is but one will, but one law; that is the will and law of the king!" And, without further greetings, he passed on.

The Wreeckies stood pale and trembling, and the face of Pöllnitz was radiant with contentment. "Well, those poor fellows will not receive my house in Jäger Street," he said to himself, "they have fallen into disgrace; it appears the king wants to punish all those who rendered good service to the prince royal. Louis the Fourteenth said: 'It is most unworthy of a French king to punish any wrong done to the crown prince;' here the rule is reversed—the King of Prussia deems it unworthy to reward the services rendered the prince royal. But what is the meaning of that crowd over there?" he exclaimed, interrupting himself, "why is the lord marshal approaching his majesty with such an eager, joyful air? I must know what is going on." Again Pöllnitz made his way through the courtiers and arrived safely, right behind the king, just as my lord marshal was saying in an excited voice: "Your majesty, there is a young man in the next room who begs your highness to allow him to throw himself at your feet and take the oath of allegiance; he has come from America to greet you as king. So soon as he heard of the illness of your father, he left his asylum and has travelled night and day; he has finished his journey at a most fortunate moment."

The eye of the king rested coldly, unmoved on the speaker; and even after he ceased speaking, regarded him sternly. "What is the name of this young man, for whom you show so lively an interest?" said the king, after a pause.

The lord marshal looked perplexed and frightened; he thought the king's heart should have told him who stood without; who it was that had left his asylum in America and longed to greet the young king. "Sire," he said, hesitatingly, "your majesty demands to know the name of this young man?"

"I demand it."

The lord marshal breathed quickly. "Well, your majesty, it is my nephew; it is Lieutenant Keith, who has come from America to throw himself at your majesty's feet."

Not a muscle of the king's countenance moved. "I know no Lieutenant Keith," he said, sternly; "he who was once known to me by that name, was stricken from the officers' roll with the stigma of disgrace and shame, and was hung by the hangman in effigy, upon the gallows. If Mr. Keith is still living, I advise him to remain in America, where no one knows of his crime, or of his ignominious punishment."

"Your majesty will not receive him, then?" said the lord marshal, with a trembling voice.

"You may thank God, sir, that I do not receive him—above all, that I ignore his being here; if I should know that he still lived, I should be forced to execute the sentence to which he was condemned by the court-martial." Slightly nodding to the lord marshal, the king passed on and spoke a few indifferent words to some gentlemen standing near.

"Well, Mr. Keith will not get my house in the Jäger Street," said Pöllnitz, laughing slightly. "What is the matter with this king, he seems to have lost his memory? God grant he may not forget who it was that induced Frederick William to pay the debts of the prince royal, and to present him with the Trakener stud."

CHAPTER IX.

DORRIS RITTER.

WHEN the king had left the balcony, a poor young woman, who had been sitting on the steps of the cathedral, arose and looked fearfully around her. The sight of the king had carried her far away, she had been dreaming of the blissful days of the past. His disappearance brought her back to the present—the sad, comfortless present. The king had left the balcony. What had she to do in this mob, that might again mock, insult, or commiserate her! the could stand neither their sneers nor their pity, she must flee from both.

With a hasty movement she drew her shawl tighter around her poor slender figure, and hurried through the crowd. She came at last to a miserable small house. The low narrow door seemed unfriendly, inhospitable, as if it would permit no one to pass its threshold and enter its dreary, deserted rooms, from which no sound of life proceeded. But this small, quiet dwelling ought to have been a house of labor and occupation, and would not have been so poor and pitiful looking if the large iron bell hanging over the door had been oftener in motion, and filled the silent space with its cheerful sound.

Behind this door there was a shop, but the bell was generally silent, and purchasers rarely came to buy in this miserable little store the articles which could be purchased more reasonably in one of the large shops belonging to wealthy merchants. The house seemed to have seen better days; it had some claims to comfort and respectability. In the windows were placed bright shells and cocoanuts; there were the large blue china pots, in which the costly ginger is brought; there were quantities of almonds, raisons, citron, and lemons in glass shells; neat paper-bags for coffee, and small Chinese chests that had held real Chinese tea. But these bags and chests were empty; the lemons and fruits were dried and hard; the ginger-pots held no more of their strengthening contents; even the dusty, faded sign over the door, which represented a wonderfully-ornamented negro engaged in unrolling dried tobacco leaves, was but a reminiscence of the past, for the tobacco had long since disappeared from the chests, and the little that was left had fallen to dust. The store contained but a few unimportant things: chicory for the poor, who could not pay for coffee; matches, and small home-made penny lights, with which poverty illuminated her misery and want; on the table, in glass cans, a few hardened, broken bits of candy; a large cask of old herring, and a smaller one of syrup. This was the inventory of the shop, these the possessions of this family, who alone occupied this house with their misery, their want, and their despair; whose head and only stay was the poor young woman now leaning wearily against the steps, dreading to enter her house of woe and wretchedness. She arose at length and hastily entered. The bells' hoarse creaking ring was heard, and a poor, pale boy hastened forward to inquire the comer's wants. He stopped and looked angrily at the poor woman who had entered.

"Ah, it is you, mother," said he, peevishly. "I hoped it was some one wishing to buy, then I could have bought some bread."

"Bread!" said the mother anxiously; "did I not, before I went out, give you money to buy bread for you and your little sister?"

"Yes, but when father came home he threatened to beat me if I did not give up the money at once; I was frightened, and gave it; then he left, and Anna and I have been crying for bread, while our father is amusing himself at the ale-house, and our mother has taken a holiday, and has been looking at the festivities which I also would have been glad to see, but could not, because I must stay at home and watch the shop into which no one has entered, and take care of my little sister, who cries for bread, which I cannot give her." As he finished he threw an angry look at his mother, who, deeply grieved, had fallen back on a wooden bench. She looked lovingly at her son, and holding out her arms to him, said:

"Come, give me a kiss, and reward me for all my pain and suffering."

"Give us bread, then perhaps I will kiss you," said he, harshly.

She looked terrified into his hard, cold face. She pressed her hand to her high, pale forehead, as if she would force back the madness that threatened her; she held the other hand to her heart, whose wild, feverish throbbings were almost choking her.

"My God! my God!" murmured she, "am I then already mad? Am I dreaming? Is this my son, my Karl, who loved me so dearly—my boy, who was the only comfort in my misery, the confidant of my tears and wretchedness? Can I, whom he looks at with such dark glances, be his mother—his mother, who joyfully bears for him the scorn of the world, who has suffered and hungered for him, worked for him during the long, cold winter nights—his mother, whose love for him was so great that she was willing not to die, but for his sake to live on in her woe? Karl, my son, come to your mother, for you well know how tenderly she loves you, and that she will die if you do not love her."

"No, mother," said he, not moving, "you do not love me, nor my little sister Anna; for if you loved us, you would not have left us to-day, and joined the gay people who were making merry while your poor children were at home groaning and crying."

"Oh, my child! my child! I did not go, out of idle curiosity," said she, sadly. "I went to consult the oracle of your future, and to see if there was not to be some hope, some comfort for my children; if this would not be the beginning of brighter days. I wished to read all this in a man's face; I wished to see if he still had a heart, or if, like all princes, he had become hard and pitiless."

She had forgotten that she was speaking to her son; she was addressing herself, and had entirely forgotten that he was present.

"Ah," said he, sneeringly, "you thought he would now give you money for your shame; but father told me that all the gold in the world would not wipe out this shame, and that brandy was the only way besides death that could make us forget that we are despised and accursed. Father told me—"

The boy stopped and retreated a few steps; his mother had risen from her seat and stood before him, deadly pale, with widely-opened, flashing eyes, with trembling lips; every muscle of her face in play; her whole form trembling in a paroxysm of rage and frightful torture. It was not the head of a woman, but a Medusa; not the look of a tender, loving mother, but of a wild, angry, threatening mad woman.

"What did your father tell you?" cried she, wildly, to the trembling boy before her. "What did he say? I will, I must know! You are silent; speak, or I dash my brains out against the wall, and you will be guilty of your mother's death."

"You will beat me if I tell you," said he insolently.

"No, no, I will not beat you," said she, breathlessly; and folding her hands as if to pray, she continued: "my child, my child, have mercy on your mother. Tell me what he said; with what words he poisoned your heart, and made the love for your poor mother die so quickly. Tell me all, my son; I will not beat but bless you, though your words should cut my heart like a knife."

She wished to press him to her heart, but he resisted passionately.

"No," said he, "you shall not kiss me; father said·you made all you touched unhappy and despised, and that we would be well, happy, and rich if you were not our mother."

She shuddered; her arm fell powerless to her side, a hollow groan escaped her, her eyes were fixed and tearless.

"What more did he tell you?" murmured she; "with what other tales did he amuse my child?" She looked at him with such a sad, painful smile, that he trembled and glanced timidly down; he now saw what torture he was preparing for her.

"Father was drunk," said he; "when he heard that you had gone out, he was furious; he cursed you so dreadfully that Anna and I both cried, and I begged him not insult you so, for it hurt me, for then I still loved you."

"Then he still loved me!" said his mother, wringing her hands.

"But he laughed at me, and said you did not deserve our love; that you were the cause of all our misery and want; he had become poor and wretched because he had married you, and taken to drink so as not to hear or see men pointing and laughing at you when you passed. But, mother, you look so pale, you tremble so! I will say no more; I will forget all father said; I will love you, mother; but do not look at me so dreadfully, and do not tremble in that way."

The boy wept from grief and terror. His old love had awakened; he approached his mother to kiss her, but now she pushed him back.

"I do not tremble," said she, though her teeth were chattering. "I do not tremble, and you must not forget what your father said; you must tell me all again. Speak on, speak! I must hear all, know all. What more did he say?"

The boy looked at her sadly. His voice, which before

had been insolent and rude, was now quiet and gentle, and his eyes were full of tears.

"He said he married you out of pity, and because you brought him a few thousand dollars. But this gold brought no blessing with it, but a curse; and that since then it had gone worse with him than with the executioner, whom all despise, and who dares not enter an honest man's house. But that you were more despised and disgraced than the miserable man who had stripped you in the open market and whipped you through the streets; that the boys had pelted you with mud, and that the streets became red with the blood that flowed down your back."

The poor woman gave a piercing shriek, and fell as if struck by lightning to the floor. The boy threw himself weeping by her side; and the little girl, who had been sleeping in another corner of the room, awakened by the scream, came running toward them crying for bread.

But the mother moved not; she lay there pale, with closed eyes; she was cold and lifeless; she did not hear her poor little girl cry; she did not feel the hot kisses and tears of her son, who was imploring her in anxious, tender, loving words, to open her eyes, to tell him that she was not angry, that she had forgiven him. But he suddenly stopped and listened eagerly; he thought he heard the well-known sound of the bell.

"There it was again; if it is father, he will beat me to death," murmured he, as he went toward the shop door. "He forbade me to repeat a word of all that to mother."

He opened the door, and there stood not his father but a richly-dressed gentleman, who, with a friendly gesture, pushed the boy aside and entered the shop.

"I want some tobacco, my little fellow," said he; "therefore call Mr. Schommer to give me some from his best canister."

"My father is not at home," said the boy, staring at the handsome, friendly gentleman.

"Well I did not come precisely on his account," said the gentleman, with a strange laugh. "Call your mother, Madame Schommer, and tell her I wish to make a purchase."

"Mother is lying in the back room on the floor, and I believe she is dead!" said Karl, sobbing.

The gentleman looked at him with amazement. "Did you say dead? That would be very inconvenient, for I have greatly counted on her life. What did she die of? Is a physician with her?"

"No one is with her but my little sister; you can hear her crying!"

"Yes, I can hear her; and it is in truth no edifying music. No one else, did you say? Where, then, are your friends? where is your father?"

"Father is at the ale-house, and friends we have none; we live all alone, for no one will live with us."

"Well, if you are alone, I may go to your mother," said he, with a careless laugh. "It is likely your mother has fainted; and as I am learned in these feminine swoons, it is very possible I may call her back to life. Show the way, little Cupid, and lead me to your mother, the fainting Venus." And laughing, he followed the astonished boy into the back room.

She still lay without movement on the floor, and little Anna, kneeling by her side, was praying for bread.

"That is your mother, Madame Schommer?" asked the strange gentleman, looking curiously at the pale woman.

"Yes, that is my mother," said the boy. "Mother, mother, wake up!" said he, covering her face with kisses. "Wake up, I do not believe what father said. I will love you! He was drunk! Ah, my dear, dear mother, only wake up!"

"She will awake," said the stranger, who was bending over her, laying his hand on her heart and temples, "she is, as I thought, not dead but in a swoon."

The boy laughed aloud with glee. "My mother is not dead," said he, crying and laughing at once. "She will wake up and love me; we will all be so happy!"

"Mother, mother, give me some bread!" whimpered poor little Anna.

"Are you then so hungry?" said the stranger, who was getting tired of this scene.

"Yes," said the boy, "she is hungry; we are both hungry. We have had nothing to eat all day. Mother gave us money before she went out to buy bread and milk, but father came and took it to buy brandy for himself."

"A worthy father," said the stranger, handing him something. "Here, my son, is some money. Take your sister, go to the baker's, and get something to eat, then seat yourselves and eat; and do not come back here until I call you. But if you see your father coming, then come and tell me."

The children joyfully hurried to the door; they were not now thinking of their poor, fainting mother, but of the bread they would buy to satisfy their hunger.

"But who," said the boy, turning around, "will watch the shop?"

"Well, I will," said the stranger; "I will watch your mother and your shop; go!"

The children hurried away, and the stranger was alone with the fainting woman.

CHAPTER X.

OLD AND NEW SUFFERING.

THE cavalier stood quietly some minutes, showing no sympathy for the poor insensible woman, and making no effort to arouse her to consciousness; he examined her face searchingly and curiously, not from sympathy for her sad condition, but with cold egotism, thinking only of his own special object.

"Hum," murmured he, " in spite of palor and attenuation, there are yet traces of great beauty. I am sure if well nourished and well clothed she may yet allure the heart which must be ever touched with pity for her mournful fate; besides, she is poor—hopelessly, despairingly poor. The husband is a drunkard, the children cry for bread; she is so poorly clad, so pale, so thin; hunger has been her only lover. Under these circumstances she will readily adopt my plans, and be my willing tool; she will acknowledge me as her master, and by God I will teach her how to bind this head-strong fool in chains. He has so far escaped all the pitfalls which Fredersdorf and myself have so adroitly laid for him. Dorris shall be the Delilah who will tame this new Samson. Truly," he continued, as he cast a look of contempt upon the senseless form lying before him, " truly it is a desperate attempt to transform this dirty, pale, thin woman into a Delilah. But the past is powerfully in her favor, and my Samson has a heart full of melting pity and sensibility; moreover all previous efforts have failed, and it is pardonable to seek for extraordinary means in our despair. So to work! to work!"

He took from his pocket a small phial of English salts, held it to her nose, and rubbed her temples with a small sponge. "Ah, she moves," he said, resting for a moment from his work, and looking coldly and curiously upon the poor woman, who, with the shudder of newly-awakened life, now turned her head, and whose convulsed lips uttered short sighs and piteous complaints. Pöllnitz rubbed her temples again with the strong salts, and then, as he saw that consciousness was more and more restored, he raised her from the floor, and placed her softly in a chair. "*Auso armes, auso armes,*" muttered he "*La battaille commencera.*"

The woman opened her eyes, and they wandered with an anxious and questioning look here and there, then fell upon the stranger, who, with a smiling and observant glance, followed every movement. Her eyes were fixed and staring, her features expressed terror and scorn, her whole form was convulsed, she was still half dreaming, half unconscious. But her eye was immovably placed upon him, and she murmured in low tones, "I know this face—yes, I know this cold, smiling face, I have *felt* it twice! When was it? was it only in fearful dreams, or was it a frightful reality? When, where did I see this cold, devilish smile, this face so cold and heartless, so full of iron egotism?"

"Truly, she does not flatter," murmured Pöllnitz, but without changing for one moment his watchful but friendly mien. "I am curious to see if she will at last recognize me."

"Pollnitz!" cried she at last, with flaming eyes. "Yes, it is you! I know you! you are Baron Pöllnitz! Who gave you the right to enter this house? what brings you here?"

"I repeat your question," he replied, smiling, "what brought you here, here in this gloomy, miserable room; here where hunger and wailing have their dwelling; here where misery grins upon you with hollow-eyed terror? What do you here, Dorris Ritter?"

She trembled convulsively at this name, her cheeks

were dyed purple, and in another moment became ghastly pale. "Why do you call me Dorris Ritter?" she cried, with gasping breath, "why remind me of the past, which stands like a dark specter, ever behind me, and grins upon me with bloody and shameful horrors?" Lost wholly in these fearful remembrances, she stared before her, thinking no more of Pöllnitz, forgetting that his watchful and heartless eyes were ever fixed upon her. "Dorris Ritter!" she cried, slowly, "Dorris Ritter! where are you? why do they call you by thy name? Can they not remember that you are a sleep walker wandering on the edge of a precipice, into which you must fall headlong if awakened by the sound of your name, Dorris Ritter?" she said, more loudly, fixing her eye upon Pöllnitz; "how dare you call my name, and tear me shrieking from my grave!"

"Now, that is exactly what I wish," said Pöllnitz; "I will raise you from this lowly and forgotten grave; you shall forget what you have suffered; you shall be rich, happy, distinguished, and envied."

"I!" cried she, with mocking laughter, "and you will make that of me! You, Baron Pöllnitz, you, who were partly the cause of my misery, and who looked smilingly upon my shame! What then, what have I done to deserve so much shame and sorrow? My God!" cried she, in heart-rending tones, "my heart was pure and innocent; I dared raise my head without fear, and look God and my parents in the face; even before *him* my prince, I needed not to cast down my eyes; I was innocent, and he loved me because he could also respect me. Alas! it was so silent, so resigned a love; it asked for nothing, it had no speech. Was it our fault that others saw and pointed out this love without words, and which eyes of innocence only expressed? We stood far removed from each other, and a gulf lay between us, but heavenly music formed a golden starry bridge over this abyss, and the holy and melodious tones whispered to our young hearts, the complaints and longings of a speechless, self-renouncing love. Only thus, only thus, a sweet dream, and nothing more! Then you came to awaken us, to accuse the prince of high treason, to make of me a miserable prostitute. You cast my love, which I had only confessed to my Father in heaven, like a dirty libel and foul fruit in my face; you wished to spot and stain my whole being, and you succeeded; you crushed my existence under your feet, and left me not one blossom of hope! Oh I will never forget how you tore me from the arms of my poor father! how you cast me into prison and chained my hands, because in the anguish of my shame and my despair I tried to take that life which you had dishonored! They came at last, and dragged me before the king. Two men were with him, one with a common red and swollen visage, with thick, lascivious lips, with red and watery eyes—that was Grumbkow; the other, with the fine friendly face, with the everlasting deceitful smile, the cold, contemptuous, heartless glance, that was you, Baron Pöllnitz. Ah, with what horrible glances did these three men look upon me! what mockery and contempt did their cruel voices express! I threw myself at the feet of the king; I prayed to him for mercy and grace; he kicked me from him, and shamed me with words and accusations which made my soul blush.* I swore that I was innocent; that no sin lay upon me; that I had never been the beloved of the prince; that I had never spoken to him but in the presence of my father. Then laughed they, and mocked me, and loudest of all laughed Baron Pöllnitz, and his words of scoffing and insult pierced my heart like a poisoned arrow, and checked my flowing tears. "

"It is true," murmured Pöllnitz; "she has forgotten nothing."

"Forgotten!" cried she, with a wild laugh, " can I forget that I was driven through the streets like a wild beast, that I was stripped by the rough hands of the hangman's boy; that I heard behind me the scoffings and insults of the wild mob hired for the occasion; that I felt upon my naked back the cruel blows of the executioner's whip! Oh I have borne, and I have suffered; I did not become a maniac, I did not curse God, but I prayed to my Father in heaven as I ran like a baited wild beast through the streets. I saw that all the houses were closed, that no one stood at the windows; no one had the courage to look upon my path of martyrdom, and it comforted me even in the midst of my torture, and I blessed those men who were pitiful to me, and who appeared to bear testimony to my innocence by refusing to witness my cruel punishment, and I ran further, and the hot blood flowed down my back. Suddenly I came upon a house which was not closed, the door was open, before it stood the servants and pointed the finger of scorn at me, and mocked and jeered at me. On the balcony stood Baron Pöllnitz, with his stony, heartless face! Then I uttered a cry of rage and revenge, then my prayers were hushed or changed into wild curses, and I yelled and howled in my heart: he is guilty of my shame, he with his cruel jests, his pitiless sneers, has poisoned the ear of the king, has destroyed the last doubt of my guilt in the heart of his majesty. Disgrace and shame upon Baron Pöllnitz! may he be despised, lonely, and neglected in the hour of death; may remorse, the worm of conscience, feed upon his soul, and drive him hither and thither, restless and homeless all his life long!"

She uttered a wild cry, and sank back powerless and broken in her chair.

Baron Pöllnitz was self-possessed and smiling throughout; he laid his hand upon the nerveless arm of the sobbing woman, and said with a soft, flattering tone:

"It is true I have done you injustice, but I have come to make amends for the past. You shall yet raise your head proudly, and no one shall doubt of your innocence."

She shook her head sadly. "How can that help me? My father died of shame; my husband, who married me from pity and because I had a poor two thousand crowns, could not bear that men should flee from me as from a branded culprit; this grief drove him to drink, and when he comes home drunk at night, he beats me and shames me; the next morning he prays, with strong crying and tears, for forgiveness, but goes again and begins anew the same sad existence. My children!"

She could say no more; her words were choked with tears, as she thought of the hard and frightful language her little boy had used to her that morning.

Pöllnitz was weary of the complaints and sobs of this wretched woman.

"Weep no more," said he; "weeping makes the eyes red, and you must henceforth be lovely and attractive; if you will follow my advice you and your children will once more be joyful and happy. I will send you beautiful clothing, and I know an adroit person who will make you charmingly attractive, and at the same time arrange your toilet with such enchanting grace, that you will pass for the 'Mater dolorosa' and the beautiful Magdalen in the same person. Then will I lead you to the king; then will he read in your lovely and noble face the touching and innocent story of his first love; it will then rest with you, who have so long been covered with dust and ashes, to kindle again the spark of your dead love, and to find in his tenderness the reward and compensation for all the bitter past."

She looked at him with flaming eyes, and her glance was so piercing that even Pöllnitz felt a little embarrassed, and involuntarily cast his eyes to the ground.

"Has the king sent you here with this message?"

"No, not the king; but I know that he thinks of you with love and pity, and that he would be happy to find you."

"If that is so, let him come to seek me. I will not go to him—I am the injured and dishonored one; it is his duty to repair my wrongs. But he will not come—I know it. I read it to-day in his face. The world has killed his heart; it has turned to stone in his breast—a gravestone for his dear-loved Katt. and for Dorris Ritter."

"He will come; I say to you he will! Hear me, Dorris; you will not go to him? Well, then, expect him here, and prepare yourself in such a way to receive him as to make an impression upon his heart; study carefully your part; revolve every word which you will say to him; consider every glance with which you will look upon him; put on the clothes which I will send you, and banish your husband and your children."

"My children!" cried she, trembling; "no, no, only as a mother—only under the protection of their innocent presence will I ever see him; only for my children will I receive his sympathy and grace."

Pöllnitz stamped involuntarily with his feet upon the floor, and muttered curses from between his tightly-pressed lips.

"Do you not understand that our whole scheme will fail, unless you do exactly as I tell you; that you will attain nothing unless you begin wisely and prudently? You say the king has no heart; well, then, he has intellect, and this you must flatter; through this you may, perhaps, warm his stony heart; you must not trust wholly to the majesty of your misfortunes, but advance to meet him in the grace and glory of your beauty; by your soft eyes you must work upon his heart; not with your tears, but by enchanting smiles, he may be won."

She looked at him with proud and contemptuous glances.

"Go!" said she; "go! we have nothing to do with each other. I would curse you and seek to revenge myself upon you for the new dishonor which you have put upon me by your shameless words, but I know I have not the right to resent. I am a degraded, dishonored woman, and all men believe they have the right to insult me and to mock at my misfortunes. Go!"

"You command me, then, to leave you; you will not heed the voice of a well-meaning friend; you—"

"Baron Pöllnitz," said she, with a voice tremulous with scorn, "I say go! drive me not to extremity. Shall I call upon the neighbors to relieve me from the presence of one I abhor, who disregards the sanctity of my poor house, and abuses and sneers at a woman who hates him? Go, and let me never see your face or hear your voice again!"

"Well, then, I will go; farewell, dear Madame Schömmer; but I will come again, and perhaps I may be so happy as to find in your place the enchanting Dorris Ritter, that sentimental young maiden of the past, who loved the crown prince so passionately, and was so well pleased to receive his love and his presents."

He laughed aloud, and left the dreary room with a courtly pirouette; with quick steps he hastened through the shop, and opening the door which led into the street, he kicked the two children who were sitting on the threshold to one side, and rushed into the street.

"She is truly proud yet," murmured he, shrugging his shoulders. "The hangman's whip did not humble her— that pleases me; and I am more than ever convinced we will succeed with her; she must and shall be beloved of the king; and as she will not go to him, well, then, I will bring him to her. To-morrow the king will visit the site chosen for the palace of the queen-mother, that will be a glorious opportunity to induce him to enter her hut."

Dorris Ritter had risen, and with uplifted arm and a proud glance she had followed Pöllnitz. Her whole being was in feverish excitement. In this hour she was no more a poor, disheartened woman, from whom all turned away with contempt, but a proud wife conscious of her honor and her worth, who commanded her persecutor from her presence; who asked no mercy or grace, and demanded a recognition of her purity.

As the steps of the baron faded away, and Dorris was again alone, her feverish excitement subsided, and she was again a poor, pallid, trembling, humble woman. With a cry of the most profound woe she sank back in her chair, and stared long before her. Suddenly she murmured from between her tightly-compressed lips: "Woe to him! woe to him! when he forgets what I have suffered for him; woe to him, if he does not remove the shame which crushes me! woe to him, if he despises me as others do! Then will Dorris Ritter be his irreconcilable enemy, and she will take vengeance so true as there is a God over us!"

CHAPTER XI.

THE PROPOSAL OF MARRIAGE.

"COURAGE, my dear friend," said Madame von Brandt to Count Voss, who stood before her with the most mournful expression, and seemed so lost in grief as to be scarcely aware of the presence of his charming and bewitching Armida.

"I do not understand how you can laugh and be gay, if you love me," he said, sadly.

"I love you truly, and therefore I am gay. We have almost gained our end; soon the suspicions of the world will be lulled, for who would dream that the husband of the young and beautiful Laura von Pannewitz could possibly love the old and ugly Madame von Brandt?"

"You old! you ugly!" cried the young count, indignantly. "It is well that it is you who utter such a blasphemy; if any other did, I should destroy him."

"You would do very wrong, dear count, for that would betray our love to the world. No, no, if any one should speak so to you, you must shrug your shoulders, and say, 'I am not acquainted with Madame von Brandt, I am indifferent whether she is handsome or ugly. She may be as old as Methuselah, it does not concern me.'"

"Never will I say that, never will I be induced to utter so miserable and dishonorable a falsehood. No, dearest, you cannot demand that. You see your power over me, and treat me most cruelly. You condemned me to be married, and I have obeyed your commands, although my heart was breaking as I made my proposal to the queen. Now I entreat that you will not torture me by demanding that I shall revile and calumniate you. No, no, I pray on my knees that you will be kind and merciful!"

He threw himself on his knees before her, leaning his head upon the divan on which she was sitting.

She placed her hand upon his head and played with his fair hair. "I am not cruel, I am only cautious," she whispered, almost tenderly. "Trust me, Alexander, you must not doubt my boundless love."

"No, no, you do not love me," he sighed; "you are always hard and cruel, you have never granted me the smallest favor, you have never accepted one of my presents."

A slight but scornful smile played upon the lips of this beautiful woman, while the enthusiastic and impassioned young man spake thus. She turned aside her face, that he might not see its expression.

But he thought she was again angry with him. "Ah," he said, despairingly, "you will not allow me even to behold your heavenly countenance; do you wish to drive me to distraction? What have I done to deserve this new torture? Are you so offended because I entreated you to accept a gift from me? Oh, it is so sweet to compel the one we love to think of us; to place a ring upon her finger, and bid her dream of him who loves her when she looks upon it; to bind a chain upon her neck, and whisper, 'You are fettered, my love enchains you, you are mine!' A man can only believe in the affection of his beloved when she condescends to accept something from him."

"And would that give you faith in my love?" she said, in a tender, melting voice, as she turned smilingly toward him.

"Yes!" he exclaimed, "it would increase my faith."

"Well, then, give me some little thing that will remind me of you, that I can wear, as the spaniel wears the collar which bears the name of its master."

She offered him her hand, which he covered with fervent kisses, and then drew from his bosom a large and heavy *etui*, which he placed in her hands.

"But this contains not merely a ring," she said, reproachfully; "you have deceived me, misused my kindness; instead of presenting me with a small souvenir, with the pride of a king you wish to overwhelm me with your rich gifts. Take back your case, count, I will not look at its contents; I will not behold how far your extravagance and pride have led you; take your treasures, and give me the simple ring that I promised to accept." She stood up, and handed him the *etui* with the air of an insulted queen, without once glancing at its contents, and only divining their value by the size and weight of the case.

Her poor lover regarded her with a truly despairing ex-

pression. "If you desire to destroy me, do it quickly and
at once, not slowly, day by bay, and hour by hour," he
said, almost weeping. "I fulfil your smallest desire, I marry at your command, and you refuse to show me the slightest kindness." He was now really weeping, and turned
aside that she might not behold his tears. Then suddenly
recovering himself, he said with the boldness of despair: "I
will learn from you the use of the word no. If you refuse
to accept this case, then will I refuse to marry Mademoiselle
von Pannewitz. If you compel me to receive again those
miserable stones, I will go at once to the queen, and tell her
that I was mistaken, that I cannot and will not marry
Mademoiselle von Pannewitz; that I have given up my plan,
and am determined to leave Berlin immediately."

"No! no! you must not go! you shall not leave me!"
she cried, with every appearance of terror; "give me the
case, I will accept it. You must not leave Berlin!"

The young count uttered a cry of delight, and hurried to
her side.

"I will accept this *etui*," she said smiling, "but will not
open it while we are together, for fear we might again dis-
agree."

Count Voss was beside himself with joy and gratitude,
and vowed he would marry Mademoiselle von Pannewitz that
very day, to obtain the kiss which Madame von Brandt had
promised him at his wedding.

"Love might perhaps remove mountains," she said,
"but it cannot give wings to the tongue of a queen. You
have placed your proposals in the hands of her majesty, you
selected this lofty lady to sue for you, and now you must
wait until it pleases her to make your proposals known to
the lady."

"The queen promised to do that to-day. It was necessary for me to make my proposals to her, for the family of

Mademoiselle von Pannewitz demanded that I should obtain the consent of the queen to my marriage, before I could hope for theirs."

" And Laura, have you obtained her consent ? "

" Oh," said the vain count, shrugging his shoulders, " I. am certain of that ; she is poor and entirely dependent on the proud dowager-queen ; I will make her a countess, and insure her freedom ; she will live independently upon her estates, and be surrounded with wealth and luxury ; she will have every thing but a husband."

" Poor Laura ! " said Madame von Brandt, softly. " But you have been with me already too long ; it might be remarked, and give rise to suspicion ; go now, I will work for you, and you must work for yourself. Let no difficulties frighten you."

The count left her slowly, while Madame von Brandt was scarcely able to conceal her impatience to be alone. She looked after him with a contemptuous smile, and murmured to herself: " Vain fool, he deserves to be deceived. But now at last I will see what this precious *etui* contains." She flew to the table and hastily lifted the cover of the case. A cry of astonishment arose to her lips, and her eyes beamed as clearly and brightly as the diamonds resting upon the satin cushion within. " Ah ! this is really a royal present," she whispered, breathlessly, " more than royal, for I am confident King Frederick would never present any woman with such diamonds ; but I deserve them for my wonderful acting. This poor count is convinced that I am the noblest, most unselfish, and most loving of women. How well conceived, how wise it was to decline his first gift ! I knew that he would replace it with somethimg more costly and elegant, hoping to move me to change my resolution. How my heart bounded with delight when he drew forth this great case ! I could scarcely withhold my hands from grasping the costly treasure. I concealed my impatience, and would not open the case in his presence, fearful that he might read my delight in my eyes, and that might have undeceived the poor fool as to my disinterestedness. Truly it was very wise and very diplomatic in me; even Manteuffel could not have acted more discreetly." She bent again over the flashing diamonds, and pressed her burning lips to the cold stones. "Beautiful stones," she whispered tenderly, "your cold kiss animates my whole frame; I love you more than any human being, and when you are upon my neck I will desire no warmer embrace. Welcome, then, beloved, to my house and my bosom. You shall be well cared for, I shall exert myself to provide you with worthy companions; many of your family are lying loosely about in the world, and you doubtless desire the company of your brothers and sisters. I myself share that desire, and will seek to accomplish it by bringing together more and more of your relations; I will invite your cousins, the pearls, and you shall be united. My diamonds and pearls shall have a gayer and more splendid wedding than Count Voss and beautiful Laura von Pannewitz." She laughed aloud in the joy of her heart, then closed the case and locked it carefully in her writing-desk. "And now to the queen-mother," she said; "the train is laid, it is only neccessary to apply the match and await the explosion. I must point out to the queen that this marriage of the lovely Laura with Count Voss is necessary to prevent a difficulty in the royal family, I must—*eh bien! nous verrons.* I hear the voice of the queen; she is taking her promenade, and I must not fail to be present." She took her hat and shawl, and hurried to the **garden.**

10

CHAPTER XII.

THE QUEEN AS A MATRIMONIAL AGENT.

THE queen-mother was taking a walk ·in the garden of Monbijou. She was unusually gay to-day, and her countenance wore an expression of happiness to which it had long been a stranger. And the queen had good reason to be gay, for she seemed on the point of realizing the proud anticipations she had indulged in for so many weary years. Her son was carrying into execution the promises which he had made on his first visit, and in which she had hardly dared to believe. She had already received the first monthly payment of her income as queen-dowager, which her son had largely increased. New appoinments had been made to her court, and it had been placed on a truly royal footing; and yesterday the king had told her that he had already chosen a site for her new palace. Moreover, the homage she received from the entire court, and more especially from the king's favorites, bore evidence to the fact that her influence was considered great, and that much importance was attached to her grace and favor. While Queen Elizabeth was passing her time joylessly at the Castle of Schönhausen, to which she had retired, the entire court was assembling at Monbijou, and hastening to do homage to the queen-mother. Even the young king, who had not yet paid a single visit to his wife at Schönhausen, waited on the queen his mother daily, accompanied by a brilliant suit of cavaliers.*

The queen Sophia Dorothea had good reason to be gay, and to entertain the happiest anticipations in regard to the future. To-day for the first time she could take her morning walk attended by her brilliant suite, for the last appoint-

* Thiébault, ii., page 84.

ments had only been made on the preceding day. When the queen now looked around, and she did so from time to time, she no longer saw the two maids of honor of earlier days walking languidly behind her. Six of the most beautiful ladies, all of the first nobility, had been appointed to the queen's service, and were now engaged in a merry conversation with the four cavaliers in attendance on the queen, who had been selected for this office by the king himself. While conversing with her marshal, Count Rhedern, she could hear the merry laughter of the newly-appointed maid of honor Louise von Schwerin. and the soft, melodious voice of the beautiful Laura von Pannewitz, whose grace and loveliness had even excited the admiration of her husband the king, and for a few weeks thrown him into a state to which he was entirely unaccustomed.*

The queen, as we have said, was unusually gay, for she had just received a new proof of her own importance, and of the influence she was supposed to exert on the young king her son.

Count Rhedern had solicited the assistance of the queen-mother in a very delicate and important matter, and had requested her to advocate his cause with King Frederick. The count. desired to marry, but the permission of the king was still wanting, and would probably be very difficult to obtain, for the count's chosen was unfortunately not of a noble family, but had the misfortune to be the daughter of a Berlin merchant.

" But," said the queen, after this confidential communication, " I do not understand why it is that you wish to marry this girl. I should think the nobility of our kingdom was not so poor in beautiful and marriageable ladies that a Count Rhedern should find it necessary to stoop so low in search of a wife. Look behind you, count, and you will see

* Mémoires de Frederique Wilhelmine de Baireuth, vol. ii., p. 380.

the loveliest ladies, all of whom are of pure and unblemished descent."

"True, your majesty. These ladies are beautiful, of good birth, young and amiable, but one thing is wanting to make them perfect. Mademoiselle Orguelin is neither beautiful nor of good birth, neither young nor amiable, but she has the one thing which those fairies lack, and for the sake of this one thing I am forced to marry her."

"Count, you speak in riddles, and as it seems to me in riddles of doubtful propriety," said the queen, almost angrily. What is this one thing which Mademoiselle Orguelin has, and on account of which you are compelled to marry her?"

"Your majesty, this one thing is money."

"Ah, money," said the queen, smiling; "really, it well becomes a cavalier to marry beneath him for the sake of money!"

"Your majesty, it is because I am mindful of the duties which my rank impose on me, and of the demands which a cavalier of my standing should meet, that I have determined to make this misalliance. Your majesty will be indulgent if I dare open before you the skeleton closet, and unveil the concealed misery of my house. The Counts Rhedern are an old and illustrious race. My ancestors were always rich in virtues but poor in gold. Economy seems to have been the one virtue they never possessed; they were too generous to reject any appeal made to them, and too proud to limit their expenditures to their small income. Outwardly they maintained the pomp suitable to their standing, while they gnawed secretly and unseen at the hard crust of want. Thus from father to son the debts were constantly increasing, and the revenues becoming smaller and smaller. If I do not make an end of this, and sever the Gordian knot like Alexander, instead of attempting the wearisome task of untying it, I shall soon present to the court and nobility the sad speectacle of a Count Rhedern who is compelled to give up his hotel, his equipage, his furniture, and his servants, and live like a beggar."

"Ah, this is really a sad and pressing affair!" exclaimed the queen, sympathizingly, "but are there no heiresses among the nobility, whose fortunes might save you?"

"None, your majesty, who like Mademoiselle Orguelin would bring me a fortune of three millions."

"Three millions! That is a great deal, and I can now perfectly well understand why you are compelled to marry this Orguelin. You have my consent, and I think I can safely promise you that of my son the king. Make your arrangements and fear nothing. I guarantee that the king will not refuse your request."

"After what your majesty has said, I feel assured on this point," exclaimed Count Rhedern, with a sigh.

"How, and you still sigh, count?"

"Your majesty, I need the permission of one other person—the acceptance of the bride. And to this acceptance is appended a condition, the fulfilment of which again depends upon your majesty's kindness.

"Well, truly, this is a strange state of affairs. You speak gravely of your approaching marriage, and as yet are not even engaged. You speak of your bride, but Mademoiselle Orguelin has not yet accepted you, and whether she will or not, you say, depends on me."

"Yes, on your majesty, for this girl, who is as proud of her three millions as if it were the oldest and most illustrious pedigree, consents to be my wife only on the condition that she is acknowledged at court, and has access, as Countess Rhedern, to all court festivities."

"Truly, this is a great pretension!" exclaimed the queen, angrily. "A pedlar's daughter who carries arrogance so far as to wish to appear at the court of the King of Prussia! This can never be, and never could I advocate such an innovation: it is destructive, and only calculated to diminish the prestige of the nobility, and to deprive it of its greatest and best privilege—that privilege which entitles it alone to approach royalty.   It was this view which prevented me from receiving the so-called Count Néal at my court, although my son the king admits him to his presence, and desires that I also should recognize this count of his creation.   But, as a queen and a lady, I can never do this.   There must be a rampart between royalty and the low and common world, and a pure and unblemished nobility alone can form this rampart.   You see, therefore, my poor count, that I cannot accede to this request."

"Have compassion on me, your majesty.   If your majesty will but remember that I am ruined; that I am a beggar if this union does not take place, if I do not marry the three millions of Mademoiselle Orguelin."

"Ah, certainly, I had forgotten that," said the queen, thoughtfully.

"Moreover," continued the count, somewhat encouraged, "this is a different affair altogether, and I do not believe that a principle is here at stake, as was the case with the so-called Count Néal.   A man represents himself and his house, and no power on earth can give him better or nobler blood than already flows in his veins.   But with a woman it is different. She receives her husband's name and his rank; she becomes blood of his blood, and can in no manner affect his nobility. The sons of Countess Rhedern will still be the Counts Rhedern, although the mother is not of noble birth."

"True," said the queen, "this case is different from that of the adventurer Néal.   The rank of her husband would be sufficient to permit us to draw a veil over the obscure birth of this new-made countess."

"And your majesty would then be the noble protectrice of our family," said the count, in a sweet and insinuating tone; "your majesty would not only restore my house to its ancient prestige, but you would retain the three millions of Mademoiselle Orguelin in Prussia; for if I should not be able to fulfil the condition which this lady has made, Mademoiselle Orguelin will marry a rich young Hollander, who is the commercial friend of her father, and has come here for the especial purpose of suing for the hand of his daughter."

"Ah, if that is the case, it becomes almost a duty to give you this girl, in order to prevent her millions from leaving the country," said the queen, smiling. "Be hopeful, count, your wish will be granted, and this little millionnaire who longs to appear at court, shall have her desire. I will speak with my son on this subject to-day; and you may take it for granted that your request will meet with a favorable response."

And the queen, who was proud and happy to have an opportunity of showing the count how great was her influence withher royal son, graciously permitted him to kiss her hand, and listened well pleased to his exclamations of gratitude and devotion.

She then dismissed him with a gracious inclination of her head, requesting him to inform Madame von Brandt, whose laughing voice could be heard at a short distance, that she desired to see her.

While the count hurried off to execute the commission of his royal mistress, the queen walked on slowly and thoughtfully. Now that she was permitted to be a queen, her woman's nature again made itself felt; she found it quite amusing to have a hand in the love affairs which were going on around her, and to act the part of the beneficent fairy in making smooth the path of true love. Two of the first noblemen of her court had to-day solicited her kind offices in their love affairs, and both demanded of her the reëstablishment of the prosperity and splendor of their houses.

The queen, as before said, felt flattered by these demands, and was in her most gracious humor when Madame von Brandt made her appearance. Their conversation was at first on indifferent subjects, but Madame von Brandt knew very well why the queen honored her with this interview, and kept the match in readiness to fire the train with which she had undermined the happiness and love of poor Laura von Pannewitz.

"Do you know," asked the queen suddenly, "that we have a pair of lovers at my court?"

"A pair of lovers!" repeated Madame von Brandt, and so apparent was the alarm and astonishment depicted in her countenance, that the queen was startled.

"Is this, then, so astonishing?" asked the queen, smiling. "You express so much alarm that one might suppose we were living in a convent, where it is a crime to speak of love and marriage. Or were you only a little annoyed at not having heard of this love affair?"

"Your majesty," said Madame von Brandt, "I knew all about this affair, but had no idea that you had any knowledge of it."

"Certainly you must have known it, as Mademoiselle von Pannewitz is your friend, and has very naturally made you her confidant."

"Yes, I have been her confidant in this unhappy and unfortunate love," said Madame von Brandt, with a sigh; "but I can assure your majesty that I have left no arguments, no prayers, and even no threats untried to induce this poor young girl to renounce her sad and unfortunate love."

"Well, you might have saved yourself this trouble," said the queen, smiling; "for this love is not, as you say, a sad and unfortunate one, but a happy one! Count Voss came to me this morning as a suitor for the hand of Mademoiselle von Pannewitz."

"Poor, unhappy Laura!" sighed Madame von Brandt.

"How!" exclaimed the queen, "you still pity her, when I assure you that hers is not an unhappy, but a happy love, reciprocated by Count Voss, who is a suitor for her hand?"

"But what has Count Voss to do with Laura's love?" asked Madame von Brandt, with such well-acted astonishment, that the unsuspecting queen might very well be deceived.

"Truly this is a strange question," exclaimed the queen. "You have just told me that Mademoiselle von Pannewitz entertains an unfortunate attachment for Count Voss; and when I inform you that so far from hers being an unfortunate attachment, it is returned by Count Voss, who is at this moment a suitor for her hand, you ask, with an air of astonishment, 'What has Count Voss to do with Laura's love?'"

"Pardon me, your majesty, I did not say that my poor friend loved Count Voss."

"How!" exclaimed the queen, impatiently; "it is then not Count Voss? Pray, who has inspired her with this unfortunate love? Who is he? Do you know his name?"

"Your majesty, I know him; but I have vowed on the Bible never to mention his name."

"It was very inconsiderate in you to make such a vow," exclaimed the queen, impatiently.

"Your majesty, she who demanded it of me was my friend, and in view of her sorrow and tears I could not refuse a request by the fulfilment of which she would at least have the sad consolation of pouring out her sorrow and anguish into the bosom of a true and discreet friend. But the very friendship I entertain for her makes it my bounden duty to implore your majesty to sustain the offer of Count Voss with all the means at your command, and, if necessary, even to compel my poor Laura to marry him."

10*

"How! You say she loves another, and still desire that I should compel her to marry Count Voss?"

"Your majesty, there is no other means of averting evil from the head of my dear Laura; no other means of preserving two noble hearts from the misery their unfortunate passion might produce. Laura is a noble and virtuous girl, but she loves, and would not long be able to withstand the passionate entreaties of her lover; she would hear no voice but that of him she loves."

"This love is then returned?" asked the queen.

"Oh, your majesty, Laura's maidenly pride would preserve her from an unrequited love."

"And still you call this love an unfortunate one?"

"I call it so because there are insurmountable obstacles in its way; an abyss lies between these lovers, across which they can never clasp hands. In order to be united they would have to precipitate themselves into its depths! Every word of love which these unfortunates utter is a crime—is high treason."

"High treason!" exclaimed the queen, whose eyes sparkled with anger. "Ah, I understand you now. This proud, arrogant girl raises her eyes to a height to which a princess of the blood alone can aspire. In her presumption this girl thinks to play the *rôle* of a La Vallière or a Maintenon. Yes, I now comprehend every thing—her pallor, her sighs, her melancholy, and her blushes, when I told her I expected the king and his court here to-day. Yes, it must be so, Mademoiselle von Pannewitz loves the—"

"Your majesty," exclaimed Madame von Brandt, imploringly, "have the goodness not to mention the name. I should have to deny it, and that would be an offence to your majesty; but if I should acknowledge it, I would be false to my vow and my friendship. In your penetration, your majesty has divined what I hardly dared indicate, and my noble queen now comprehends why an early marriage with Count Voss would be the best means of preserving the happiness of two noble hearts."

"Mademoiselle von Pannewitz will have to make up her mind to become the bride of Count Voss within the hour!" exclaimed the queen, imperiously. "Woe to her if in her arrogance she should refuse to give up a love against. which the whole force of my royal authority shall be brought to bear."

"May your majesty follow the suggestions of your wisdom in all things! I only request that your majesty will graciously conceal from poor Laura that you discovered her unhappy secret through me."

"I promise you that," said the queen, who, forgetful of her royal dignity, in her angry impatience turned around and advanced hastily toward her suite, who, on her approach, remained standing in a respectful attitude.

At this moment a lacquey, dressed in the royal livery, was seen advancing from the palace; he approached the maid of honor then on duty, Mademoiselle von Pannewitz, and whispered a few words in her ear.

Hurrying forward, this young lady informed the queen that her majesty, the reigning queen, had just arrived, and desired to know if her majesty would receive her. The queen did not reply immediately. She looked scornfully at the young girl who stood before her, humbly and submissively, with downcast eyes, and although she did not look up at the queen, she seemed to feel her withering and scornful glances, for she blushed deeply, and an anxious expression was depicted on her countenance.

The queen observed that the blushing Laura was wonderfully beautiful, and in her passionate anger could have trodden her under foot for this presumptuous and treasonable beauty. She felt that it was impossible longer to remain silent, longer to defer the decision. The queen's anger fairly flamed within her, and threatened to break forth; she was now a passionate, reckless woman, nothing more; and she was guided by her passion and the power of her angry pride alone.

"I am going to receive her majesty," said Sophia Dorothea, with trembling lips. "Her majesty has presented herself unceremoniously, and I shall therefore receive her without ceremony. All of you will remain here except Mademoiselle von Pannewitz, who will accompany me."

CHAPTER XIII.

PROPOSAL OF MARRIAGE.

THE greeting of the two queens was over; the inquiries of politeness and etiquette had been exchanged; Sophia had offered Queen Elizabeth her hand and conducted her into the small saloon, where she was in the habit of receiving her family.

The door leading to the conservatory was open, and the two maids of honor could be seen within, standing with Laura, and asking questions in a low tone, to which she replied, almost inaudibly. She felt that the decisive hour of her destiny was at hand, and she prayed that God would strengthen her for the coming trial. She trembled not for herself, but for her lover; for his dear sake she was determined to bear the worst, and bravely meet the shock; she would not yield, she would not die, for he would perish with her; in her heart of hearts, she renewed the oath of eternal love and eternal faith she had taken, and nerved herself for persecution and endurance. Suddenly she heard the harsh voice of the queen calling her name; she looked up, and saw her standing in the door.

"I beg the maids of honor to join the ladies in the garden ; you, mademoiselle, will remain here, I have a few words to say to you."

The ladies bowed and left the conservatory. Laura remained alone ; she stood with folded hands in the middle of the room ; her cheek was deadly pale, her lips trembled, but her eyes were bright, and filled with a heroic and dreamy excitement. As Sophia called her name, Laura laid her hand upon her heart, as if to suppress its stormy beating, and with her head bowed meekly upon her breast she advanced submissively at the call of her mistress. At the door of the second saloon she remained standing, and awaited the further commands of the queen. As Sophia did not speak, Laura raised her eyes and looked timidly at the two queens, who were seated on a sofa opposite the door ; they were both gazing at her, the queen-mother severely, with a proud and derisive smile, but Queen Elizabeth regarded with unutterable pity this poor girl, who reminded her of a broken lily.

"Mademoiselle von Pannewitz," said Sophia, after a long silence, "I have a matter of great importance to communicate to you, and as it admits of no delay, her majesty has allowed me to speak to you in her presence. Listen attentively, and weigh well my words. I have treated you with affectionate kindness ; you have always found in me a friend and mother. I therefore require of you unconditional and silent obedience—an obedience that as your queen and mistress I have a right to demand. You are of a noble but poor family, and your parents cannot support you in the style suitable to your birth. I have adopted you, and will now establish for you a future which will be both splendid and happy. A rich and gallant cavalier has proposed for your hand, and as it is a most fitting and advantageous offer, I have accepted it for you, and promised your consent."

The queen ceased, and looked piercingly at the young girl, who was still leaning against the door, silent and dejected. This dumb submission, this weak resignation revolted the queen; instead of softening her anger, she took this silence for defiance, this humility for stubbornness.

"You are not at all anxious, it appears, to learn the name of your future husband," she said, sharply; "perhaps the rapture of joy binds your tongue, and prevents you from thanking me for my motherly care."

"Pardon, your majesty," said Laura, raising her soft eyes to the harsh and severe countenance of the queen; "it was not joy that closed my lips, but reverence for your majesty; I feel no joy."

"You feel no joy!" cried the queen, with the cruel rage of the lion who seizes his prey and tears it in pieces when there is none to deliver. "Well, then, you will marry without joy, that is decided; and as you are too far above all womanly weakness to appear curious, I shall be obliged to name the happy man whose loving bride you are soon to be, that you make no mistakes, and perhaps, in the tenderness of your heart, render another than your appointed husband happy in your embraces." Laura uttered a low cry of anguish, and her cheeks, colorless until now, were dyed red with shame."

"Have pity, your majesty," murmured Elizabeth Christina, laying her hand softly on the shoulder of the queen; "see how the poor girl suffers."

Sophia shrugged her shoulders contemptuously. "Nonsense! do we not all suffer? have not I suffered? Is there a woman on God's earth whose heart is not half melted away with hot and unavailing tears?"

"It is true," said Elizabeth; "we have but one exclusive privilege—to weep and to endure."

The queen-mother turned again to Laura, who had

checked her tears, but was still standing bowed down, and trembling before her.

" Well," said Sophia, " it still does not suit you to inquire the name of your lover, then I shall name him ; mark well my words : it is Count Voss who has chosen you for his wife, and to him alone you have now to direct your heart and your tenderness."

Laura now raised her eyes and fixed them steadily upon this cruel mistress ; her glance was no longer soft and pleading, but determined. The imperious manner of the queen, instead of intimidating the pale and gentle girl, awakened her to the consciousness of her own dignity. " Majesty," she said, with cool decision, " love is not given by command, it cannot be bestowed arbitrarily."

" By that you mean to affirm that you do not and cannot love Count Voss," said the queen, suppressing her fury with difficulty.

"Yes, your majesty, I do not, I cannot love Count Voss."

" Well, then," cried Sophia, " you will marry him without love, and that speedily ! "

Laura raised her head passionately ; her eye met the queen's, but this time not humbly, not timidly, but decisively. From this moment, Sophia Dorothea was to her no longer a queen, but a cruel, unfeeling woman, who was trampling upon her soul, and binding it in chains.

" Pardon, your majesty, as I have said that I do not love Count Voss, it follows of course that I will never marry him."

The queen sprang from her seat as if bitten by a poisonous reptile. " Not marry him ! " she shrieked ; " but I say you shall marry him ! yes, if you have to be dragged with violence to the altar ! "

" Then at the altar I will say no ! " cried Laura von

Pannewitz, raising her young face, beaming with courage and enthusiasm, toward heaven.

The queen uttered a wild cry and sprang forward; the lion was about to seize upon its prey and tear it to pieces, but Elizabeth Christina laid her hand upon the raised arm of the queen and held her back. "Majesty," she said, "what would you do? you would not force this poor girl to marry against her will; she does not love Count Voss, and she is right to refuse him."

"Ha! you defend her?" cried Sophia, brought to extremities by the resistance of the queen; "you have then no presentiment why she refuses the hand of Count Voss; you do not comprehend that when a poor dependent maid of honor refuses to marry a rich and noble cavalier, it is because she believes she has secured her future in another direction—because in the haughtiness of her vain, infatuated heart, she hopes through her beauty and well-acted coquetry to secure for herself a more brilliant lot. But, mark me! however charming and alluring that prospect may appear outwardly, even in its success there would be found nothing but infamy! She can never have the madness to believe that any priest in this land would dare to bind with the blessings of the Holy Church a love so boldly impudent, so traitorous; she can never hope to set her foot where only the lawful wife of a king can stand—where the sister of the King of England has stood! yes, where she still stands, and from whence she is resolved to repulse this miserable coquette, who hopes to conquer a throne through her shameless allurements."

Laura uttered a piercing scream, and with hands raised to heaven, she exclaimed, "My God! my God! can I bear this and live?"

The queen broke into a wild, mocking laugh. Elizabeth Christina looked, questioningly, at this scene, which she did not comprehend, but which touched her heart by its tragic power.

"It is a hard and cruel accusation which your majesty is bringing against this young girl; let us hope that Laura will know how to defend herself."

"Defend herself! look at her! look how my words have crushed her! how her proud, aspiring soul is checked! Believe me, Elizabeth, she, whom you so generously pity, understands my words better than your majesty; and she knows well of what I accuse her; but you, my daughter, shall know also; you have a right to know."

"Mercy! your majesty, mercy!" cried Laura, falling upon her knees and raising her arms pleadingly toward the queen; "speak no more! humble me no further! Do not betray my secret, which in your mouth becomes a denunciation! Let me remain even on the brink of the precipice, where you have dragged me! that is appalling, but cast me not down! So low and dust-trodden a creature is no longer worthy of the honor of approaching your majesty, I see that, and beg humbly for my dismissal, not as your majesty supposes, to lead an independent and happy, if still a shameful life, but to flee to some corner of the world, where alone and unseen I may weep over the beautiful and innocent dreams of my life, from which your majesty has awakened me so cruelly."

She was wonderfully beautiful in this position; those raised arms, that noble, transparently pale, tear-stained countenance. Sophia Dorothea saw it, and it made her feel more bitter, more cruel.

"Ah, she dares to reproach me," she cried, contemptuously; "she still has a slight consciousness of her shame; she trembles to hear what she did not tremble to do! Listen, my daughter, you that have for her so warm, so pitiful a heart; you, who when I have spoken, will detest and curse

her, as I do, and as you are entitled to do. Believe me, Elizabeth, I know all your suffering, all your sorrow; I know the
secret history of your noble, proud, and silent heart. Ask
that girl there of your grief and misery; ask her the reason
of your lonely, tearful nights; demand of her your broken
happiness, your crushed hopes; demand of her your husband's love, your soul's peace. Mademoiselle von Pannewitz
can return them all to you, as she has taken them from you,
for she is the mistress of the king."

"Mistress of the king!" said Elizabeth, with a painful
cry, while Laura let her hands glide from her face, and looked
at the queen with an astonished expression.

"Yes," repeated Sophia Dorothea, whose hot blood
rushed so violently through her veins, that her voice faltered,
and she was scarcely able to retain an appearance of self-
control; "yes, she is the mistress of the king, and therefore
refuses to marry Count Voss! But patience, patience, she
shall not triumph! and if she dares to love my son, the son
of the queen, King Frederick of Prussia, I will remind her
of Dorris Ritter, who loved him, and was beloved by him!
This Dorris was flogged through the streets of Berlin, and
cast out from amongst men."

Laura uttered so loud and fearful a cry, that even the
queen-mother was startled, and for a moment touched with
pity for the poor, broken-hearted girl who lay at her feet,
like a poor, wounded gazelle in the convulsive agonies of
death.

But she would not give way to this pity; would not betray a weakness, of which she was ashamed. Taking the hand
of the young queen and casting a look of disdain at Laura,
she said, "Come, my daughter, we will no longer bear the
presence of this person, whose tears, I hope, spring from repentance and acknowledgment of her offence; may she obtain our pardon by resolving to-day, of her own free will, and

without forcing us to harsher measures, to accept the hand of Count Voss; come, my daughter."

The two queens stepped to the door. Sophia threw it open violently, and passed immediately into the boudoir, but Elizabeth did not follow her. She looked back at the poor sobbing girl lying upon the floor. The pale and noble face touched her womanly heart.

"Pardon, your majesty, if I do not follow immediately; I should like to say a few words to Mademoiselle von Pannewitz; I think I have a right to do so."

The queen-mother experienced a cruel pleasure at these words.

"Oh, my daughter, even your forbearance is exhausted, and you feel that forgiveness is impossible; yes, speak to her, and let her feel the whole weight of your righteous indignation. Words of reproach and accusation from your gentle lips will have a crushing power. But no delay—you know the king will soon be here."

The queen closed the door. She wished to hear nothing that passed between Elizabeth and Laura; she needed rest, in order to receive the king with composure.

CHAPTER XIV.

THE MISUNDERSTANDING.

THE young queen, the reigning queen, as she was called, was now alone with Laura von Pannewitz. She was for a moment speechless; strange, tempestuous feelings burned in the bosom of this gentle woman; she felt all the torments of rage and jealousy, and the humiliation of unrequited love.

Leaning against the wall, she looked frowningly at Laura,

who was kneeling before her, wringing her hands and weeping piteously. How could a woman weep who could call that happiness her own—to possess which Elizabeth would cheerfully give years of her life? She had at last found the rival for whom she was despised; the destroyer of her happiness; the envied woman loved by Frederick!

As she saw this woman bathed in tears at her feet, an exulting joy for one moment filled her heart. But this violent emotion soon disappeared. Elizabeth was too true and noble a woman to give herself up long to such resentment. She felt, indeed, a melancholy pleasure in knowing that it was not coldness of heart, but love for another, which estranged the king from her; in the midst of her wild grief she was still just; and she acknowledged that this woman, whom the king loved, was more charming and more beautiful than herself.

The love Elizabeth bore her husband was so unselfish, so resigned, so magnanimous, that she felt grateful to the woman who could impart a happiness to the king it had never been in her power to bestow.

With a truly noble expression she approached the maid of honor, who, unconscious of the queen's presence, was still lying on the floor and weeping bitterly.

"Arise, Laura," said Elizabeth, gently. "How can a woman loved by the king be sad, or shed tears?"

Laura's hands fell slowly from her face; she checked her tears and looked piteously at the queen. "God, then, has heard my prayers," she said; "He does not wish your majesty to despise and condemn me; He permits me to clear myself before you!"

"Clear yourself," said Elizabeth. "Oh, believe me, in my eyes you need no justification. You are young, gay, beautiful, and witty; you have the rare art of conversation; you are cheerful and spirited. This has attracted Frederick; for this he loves you; in saying this, all is said. It s impossible for a woman to resist his love. I forgive you freely, fully. I have but one prayer to make you: resolve all your duties into one; fill your soul with one thought, make the king happy! This is all. I have nothing more to say; farewell!"

She was going, but Laura held her back. "Oh, your majesty, she cried imploringly, "listen to me! do not leave me under this cruel misconception—these insulting suppositions. Do not think I am so degenerate, so base, so entirely without womanly feeling, as not to feel myself amenable to the laws of the land and of the Church. Oh, believe me, the husband of my queen is sacred in my eyes! and even if I were so unhappy as to love the king, otherwise than as a true, devoted subject, I would rather die than cast one shadow on the happiness of your majesty. Unhappy and guilty as I am, I am no criminal. His majesty never distinguished me by word or look. I honored him, I revered him, and nothing more."

"Alas!" said the queen, "you are faint-hearted enough to deny him. You have not the courage to be proud of his love; you must, indeed, feel guilty."

"My God! my God!" cried Laura, passionately, "she does not believe me!"

"No, I do not believe you, Laura. I saw how you trembled and paled when the queen charged you with your love to her son, but I did not hear you justify yourself."

"Alas, alas!" murmured Laura, in so low a voice as not to be heard by the queen, "I did not know her majesty was speaking of her son Frederick."

"Deny it no longer," said Elizabeth; "acknowledge his love, for which all women will envy you, and for which I forgive you."

"Do not believe what the queen-mother told you!" cried Laura, passionately; "I have done you no wrong, I have no pardon to ask!"

"And I," said Elizabeth—"I make no reproaches; I do not wail and weep; I do not pass my nights, as the queen said, sleeplessly and in tears; I do not mourn over my lost happiness. I am content; I accept my fate—that is, if the king is happy. But if, perchance, this is not so, if you do not make his happiness your supreme object, then, Laura, I take back the forgiveness so freely given, and I envy you in my heart. Farewell."

"No, no, you must not, you shall not go! believe my words! have some pity, some mercy on me! O Heavenly Father, I have suffered enough without this! It needed not these frightful accusations to punish me for a love which, though unwise, yes mad, is not criminal. As truly as God reigns, it is not the king I love. You turn away, you do not believe me still! Oh, your majesty—" She stopped, her whole frame trembled—she had heard her lover's voice; God had sent him to deliver her, to clear her from these disgraceful suspicions.

The door opened, and Prince Augustus William entered; his countenance was gay and careless, he had come to see the queen-mother, and had been directed to this saloon. Already sportive and jesting words were on his lips, when he perceived this strange scene; Laura on her knees, pale and trembling, before the proud queen, who left her disdainfully in her humble position. It was a sight that the proud lover could not endure. The hot blood of the Hohenzollerns was raging. Forgetful of all consequences, he sprung to her side, raised her from the floor and clasped her to his heart. Then, trembling with anger, he turned to the queen. "What does this mean? Why were you in that position? Why were you weeping, Laura? You on your knees, my Laura! You, who are so innocent, so pure, that the whole world should kneel before and worship you! And you, Madame,"

turning to Elizabeth, "how can you allow this angel to throw
herself in the dust before you ?   How dared you wound her ?
What did you say to bring anguish to her heart and flood
her face with tears ?   Madame, I demand an answer !   I demand it in the name of honor, justice, and love.   Laura is
my bride, it is my right to defend her."

"Now, now," said Laura, clinging wildly to her lover,
" she will no longer believe that I love her husband."

"Your bride ! " said the queen, with a sad sweet smile ;
" how young and trusting you are, my brother, to believe in
the possibility of such a marriage."

"She will be my wife ! " cried he passionately ; " I
swear it, and as truly as there is a God in Heaven I will
keep my oath !   I have courage to dare all dangers, to trample under foot all obstacles.   I do not shun the world's verdict or the king's power.   My love is pure and honest, it
has no need to hide and veil itself; it shall stand out boldly
before God, the king, and the whole world !   Go, then—go,
Madame, and repeat my words to the king ; betray a love
which chance, undoubtedly, revealed to you.   It was, I suppose, the knowledge of this love which led you to wound
and outrage this noble woman."

"It is true," said the queen, gently ; " I did her injustice—I doubted her words, her protestations; but Laura
knows that this offence was involuntary, it all arose from a
mistake of the dowager queen."

"How ! my mother knows of our love ! " said the prince,
in amazement.

"No, she is convinced that Laura von Pannewitz loves
and is beloved by the king; for this reason she heaped reproaches upon her, and commanded her to marry Count
Voss, who has just proposed for her hand."

The prince clasped Laura more firmly.   "Ah, they
would tear you from me; but my arms will hold you and

my breast will shield you, my darling. Do not tremble, do not weep, my Laura; arm in arm we will go to the king. I will lead you before my mother and the court, and tell them that you are my betrothed—that I have sworn to be true to you, and will never break my oath."

"Stop—be silent, for God's sake!" said Elizabeth; "do not let your mother hear you—do not let the king know your sad, perilous secret. If he knows it you are lost."

"Your majesty does not then intend to make known what you have heard," said the prince. "Have you the courage to conceal a secret from your husband?"

"Ah!" said she queen, with a sigh, "my life, thoughts, and feelings are a secret to him; I will but add this new mystery to the rest. Guard this secret, which will in the end bring you pain and sorrow. Be cautious, be prudent. Let the dowager queen still think that it is the king whom Laura loves, she will be less watchful of you. But now listen to my request; never speak to me of this love that chance revealed, and which I will seek to forget from this moment; never remind me of an engagement which in the eyes of the king and your mother would be unpardonable and punishable, and of which it would be my duty to inform them. As long as you are happy—that will be as long as your love is under the protection of secrecy—I will see nothing, know nothing. But when disaster and ruin break over you, then come to me; then you, my brother, shall find in me a fond, sympathizing sister, and you, poor, wretched girl, will find a friend who will open her arms to you, and will weep with you over your lost happiness."

"Oh, my queen!" cried Laura, pressing her hand to her lips; "how noble, how generous you are!"

Elizabeth drew the poor trembling girl to her heart and kissed her pale brow. "For those who weep and suffer there is no difference of rank, a strong bond of human sym-

pathy unites them. I am for you, not the queen, but the
sister who understands and shares your griefs. When you
weary of hidden agony and solitary weeping come to me at
Schönhausen; you will find there no gayeties, no worldly distractions, but a silent shady garden, in which I sometimes
seem to hear God's voice comforting and consoling me.
Here you can weep unnoticed, and find a friend who will
not weary you with questions."

"I thank you, and I will come. Ah! I know I shall
soon need this comfort, my happiness will die an early
death!"

"And may I also come, my noble sister?" said the
prince.

"Yes," said Elizabeth, smiling, "you may also come,
but only when Laura is not with me. I now entreat you,
for your own safety, to close this conversation. Dry your
eyes, Laura, and try to smile, then go to the garden and call
my maids of honor; and you, brother, come with me to the
queen-mother, who is in her boudoir."

"No!" said the prince, fiercely; "I cannot see her now,
I could not control myself. I could not seem quiet and indifferent while I am suffering such tortures."

"My brother," said the queen, "we princes have not
the right to show how we suffer, it is the duty of all in our
station to veil our feelings with a smile. Come, the queen,
who is indignant and angry, will yet receive us with a smile;
and we, who are so sorrowful, will also smile. Come."

"One word more to Laura," said the prince; and leading
the young girl, who was endeavoring to suppress her emotion, to another part of the room, he threw his arm around
her slender form, and pressed a kiss upon her fair cheek.
"Laura, my darling, do you remember your oath?
Will you be true and firm? Will my mother's threats
and commands find you strong and brave? You will not

11

falter? You will not accept the hand of Count Voss? You will let no earthly power tear you from me? They can kill me, Laura, but I cannot be untrue to myself or to you!" Augustus laid his hand upon her beautiful head; the whole history of her pure and holy love was written in the look and smile with which she answered him. "Do you remember that you promised to meet me in the garden?"

"I remember," said she, blushing.

"Laura, in a few days we will be separated. The king wishes to make an excursion incognito—he has ordered me to accompany him; I must obey."

"Oh, my God! they will take you from me! I shall never see you again!"

"We will meet again," said he encouragingly. "But you must grant me the comfort of seeing you once more before my departure, otherwise I shall not have the courage to leave you. The day for our journey is not yet determined; when it is fixed I will come to inform my mother of it in your presence. The evening before I will be in the conservatory and await you; will I wait in vain?"

"No," whispered Laura, "I will be there;" and as if fleeing from her own words, she hurried to the garden.

Prince Augustus William looked for his sister-in-law to accompany her to the queen; but she had withdrawn, she did not wish to witness their parting. Seeing this, the prince was on the point of following Laura to the garden, when the beating of drums was heard from without.

CHAPTER XV.

SOIRÉE OF THE QUEEN DOWAGER.

"THE king is coming," whispered Augustus William, and he stepped towards the cabinet of the queen-mother. But the door was already opened, and the two queens hastened out; they wished to reach the garden saloon and there to welcome the king.

The expression of both ladies was restless and anxious. Sophia Dorothea feared the meeting with her son, who would, perhaps, in the inflamed eyes of his beloved, read the history of the last hours; his kingly anger would be kindled against those who brought tears to her eyes. The queen confessed that she had gone too far—had allowed herself to be mastered by her scorn; she was embarrassed and fearful.

Elizabeth Christina was not restless, but deeply moved; her heart beat quickly at the thought of this meeting with her husband; she had not seen him since the day of the coronation, had not exchanged one single word with him since the ominous interview in her chamber at Rheinsberg. Not once on the day of the coronation had the king addressed her; and only once had he taken her hand. After the coronation he led her in the midst of the assembled court, and said with a clear and earnest voice: "Behold, this is your queen."

These ladies were so excited, so filled with their own thoughts that they hastened through the saloons, scarcely remarking the prince, who had stepped aside to allow them to pass. The queen-mother nodded absently and gave him a passing greeting, then turned again to Elizabeth, who had scarcely patience to conform her movements to the slow and measured steps of the queen-mother; she longed to look upon her husband's face once more.

"If Laura von Pannewitz complains to the king, we will have a terrific scene," said Sophia.

"She will not complain," replied Elizabeth.

"So much the worse, she will play the magnanimous, and I could less readily forgive that, than a complaint."

At this moment the door opened. The king, followed by his attendants and those of the two queens, entered the saloon. The two ladies greeted the king with smooth brows and thoughtless laughter; nothing betrayed the restless anxiety reigning in their hearts. Frederick hastened to meet his mother, and bowing low he greeted her with loving and respectful words, and tenderly kissed her hand; then turning to his wife he bowed stiffly and ceremoniously; he did not extend his hand, did not utter a word. Elizabeth bowed formally in return, and forced back the hot tears which rushed into her eyes.

The face of the queen-mother was again gay and triumphant. The king knew nothing as yet; she must prevent him from speaking with Laura alone. She glanced around at the maid of honor, and saw that the young maiden, calm and unembarrassed, was conversing with the Prince Augustus William; her majesty was more than happy to see her son William entertaining the beautiful Laura. "Ah! now I know how to prevent the king from speaking to her alone," thought she.

Sophia was never so animated, so brilliant; her sparkling wit seemed even to animate the king. There was a laughing contest, a war of words, between them; piquant jests and intellectual *bon mots*, which seemed to the admiring courtiers like fallen stars, were scattered to right and left. The queen would not yield to her son, and indeed sometimes she had the advantage.

Queen Elizabeth stood sad and silent near them, and if by chance the eye of the king fell upon her, she felt that his glance was contemptuous; her pale cheeks grew paler, and it was with great effort she forced her trembling lips to smile.

The queen-mother proposed to her son and Elizabeth to walk in the garden, and then to have a simple dance in the brilliant saloons. The court mourning would not allow a regular ball at this time.

"But why should we seek for flowers in the garden," said the king; "can there be lovelier blossoms than those now blooming on every side?" his eye wandered around the circle of lovely maids of honor, who cast their eyes blushingly to the ground.

Six eyes followed this glance of Frederick with painful interest.

"He scarcely looked at Laura von Pannewitz," said the queen, with a relieved expression.

"He did not once glance toward me," thought Elizabeth, sighing heavily.

"His eye did not rest for more than a moment upon any woman here," thought Pöllnitz; "so it is clear he has no favorite in this circle. I will, therefore, succeed with my beautiful Dorris."

Frederick wished to spare his mother the fatigue of a walk in the garden—she was lame and growing fleshy; he therefore led her to a seat, and bowing silently, he gave his left hand to his wife and placed her by his mother.

Sophia, who watched every movement and every expression of her royal son, observed the cruel silence which he maintained toward his wife, and she felt pity for the poor, pale, neglected queen. Sophia leaned toward the king, who stood hat in hand behind her divan, and whispered:

"I believe, my son, you have not spoken one word to your wife!"

The king's face clouded. "Madame," said he, in a low but firm tone, "Elizabeth Christine is my queen, but not my wife!" and, as if he feared a further explanation, he nodded to the Marquis Algarotti and Duke Chazot to come forward and take part in the conversation.

Suddenly a lady, who had not before been seen in the court circle, approached the two queens. This lady was of a wondrous pallor; she was dressed in black, without flowers or ornament; her deep sunken eyes were filled with feverish fire, and a painful smile played upon her lips, which were tightly pressed together, as if to force back a cry of despair.

No one recognised in this pale, majestic, gentle lady, the "Tourbillon," the joyous, merry, laughing Madame von Morien; no one could have supposed that her fresh and rosy beauty could, in a few months, assume so earnest and sad a character. This was the first time Madame von Morien had appeared at the court of the queen-mother; she was scarcely recovered from a long and dangerous illness. No one knew the nature of her disease, but the witty and ill-natured courtiers exchanged many words of mockery and double meaning on the subject.

It was said Madame von Morien was ill from the neglect of the king. She suffered from a chill, which, strange to say, had attacked the king, and not the beautiful coquette. Her disease was a new and peculiar cold, which did not attack the lungs, but seized upon the heart; the same disease, indeed, which prostrated Dido upon the departure of the cruel Æneas.

The queen-mother received this pale, but still lovely woman, most graciously; gave her the royal hand to kiss, and smiled kindly.

"It is an age since we have seen you, fair baroness; it appears as if you will make yourself invisible, and forget entirely that we rejoice to see you."

"Your royal highness is most gracious to remind me of that," said Madame von Morien, in a low tone; "death had almost made me forget it, and assuredly I had not dared to approach you with this pale, thin face, had not your majesty's flattering command given me courage to do so."

There was something in the low, suffering voice of Madame von Morien which awakened sympathy, and even disarmed the anger of the queen Elizabeth. What bitter tears had she shed, what jealous agony endured, because of this enchanting woman! She saw her now for the first time since the *fête* at Rheinsberg. Looking into this worn and sorrowful face, she forgave her fully. With the instinct of a loving woman, the queen understood the malady of her rival; she felt that Madame von Morien was suffering from unrequited affection, and that despair was gnawing at her heart.

The king had now no glance, no greeting for his "enchanting Leontine;" he continued the conversation with Algarotti and Chazot quietly, and did not consider her profound and reverential salutation as worthy of the slightest notice.

Elizabeth Christine was pitiful; she gave her hand to be kissed, and spoke a few friendly, kindly words, which touched the heart of the beautiful Morien, and brought the tears to her eyes. The king, although standing near, did not appear even to see her

"I have some news to announce to your majesty," he said, turning to the queen-mother. "We are about to make Berlin a temple of science and art, the seat of learning and knowledge. The Muses, should they desire to leave Olympus, shall receive a most hospitable reception. Now listen to the great news. In autumn Voltaire will visit us; and Maupertius, the great scholar, who first discovered the form of the earth, will come, as President of our Academy; and Buncauson, who understands some of the mysteries of God, will also come to Berlin. The celebrated Eulert will soon belong to us."

"This is indeed glorious news," said Sophia; "but I fear that your majesty, when surrounded with so many scholars, philosophers, and historians, will entirely forget the poor ignorant women, and banish them from your learned court."

"That would be to banish happiness, beauty, mirth, and the graces; and no one would expect such barbarism from the son of my noble and exalted mother," said Frederick. "Even the Catholic Church is wise enough to understand that in order to draw men into their nets, the Trinity, Father, Son, and Holy Ghost is not sufficient, they have also called a lovely woman to their assistance, whose beauty and pure mysterious maidenhood is the finest, most piquant and intoxicating perfume of their gaudy religion. And what would the great painters have been without women—without their lovely, their bewitching sweethearts, whom they changed into holy maidens? From luxurious women were designed the modest, shrinking Magdalens, before whose mysterious charms the wise children of men bow the knee in adoration. Ah, how many Madonnas has Raphael painted from his Fornarina! and Correggio had the art to change his bewitching wife into a holy saint. I must confess, however, we owe Correggio but small thanks; I should have been more grateful had he painted us a glowing woman, radiant with beauty, grace, and love. I, for my part, have a true disgust for weeping, sighing Magdalens, who, when wearied with earthly loves and passions, turn half way to heaven, and swear to God the same oaths they have a thousand times sworn to men and a thousand times broken. Now, if I were in God's place, I would not accept these wavering saints. For my part I hate these pale, tearful, sighing, self-destroying beauties, and the farcical exhibition of their sufferings would never soften my heart."

While the king was speaking his eye turned for the first time toward Madame von Morien, and his glance rested long, with a cold and piercing expression, upon her. She had heard every word he had spoken, and every word was like a cold poisoned dagger in her heart; she felt, although her eyes were cast down, that his stern look rested upon her; she was conscious of this crushing glance, although she saw it not; she had the power not to cry out, not to burst into passionate tears, but to reply quietly to the queen, who in fact questioned her, only with the good-humored intention of drowning the hard and cruel words of the king.

The queen wished to lead the conversation from the dangerous topic of religion and give it another direction. "My son," she said, "you have forgotten to mention another great surprise you have prepared for us. You say nothing of the German and French journals which you have presented to our good city of Berlin; but I assure you I await with true impatience the day on which these journals appear, and I am profoundly interested in these new and charming lectures which make of politics an amusing theme, and give us all the small events of the day."

"Let us hope," said Frederick, "that these journals will also tell us in the future of great events." Then assuming a gay tone he said: "But your majesty forgets that you promised the ladies a dance, and see how impatiently the little princesses look toward us; my sister Amelia is trying to pierce me with her scornful glances, because I have forced her to sit in her arm-chair like a maid of honor, for such a weary time, when she longs to float about like a frolicksome zephyr. To put a stop to her reproaches I will ask her to give me the first dance." The king took his sister's hand and led her into the dancing saloon.

11*

The queens and court followed. "Now without doubt he will seek an opportunity to speak to Laura von Pannewitz," thought the queen-mother; "I must take measures to prevent it." She called Prince Augustus William to her side. "My son," said she, "I have a favor to ask of you."

"Oh, your majesty has only to command."

"I know that you are a good son, willing to serve your mother. Listen; I have important reasons for wishing that the king should not converse to-night, at least not alone, with Laura von Pannewitz; I will explain my reasons to you another time. I beg you, therefore, to pay court to Laura, and not to leave her side should the king draw near. You will appear not to see his angry glances, but without embarrassment join in the conversation, and not turn away from Laura until the king has taken leave. Will you do this for me, my son?"

"I will fulfil your royal commands most willingly," said the prince, "only it will be said that I am making love to Laura von Pannewitz."

"Well, let them say so, Laura is young and lovely, and does credit to your taste. Let the court say what it will, we will not make ourselves unhappy. But hasten, my son, hasten; it appears to me the king is even now approaching Laura."

The prince bowed to his mother, and with joy in his heart he placed himself by the side of his beloved.

The queen-mother, entirely at ease, took her seat at the card-table with her daughter-in-law and their cavaliers, while the king amused himself in the ball-room, and danced a tour with almost every lady. He did not dance with Leontine; not once did his eye meet hers, though her glances followed him everywhere with a tender, beseeching, melancholy expression.

"So sad," whispered Madame von Brandt, who, glowing

with beauty and merriment, having just danced with the king, now took a seat by her side.

Madame von Morien with a sigh held out her small hand. "Dear friend," said she, in a low voice, "you were right. I should not have come here; I thought myself stronger than I am; I thought my mourning would touch him, and awaken at least his pity."

"Pity!" laughed Madame von Brandt; "men never have pity for women: they worship or despise them; they place us on an altar or cast us in the dust to be trodden under foot. We must take care, dear Leontine, to build the altar on which they place us so high, that their arms cannot reach us to cast us down."

"You are right; I should have been more prudent, wiser, colder. But what would you? I loved him, and believed in his heart."

"You believed in the heart of a man! Alas! what woman can boast that she ever closed that abyss and always retained the key?"

"Yes, the heart of a man is an abyss," said Madame von Morien; "in the beginning it is covered with flowers, and we believe we are resting in Paradise; but the blossoms wither, and will no longer support us; we fall headlong into the abyss with wounded hearts, to suffer and to die."

Madame von Brandt laid her hand, glittering with jewels, upon the shoulder of her friend, and looked derisively into the poor pale face. "Dear Morien," said she, "we cannot justly cast all the blame upon the men, when the day comes in which they make themselves free from the bonds of love. The fault is often the woman's. We misuse our power, or do not properly use it. It is not enough to love and to be loved. With love we must also possess the policy of love. This policy is necessary. The women who do not know how to govern the hearts which love them, will soon lose their power. So was it with you, my dear friend; in your love you were too much the woman, too little the politician and diplomatist; and instead of wisely making yourself adored, by your coldness and reserve you yielded too much to your feelings, and have fallen into that abyss in which, poor Leontine, you have for the moment lost your health and strength. But that must not remain the case; you shall rise from this abyss, proud, triumphant, and happy. I offer you my hand; I will sustain you: while you sigh I will think for you; while you weep I will see for you."

Madame von Morien shook her head sadly. "You will only see that he never looks at me—that I am utterly forgotten."

"But when I see that, I will shut my eyes that I may not see it; and when you see it, you must laugh gayly and look the more triumphant. Dear friend, what has love made of you? Where is your judgment and your coquetry? My God! you are a young maiden again, and sigh like a child for your first love. However tender we may be, we must not sacrifice all individuality; besides, being a woman you must still be a coquette, and in a corner of your most tender and yielding heart you must ever conceal the tigress, who watches and has her claws ready to tear in pieces those whom you love, if they ever seek to escape from you. Cease, then, to be the neglected, tear-stained Magdalen, and be again the revengeful, cruel tigress. You have, besides, outside of your love, a glittering aim—a member of the Female Order of Virtue. To wear the cross of modesty upon your chaste breast, what an exalted goal! And you will reach it. I bring you the surest evidence of it; I bring you, as you wished, a letter from the empress, written with her own hand. You see all your conditions are fulfilled. The empress writes to you and assures you of her favor; she assures you that the Order of Virtue will soon be established. The king has not separated from his wife, and for this reason you receive a letter from the empress. Now help to bring about the marriage of the Prince Augustus William with the Princess of Brunswick, and you will be an honored member of the Austrian Order of Virtue. Here, take at once this letter of the empress."

Madame von Brandt put her hand in her pocket to get the letter, but turned pale, and said, breathlesly: "My God! this letter is not in my pocket, and yet I know positively that I placed it there. A short time before I joined you I put my hand in my pocket, and distinctly felt the imperial seal. The letter was there, I know it. What has become of it? Who has taken it away from me? But no, it is not possible, it cannot be lost! I must have it; it must still be in my pocket."

Trembling with anxiety, with breathless haste Madame von Brandt emptied her pocket, hoping that the luckless letter might be sticking to her gold-embroidered handkerchief, or fastened in the folds of her fan. She did not remember that her anxiety might be observed; and truly no one noticed her, all were occupied with their own pleasures. All around her was movement, life, and merry-making; who would observe her? She searched again in vain, shook her handkerchief, unfolded the large fan; the letter could not be found. An indescribable anxiety overpowered her; had she lost the letter? had it been stolen from her? Suddenly she remembered that while engaged a short time before with Pöllnitz, she had drawn out her fan; perhaps at the same time the letter had fallen upon the floor, and Pöllnitz might have found it, and might now be looking for Madame von Morien in order to restore it. She searched in every direction for Pöllnitz.

Madame von Morien had not remarked the anguish of her friend, or had forgotten it. She was again lost in dreams; her eyes fastened on the face of the young king, she envied every lady whose hand he touched in the dance, to whom he

addressed a friendly word, or gave a gracious smile. " I see
him no more," said she sadly.

" Who ? " said Madame von Brandt, once more searching
her pocket.

" The king," Morien answered, surprised at the question ;
" he must have left the saloon, I saw him a few moments
since in conversation with Pöllnitz."

" With Pöllnitz," said she eagerly, and she searched
again in every direction for him.

Suddenly Madame von Morien uttered a low cry, and a
rosy blush overspread her fair pale face; she had seen the
king, their eyes had met; the sharp, observant glance of
the king was steadily and sternly fixed upon her.

The king stood in a window corner, half hidden by the
long, heavy silk curtains, and gazed ever steadily at the two
ladies.

" I see the king," murmured Madame von Morien.

" And I see Pöllnitz standing near him," said Madame von
Brandt, whose eyes had followed the direction of her friend's.
She thrust her handkerchief into her pocket and opened her
fan in order to hide her reddened face behind it ; the king's
piercing look filled her with alarm. " Let us walk through
the saloons, dear Morien," said she, rising up, " the heat
chokes me, and I would gladly search a little for the letter;
perhaps it may yet be found."

" What letter ? " said Madame von Morien, indifferently.
Her friend stared at her and said :

" My God! you have not heard one word I have said to
you!"

" Oh, yes, that you had a letter to give me from the Empress of Austria."

" Well, and this letter I have lost here in these saloons."

" Some one will find it; and as it is addressed to me, will
immediately restore it."

"Dear Morien, I pray you in God's name do not seem so quiet and indifferent. This is a most important affair. If I did not leave this letter in my room, and have really lost it, we are in danger of being suspected; in fact, in the eyes of the king we will be considered as spies of Austria."

At the name of the king Madame von Morien was attentive and sympathetic.

"But no one can read this letter. Was it sealed?"

"Yes, it was sealed; but, look you, it was sealed with the private seal of the empress, and her name stands around the Austrian arms. Without opening the letter it will be known that it is from the Empress of Austria, and will awaken suspicion. Hear me further; this letter was enveloped in a paper which had no address, but contained some words which will compromise us both if it is known that this letter was addressed to me."

"What was written in this paper?" said Madame von Morien, still looking toward the king, who still stood in the window niche, and kept his eyes fixed upon the two ladies.

"The paper contained only the following words: 'Have the goodness to deliver this letter; you see the empress keeps her word, we must do the same and forget not our promises. A happy marriage is well pleasing in the sight of God and man; the married woman is adorned, the man crowned with virtue.'"

"And this letter was signed?"

"No, it was not signed; but if it falls into the hands of the king, he will know from whom it comes; he is acquainted with the handwriting of Manteuffel."

"Come! come! let us look to it!" said Madame von Morien, now full of anxiety; "we must find this unfortunate paper; come!"

She took the arm of her friend and walked slowly through

the saloons, searching everywhere upon the inlaid floor for something white.

"You are right," said the king, coming from the window and following the ladies with his eyes; "you are right. They are both searching anxiously, and it was surely Madame von Brandt to whom the outer covering of this letter was directed. Let them seek; they will find as little as the eleven thousand virgins found. But now listen, baron, to what I say to you. This whole affair remains a secret known to no one. Listen well, baron; known *to no one!* You must forget that you found this letter and gave it to me, or you will believe it to be a dream and nothing more."

"Yes, your majesty," said Pöllnitz, smiling; "a dream, such as Eckert dreamed, when he supposed the house in Jäger Street to be his, and awaked and found it to belong to your highness!"

"You are a fool!" said the king, smiling; he nodded to Pöllnitz and joined the two queens, who had now finished their game of cards and returned to the saloon.

The queen-mother advanced to meet her son, and extended her hand to him; she wished now to carry out her purpose and fulfil the promise given to Duke Rhedern. She did not doubt that the king, who received her with so much reverence and affection, would grant her request, and the court would be again witness to the great influence, and indeed the unbounded power which she had over her son. She stood with the king directly under the chandelier, in the middle of the saloon; near them stood the reigning queen and the princes and princesses of the royal house. It was an interesting picture. It was curious to observe this group, illuminated by a sharp light, the faces so alike and yet so different in expression; blossoms from one stem, and yet so unlike in greatness, form, and feature. The courtiers drew near, and in respectful silence regarded the royal family, who, bathed in a sea of light, were in the midst of them but not of them.

"My son," said the queen, in a clear, silvery voice, "I have a request to make of you." The king kissed his mother's hand.

"Madame, you well know you have no need of entreaty; you have only to command." Sophia smiled proudly.

"I thank your majesty for this assurance! Listen, then, my chamberlain, Duke Rhedern, wishes to marry. I have promised him to obtain your consent."

"If my royal mother is pleased with the choice of her chamberlain, I am, of course, also content; always provided that the chosen bride of the duke belongs to a noble family. What is the rank of the bride?"

The queen looked embarrassed, and smiling, said: "She has no rank, your majesty."

The king's brow darkened. "She was not born, then, to be a duchess. Your chamberlain would do better to be silent over this folly, than to force a refusal from me. I hate misalliances, and will not suffer them at my court."

These loudly spoken and harsh words produced different impressions upon the family circle of the king; some were cast down, others joyful; some cheeks grew pale, and others red. Sophia blushed from pleasure; she was now convinced that the king would not seek a divorce from his wife, in order to form a morganatic marriage with Laura von Pannewitz; and the queen-mother was of too noble and virtuous a nature herself to believe in the possibility of a mistress at the court of ·Prussia. The love of the king for the lovely Laura appeared now nothing more than a poetical idyl, which would soon pass away—nothing more! The words of the king made a painful impression upon Angustus William; his brow clouded, his features assumed a painful, but threatening expression; he was in the act of speaking, and opposing in the name of

humanity and love those cruel words of the king, as Elizabeth Christina, who stood near him and observed him with
tender sympathy, whispered lightly:

"Be silent, my brother; be considerate."

The prince breathed heavily, and his glance turned for
comfort toward the maids of honor. Laura greeted him with
her eyes, and then blushed deeply over her own presumption. Strengthened by this tender glance from his beautiful
bride, Augustus was able to assume a calm and indifferent
mien.

In the mean time the queen-mother was not silenced
by the words of the king. Her pride rebelled against this
prompt denial in the face of her family and the court. Besides, she had given her royal word to the count, and it must
be redeemed. She urged, therefore, her request with friendly
earnestness, but the king was immovable. Sophia, angry at
the opposition to her will, was even the more resolved to
carry out her purpose. She had a few reserved troops, and
she decided to bring them now into the field.

"Your majesty should, without doubt, protect your nobles from unworthy alliances; but there are exceptional cases,
where the interest of the nobility would be promoted by allowing such a union." Sophia Dorothea drew nearer to her
son, and whispered lightly: "Count Rhedern is ruined, and
must go to the ground if you forbid this marriage."

The king was now attentive and sympathetic. "Is the
lady very rich?"

"Immensely rich, sire. She will bring the duke a million dollars; she is daughter of the rich silk merchant Orguelin."

"Ah, Orguelin is a brave man, and has brought much
gold into Prussia by his fabrics," said the king, who was evidently becoming more yielding.

"It would be a great pity if this gold should be lost to
Prussia," said the queen.

" What do you mean, Madame ? "

" This Mademoiselle Orguelin, thanks to her riches, has many lovers, and at this time a young merchant from Holland seeks her hand ; he has the consent of her father, and will also obtain hers, unless the count knows how to undermine him," said the queen, thus springing her last mine.

" This must not be," said the king ; " this Orguelin shall not marry the rich Hollander ! Those millions of crowns shall not leave Prussia ! "

" But your majesty cannot prevent this girl from marrying the man of her choice, and you cannot forbid her father to give her a portion of his fortune."

The king was silent a moment, and appeared to consider. He then said to his mother : " Madame you are an eloquent advocate for your client, and no man can withstand you. I give way, therefore ; Count Rhedern has my consent to marry the Orguelin."

" But even *that* is not sufficient," said the queen ; " there is yet another condition, without the fulfilling of which this proud millionnaire refuses to give her hand to the duke."

" Ah, look you, the little bourgeoise makes conditions before she will wed a count."

" Yes, sire, she will become the wife of the count only with the count's assurance that she will be presented at court, and be received according to her new rank."

" Truly," said the king, with ironical laughter, " this little millionnaire thinks it an important point to appear at my court."

" It appears so, sire ; it seems that this is a greater glory than to possess a count for a husband."

The king looked thoughtfully before him, then raised his eyes to his mother with a mocking smile. " Mother, you know I can refuse you nothing ; and as you wish it, Mademoiselle Orguelin, when she is married, shall be received at my court as a newly *baked countess*. But petition for petition, favor for favor. I promise you to receive this new baked countess if you will promise me to receive the Count Néal at your court ? "

" Count Néal," said the queen, " your majesty knows—"

" I know," said the king, bowing, " I know that Count Néal is of as good family as the new Countess of Rhedern ; that he possesses many millions which I have secured to Prussia by granting him his title. So we understand each other. The new baked countess will be as well received at my court as Count Néal will at yours."

He gave the queen his hand, she laid hers unwillingly within it, and whispered : " Ah, my son, you have cruelly overreached me."

" Madame, we secure in this way three millions for Prussia, and they weigh more than a few countly ancestors. The Prussia of the future will triumph in battle through her nobles ; but she will become greater, more powerful, through the industry of her people than by victory on the battle-field."

CHAPTER XVI.

UNDER THE LINDENS.

LINDEN STREET, of Berlin, which is now the most brilliant and most beautiful thoroughfare of that great city, was, in the year 1740, a wild and desolate region.

Frederick the First loved pomp and splendor. His wife, when told upon her death-bed how much the king would mourn for her, said, smiling : " He will occupy himself in arranging a superb funeral procession ; and if this ceremony is very brilliant, he will be comforted."

Frederick the First planted the trees fro.n which this street takes its name, to render the drive to the palace of Charlottenburg more agreeable to the queen, and to conceal as much as possible the desolate appearance of the surroundings ; for all this suburb lying between the arsenal and the zoological garden, was at that time a desolate and barren waste. The entire region, extending from the new gate to the far-distant Behren Street, was an immense mass of sand, whose drear appearance had often offended Frederick while he was still the prince royal. Nothing was to be seen, where now appear majestic palaces and monuments, the opera house and the catholic church, but sand and heaps of rubbish. Frederick William the First had done much to beautify this poor deserted quarter, and to render it more fitting its near neighborhood to the palaces, which were on the other side of the fortifications ; but the people of Berlin had aided the king very little in this effort. None were willing to banish themselves to this desolate and remote portion of the city, and the few stately and palatial buildings which were erected there were built by the special order of the king, and at his expense. Some wealthy men of rank had also put up a few large buildings, to please the king, but they did not reside in them, and the houses themselves seemed almost out of place. One of these large and stately houses had not been built by a Count Dohna, or a Baron von Pleffen, or any other nobleman, but by the most honorable and renowned court tailor Pricker ; and for the last few days this house had rejoiced in a new and glittering sign, on which appeared in large gilt letters, "Court Tailor to her majesty the dowager queen, and to her majesty the reigning queen." But this house, with its imposing inscrip tion, was also surrounded by dirty, miserable cabins. In its immediate neighborhood was the small house which has already been described as the dwelling of poor Anna Schommer.

A deep and unbroken silence reigned in this part of
Berlin, and the equipages of the royal family and nobility
were rarely seen there, except when the king gave an entertainment at Charlottenburg.

But to-day a royal carriage was driven rapidly from the
palace through this desolate region, and toward the Linden
Avenue. Here it stopped, and four gentlemen alighted.
They were the king; the royal architect, Major Knobelsdorf;
the grand chamberlain, Von Pöllnitz; and Jordan, the head
of police and guardian of the poor.

The king stood at the beginning of the Linden Avenue
and looked earnestly and thoughtfully at the large, desolate
surface spread out before him; his clear bright glance flew
like lightning here and there.

"You must transform this place for me, Knobelsdorf;
you must show yourself a very Hercules. You have the
ability, and I will furnish the money. Here we will erect a
monument to ourselves, and make a glorious something of
the nothing of this desert. We will build palaces and temples of art and of religion. Berlin is at present without
every thing which would make it a tempting resort for the
Muses. It is your affair, Knobelsdorf, to prepare a suitable
reception for them."

"But the Muses are willing to come without that," said
Pöllnitz, with his most graceful bow, "for they would discover here the young god Apollo, who, without doubt, found
it too tiresome in heaven, and has condescended to become
an earthly king."

The king shrugged his shoulders. "Pöllnitz," he said,
"you are just fitted to write a book of instructions for
chamberlains and court circles; a book which would teach
them the most honied phrases and the most graceful flat-
teries. Why do you not compose such a work?"

"It is absolutely necessary, your majesty, in order to

write a book to have a quiet study in your own house, where you can arrange every thing according to your own ideas of comfort and convenience. As I do not at present possess a house, I cannot write this book."

The king laughed and said : " Well, perhaps Knobelsdorf can spare a small spot here, on which to erect your Tusculum. But we must first build the palace of the queen-mother, and a few other temples and halls. Do you not think, Jordan, that this is a most suitable place on which to realize all those beautiful ideals of which we used to dream at Rheinsberg? Could we not erect our Acropolis here, and our temples to Jupiter and Minerva ? "

" In order to convince the world that it is correct in its supposition," said Jordan, smiling, "that your majesty is not a Christian, but a heathen, who places more faith in the religion of the old Greeks than in that of the new Church fathers."

" Do they say that ? Well, they are not entirely wrong if they believe that I have no great admiration for popery and the Church. This Church was not built by Christ, but by a crafty priesthood. Knobelsdorf, on this spot must stand the temple of which I have so often dreamed. There is space to accomplish all that fancy could suggest or talent execute."

" Then the palace of the dowager queen must not be placed here? " asked Knobelsdorf.

" No, not here; this place has another destination, of which I will speak further to you this evening, and learn if my plan has your approval. I dare say my most quarrelsome Jordan will make some objections. *Eh bien, nous verrons.* We will proceed and seek a situation for the palace of the queen."

" If your majesty will permit me," said Pöllnitz, while the king with his three companions passed slowly down the Linden Avenue, " I will take the liberty of pointing out to you a

spot, which appears most suitable to me for this palace. It
is at the end of the avenue, and at the entrance to the park;
it is a most beautiful site, and there would be sufficient room
to extend the buildings at will."

"Show us the place," said the king, walking forward.

"This is it," said Pöllnitz, as they reached the end of the
avenue.

"It is true," said the king, "here is space enough to
erect a palace. What you do think, Knoblesdorf, will this
place answer?"

"We must begin by removing all those small houses,
your majesty; that would, of course, necessitate their pur
chase, for which we must obtain the consent of the possessors,
who would, many of them, be left shelterless by this sudder.
sale."

"Shelterless!" said the king; "since Jordan has become
the father of the poor, none are shelterless," as he glanced
toward his much-loved friend. "This spot seems most suitable to me. The palace might stand on this side; on that a
handsome public building, perhaps the library, and uniting
the two a lofty arch in the Grecian style. We will convert
that wood into a beautiful park, with shady avenues, tasteful
parterres, marble statues, glittering lakes, and murmuring
streams."

"Only a Frederick would dream it possible to convert
this desolate spot into such a fairy land," said Jordan, smiling.
"For my part, I see nothing here but sand, and there a wood
of miserable stunted trees."

The king smiled. "Blessed are they who believe without having seen," he said. "Well, Knobelsdorf, is there
room here to carry out our extensive plans?"

"Certainly; and if your majesty will furnish me with the
requisite funds, the work can be begun without delay."

"What amount will be required?"

" If it is all executed as your majesty proposes, at least a million."

" Very well, a million is not too much to prepare a pleasure for the queen-mother."

" But," said Pöllnitz, " will not your majesty make those poor people acquainted with their fate, and console them by a gracious word for being compelled to leave their homes? It has only been a short time since I was driven by the rain to take shelter in one of those houses, and it made me most melancholy, for I have never seen such want and misery. There were starving children, a woman dying of grief, and a drunken man. Truly as I saw this scene I longed to be a king for a few moments, that I might send a ray of happiness to brighten this gloomy house, and dry the tears of these wretched people."

" It must have been a most terrible sight if even Pöllnitz was distressed by it," cried the king, whose noble countenance was overshadowed with sorrow. " Come, Jordan, we will visit this house, and you shall assist in alleviating the misery of its inhabitants. You, Knobelsdorf, can occupy yourself in making a drawing of this place. Lead the way, Pöllnitz."

" My desire at last attained," thought Pöllnitz, as he led the king across the common. " It has been most difficult to bring the king here, but I am confident my plan will succeed. Dorris Ritter doubtless expects us; she will have considered my words, and yielding to her natural womanly coquetry, she will have followed my counsel, and have made use of the clothing I sent her yesterday."

They now stood before the wretched house which Pöllnitz had indicated.

" This house has truly a most gloomy appearance," said the king.

12

"Many sad tears have been shed here," said Pöllnitz, with an appearance of deep sympathy.

The door of the shop was merely closed; the king pushed it open, and entered with his two companions. No one came forward to meet them, silence reigned in the deserted room.

"Permit me, your majesty, to go into that room and call the woman; she probably did not hear us enter."

"No, I will go myself," said the king; "it is well that I should occasionally seek out poverty in its most wretched hiding-place, that I may learn to understand its miseries and temptations."

"Ah! my king," said Jordan, deeply touched, "from to-day your people will no longer call you their king, but their father."

The king stepped quickly to the door which Pöllnitz had pointed out; the two gentlemen followed, and remained standing behind him, glancing curiously over his shoulder.

The king crossed the threshold, and then stood motionless, gazing into the room. "Is it possible to live in such a den?" he murmured.

"Yes, it is possible," replied a low, scornful voice; "I live here, with misery for my companion."

The king was startled by this voice, and turned toward that side of the room from which it proceeded; only then seeing the woman who sat in the farthest corner. She remained motionless, her hands folded on her lap; her face was deadly pale, but of a singularly beautiful oval; the hair encircling her head in heavy braids, was of a light, shining blond, and had almost the appearance of a halo surrounding her clear, pale face, which seemed illumined by her wonderful eyes.

"She has not made use of the things which I sent," thought Pöllnitz; "but I see she understands her own advan tages. She is really beautiful; she looks likes a marble statue of the Virgin Mary in some poor village church."

The king still stood gazing, with an earnest and thought-ful expression, at this woman, who looked fixedly at him, as if she sought to read his thoughts. But he remained quiet, and apparently unmoved. Did the king recognize this woman? did he hear again the dying melodies of his early youth? was he listening to their sweet, but melancholy tones? Neither Pöllnitz nor Dorris Ritter could discover this in his cold, proud face.

Jordon broke this silence by saying gently, "Stand up, my good woman, it is the king who is before you."

She rose slowly from her seat, but her countenance did not betray the least astonishment or pleasure.

"The king," she said; "what does the king desire in this den of poverty and misery?"

"To alleviate both poverty and misery if they are unde-served," said the king softly.

She approached him quickly, and made a movement as if she would offer him her hand. "My wretchedness is un-deserved," she said, "but not even a king can alleviate it."

"Let me, at least, attempt to do so. In what can I assist you?"

She shook her head sadly. "If King Frederick, the son of Frederick William the First, does not know, then I do not."

"You are poor, perhaps in want?"

"I do not know—it is possible," she said absently; "how can I among so many pains and torments distinguish be-tween despair and anguish, and want and privation."

"You have children?"

"Yes," she said, shuddering, "I have children, and they suffer from hunger; that I know, for they often pray to me for bread, when I have none to give them."

" Why does not their father take care of them; perhaps he is not living? "

" He lives, but not for us. He is wiser than I, and forgets his grief in drink, while I nourish the gnawing viper at my heart."

" You have, then, nothing to ask of me?" said the king, becoming indignant.

She gazed at him again long and searchingly, with her great, piercing eyes. " No," she said harshly, " I have nothing to ask."

At this moment the door was thrown open, and the two children, Karl and Anna, ran in, calling for their mother; but they became silent on perceiving the strangers, and crept shyly to her side. Dorris Ritter was strangely moved by the appearance of her children; her countenance, which had borne so hard an expression, became mild and gentle. She grasped the hands of the two children, and with them approached the king.

" Yes, your majesty, I have a petition to make. I implore your pity for my children. They are pure and innocent as God's angels; let not the shame and misery of their parents fall upon their heads. King Frederick, have pity on my children!"

And overcome by her emotions and her anguish, this unhappy woman sank with her children at the feet of the king. The king regarded her thoughtfully, then turned to Jordan.

" Jordan," said he, " to you I intrust the care of these children."

The wretched woman started to her feet, and pressed her children to her arms with an expression as terrified and full of agony as that of the noble and touching statue of the Greek Niobe.

" Ah! you would tear my children from me! No, no, I ask nothing; we need no mercy, no assistance; we will suffer together; do not separate us. They would cease to love me; they would learn to despise me, their mother, who only lives in their presence; who, in the midst of all her sorrow and grief, thanks God daily upon her bended knees that he gave her these children, who alone have saved her from despair and death."

"You have uttered very wild and godless words," said the king. "You should pray to God to make your heart soft and humble. To be poor, to suffer from hunger, to have a drunken husband, are great misfortunes, but they can be borne if you have a pure conscience. Your children shall not be parted from you. They shall be clothed and taught, and I will also see what can be done for you. And now farewell."

And the king, bowing slightly, turned toward the door, and in doing so placed a few pieces of gold on the table. Dorris had watched every movement; she started wildly forward and seized the gold, which she handed to the king.

"Your majesty," she said, with flashing eyes, "I only implored mercy for my children; I did not beg for myself. My sufferings cannot be wiped out with a few pieces of gold."

The countenance of the king assumed a most severe expression, and he threw an annihilating glance on this bold woman, who dared to oppose him.

"I did not give the gold to you, but to your children," he said; "you must not rob them." He then continued more gently: "If you should ever need and desire assistance, then turn to me; I will remember your poverty, not your pride. Tell me your name, therefore, that I may not forget."

The poor, pale woman glanced searchingly at him. "My name," she said thoughtfully, as if to herself, "King Frederick wishes to know my name. I am called—I am called Anna Schommer."

And as she replied, she placed her hand upon the head of her little daughter, as if she needed a support. Thus she

stood trembling, but still upright, with head erect, while the
king and his suite turned toward the door.   Her son, who
had kept his eyes upon the king, now followed him and
lightly touched his mantle.

His mother saw it, and raising her arm threateningly,
while with the other she still supported herself by leaning on
her child, she cried: " Do not touch him, my son.   Kings
are sacred."

Frederick, already standing on the threshold, turned once
more; his great, luminous eyes rested inquiringly on this
pale, threatening figure.   An indescribably sad smile played
upon his features, but he spoke no word ; and slowly turning,
he passed through the door, and hurried silently from the
shop.

Dorris Ritter uttered a low cry when she no longer saw
him ; her hands slid powerless from the head of her child,
and hung heavily at her side.   The child, thus set at liberty,
hurried out to gaze at the king and his escort.

The poor woman was all alone—alone with her grief and
painful memories.   She stood for a long time motionless and
silent, as if unconscious, then a dull, heavy groan escaped
from her breast, and she fell as if struck by lightning.   " He
did not even know me," she cried.   " For him I suffer pain and
misery, and he passes by, and throws me the crumbs of
benevolence which fall from his bountiful table."   For many
minutes she lay thus broken and trembling ; then, suddenly
excited by pride and revenge, she arose, with a wild gleam
in her eyes.   She raised her hand as if calling upon God to
witness her words, and said solemnly, " He did not recognize
me to-day, but a day will come on which he shall recognize
me—the day on which I avenge my wretched and tormented
life !   He is a royal king and I a poor woman, but the sting
of a venemous insect suffices to destroy even a king.   Revenge
I will have ; revenge for my poisoned existence."

CHAPTER XVII.

THE POLITICIAN AND THE FRENCH TAILOR.

WITHOUT, the scene had changed in the meanwhile. The attention of the people had been attracted to the king's presence by the royal equipage which was slowly driving down the street, and one and all hurried from their houses to see and greet their handsome young monarch. Men and women, young and old, were running about confusedly, each one inquiring of his neighbor why the king had come, and where he might now be, as his carriage was apparently awaiting him. And why was that fat man, who was seated on the sidewalk, sketching this sandy place with its poor little houses?

Even the proud and self-satisfied Mr. Pricker had not considered it beneath his dignity to descend to the street door, where he took his stand surrounded by his assistants and apprentices.

"It is said the king has gone into the house of Schommer, the grocer," said one of his assistants, returning from a reconnoissance he had made among the noisy and gossiping multitude.

Mr. Pricker shook his head gravely. "He must have been misinformed, for he undoubtedly intended coming to this house and paying me a visit, an intention which would be neither novel nor surprising in my family. None of the rulers of the house of Hohenzollern have as yet neglected to pay a visit to the house of Pricker. The present king will not fail to observe this noble custom, for—"

The worthy Mr. Pricker was interrupted by the shouts of the people. The king had appeared upon the streets, and was greeted with vociferous cheers, amid the waving of hats and handkerchiefs.

Mr. Pricker, observing with intense satisfaction that the king had turned and was advancing in the direction of his house, stepped forward with a self-gratulatory smile, and placed himself immediately at the side of the king's path But the king passed by without noticing him. On this occasion he did not return the greeting of the people in quite so gracious a manner as usual; his eye was dim, and his brow clouded. Without even favoring the smiling and bowing Pricker with a glance, he passed on to the carriage which awaited him in front of the court dressmaker's. The king entered hastily, his cavaliers following him, and the carriage drove off. The shouting of the populace continued, however, until it disappeared in the distance.

"Why do these poor foolish people shout for joy?" grumbled Mr. Pricker, shrugging his shoulders. Now that the king had taken no notice of him, this man was enraged. "What do they mean by these ridiculous cries, and this waving of hats? The king regarded them as discontentedly as if they were vermin, and did not even favor them with a smile. How low-spirited he is; his not recognizing me, the court dressmaker of his wife, shows this conclusively. It must have been his intention to visit me, for his carriage had halted immediately in front of my door; in his depression he must have entirely forgotten it."

The crowd had begun to disperse, and but a few isolated groups could now be seen, who were still eagerly engaged in discussing the king's appearance.

At a short distance from Mr. Pricker were several grave and dignified citizens, dressed in long coats ornamented with immense ivory buttons, and wearing long cues, which looked out gravely from the three-cornered hats covering their smooth and powdered hair.

Mr. Pricker observed these citizens, and with a friendly

greeting, beckôned to them to approach. "My worthy friends, did you also come to see the king?"

"No, we were only passing, but remained standing when we saw the king."

"A very handsome young man."

"A very wise and learned young king."

"And still—"

"Yes, and still—"

"Yes, that is my opinion also, worthy friends," sighed Mr. Pricker."

"The many innovations and ordinances: it terrifies one to read them."

"Every day something new."

"Yes, it is not as it was in the good old times, under the late lamented king. Ah, we then led a worthy and respectable life. One knew each day what the next would bring forth. He who hungered to-day knew that he would also do so on the morrow; he who was rich to-day knew that he would still be so on the morrow. Ours was an honest and virtuous existence. Prudence and propriety reign-ed everywhere; as a husband and father, the king set us an exalted example."

"It is true, one ran the risk of being struck occasionally; and if a man had the misfortune to be tall, he was in danger of being enrolled among the guards," said another. "But this was all. In other respects, however, one lived quietly enough, smoked his pipe, and drank his pot of beer; and in these two occupations we could also consider the king as our model and ideal."

"But now!"

"Yes, now! Every thing changes with the rapidity of the wind. He who but yesterday was poor, is rich to-day; the man who was rich yesterday, is to-day impôverished and thrown aside; this was the fate of the Privy Counsellor von

Eckert. I worked for him, and he was a good customer, for he used a great many gloves, almost a dozen pair every month; and now I have lost this good customer by the new government."

"But, then, Eckert deserved it," said the fat beer brewer "He oppressed the people, and was altogether an arrogant, puffed-up fellow, who greeted nobody, not even myself. It serves him right that the king has taken the new house in Jäger Street away from him; there was justice in that."

"But the late lamented king had given it to him, and his last will should have been honored."

"Yes, that is true; the last will of the late lamented monarch should have been honored," they all exclaimed with earnest gravity.

"Oh, we will have to undergo a great many trials," sighed Mr. Pricker. "Could you believe, my friends, that they con template depriving us of our respectable cue, and replacing it with a light, fantastic, and truly immoral wig?"

"That is impossible! That can never be! We will never submit to that!" exclaimed the assembled group, with truly Grecian pathos.

"They wish to give us French fashions," continued Pricker; "French fashions and French manners. I can see the day coming when we will have French glovemakers and shoemakers, French hair-dressers and beer-brewers; yes, and even French dressmakers. I see the day coming when a man may with impunity hang out a sign with French inscriptions over his shop door, and when he who intersperses his honest German with French phrases, will no longer be well beaten. Ah, the present king will not, like his lamented predecessor, have two girls arrested because they have said 'charmant;' he will not, with his own hands, belabor the young lads who have the assurance to appear on the streets in French costumes, as the deceased king so often did. Every thing will be different, but not better, only more French."

"Yes, could it be believed," exclaimed the fat beer-brewer, "that they think of crying down beer, the favorite beverage of the late lamented king, which, at all events, should be holy in the sight of his son? At court no more beer will be drank, but only French wines; and he who wishes to be modern and acceptable at court will turn up his nose at the beer-pot, and drink mean and adulterated wines. Yes, even coffee is coming into fashion, and the coffee-house keeper in the pleasure-garden, who, up to the present time, was only permitted to make coffee for the royal family and a few other rich people at court, has not alone received permission to serve coffee to everybody, but every innkeeper may do the same thing."

"And have you heard," asked the glovemaker gloomily, "that the two hotel-keepers in Berlin, Nicolai and St. Vincent, have their rivals, and will no longer keep the only houses where a good dinner can be had for money? Two French cooks have already arrived, and one of them has opened a house in Frederick Street, the other one in King Street, which they call 'Restauration.'"

"Yes," said the shoemaker with a sigh, "I went to the French house in Frederick Street yesterday, and ate a meal out of curiosity. Ah, my friends, I could have cried for rage, for I am sorry to say that it was a better meal than we could ever get at Nicolai's or St. Vincent's; moreover I paid less for it."

"It is a shame. A Frenchman comes here and gives a better and cheaper dinner than a native of Berlin," said Mr. Pricker. "I tell you we will all have much to endure; and even my title is insufficient to protect me from insult and humiliation, for it might happen that—"

Mr. Pricker suddenly became silent and stared toward the centre of the street, astonishment and curiosity depicted on his countenance and on that of his friends, who followed the direction of his glances.

And in truth a very unusual spectacle presented itself to these worthy burghers. A carriage was slowly passing along the street drawn by two weary and smoking horses. This carriage was of the elegant and modern French make, now becoming fashionable at court, and was called a chaise. As the top was thrown back, its occupants could very well be seen.

On the front seat were three persons. The first was a man of grave and earnest demeanor and commanding appearance. His tall and well-made figure was clad in a black velvet coat with little silver buttons, ornamented on the sleeves and breast with elegant lace ruffles. His hair, which was turning gray, was twisted in a knot at the back of his head, from which a ribbon of enormous length was pendant. A small three-cornered hat, of extraordinary elegance, rested on the toupet of curls which hung down on either side of his head and shaded the forehead, which displayed the dignity and sublimity of a Jupiter.

At his side sat two females, the middle one an elderly, grave-looking lady; the other a beautiful young girl, with smiling lips, glowing black eyes, and rosy cheeks. The elegant and graceful attire of these ladies was very different from the grave and sober costume of the women of Berlin. Their dresses were of lively colors, with wide sleeves bordered with lace, and with long waists, the low cut of which in front displayed in the one the beauty and freshness of her neck; and in the other, the richness of a guipure scarf, with which her throat was covered. Their heads were covered with immense toupets of powdered hair, surmounted by little velvet hats, from which long and waving ribbons hung down behind.

On the back seat were three other young ladies dressed in the same style, but less richly. This first carriage was followed by a second, which contained six young men in French

costumes, who were looking around with lively curiosity, and
laughing so loudly, that the worthy burgher who stood in
front of Pricker's house could hear every word they uttered,
but unfortunately could understand nothing.

"Frenchmen!" murmured Mr. Pricker, with a slight
shudder.

"Frenchmen!" echoed his friends, staring at this novel
spectacle.

But how? Who was that standing by the first carriage which had halted in front of Mr. Pricker's house?
Who was that speaking with the young girl, who smilingly
leant forward from the carriage and was laughing and jesting
with him? How? Was this young man really the son and
heir of Mr. Pricker? Was he speaking to these strangers,
and that, too, in French? Yes, Mr. Pricker could not deceive himself, it was his son; it was William, his heir.

"How? Does your son speak French?" asked the glovemaker, in a reproachful tone.

"He so much desired to do so," said Mr. Pricker, with a
sigh, "that I was forced to consent to give him a French
teacher."

William, who had observed his father, now hurried across
the street. The young man's eyes glowed; his handsome
face was enlivened with joy; his manner denoted eagerness
and excitement.

"Father," said he, "come with me quickly! These
strangers are so anxious to speak with you. Just think how
fortunate! I was passing along the Charlottenburg road
when I met the travellers. They addressed me in French,
and inquired for the best hotel in Berlin. It was lucky that
I understood them, and could recommend the 'City of Paris.'
Ah, father, what a beautiful and charming girl that is; how
easy and graceful. In the whole city of Berlin there is not
so beautiful a girl as Blanche. I have been walking along by

the side of the carriage for half an hour, and we have been laughing and talking like old friends; for when I discovered who they were, and why they were coming to Berlin, I told them who my father was directly, and then the old gentleman become so friendly and condescending. Come, father, Mr Pellissier longs to make your acquaintance."

"But I do not speak French," said Mr. Pricker, who notwithstanding his antipathy to Frenchmen, still felt flat tered by this impatience to make his acquaintance.

"I will be your interpreter, father. Come along, for you will also be astonished when you hear who this Mr. Pelissier is." And William drew his father impatiently to the carriage.

Mr. Pricker's friends stood immovable with curiosity, awaiting his return with breathless impatience. At last he returned, but a great change had taken place in Mr. Pricker. His step was uncertain and reeling; his lips trembled, and a dark cloud shaded his brow. He advanced to his friends and regarded them with a wild and vacant stare. A pause ensued. The hearts of all beat with anxiety, and an expression of intense interest was depicted on every countenance. At last Mr. Pricker opened his trembling lips, and spoke in deep and hollow tones:

"They are Frenchmen! yes, Frenchmen!" said he. "It is the new tailor, sent for by the king. He comes with six French assistants, and will work for the king, the princes, and the cavaliers of the court. But he is not only a tailor but also makes ladies' clothing, and his wife and daughter are the most celebrated dressmakers of Paris; they also are accompanied by three female assistants, and expect to work for the queen, the princesses, and the entire court.

"But that is impossible," exclaimed his friends. "The laws of our guild protect us. No woman can carry on the business of a tailor."

"Nevertheless they will do so," said Pricker; "the king has accorded them this privilege. Yes, every thing will now be different, handsomer, and better. The king summons these French dressmakers to Berlin, and the monsters ask my advice. They wish to know of me how they are to demean themselves toward the members of the guild. The new French dressmaker asks advice of me, of the court dressmaker Pricker! Ha, ha, ha! is not that laughable?" And Mr. Pricker broke out into a loud, wild laugh, which made his friends shudder, and then sunk slowly into the arms of the glover. His son William, who had been a witness of this scene, hurried to his father's assistance, and carried him into the house.

From his carriage Mr. Pelissier looked proudly down upon the poor tailor. "The good master has fainted," said he with an olympic smile. "And he has good reason, for ruin is before him. He is a lost man; for how could he, an unknown German tailor, dare to compete with Pelissier, the son of the celebrated tailor of Louis the Fourteenth? That would evince an assurance and folly with which I could not credit even a German brain."

CHAPTER XVIII.

THE DOUBLE RENDEZVOUS.

THE little maid of honor, Louise von Schwerin, was walking with quick steps up and down her room; she had locked her door to secure herself from interruption. She wished to read once more the mysterious note found yesterday in the bunch of flowers, and once more to meditate undisturbed upon its contents. Louise knew the note was from the handsome gardener Fritz Wendell; from him came the beautiful flowers she found daily upon the sill of her window, and he only could have concealed the note amongst them. There were but a few lines, entreating her to meet him that night at eight o'clock, in the grotto of the conservatory, where she should learn an important and dangerous secret.

"What can the secret be?" asked Louise of herself, after reading the note again and again. "Perhaps," she said, with a roguish smile, "perhaps he thinks that his love for me is a secret. Dangerous it certainly is for him and for me, but a secret it is not. I am certain that he loves me, but it must be very sweet to·be told so; to hear his lips confess at last what until now I have only read in those eloquent eyes Alas! is it not fearful, intolerable, to wait so long for a dec laration of love? Two months so near each other, but not one moment of sweet, unrestrained intercourse; always hemmed in by this cold, ceremonious, stupid court life; surrounded by spies and eavesdroppers; never alone, never free. Is it not terrible to have a sweetheart, and never to have refused him a kiss, because he has never had the opportunity to demand one? They say there is rapture in the first kiss of your lover—in his first embrace. I must know this for myself, that they may no longer laugh and say I am a silly child without experience. I will have my experience! I will have my love affairs as well as the other ladies of the court, only mine shall be more extraordinary, more romantic. To be loved by a baron, or a count, is indeed commonplace; but to be adored by a gardener, who is beautiful as the god Apollo, and whose obscure birth is his only fault—this is original, this is piquant. Ah, Madame von Brandt laughed at me yesterday, at my stupidity and innocence; she was merry at my expense, because I had never been kissed, never received a stolen embrace, which she declared to be the most charming event in a woman's life. All the ladies laughed at me as she said this, and called me an unbaked roll left out in the cold— which never felt the fire. They shall laugh at me no longer," cried Louise, with spiteful tears in her eyes and stamping her little foot. " No one shall mock at me again ; and if they do, I will tell them I too have a lover; that I have had a declaration of love, and have received my lover's first kiss. I must be able to say this, and therefore I will meet Fritz this evening in the grotto of the conservatory." Even while saying this she was seized with a cold trembling ; one moment her heart stood still, and then almost suffocated her with its rapid beating. A soft voice seemed to warn her against this imprudence ; she seemed to see the pale face of her mother, and to hear her living counsels : " Do not go, Louise, Fritz Wendell is no lover for Louise von Schwerin." Her guardian angel spread once more his white wings around her, longing to protect and save. But, alas ! she heard another voice, breathing flattering words and sweet promises. She saw a beautiful youth with his soft, large, hazel eyes fixed imploringly upon her. Louise felt the irresistible charm of the forbidden, the disallowed, the dangerous. Louise closed her ear to the warning voice, her good genius had no power over her. " I will go," she said, and a rosy blush suffused her childish cheeks ; " nothing shall prevent me !" Louise was now quite resolved ; but she was not at peace with herself, and from time to time she hoped some unexpected occurrence, some unconquerable obstacle, would prevent her from taking this imprudent step. No difficulty arose, chance seemed to favor her meeting with her obscure lover.

Sophia Dorothea was to visit her daughter-in-law at Schönhausen, not as a queen, but without pomp and splendor. The two eldest maids of honor only would accompany her. Neither Louise von Schwerin nor Laura von Pannewitz were to be of the party. Sophia was glad that at least for a few hours she would not see the lovely, sad face, and soft, melancholy eyes of Laura, nor hear the low and plaintive tones of her accusing voice. The king had gone to Potsdam, it was therefore unnecessary to watch Laura. Indeed, of late the queen scarcely believed in this love, of which she had been so confident; she had tried in vain to discover any trace of an understanding between Laura and the king. Frederick scarcely noticed Laura, and had spoken to her but once since that stormy day; then he had laughingly asked her why she was so pale and languishing, and if it was an unhappy love which made her look so mournful. Since that day the queen no longer believed in the passion of the king for Laura, and she reproached Madame von Brandt with having misled her.

Madame von Brandt smiled mysteriously. "I did not say, your majesty, that the king loved Laura ; your suspicions fell upon him, and I did not undeceive you."

"And why not ?" said the queen angrily; "why did you not make known to me the name of Laura's lover ?"

"Because I had solemnly sworn not to disclose it," said Madame von Brandt.

"Is it not the king? then all the better for my poor Laura."

"Still, I venture to implore your majesty to induce my dear young friend to accept the hand of Count Voss ; she will thus perhaps be cured of her unhappy and hopeless passion."

Sophia was resolved to follow this advice ; she therefore drove to Schönhausen to see the young queen, and consult with her as to the most efficacious means of accomplishing this result. Louise von Schwerin thought the queen might still change her mind and command her to accompany her; she hoped and feared this at the same time. She would have wept bitterly at this result, but she knew it would be best for her. Between anxiety and hope, doubts and fears, the time passed slowly.

"There rolls a carriage from the court," said Louise; she heard the loud cries of the guard and the beating of the drums.

It was the queen leaving for Schönhausen. Louise was now free, now unobserved; nothing could prevent her from going to the grotto. With trembling steps and a quickly beating heart she slipped through the dark alleys of the garden and entered the conservatory. All was still and wrapped in a sweet twilight. The delightful odor of orange blossoms filled the place; which, like the subtle vapor of opium, intoxicated her senses. Breathless with fear and expectation she entered the grotto; her eyes were blinded by the sudden darkness, and she sank to the ground.

"Thank God," she murmured softly, "I am alone, he is not here! I shall have time to recover, and then I can return; I am so frightened—I ought not to have come. Perhaps the ladies of the court have arranged this practical joke at my expense. Yes, that is it. It was folly to believe he would dare to ask me to meet him; he is too timid—too humble. Yes, it is a trap laid for me, and I have fallen into it."

She rose hastily to fly back to the palace; but it was too late, a strong arm was gently thrown around her neck, and she was drawn back to her seat. She tried to free herself, but could not; she heard the loud beating of his heart, which found an echo in her own; she felt his lips pressed to hers, but her childish modesty was aroused; she found she had the wish and courage to free herself.

"Let me go!" she cried breathlessly; "let me go! do not hold me a moment! I will go! I will go this instant! How dare you treat me in this manner? How and why did you come?" and Louise, who was now free, remained standing to hear his reply.

"How did I come here?" said the handsome gardener, in a submissive, but pleading tone. "Every night for four weeks I have worked upon this subterranean alley; this dark path, which should lead me here unseen. While others slept and dreamed I worked; and also dreamed with waking eyes. Mine were happy dreams. My work was done, and I could reach this consecrated spot unseen. I saw in my vision an angel, whom I adore, and to whom I have consecrated every hour, every moment of my life. Look, Mademoiselle, at the opening behind that large orange tree, that is the way to my paradise; through that opening I can reach a staircase, leading to a small cellar; another pair of steps takes me to a trap-door leading directly to my room. You can well imagine it required time, and strength, and courage to prepare this way."

Louise approached the opening curiously. This strange path made for her sake affected her more than all Fritz Wendell's words. Only a mighty love could have moved a man in darkness and alone to such a task. Louise wished to conquer her confusion and to hide her embarrassment with light mockery and jesting.

"Truly," she said, laughing, "this is a dark and mysterious passage, but any one with a light would discover it. You know her majesty has the saloon illuminated occasionally in the evening, and takes her tea here."

"No one will find this opening," said the gardener. He pushed the wooden tub, in which the orange tree grew, with his foot; it gave way to a slight touch, and turned round over the opening. "Look, Mademoiselle, the tree covers my secret."

"Open it! open it! I pray you, I must see it!"

"I will do so if you promise me not to leave me immediately."

"I promise! I promise!"

Fritz Wendell pushed back the orange-tree, then lifting Louise gently in his arms, he carried her to the grass-plot, and seating her, he threw himself on his knees before her, and bowed, as if in adoration.

"You are my queen, the sovereign of my soul! I lay myself at your feet, as your slave. You alone can decide my fate. You can raise me to the heaven of heavens, or cast me in the dust. Say only the little words 'I love you!' this will give me strength and power to brave the whole world. I will acquire fame and honor, and at no distant day before God and the whole world I will demand your hand! If you say, 'Remain where you are, at my feet is your proper place; I despise the poor gardener, who dares to love the high-born lady!' then I will die; if I live I shall go mad. My brain reels at the thought of such wretchedness. I can die now, and bless you in dying; if I live in my madness I shall curse you for your cruelty."

He ceased, and raised his handsome face pleadingly to hers. Louise was speechless; she was intoxicated with the music of his voice and impassioned words.

"You do not answer me! Oh! before you cast me off consider my agony. The heart you despise contains a treasure of love and tenderness. No other man can love you as I do. You are my light and life. You are beautiful and fascinating many will love you and seek your hand. Who but the poor gardener will die for you if you say no? To me you are more than the most lovely of women, you are a goddess! Oh, you know not what you have already made of me! what you can still make of me! When I saw you for the first time I was a poor, ignorant gardener, loving nothing but my flowers; knowing no language. The great book of nature was my only study. Since that glorious day in which I looked upon you as a radiant, heavenly vision, I have realized poverty; I have blushed at my ignorance. My life has been one great effort to make myself worthy of you. Now, Louise, command me. What shall I do? What shall I become? If you do not despise and laugh at my love, if you love me a little in return, if you have hope, courage, and patience to wait, I will be worthy of you!"

"Alas!" said Louise, "this is the dream of a madman. The king and my noble and proud family would never consent that I should become your wife."

"As to the king," said Fritz, carelessly, "I would find means to obtain his consent, and honor and distinction at his hands.

"I understand," said Louise, "the secret you intended to tell me—tell it now," she exclaimed, with a child's eager curiosity.

"Listen," said he, rising from his knees—"listen, but do not let us betray ourselves by loud words or exclamations."

"I hear steps," said Louise. "Oh, if we should be discovered!"

"Fear nothing; look there, Louise!" Her eye followed the direction of his hand.

Under the laurel-tree sat Laura von Pannewitz, and before her knelt Prince Augustus William, radiant with happiness, and covering her hands with kisses.

"Laura, my bride, my darling, when will the day come in which I can call you mine to all eternity?"

"That day will come when I am dead," said Laura, with a sad smile. "Yes, my prince, only when I am dead shall I be free to love you, and to pray for you. My freed spirit shall hover around you as your guardian angel, and protect you from all dangers. Oh, if I could die now, and fulfil this noble mission!"

Louise was so absorbed in this scene that she did not notice Fritz Wendell as he drew near and again threw his arm around her.

"Look at them," he murmured; "he is a royal prince, and she only a poor maid of honor; he loves her, and she accepts his love, and fears no shame."

Louise laid her hand impatiently upon his lips and whispered, "Hush!" he covered her hand with kisses; they listened with subdued breathing to the pure and ardent vows of the two lovers.

For one moment Laura, carried away by her own feelings and the earnest words of her lover, allowed him to press his lips to her cheek, and returned his vows of love and constancy. But at this moment Louise heard the soft voice of Laura entreating her lover to leave her, and not to make her blush for herself.

"Promise me," she cried, "never again to embrace me; our love must remain pure, and only when we fear not God's holy eye, dare we pray to Him for assistance. Let us retain the right to shed innocent tears over our unhappy love, and lay it as a sacrifice at the foot of God's throne in that day when the world shall separate and despise us."

"No one shall dare do that, Laura; you are my future wife; I shall be ever near to defend you with my life's blood! But I promise what you ask; I will restrain my heart; only in dreams will I embrace you; I swear this, my beloved. But the day will come when you will cancel this vow—the day when I will claim you before God and man as my wife!"

Laura took his hand with a sweet, confiding smile: "I thank you, darling: I thank you, but now we must part."

"Part! alas, we shall not meet again for weeks. I am commanded to accompany the king on a pleasure trip; for me there is but one earthly pleasure, to see you—to be at your side."

"Go," she said, smiling; "go without fear; we can never forget each other; however widely separated, you are always before me; I am always with you, although you see me not."

"Yes, Laura, there is not one moment of my life in which I do not see and hear you!"

"Well, then, go cheerfully with the king. Our hearts understand each other; our souls are inseparable."

The prince took her hand and pressed it to his heart, then silently they left the saloon.

Louise had long since freed herself from her lover, and she now arose, resolved to return to the palace. Fritz Wendell tried to detain her, but the weak and foolish child had gathered courage from the modest words and dignified example of Laura.

"If you touch me again, you have seen me for the last time! I will never again return to this grotto!" Fritz Wendell was encouraged by her words; he had not asked her to return, and she had half promised to do so.

"I will not dare to touch you again," he said, humbly; "but will you not promise me to come again?"

"Well, I suppose I shall have to come again to hear the end of poor Laura's romance."

"This romance can be of great use to us," he said, seizing her hand and pressing it to his lips; "if mademoiselle accepts my love and allows me to hope I may one day become her husband, I will sell this secret to the king, and thus obtain his consent."

"You would not be so cruel as to betray them to the king?"

"Yes, there is nothing I would not do to obtain your hand."

BOOK III.

CHAPTER I.

THE INTRIGUING COURTIERS.

"You are right," said Baron Pöllnitz, "yes, you are right, dear Fredersdorf; this is not the way to vanquish our Hercules or to influence him. He has no heart, and is not capable of love, and I verily believe he despises women."

"He does not despise them," said Fredersdorf, "he is wearied with them, which is far worse. Women are always too ready to meet him; too many hearts have been given him unasked; no woman will ever have power over him."

"How, what then, my dear friend?" cried Pöllnitz. "There are means to tame every living creature; the elephant and the royal lion can be tamed, they become under skilful hands gentle, patient, and obedient: is there no way to tame this king of beasts and hold him in bondage? Unless we can ensnare him, we will be less than nothing, subject to his arbitrary temper, and condemned to obey his will. Acknowledge that this is not an enviable position, it does not correspond with the proud and ambitious hopes we have both been for some time encouraging."

" Is it possible that when the king's chamberlain and a
13

cunning old courtier like myself unite our forces the royal game can escape our artful and well-arranged nets ? "

"Dear Fredersdorf, this must not, this shall not be. It would be an everlasting shame upon us both."

"What an unheard-of enormity, a king without a powerful and influential favorite ! "

"Frederick shall have two, and as these places are vacant, it is but natural that we should strive to occupy them."

"Yes," said Fredersdorf, "we will seize upon them and maintain our position. You called the king a young Hercules—well, this Hercules must be tamed."

"Through love of Omphale."

"No, not exactly, but Omphale must lead him into a life of luxury, and put him to sleep by voluptuous feasts. Call to mind how the Roman Emperor Heliogabalus killed the proud and ambitious senators who wished to curtail his absolute power."

"I am not so learned as you are, my dear friend, and I confess without blushing that I know nothing of Heliogabalus."

"Listen, then : Heliogabalus was weary of being but the obedient functionary of the senate ; he wished to rule, and to have that power which the senate claimed as its own. He kept his ambitious desires to himself, however, and showed the senators' a contented and submissive face. One day he invited them to a splendid feast at his villa ; he placed before them the most costly meats and the choicest wines. They were sitting around this luxurious table, somewhat excited by drink, when the emperor arose and said with a peculiar smile : 'I must go now to prepare for you an agreeable surprise and practical joke, which you will confess has the merit of originality.' He left the room, and the tipsy senators did not observe that the doors were locked and bolted from without. They continued to drink and sing merrily ; suddenly a glass door in the ceiling was opened, and the voice of Helio-gabalus was heard, saying: 'You were never satisfied with your power and glory, you were always aspiring after new laurels; this noble thirst shall now be satisfied.' A torrent of laurel wreaths and branches now fell upon the senators. At first they laughed, and snatched jestingly at the flying laurels. The most exquisite flowers were now added, and there seemed to be no end to the pelting storm. They cried out, 'Enough, enough,' in vain; the wreaths and bouquets still poured upon them in unceasing streams; the floor was literally a bed of roses. At last, terror took possession of them; they wished to escape, and rushed to the doors, but they were immovable. Through the sea of flowers, which already reached their knees, they waded to the window, but they were in the second story, and below they saw the Roman legions with their sharp weapons pointed in the air. Flight was impossible; they plead wildly for mercy, but the inexorable stream of flowers continued to flow. Higher and higher rose the walls around them, they could no longer even plead for pity; they were literally buried in laurels. At last nothing was to be seen but a vast bed of roses, of which not even a fragrant leaf was stirred by a passing breeze. Heliogabalus had not murdered his senators; he had suffocated them with sweets, that was all. Well, what do you think of my story?" said Fredersdorf.

"It is full of interest, and Heliogabalus must have been poetical; but I do not see the connection between the emperor and ourselves."

"You do not?" said his friend impatiently; "well, let us follow his example. We will intoxicate this mighty king with enervating pleasures, we will tempt him with wine and women, we will stifle him with flowers."

"But he has no taste for them," said Pöllnitz, sighing.

"He does not care for the beauty of women, but he has

other dangerous tastes; he has no heart, but he has a palate; he does not care for the love of women, but he enjoys good living—that will make one link in his fetters. Then he loves pomp and splendor; he has so long been forced to live meanly that wealth will intoxicate him; he will wish to lavish honors and rain gold upon his people. Frederick William has stowed away millions; we will help the son to scatter them."

"This will be a new and thrillingly agreeable pastime, in the ordering of which he could not have a better adviser than yourself, baron."

"While Frederick and yourself are building new palaces and planning new amusements, I will rule, and help him to bear the burden of state affairs."

"You will help him to scatter millions, and I will collect from the good Prussians new millions for him to scatter. It is to be hoped that some heavy drops from this golden shower will fall into my purse," said Pöllnitz. "My finances are in an unhealthy state, and my landlord threatens to sell my furniture and my jewels, because for more than a year I have not paid my rent. You see now, Fredersdorf, that I must have that house in the Jäger Street. I count upon it so surely that I have already borrowed a few thousand dollars from some confiding noble souls, whom I have convinced that the house is mine."

"You shall have it," said Fredersdorf; "the king will give it to you as a reward for the plans you have drawn for the new palaces."

"Has he seen them?"

"Yes, and approves them. The papers are in his desk, and need but his royal signature."

"Ah!" said Pöllnitz, "if they were but signed! What a glorious life would commence here! we would realize the Arabian Nights; and Europe would gaze with dazzled eyes

at the splendor and magnificence of our court. How vexed
the treasurer, Boden, will be when the king commands him
to disburse for our revels and vanities the millions which he
helped the late king to hoard together for far different purposes! This Boden," said Pöllnitz thoughtfully, " will be
our most dangerous opponent: you may believe this; I am
somewhat versed in physiognomy. I have studied his countenance; he is a bold, determined man, who, when irritated,
would even brave the king. All the other ministers agree
with our plans, and will not stand in our way. They are not
dangerous; I have made a compromise with them; they
have resolved to think all we do right. But Boden was in
flexible; he would not understand my secret signs or hints;
flattery has no power over him, and he is alike indifferent to
promises and threats. All my dexterously aimed arrows re-
bounded from the rough coat-of-mail with which his honesty
has clothed him."

" Do not concern yourself about Boden," cried Fredersdorf, "he is a lost man; he falls without any aid from us.
The king hates him, and is only waiting for an opportunity
to dismiss him. Have you not noticed how contemptuously
he treats him—never speaks to him or notices him, while
he loves to chat with his other ministers? Frederick did not
dismiss him from office at once, because the old king loved
him. Boden was his treasurer and confidential friend, from
whom he had no secrets; the king has therefore been patient;
but his sun is set, of that you may be convinced. The king,
though he seems not to notice him, watches him closely;
one incautious movement and he will be instantly dismissed.
This may happen this very day."

" How ? " said Pöllnitz.

" The king has adopted the plan, which he had ordered
Knobelsdorf to sketch for him, for the new palace of the
dowager-queen. It is to be a colossal wonder—the capitol

of the north! the building of which will cost from four to
five millions! These millions must come from Boden's
treasury; he must respect the royal order. If he does, he
is an unscrupulous officer, and the king can no longer put
faith in him. If he dares oppose the royal command, he is
a traitor, and the king, who demands silent and unconditional
obedience from his officers, will dismiss him. The king feels
this himself, and when he gave me these documents, he said,
with a peculiar smile, ' This is a bitter pill for Boden—we will
see if he is able to swallow it.' You see, now, that our good
Boden stands between two pitfalls, from both of which he
cannot hope to escape alive."

"Ah, if this be true," said Pöllnitz, gayly, " our success
is assured. The house in Jäger Street will be mine, and you
will be an influential minister. We will govern the ruler of
Prussia, and be mighty in the land. Only think how all the
courtiers will bow before us! The king will do nothing without our advice. I will make more debts. I will be as generous as Fouquet, and as lavish and luxurious as Lucullus;
and if at last all my resources fail, I will do as Heliogabalus
did; if my creditors become troublesome, the old Roman
shall teach me how to silence them by some refinement in
hospitality."

"And I, the lowly born," said Fredersdorf, " who have so
long been a slave, will now have power and influence. The
king loves me; I will be a true and faithful servant to him.
I will be inflexible to those who have scorned me; those
proud counts and barons, who have passed me by unnoticed,
shall now sue to me in vain. The king's heart is mine, and I
will be sustained by him. This tamed lion shall be drawn by
prancing steeds in gilded chariots; we will anoint him with
honey and feed him with nightingales' tongues; he shall
bathe in Lachrymæ Christi, and all that the most fantastic
dream and the wildest flights of fancy can imagine shall be

set before him. Those good epicurean Romans, who threw young maidens into their ponds for their eels to feed upon, in order that their meat might be tender and juicy, were sickly sentimentalists in comparison with what I shall be—" he stopped, for the door opened, and Boden, their hated enemy, stood before them. They looked upon him indifferently, as a doomed adversary. Boden approached quietly, and said to Fredersdorf:

" Have the kindness to announce me to his majesty."

" Has his majesty sent for you?" said Fredersdorf, carelessly.

" He has not sent for me, but please say to his majesty that I am come to speak with him on important business."

Fredersdorf stepped into the adjoining room, and returned quickly, saying, with a triumphant and malicious smile: " The king says he will send for you when he wishes to speak with you. These were his exact words; accommodate yourself to them in future."

The minister's countenance was perfectly calm; his lip slightly trembled; but he spoke in his usual grave, composed manner: " The king may not desire to see me; but I, as an officer and minister of state, have the most urgent reasons for desiring an audience. Go and tell him this."

" These are proud, disrespectful words," said Pöllnitz, smiling blandly.

" Which I will faithfully report to his majesty," said Fredersdorf.

" I fear your excellency will pay dearly for this speech," whispered Pöllnitz.

" Fear nothing for me," said Boden, with a quiet smile.

" His majesty awaits you," said Fredersdorf, still standing at the door. Boden walked proudly by Fredersdorf, casting upon him a look of contempt, who returned it with a mocking grin.

"The fox is caught," he whispered, as the door closed upon him.

"Do you think so?" said Pöllnitz. "I am surprised and somewhat anxious at the king's receiving him."

"Fear nothing, he is but received to be *dismissed*. The king's eye flamed, and his brow, usually so clear, was heavily clouded; this betokens. storms; may they break upon Boden's devoted head! Come, let us watch the tempest; there is nothing more instructive than a royal hurricane."

"Let us profit by the occasion, then."

The two courtiers slipped noiselessly to the door and pushed the curtains carefully to one side, so as to see and hear clearly.

CHAPTER II.

THE KING AND SECETARY OF THE TREASURY.

THE king received the secretary with a solemn and earnest bow. He stood leaning upon his writing-table, his arms folded, and his eyes fixed upon Boden. Many a bold man had trembled at the eagle glance of Frederick, but Boden looked up clear, and betrayed neither confusion nor hesitation.

"You insisted positively upon seeing me," said Frederick, sternly; "let me hear now what you have to say."

"I have much to say, and I must bespeak patience and indulgence; I fear that my words will seem dry and tedious to your majesty."

"Speak; I will myself determine how far I can grant you patience and indulgence."

"Your majesty is a fiery but noble and learned gentleman; besides this, you are young, and youth has a daring will—can renew the old and lumbering wheel and push the world forward in her progress. Your majesty will, can, and must do this; God has given you not only the power, but the intellect and strength. Your majesty will change many things and inaugurate new measures. The old times must give way before the new era. I saw that the first time I looked into my young king's eye—in that bold eye in which is written a great and glorious future for Prussia; I understood that we, who had served the sainted king, might not appear worthy or young enough to carry out the purposes of the royal successor of Frederick William. I waited, also, for my dismissal; but it came not. Your majesty did not remove me from my office, and I confess this gave me pleasure. I said to myself, 'The king will not destroy, he will improve; and if he believes that his father's old servants can help him in that, so will we serve him and carry out his purposes with a holy zeal. I know the secret machinery of state. The king concealed nothing from me. I will explain all this to the young king; I will make him acquainted with this complicated and widely spread power; I will have the honor to make known to him my knowledge of the revenue and its uses. I rejoiced in the hope that I might yet serve my fatherland.'"

"These are very friendly and perhaps well-meant propositions which you are making me," said the king, with a light laugh. "Happily, however, I do not need them. I know already what is necessary, and as I have found amongst the papers of my father all the accounts of the states-general, you can understand that I know exactly what I receive as revenue and what I am to disburse. Besides all this, I will not fatigue myself in minute details on this subject; I do not deem it of sufficient importance. My time is much occupied, and I have more important and better things to do than to weary myself over dull questions of finance."

"No, majesty," cried Boden, "you have nothing more important or better to do. The finances are the blood vessels of the State, and the whole body would sicken and die if these vessels should be choked or irregular in their action."

"Then must we call the lancet to our aid," said the king. "I am the physician of this revenue, you are the surgeon only when I need the lancet; then will you strike the vein, and allow so much golden blood to flow as I think good and necessary."

"No, this will I not do!" said Boden, resolutely; "your majesty can dismiss me, but you cannot force me to act against my conscience."

"Boden!" cried the king, in so loud and angry a tone, that even the two listening courtiers trembled and turned pale.

"This man is already a corpse," whispered Pöllnitz. "I already smell, even here, the refreshing fragrance of his body. We will bury him, and be his smiling heirs."

"Look, look at the fearful glance of the king!" whispered Fredersdorf; "his eyes crush the over-bold, even as the glance of Jove crushed the Titans. Yes, you are right, Boden is a dead man. The king is so filled with scorn, he has lost the power of speech."

"No, he opens his lips, let us listen."

"Boden," said the king, "you forget that you speak with the son, and not with the father. You were the favorite of Frederick William, but you are not mine; and I will not suffer this inconsiderate and self-confident manner. Remember that, and go on."

"So long as I am in your service," said the minister, with a slight bow, "it is my first and my holiest duty to express my opinions freely to your majesty, to give you counsel according to the best of my strength and my ability. It remains with your majesty to reject my advice and to act differently, but still according to the constitution of the State."

"The first duty of a servant is to give his counsel only when it is demanded; as I did not desire yours, you might have spared yourself this trouble."

"Your majesty did not ask my counsel, that is true," said the minister; "you only remembered me when you had commands to give as to the emptying of the royal treasury. Your majesty thought you had no use for your finance minister, as you had all the papers relating to the states general. Every one of your majesty's ministers is acquainted with these matters, and yet they would not feel able to decide the question of the disbursing of the kingly revenue, to say under what circumstances, and conformably to the powers of the States, this revenue should be disposed of. This, my king, requires a special knowledge, and I, as minister of finance, dare boast that I understand this matter."

The king's brow became more and more clouded. "That may be," said he, impatiently, "but I am not willing to be restrained in my operations by narrow-minded laws; I will not live meanly like my father, and think only of gathering millions together."

"Nor did King Frederick William live for that," said the minister, boldly; "he lived economically, but where there was want, he knew how to give with a truly royal hand; this is proved by the provinces, by the cities and villages which he built out of dust and ashes; this is proved by the half million of happy men who now inhabit them in peace and comfort. More than three millions of dollars did the king give to Lithuania, which was a howling wilderness, filled with famine and pestilence, until relieved by the generosity of their monarch; and while doing this he watched with close attention the accounts of his cook and spent but little money on the royal table. No! The king did not only gather millions together; he knew how to disburse them worthily."

"This man must be crazy," whispered Pöllnitz; "he dares to praise the dead king at the expense and in the teeth of the living; that is indeed bold folly, and must lead to his destruction. The king has turned away from him; see, he goes to the window and looks without; he will give himself time to master his scorn and conquer the desire which he feels to crush this daring worm to the earth. I tell you," said Pöllnitz, "I would give Boden a hundred glasses of champagne from my cellar in the Jäger Street if I could see the king punish him with his own hands."

The king turned again to the minister, who looked at him like a man who dared all and was resigned to all; he thought, with Pöllnitz and Fredersdorf, that the king would crush him in his wrath. But Frederick's face was calm, and a strangely mild glance beamed in his eye.

"Well, if you praise my father for disbursing millions, so will you also be content with me, for it is my purpose zealously to imitate him. I will begin by putting my court upon a truly royal footing; I will live as it becomes the King of Prussia. The necessary preparations are already commenced, and a detailed plan lies now upon the table; I will sign it to-day."

"May I read it, your majesty?" said Boden.

The king nodded. Boden took the paper and glanced hastily over it, while the king folded his arms behind him and walked backwards and forwards.

"I find the king wondrously wearisome and patient," murmured Fredersdorf; "it is not his manner generally to withhold so long his crushing glances."

"And with what derisive laughter that man there reads my plan," said Pöllnitz, gnashing his teeth; "truly one might think he was making sport of it."

"Have you read it?" said the king, standing still before Boden, and looking at him sharply.

"Yes, your majesty, I have read it."

"Well, and what think you of it?"

"That only Pöllnitz, who it is well known has no gold, and is only acquainted with debt, could have drawn out such a plan, for the realization of which, not only Prussian gold, but a fountain of gold from the Arabian Nights, would be necessary."

"I swear I will break this fellow's neck!" said Pöllnitz.

A faint smile might be seen on the lips of Frederick. "You do not approve of this plan?" said he.

"Your majesty, we have no strong box from which this sum can be abstracted, and if you are resolved to take from the State treasury the sum necessary for this purpose, so will this also be exhausted during the first year."

"Well, let us leave this plan for the present, and tell me how you stand as to the means necessary to build the palace of the queen-mother. Have you received my instructions?"

"I have received them."

"And you have disbursed the sum necessary?"

"No, sire, I cannot."

"How! cannot, when I your king and lord command it?"

Boden bowed respectfully. "Your majesty, there is a greater lord—that is, my conscience; my conscience forbids me to take this sum from the strong box designated. You require four millions of dollars, and you desire that this sum shall be taken from the money set apart for the maintenance of the army and the assistance of famished and suffering villages and towns. I acknowledge that the court of his sainted majesty was somewhat niggardly, and that you, sire, may justly find some changes necessary. If, however, it is determined to use for this purpose the funds set apart for other important objects, then must your majesty impose new and heavy taxes upon your subjects, or you must diminish the army."

"Diminish my army!" said the king; "never, never shall that be done!"

"Then, sire, if the building of a palace is absolutely necessary, take the sum for this purpose from your royal treasury; it contains now seven millions of dollars, and as there is no war in prospect, you may well use four millions of the seven in building a castle.

"No, this will not do!" said Frederick. "This money is set apart for other objects; you shall take these four millions from the designated sources."

"I have had already the honor to show your majesty the consequences of such a course. You declare you will not diminish the army: it only remains then to impose a new tax."

"Do that, then," said the king, indifferently; "write a command for a new tax; that is your affair."

The minister looked at the king in painful surprise, and a profound sorrow was painted in his face.

"If this must be so, your majesty," said he, with a deeply moved voice, "then is the hour of my dismissal at hand, and I know what I have to do; I am no longer young enough to bear the burden of a *portfolio;* I belong to the old and cautious time, and my ideas do not suit the young era. I ask your majesty, in all humility and submission, to give me my dismissal. Here is the paper which contains the plan of the palace; you will readily find another who will obey your commands. I am not sufficiently *grown* for this post of finance minister. I beg also for my dismissal."

"*At last,*" said the king, with glistening eyes.

"At last!" repeated Pöllnitz; "truly it was a long time before this cowardly man could be brought to the point."

"Did I not tell you that the king was resolved to get rid of Boden?" said Fredersdorf; "but let us listen! no, why should we listen? Boden has handed in his resignation, and the king has accepted it. I confess my back aches from this crouching position; I will go and drink a glass of champagne to the health of the new minister of finance."

"You must not go. The king asked for you as Boden was announced, and commanded that we should wait here in the ante-room until called, as he had something of importance to communicate. Without doubt he will present me to-day with the deed of the house in Jäger Street. Look! in the last window niche I see a pair of very inviting chairs; let us make ourselves comfortable."

The king had said "At last!" as Boden offered his resignation; after a short silence he added: "It seems to me that you hesitated a long time before resigning."

"It is true," said Boden sadly; "I certainly had occasion to take this step earlier, but I still hoped I might be useful to my king."

"And this hope has not deceived you," said Frederick, drawing near to Boden, and laying his hand on his shoulder; "I cannot accept your resignation."

Boden looked up amazed. The king's face was beautiful to behold—a touching and gentle expression spoke in every noble feature; his light-blue eye beamed with gladness and goodness.

"How! Your majesty will not accept my resignation?"

"No, it would be great folly in me," said Frederick, in a tone which brought tears to the eyes of the minister; "it would be great folly to deprive myself of so noble and faithful a servant. No, Boden, I am not so great a spendthrift as to cast away such a treasure. Now in order that you may understand your king, I will make you a confession: you had been slandered to me, and my distrust awakened. It was said of you that you filled the State treasury while the people hungered; it was said of you that you were resolved to hold on to your office, and therefore carried out the commands of the king, even though unjust to the people. I wished to prove you, Boden, to see if you had been *slandered* or justly charged; I handled you, therefore, contemptuously; I gave you commissions which were oppressive; I drew upon the treasury so as to exhaust it fully; I wished to know if you were only a submissive servant or an honest man; I had long to wait, and your patience and forbearance were great. To-day I put you to the extremest proof, and by God! if you had carried out my unjust and unwise instructions, I would not only have deprived you of your office, but I would have held you to a strict account. You would have been a dishonest servant, who, in order to flatter the king, was willing to sin against the people. The welfare of my people is holy to me, and they shall not be oppressed by new taxes. Praised be God! I can say I understand my duties; may every ruler do the same. May they keep their eyes steadily fixed upon their great calling; may they feel that this exaltation, this rank of which they are so proud, so jealous, is the gift of the people, whose happiness is intrusted to them; that millions of men have not been created to be the slaves of one man, to make him more terrible and more powerful. The people do not place themselves under the yoke of a fellow-man to be the martyrs of his humor and the playthings of his pleasure. No, they chose from amongst them the one they considered the most just, in order that he may govern them; *the best*, to be their father; the most humane, that he may sympathize and assist them; the bravest, to defend them from their enemies; the wisest, that they may not be dragged without cause into destructive wars—the man, in short, who seems to them the best suited to govern himself and them; to use the sovereign power, to sustain justice and the laws, and not to play the tyrant. These are my views of what a king should be, and I will fulfil my calling, so help me God! You, Boden, must stand by and give me honest help."

In the eyes of the minister might be seen joyful tears and a noble ambition; he bowed low and kissed the extended hand of the king.

"How gracious has God been to my fatherland in giving it such a prince!"

"You will not, then, insist upon your resignation?" said the king. "You are content to serve me, provided I do not diminish my army, and do not impose new taxes upon the people?"

"I will be proud and happy to serve my king," said Boden, deeply moved.

"I must tell you, Boden, this will be no light service, and my ministers will be hereafter less important personages than they have supposed themselves to be; I shall closely observe them all, and shall require much work of them, but I myself will be diligent. It seems to me an idle prince is a poor creature, that the world has little use for. I am resolved to serve my country with all my powers; but I will stand alone, independent, self-sustaining. My ministers will only be my instruments to carry out my purposes; they will have much to do, and have no influence. I will have no favorite, and never consult any other will than my own; but I shall require of them to express their opinions frankly and without fear in answer to my questions, and that they shall not fail to call my attention to any errors I may commit, either through haste or want of judgment."

"All this I will do," said Boden, deeply moved. "So truly as God will give me strength, I will serve my king and my fatherland faithfully to the end."

"We are agreed, then," said Frederick; "you will remain my minister. If you had not demanded your dismissal, I should have given it to you. I should have seen that you were justly accused, and were determined to remain minister at any price. Thank God, you have proved to me that you are an honest man! But," said the king, "you are not only an honest man, but a bold, unterrified, truthful man; a true friend, grateful for benefits received, you do not cease to love your king and benefactor, even after his death. You have had the courage to defend the dead king, and to reproach his successor. The king cannot thank you for this; but as a son, I thank you—I say, 'Come to my heart, true and faithful servant.' We kings are too poor to reward our servants in any other way than by confiding love." The king opened his arms and pressed Boden to his heart, who wept aloud. "And now," cried the king, "we understand each other, and know what we have to expect, and that is always a great gain in this world, full of disappointment, hypocrisy, and cunning. I will now give you a proof that I do not close my ear to the reasonable counsels of my minister, and that I am ready to offer up my personal wishes; I will not build this palace for my mother, you have convinced me that I have not the income to do so. I cannot take four millions from the State treasury. This money will soon be needed for a more important object. But some changes are absolutely necessary in the royal palace; it must be made more worthy of a king. Take, therefore, these plans and designs; strike from them what you consider superfluous. Let me know what additions you think it best to adopt, and from what source we can draw the necessary funds." *

CHAPTER III.

THE UNDECEIVED COURTIER.

At the time that the king was placing the extravagant plans, which Baron von Pöllnitz had drawn up, into the

---

* "History of Berlin," Thiebault.

hands of his minister of finance, the baron was waiting in the ante-room, in a state of smiling security, entertaining his friend Fredersdorf with an account of his own future splendor and magnificence, speaking especially of the entertainments which he intended giving in his new house in Jäger Street. When at length the door of the royal cabinet was opened, and the minister of finance entered the ante-room, Pöllnitz and Fredersdorf stood up, not however to greet the minister, but to pass him with a cold, contemptuous smile, on their way to the door of the cabinet. The smile died suddenly on Pöllnitz's lips, and he stood as if transfixed before the minister.

"What are those papers which you hold?" he asked, extending his hand as if he would tear the papers from Baron von Boden.

The minister pushed him back, as he carelessly shrugged his shoulders. "These are papers which his majesty handed me, that I might examine their contents, and see if they contain any thing but folly."

"Sir," said Pöllnitz, beside himself with rage, "these papers—" but he became suddenly silent, for the door of the cabinet was opened again, and the king entered the room.

He glanced scornfully at Pöllnitz, who was scarcely able to conceal his anger, and approached Baron von Boden. "One thing more, minister," said the king, "I had forgotten that I had prepared a little surprise for you; I am aware that you are not rich, although you are the minister of finance, and I understand that you live in a limited way, scarcely worthy of your rank. We must alter this, and happily I know a house which even Baron von Pöllnitz declares is worthy a nobleman. I present this house to you, with its entire contents. From this moment it is yours, and Baron von Pöllnitz must go with you, and show it to you; he can point out to you all the advantages and conveniences which he has so often praised to me."

Pöllnitz stood pale, trembling, and confused. " I do not know of what house your majesty speaks," he stammered, " of what house I can have said that it was worthy of the minister of finance."

" Not of the minister of finance, but of a nobleman, and Boden is a nobleman, not only in name but in reality ; and is entirely worthy to possess the house which I have presented to him. You are well acquainted with it, Pöllnitz ; it is the house which my father had built for Eckert, the beautiful house in Jäger Street."

" The house in Jäger Street ! " cried Pöllnitz, forgetting the restraint which the presence of the king usually imposed. " No, no, your majesty is pleased to jest. You do not mean the house in Jäger Street, that house which—"

" That house," interrupted the king, in a stern voice, " that house which pleased you so well, that you, as foolish children sometimes do, confused reality with your dreams, and imagined that this house already belonged to you, merely because you desired that it should do so. I would have smiled at this childish folly, if it had remained an amusement for your unemployed fancy ; but you have deceived others as well as yourself, and that is an unpardonable fault, and one which you must repair immediately if you do not wish to be dismissed from my service."

" I do not understand your majesty ; I do not know how I have forfeited the favor of my king."

The king glanced angrily at the pale, trembling courtier. " You understand perfectly, Baron von Pöllnitz, of which fault, amongst the many that you daily and hourly commit, I speak. You know that it has pleased you to declare the house, which I have just presented to Boden, to be yours, and that you have found credulous people who have lent you money on that representation."

"Will your majesty grant me a favor?" said Minister von Boden, glancing kindly at Pöllnitz, who stood near him crushed and trembling.

The king consented by bowing silently, and the minister proceeded:

"Your majesty has just made me most rich and happy, and I consider it my duty, as it is my pleasure, to share both riches and happiness with my fellow-creatures. Baron von Pöllnitz, by the commands of the late king, executed the plans for the house which your majesty has so kindly presented to me; he also selected the decorations and furniture, and this may have led him to believe that the house, which had been built and furnished according to his taste, might become his own. I am much indebted to Pöllnitz, for a man so plain and simple as I am would never have been able to make this house so tasteful and elegant. Permit me, therefore, your majesty, to liquidate this debt by considering the small mortgage which Baron von Pöllnitz has put upon this house, as my affair."

"What reply do you make to this proposition?" said the king, turning to Pöllnitz.

"That if your majesty allows me I will accept it with pleasure, and I merely wish to ask the minister whether he will only take up those mortgages which I have already put upon the house, or the others which I intended putting?"

"Ah!" cried the king, laughing, "you are incorrigible. If poor Boden is to satisfy not only your old creditors but your new ones, the present I have made him would probably reduce him to beggary in a few months. No, no, this one mortgage is sufficient, and as it amounts to only a few thousand dollars, it shall be paid from my purse; and that my gift to you, Boden, may have no drawback, Pöllnitz may consider himself thus repaid for his trouble about the plans and arrangements of your house. But woe to you, Pöllnitz, if

I should again hear of such folly and deceit; and if you do not give up such disgraceful conduct, and act in a manner becoming your rank and office, this is the last time that I will show any mercy for your folly. If there is a repetition of it, I will be inexorable, only a stern judge and king."

"Your majesty plunges me into an abyss of despair," said Pöllnitz, swinging his hands. "You demand that I shall create no new debts; and how is it possible to avoid that, when I have not even the money to pay the old ones? If your majesty desires that I should lead a new life, you should have the kindness to pay my old debts."

The king paced the room silently for a short time, and then stood before Pöllnitz, and said:

"You are so shameless and absurd, that I must either drive you away, or content myself with laughing at you. I will, however, remember that my father and grandfather laughed at you, and for the present I will also laugh, as I laugh at the silly pranks of merry Mr. Raths, my monkey. But even Mr. Raths was punished yesterday because he was too daring with his monkey tricks. Mark this, Baron von Pöllnitz, I will pay your debts this time; but if it should occur to you to make new ones, I will forget that you were the jester of my father and grandfather, and only remember that so reckless an individual cannot remain in my service. Now accompany the minister to the Jäger Street, and show him his house. Your audience is at an end, gentlemen."

After these gentlemen had left the room, the king stood for a long time as if lost in thought. He did not appear to be aware that he was not alone, that Fredersdorf was standing in the window, to which he had withdrawn on the appearance of the king, and had been a trembling, despairing witness to this scene, which had disturbed his plans and hopes. Suddenly the king walked rapidly through the room, and stood before Fredersdorf—his eyes, usually so clear and bright, veiled as with a cloud, and an expression of deep melancholy upon his noble face.

" Fredersdorf," he said, with a voice so mild and gentle, that his hearer trembled, and a deadly pallor overspread his countenance—" Fredersdorf, is it really true that you all think of me only as a king, never as your fellow-man ? that you have no love for your sovereign, only envy and hatred, only malice and cunning? And you, also, Fredersdorf, you whom I have loved, not as a master loves his servant, but as a dear friend, with whom I have often forgotten that I was a prince, and only remembered that I was with a friend, who had a feeling heart for my cares and sorrows, and entertained a little love not for the prince but for the man. Are you all determined to make me cold-hearted and distrustful? are you laboring to turn my heart to stone—to cut off my soul from faith and love? A day will come when you will call me cold and relentless, and no one will say that it was those I loved and trusted who made me thus."

" Mercy! mercy! my king," prayed Fredersdorf, sinking to the feet of the king. " Kill me! destroy me with your anger! only do not show me such kindness and love. Oh! your majesty does not know how I love you, how my heart is bound up in yours; but I have a wild and ambitious heart, and in the thirst of my ambition I was not satisfied to remain the servant of my king. I wished to become powerful and influential. I longed to mount high above those who now look down upon and despise me because I am a servant. This, my king, is my whole crime, the remorseful confession of my guilt."

" You did not wish to betray your king, you only desired to be the lord of your lord. You wished to reign through me. Poor Fredersdorf, do you think it such happiness to be a king? Do you not know that this royal crown, which seems so bright to you, is only a crown of thorns, which is

concealed with a little tinsel and a few spangles? Poor
Fredersdorf, you are ambitious; I will gratify you in this as
far as possible, but you must conquer the desire to control
my will, and influence my resolutions. A king is on'y answerable to God," proceeded the king, "and only from
God can he receive control or commands. I am the servant
of God, but the master of men. I will gratify your ambition, Fredersdorf, I will give you a title. You sha'l no
longer be a mere servant, but a private secretary; and that
you may be a master as well as a servant, I present you the
estate Czernihon, near Rheinsberg. There you will be lord
of your peasants and workmen, and learn if it is not a thank-
less office to rule. Are you satisfied, my poor Fredersdorf?"

Fredersdorf could not answer; he pressed his lips to the
hand of the king, and wept aloud.

CHAPTER IV.

THE BRIDAL PAIR.

JOY and exultation reigned in the house of the rich
manufacturer Orguelin. The proud daughter had consented
to become the wife of Count Rhedern; she had at last
accepted him, and the happy father, delighted at the prospect of soon becoming father-in-law to a count, busied himself with the preparations for the approaching wedding festivities, which were destined to excite the admiration and
astonishment of the entire city by their magnificence and
prodigal splendor. At this festival the future Countess
Rhedern was to appear for the last time in the circle of her

old friends, and then to take leave of them forever; for as a matter of course the Countess Rhedern would have to form new friendships and seek other society than that to which she had been accustomed as Mademoiselle Orguelin. But M. Orguelin desired to exhibit to his associates, the manufacturers and merchants, this splendid nobleman who had now become his son; he wished to excite the envy and admiration of his friends by the princely magnificence of his house.

But all this was far from being agreeable to Count Rhedern, who had other plans. His creditors and his poverty compelled him to marry this rich merchant's daughter, but he had no desire or intention of entering into any association or connection with the friends and relations of his wife; and even if it should be necessary to recognize his rich father-in-law, it did not follow that he would appear at his *fêtes* to add lustre to the entertainment and be shown off as a highly ornamental acquisition. He trembled when he thought of the ridicule of the court cavaliers, to whom it would be an inexhaustible subject of jest, that he, the marshal of the queen, and a cavalier of old nobility, had played this *rôle* at a *fête* of the bourgeoisie, and had conversed, eaten, and danced with manufacturers and tradespeople. That could not and should not be. To preserve the prestige of his house, a nobleman might marry the daughter of a merchant, if she possessed a million, but he could not stoop so low as to consider himself a member of her family, and to recognize this or that relative. Count Rhedern thought of some plan by which he could frustrate this scheme of his father-in-law in regard to the wedding festivities, which would bring him into such undesirable and disagreeable association with persons beneath his rank, as he desired to avoid as far as possible all *éclat* in this misalliance. With a smiling countenance he entered one morning into the mag-

14

nificent parlor of his affianced, who with her father's assist-
tance was engaged in making out a list of the wedding
guests. The count seated himself near his future bride,
and listened with inward horror to the terrible and barba-
rous names which were placed on the list, the possessors of
which could never appear at a knightly tournament or court
festival, and were consequently excluded from all the joys
and honors of the world.

"Well," said the father exultingly, "what do you think of
our *fête ?* It will be perfectly magnificent, will it not? The
richest merchants of Berlin will be present ; and if one were
to estimate us by our wealth, it would be found that more
millions would be assembled there than Germany has inhabitants. You will readily understand, my dear son, that in
order to do honor to such guests, great preparations are necessary, for it is not easy to excite the astonishment and
admiration of these proud merchants. It is quite easy to
surprise one of your barons or counts ; you are delighted
when entertained with champagne or fine Holstein oysters,
but a rich merchant turns scornfully from turtle-soup and
Indian birds'-nests. Nevertheless, my proud guests shall be
surprised ; they shall have a dinner, the like of which they
have never seen. For this purpose I have ordered two of the
best cooks from Paris, who will arrive in a few days. They
have written that they will need at least two weeks to make
the necessary preparations for the wedding-dinner. For
their services I will pay them a salary which is perhaps
equal to the half-yearly pay of a marshal or chamberlain.
Moreover, we will have fireworks, illuminations, splendid
music ; yes, I have even thought of having a stage erected,
and of engaging a French company to amuse our guests with
a few comedies."

"I am only afraid that but few of our guests will understand a word of these French plays," exclaimed his daughter,
laughing.

"That is quite possible; nevertheless French is now the rage, and it will attract attention if we have a French play. And you, my dear son, what do you say to all this? You look almost vexed."

"I sigh because you wish to defer the wedding for so long a time."

"Ah, that is a compliment for you, my daughter. Lovers are always impatient."

"But I did not sigh only because I would so long be deprived of the happiness of leading my dear Caroline to the altar, but because I should thereby lose the pleasure of presenting her to the court as my wife, on the occasion of the large and most magnificent court ball with which the season will be opened."

"A court ball is to take place?" asked Caroline Orguelin, with vivacity. "The king has, I believe, not yet returned from his journey."

"But will do so in a few days, and as the court mourning is now at an end, the king will give a brilliant masquerade ball, which will probably be the only one given this winter."

"A masquerade ball!" exclaimed his bride; "and I have never seen one!"

"And this is to be a most magnificent one. Moreover, the queen-mother has already promised me an invitation for my wife, and requested me to present her to the entire court on this occasion."

"And it is impossible to have the wedding any sooner?" asked Caroline, impatiently.

"Quite impossible," said M. Orguelin.

"And why impossible?" said the count. "Could we not have the wedding at an early day, and the festival later? Could we not, as is now customary in high circles, be married quietly, and have the festival at a later day? These noisy weddings are a little out of fashion at the present day, and it would be said at court that the wealthy and highy cultivated M. Orguelin showed his disregard for the customs of our young and modern court, by adhering to those of the old *régime*."

"God forbid that I should do that!" exclaimed M. Orguelin, in a terrified voice.

"Father, I detest noisy merry-makings, and insist on a quiet marriage. It shall not be said at court that Mademoiselle Orguelin, with all her acquaintances, had rejoiced over the inestimable happiness of becoming the wife of a count. I will be married quietly; afterwards the count may give a *fête* in honor of our marriage, which you, my father, can return."

As usual, M. Orguelin submitted to his daughter's will, and it was determined that a quiet wedding should take place in a few days, to be followed on a later day by a magnificent *fête* in the house of the father-in-law.

"At which I shall certainly not be present," thought Count Rhedern, while he expressed his entire satisfaction with this arrangement.

Mademoiselle Orguelin's proudest wishes were about to be accomplished. She was to be introduced at court, and the queen-mother had graciously declared her intention of presenting her to the king at the approaching masquerade. There was now wanting but one thing, and that was a suitable costume for this important occasion, and Count Rhedern assured her, with a sigh, that it would be very difficult to prepare it, as it would be almost impossible to find a tailor who would undertake to make, in so short a time, the gold-brocaded train which was necessary.

"Pelissier, the new French tailor, has even refused to make a little cloak for me," said Count Rhedern, "and his female assistants, who are the most fashionable dressmakers, have been deaf to all entreaties for the last week. They take

no more orders for the masquerade, and it was only yesterday that I met Countess Hake, who had been with the pretty
Blanche while I was with her father, descending the steps,
wringing her hands and bathed in tears, because the proud
dressmakers had replied to her prayers and entreaties with a
cruel 'Impossible!'"

"I know, however, that M. Pricker, the court dressmaker of the two queens, would not make me this reply,"
said Caroline Orguelin, proudly, "but that he would make
whatever is necessary even if he should be forced to take
several additional assistants."

"Then let us drive to M. Pricker's," said her affianced,
smiling; "but we must go at once, for we have no time to
lose, and you can well imagine that I would be inconsolable,
if, after our marriage, I could not present you to the court
as my wife on the first suitable occasion."

"Yes, we have no time to lose," repeated Caroline, ringing a bell, and ordering her carriage. When, after a few
minutes, Caroline Orguelin and the count were alone in the
carriage, she turned to him with a mocking smile, and remarked: "The wedding is, then, to take place the day after
to-morrow."

"Yes, my dearest Caroline, and on that day I will be the
happiest of men."

"Your creditors," said she, shrugging her shoulders,
"were then becoming so pressing that you suddenly experienced an ardent longing for my dowry."

"My creditors?" asked the count; "I do not understand
you, dearest Caroline."

"You understand me very well," said she, with cutting
coldness; "it is, moreover, time that we understand each
other, once for all. Know, therefore, my dear sir, that I
have not allowed myself to be deceived either by your tender protestations or by the *rôle* of an impatient lover, which

you have acted so well. I am neither young nor pretty enough to awaken a passion in the breast of so noble and excellent a cavalier as Count Rhedern. You are poor, but rich in debts, and you needed therefore a rich wife ; and as I happened to have more money than any of the beautiful and noble ladies of the court, you determined to marry me, deeming my rich dowry a sufficient compensation for the disgrace inflicted on your noble house. In a word, you chose me because you were tired of being dunned by your creditors, and of living in a state of secret misery ; and I—I bought Count Rhedern with my million, in order that I might appear at court."

"Well, truly, these confessions are very curious, highly original," said Count Rhedern, with a forced smile.

"They are, however, necessary. We need no longer trouble ourselves with this useless acting and hypocrisy. It is also but just that I should inform you why I so ardently desire to become a lady of quality, that is, why I wish to be able to appear at court, for I hope you do not consider me silly enough to buy a count for the mere sake of being called countess ? "

"I should consider this wish by no means a silly one," murmured the count.

"No," continued his bride, "I desired to become a countess that I might obtain access to court and enjoy a happiness of which thousands would be envious, although like the moth I could only flutter round the brilliant and dazzling light until it burned me to death. I told you I was no longer young. I, however, still have a young heart, a fresher heart perhaps than all your proud and beautiful ladies of the court, for mine was as hard and clear as crystal, until—"

"Well, conclude," said the count, as she hesitated ; " continue these little confessions, which are certainly rarely **made** before, but generally after marriage. You spoke of your heart having been as hard and clear as crystal, until—"

"Until I had seen the king," continued his bride, blushing, "until I had gazed in those wondrous eyes, until I had seen the smile, so proud, and yet so mild and gentle, with which he greeted his people from the balcony."

"It was then at the coronation that you formed the genial resolution of loving the king?"

"Yes, it was on the coronation day that I for the first time comprehended how grand, how noble and sublime a true man could be. And my soul bowed in humility and obedience before the commanding glance of this Titan, and my heart bowed in adoration at the feet of this man, whose smile was so wondrous, and whose eyes spoke such great things. Oh! had I been near him as you were, I would have fallen at his feet and have said to him: 'I accept you as my master and my divinity; you are my ideal, and I will adore you as such with a pure and noble worship.' But I was far off, and could only pray to him in thought. I determined that I would be near him at some day; and I, who had wished to remain single, determined in this moment to marry—but to marry only a cavalier of the court. I inquired of my companion the names of the cavaliers who stood behind the king, and the most of them were married, but you were not, and I was told that you possessed a great many debts and very small means of paying them. On this day I told my father: 'I wish to marry Count Rhedern, I desire that you should purchase him for me, as you recently purchased the handsome set of Nuremberg jewelry.'"

"Really, a very flattering and ingenious view of the matter," said the count, with a forced laugh.

Caroline continued: "My father intrusted this affair to a broker who had frequently done business for him before, and who proved to be an apt trader on this occasion, for you see he purchased the goods we desired, and the business transaction has been concluded. Count, you will now understand why I made the condition that I should be admitted at court, and recognized as your countess, before I determined to become your wife."

"I understand perfectly well," said the count, peevishly'; "you made use of me as a bridge over which you might pass from your father's shop to the royal palace, as I will make use of you to pay my debts, and to enable me to live a life worthy of a count. Ah, now that we understand one another so well, we will be perfectly at ease, and live a free and unconstrained life without annoying each other."

"Still, my dear count, you will sometimes experience a slight annoyance at my hands," said the millionnairess, gently placing her hand on the count's shoulder. "It was not only on account of your creditors that you desired so early a marriage, but mainly because the count considered it beneath his dignity to take part in the festivities of manufacturers and merchants. But I must inform you, dear sir, that I shall never forget that my father is a merchant, and that all my friends are the daughters of manufacturers and merchants. I will be a grateful daughter and a true friend, and I will compel you to show the same respect to my father and friends that I will show to yours."

"Compel!" exclaimed the count, "you will compel me?"

"I said compel, and you will soon perceive that it is in my power to do so. Listen: my father promised you that my dowry should be a million, out of which, however, your debts, and the expense of my *trousseau*, are to be defrayed. Your debts, including the mortgage on your estates, amount to two hundred thousand, and my *trousseau*, diamonds, and the furnishing of my house will cost about the same sum. There will remain, therefore, but six hundred thousand, of which you will enjoy the benefit, according to our marriage

contract. But you will readily understand that the interest
of this small capital will not support the daughter of a rich
merchant respectably, and that if I should desire to entertain the king in my house, I would perhaps expend in one
evening the half of my income."

The count regarded his bride with admiration, almost
with reverence. "You then think that we could not live
on the interest of six hundred thousand dollars?" asked he.

"I do not only think so, but am sure of it, for I needed
as much when a girl. Ah, my dear count, a great deal of
money is necessary to gratify one's humors and caprices.
My father is well aware of this fact, and has, therefore, given me as pin money a second million; this
will, however, remain in his business, and I shall only
receive the interest in monthly payments. I must, however, remark that this interest is not a part of my dowry, but
is my personal property, with which I can do as I see fit. I
can, if I wish, give *fêtes* with this money, pay your debts, purchase horses and equipages for you, or I can give it to my
father, who can make very good use of it in his business.
And now pay attention: whenever you choose to neglect the
proper and dutiful attention due to your wife, her father, or
her friends, I will relinquish my pin money to my father, and
you must look to some other source for the necessary
funds."

"But I shall always be an attentive and grateful husband,
and a dutiful son to your father," exclaimed the count,
charmed with the prospect of a second million.

"Then you will do well," said his bride, gravely, "for
your monthly income will thereby be increased by four
thousand dollars. You see I am a true merchant's daughter,
and understand accounts. I have bought you, and know
your worth, but I also desire to be properly esteemed and
respected by you. You must never think you have honored

14*

me by making me a countess, but must always remember that my father is a millionnaire, whose only daughter and heiress pays you for your amiability, your title, and her admission to court. And now enough of these tedious affairs. The carriage has stopped, and we have arrived at our destination; let us put on our masks again, and be the fond lovers who marry for pure love and tenderness."

"And in truth you deserve to be loved," exclaimed the count, pressing her hand to his lips. "You are the most discreet and charming of women, and I have no doubt that I will love you ardently some day."

"Poor count," said she, laughing, "on that day you will deserve commiseration, for I shall certainly never fall in love with you. A heart like mine loves but once, and dies of that love."

"I hope that this death will at least be a very slow one," said the count, jumping out of the carriage, and assisting his bride elect to descend.

CHAPTER V.

THE FRENCH AND GERMAN TAILORS, OR THE MONTAGUES AND CAPULETS OF BERLIN.

M. PRICKER stood at his window; his face was sad, and he looked with a troubled gaze at the house on the other side of the street. This was the house of the new French tailor, Pelissier. Many splendid equipages were drawn up before the door, and crowds of gayly dressed men and women were passing in and out. Alas for earthly grandeur! alas for popular applause! Pricker stood at his window, no one rang his bell, not a carriage was to be seen at his door, since the arrival of the French tailor. Pricker was a lost man, wounded in his ambition, his most sacred feelings trampled upon, and his just claim to the gratitude of his generation disallowed. What advantage was it to him to be the acknowledged tailor of two queens? Since, in the ardor of his patriotism, he had refused to employ French hands, not one of all those ladies who had formerly confided to him the secrets of their toilets, remembered his discretion, or his ability to hide their defects, or supply their wants. The fickle and ungrateful world had forsaken him. Even the Hohenzollerns had forgotten the great deeds and still greater services of the Prickers, and no longer knew how to reward true merit. Since Pelissier took the opposite house, Pricker's heart was broken; night and day he was consumed with anguish; but he made no complaint, he suffered in Spartan silence, and like a hero covered his bleeding wounds. One soft eye, one kindred heart discovered his silent sorrow; she, too, sorrowed as those without hope; she had not even the courage to offer consolation. In this hour of extremity poor Pricker sometimes thought of selling his house, but the next moment he would blush at his weakness and cowardice in thus abandoning the field to his foe.

In spiteful arrogance the French tailor had settled himself in the opposite house. It was a struggle for life or death offered by Pelissier, and it should not be said that a Pricker ignominiously declined the contest. Pricker must remain, he must defy his adversary, and yield only in death to this dandy Frenchman; he would therefore remain in those ancestral halls, which had so long sheltered the tailor of the two queens. He remained, but the death-worm was gnawing at his heart. Pricker still gazed across the street, and with an added pang he saw another carriage rolling in that direction; but no, this time the carriage turned to his side of the street. In the first joy of his heart he sprang forward to open the door and aid the ladies in descending; he checked himself in time, however, remembering that this would compromise the dignity of his house.

In a few moments Madame Pricker announced the rich Mademoiselle Orguelin and her future husband. Pricker advanced to meet them with calm composure, but there was tumultuous joy in his heart.

"You will be surprised, my dear Pricker, that we did not send for you, but we should have lost time by that, and our affairs demand the greatest haste."

Pricker bowed proudly. "My house is accustomed to receive noble persons; my grandfather had once the happiness to welcome a prince. In what can I serve you?"

"I need two complete court toilets," said Mademoiselle Orguelin—"the robes for a first presentation, and then for a great court ball."

"Then you wish a robe with a brocade train; I would choose blue velvet, it is most becoming to blondes, and throws a heavenly light upon their complexions."

"Then we will take sky blue," said the millionnaire, "with a train of silver. For the ball dress, my father has given me a dress woven in velvet and gold."

"Your toilets will be superb, and the appearance of the Countess Rhedern will do honor to the house of Pricker."

"You must promise to be ready in eight days."

"In four, if necessary," said Pricker, taking the long measure from his wife and approaching the lady.

"I leave the trimmings entirely to your taste, but of course my dress must be of the newest French cut."

Pricker had laid the measure around the slender waist of Mademoiselle Orguelin; he now removed it violently "You desire your dresses made after the latest French style?" he said, harshly.

"Of course; that is surely understood; no decent tailor

would work in any other style. I should indeed be ridiculous to appear at court in a stiff old German costume. You must make me the tight-fitting French waist, the long points in front, the narrow sleeves reaching to the elbow and trimmed with rich lace."

Pricker folded his measure with heroic determination and laid it upon the table.

"Your dress cannot be made in the house of Pricker, mademoiselle."

"What, you refuse to work for me?"

"I will not adopt the French fashions! that would be an insult to my ancestors. I will remain true to the good old German customs."

"Reflect," said Count Rhedern, "how much this obstinacy will cost you. You will lose all the patronage of the court; all the world adopts the new French fashions."

"That is true," said the sorrowful Pricker; he approached and pointed through the window to the house opposite. "Once all those carriages stood before my door; once I dressed all those noble people; a wink would be sufficient to recall them. Would I be untrue to the customs of my fathers, would I employ French workmen, all those carriages would be arrayed before my door. I hold the destiny of that contemptible Frenchman in my hands; a word from me, and he would be ruined; but I will not speak that word. Let him live to the disgrace and shame of the Germans who abandon the time-honored customs of their fatherland."

The count offered his arm to his bride, and said, mockingly:

"I thank you for your address. I see that a German tailor may be a consummate fool! Come, my dear Caroline, we will go to M. Pelissier."

Pricker remained alone; grand and proud he stood in

the middle of the saloon, and looked up, like a conquering hero, at the grim portraits of his ancestors.

"Be satisfied with me," he murmured; "I have made a new sacrifice to your manes. My house is German, and German it shall remain."

At this moment there arose on the air the clear, full voice of his daughter, who was practising with Quantz a favorite Italian air of the king. "Nel tue giorni felice ricordati da me," sang the beautiful Anna, while Father Pricker ran, like a madman, up and down the room, and stopped his ears, that he might not hear the hateful sound. He cursed himself for allowing the monster Quantz to come to the house.

"Alas! alas! I have closed my heart to the new era and its horrors, but I shall lose my children; they will not wish to wander in my ways."

At this moment Anna entered the room, with sparkling eyes and rosy cheeks.

"Father," she said, hastily, "the supreme desire of my heart will now be fulfilled. Quantz has at last promised that I shall sing at the next court concert. In eight days the king returns, and a concert will be arranged, at which I, your happy daughter, will sing an Italian song."

"Italian!"

"She will sing Italian," murmured Quantz, who was listening at the door. "She will give all the world an opportunity to laugh and ridicule her, and I shall be responsible; I would rather die!".

Anna was greatly excited, and did not notice her teacher; and, as her mother entered the room, she embraced her warmly.

"Mother, mother, Quantz has pronounced me worthy to sing at the court. I shall cover myself with glory, and the daughter of the tailor will fill all Germany with her fame!"

"Unhappy child, do you not know that your father is present?"

"Oh, my father shall be proud of me!" cried Anna.

Mother Pricker was frightened at the looks of her husband. Anna scarcely noticed her parents; she said:

"Father, it is high time to think of my dress; it must be new and elegant."

"You shall have it," said her father, solemnly; "it is an honor to sing before the king. I will make you a magnificent dress out of your mother's bridal robe."

Anna laughed contemptuously. "No, no, father; the time is passed when we dared to wear the clothes of our great-grandmothers. The day is gone by for family relics. How the ladies of the court would laugh at my mother's old flowered robe! Besides, the dress is too narrow for a modern hoop robe, the only style now tolerated."

"A hoop robe!" cried the father, in tones of horror; "she wishes to wear a hoop robe!"

"Yes, and why not?" said Anna. "Does not the beautiful Blanche wear one? and have not all the court ladies adopted them? No fashionable lady dare now appear without a hoop robe."

"Who is Blanche?" cried M. Pricker, rising from his chair and looking threateningly at Anna, "who is Blanche?"

"Do you not know, father? Oh, you are only pretending not to know! Dearest Blanche, whom I love like a sister, and to whom I can only pay stolen visits, for her father is furious that you have not returned his visit, and has forbidden any of his family to enter our house."

"He did right; and I also forbid you to cross his threshold. I thought, Anna, you had too much pride to enter the house of your father's enemy, or speak to his daughter."

Anna shrugged her shoulders silently, and now quick steps were heard approaching.

"Oh quel pleusir d'être amoreuse," sang a fresh, manly voice.

"French!" cried Father Pricker, wild with rage. "William singing French!"

The door was hastily opened, and William, heir to the house of Pricker, stood upon the sill. He was arrayed in most charming costume. A tight-fitting coat, short-waisted and long-tailed, wide sleeves, and large mother-of-pearl buttons; the cuffs and high-standing collar were richly embroidered in silver; his vest was "coleur de chair," and instead of a long plait, William had covered his hair with a powdered wig. A small three-cornered hat, worn jauntily to one side, was embroidered with silver, and ornamented with a black feather; in his hand he held a slight, graceful cane. William appeared before his father a complete model of a new-fashioned French dandy; rage and horror choked the old man's utterance.

"Well, father, do I please you? is not this attire worthy of a nobleman? only I cannot wear the white feather, which they say belongs exclusively to the nobility."

"Where did you get these clothes, William?" said his father, approaching him slowly; "who gave you the money to pay for them? It is a fool's costume! Who made it for you?"

"Well, you gave me the money, dear father," said William, laughing; "that is, you will give it to me. This handsome suit has not yet been paid for. The name of Pricker has a silvery sound; Pelissier knows that, and credited me willingly; though at first he refused to work for me, and I thank Blanche that I have a costume from the celebrated shop of Pelissier."

Old Pricker uttered a cry of rage, and seizing, with feverish violence, the long tails of his son's coat, he dragged him to and fro.

" So Pelissier made this ! he has dared to array my son, the son and heir of the house of Pricker, in this ridiculous manner ! And you, William, you were shameless enough to receive this suit from your father's enemy. Alas ! alas ! are you not afraid that your ancestors will rise from their graves to punish you ? "

" Dear father," said William, " it is only a costume, and has nothing to do with character or principle."

" Never will I allow my son to be lost to me in this manner," cried Pricker; " and if in the blindness of his folly he has lost himself, I will bring him back with violence, if necessary, to the right path. Off, then, with this absurd coat! off with this fool's cap! off with all this livery ! "

Pricker now began to pull and tear madly at his son's clothes; he knocked his hat off, and trampled it under his feet; he seized with both hands the lace collar, and laughed when the shreds remained in his hands. William was at first dumb with terror, but the loud laugh of his sister, who found this scene amusing, restored his presence of mind ; with mad violence he pushed his father from him.

" Father," he cried, " I am no longer a boy ! I will not bear this treatment; I will dress as I like, and as the fashions demand."

" Well spoken, my brother," said Anna, laughingly, springing to his side; " we are children of the new era, and will dress as it demands. Why did our parents give us modern educations if they wished us to conform to old-fashioned prejudice ? "

" ' Honor thy father and thy mother, that thy days may be long in the land which the Lord thy God giveth thee,' " said Pricker, solemnly.

" Another Bible verse," said Anna, mockingly. " The book is no longer fashionable ; and it is not half so amusing as Voltaire."

"Enough, enough," said Pricker; "now listen to my last determination. I command you to live and dress as your father and mother have dressed before you! Woe to you if you despise my commands! woe to you if you defy my authority! I will disown you—and my curse shall be your inheritance; remember this. If you ever enter that house again, or speak to any of its inhabitants—if I ever see you in this French livery again, or if you, Anna, ever appear before me in a hoop robe and *toupé*, from that moment you cease to be my children."

Father and mother left the room; the brother and sister remained alone.

"Well," said Anna, "do you intend to obey these commands? Will you wear the queue and the narrow, coarse frock coat?"

"Nonsense," said William, "that Blanche may ridicule me, and all the world may laugh at me. You do not know, Anna, how much Blanche and myself love each other; we have vowed eternal love and faith, and she is to be my wife!"

"You will then become an honorable tailor, as your fathers were."

William laughed. "I follow a trade! I who have received the education of a nobleman! no, no, Anna, you are not in earnest; you cannot believe that."

"Take care, William, you will be disinherited; father is in earnest."

"Oh, he will have to submit, as old Pelissier must do; he will also be furious when he first learns that I am the husband of Blanche; he has threatened her with his curse if she marries me. But in spite of all this we intend to marry; they must at last be reconciled. Oh, Blanche is beautiful as an angel!"

"Nevertheless she is a tailor's daughter," said Anna.

"Yes, like my beautiful and amiable sister Anna."

"But I shall become a celebrated singer, and the wife of a nobleman."

"Well, and who says that Blanche will not be the wife of a celebrated man, and that you will not be proud of me?"

"Will you be a man or a woman dressmaker?"

"Neither one nor the other! I shall be an actor; but silence, this is my secret and I must keep it!"

CHAPTER VI.

IN RHEINSBERG.

THE quiet castle of Rheinsberg was again alive with noise Its halls resounded with music and laughter; gay and happy faces were everywhere to be seen; bright jests to be heard on every side. The charming days of the past, when Frederick was prince royal, seemed to have returned; the same company now filled the castle; the same sports and amusements were enjoyed. All was the same, yet still, every thing was changed, transformed. Almost all of those who had left Rheinsberg with such proud hopes, such great desires, were again there, but with annihilated hopes. They had all expected to reign; they had claimed for themselves honor and power, but the young king had allowed to none the privilege of mounting the throne by his side. They were all welcome companions, loved friends. But none dared overstep the boundary of dependence and submission which he had drawn around them, and in the centre of which he stood alone, trusting to his own strength and will. They had gained nothing from the crown which rested upon Frederick's noble head; but they had lost nothing. They returned to Rheinsberg not exalted, though not humbled.

But one heart was broken, one heart was bleeding from unseen pain. It was the heart of Elizabeth, the heart of that poor rejected woman who was called the reigning queen, the wife of Frederick.

The king, on returning from his excursion to Strasburg, had reminded her of her promise to follow him with her court to Rheinsberg. And the poor sufferer, though she knew that the presence of the king would be for her a continual torment, an hourly renunciation, could not find strength to resist the desire of her own heart. She had followed her husband, saying to herself with a painful smile: "I will at least see him, and if he does not speak to me I will still hear his voice. My sufferings will be greater, but I shall be near him. The joy will help me to bear the pain. *Soffri é taci!*" Elizabeth Christina was right; the king never spoke to her, never fixed those brilliant blue eyes, which possessed for her the depth and immensity of the skies, upon her pale countenance. With a silent bow he welcomed her daily at their meals, but he did not now lead her to the table and sit beside her. The presence of the Margrave and Margravine of Baireuth seemed to impose upon him the duty of honoring his favorite sister, who was his guest, more than his wife the queen. He sat, therefore, between his sister and her husband the count, at whose side the queen was placed. He did not speak to her, but she saw him, and strengthened her heart by the sight of his proud and noble countenance.

She suffered and was silent. She veiled her pain by a soft smile, she concealed the paleness of her cheek with artificial bloom, she covered the furrows that care already showed in her lovely and youthful face, with black beauty-spots which were then the fashion. No one should think that she suffered. No one should pity her, not even the king. Elizabeth Christina joined in all the pleasures and amusements at Rheinsberg. She laughed at Bielfield's jests,

at Pöllnitz's bright anecdotes; she listened with beaming eyes
to Knoblesdorf's plans for beautifying the king's residence;
she took part in the preparations for a drama that was to
be performed. Voltaire's "Death of Cæsar," and "The
Frenchman in London," by Boissy, had been chosen by the
king to be played at Rheinsberg, and in each piece she
played a prominent *rôle*. The young queen, as it seemed,
had become an enthusiastic admirer of the theatre; she was
never missing at any of the rehearsals, and aided her beautiful maids of honor in the arrangements of their costumes.

The king was now seldom to be seen in the circle of his
friends and companions, and the tones of his flute were
rarely to be heard. He passed the day in his library, no
one dared disturb him, not even Guentz. Madame von
Brandt, who had accompanied the court to Rheinsberg,
said, in one of her secret meetings with Count Manteuffel:
" The king is unfaithful to his last sweetheart, he has aban-
doned and rejected his flute."

" But with what does the king occupy himself the entire day?" asked the count. "What is it that takes him from
his friends and fills up all his time?"

" Nothing but scientific studies," said Madame von Brandt,
shrugging her shoulder. Fredersdorf told me that he busies
himself with maps and plans, is surrounded by his military
books, and is occupied like an engineer with astrolabes and
land surveyors. You now see that these are very innocent occupations, and that they can have no influence upon
our affairs. The king, I promise you, will never be more
divorced from his wife than he now is; and concerning the
marriage of Prince Augustus William, my plans are so skil-
fully laid that there is no danger of failure, and poor Laura
von Pannewitz will surely be sacrificed. All is well, and we
have nothing to fear from the king's innocent studies."

"Ah, you call these innocent studies?" said the count; "I assure you that these studies will greatly disturb the Austrian court, and I must at once notify my friend Secken dorf of them."

"You are making a mountain of a mole hill," said Madame von Brandt, laughing. "I assure you, you have nothing to fear. It is true the king passes the day in his study, but he passes his evenings with us, and he is then as gay, as unconstrained, as full of wit and humor as ever. Perhaps he makes use of the solitude of his study to learn his *rôle*, for to-morrow, you know, we act the 'Death of Cæsar,' and the king is 'Brutus.'"

"Yes, yes," said Count Manteuffel, thoughtfully, "it strikes me the king is playing the part of Brutus; to the eye he seems harmless and gay, but who knows what dark thoughts pregnant with mischief, are hid in his soul?"

"You are always seeing ghosts," said Madame von Brandt, impatiently. "But hear! the court clock is striking six, it is high time for me to return to the castle, for at seven the last rehearsal commences, and I have still to dress." And Madame von Brandt hastily took leave of her ally, and ran gayly to the castle.

But she had no need to dress for the rehearsal. The king was not able to act; the strong will was to-day conquered by an enemy who stands in awe of no one, not even of a king—an enemy who can vanquish the most victorious commander. Frederick was ill of a fever, which had tormented him the whole summer, which had kept him from visiting Amsterdam, and which confined him to his bed in the castle of Moyland, while Orttaire was paying his long expected visit, had again taken a powerful hold upon him and made of the king a pale, trembling man, who lay shivering and groaning upon his bed, scoffing at Ellart, his physician, because he could not cure him.

"There is a remedy," said Ellart, "but I dare not give it to your majesty."

"And why not?" said the king.

"Because its strength must first be tested, to see if it can be used without danger; it must first be tried by a patient upon whose life the happiness of millions does not depend."

"A human life is always sacred, and if not certain of your remedy, it is as vicious to give it to a beggar as to a king."

"I believe," said Ellart, "as entirely in this remedy as Louis the Fourteenth, who bought it secretly from Talbot, the Englishman, and paid him a hundred Napoleons for a pound. The wife of the king of Spain was cured by it."

"Give me this remedy," said the king, with chattering teeth.

"Pardon me, your majesty, but I dare not, though I have a small quantity with me which was sent by a friend from Paris, and which I brought to show you as a great curiosity. This tiny brown powder is a medicine which was not distilled by the apothecary, but by Nature."

"Then I have confidence in it," said the king; "Nature is the best physician, the best apothecary, and what she brews is full of divine healing power. How is this remedy called?"

"It is the Peruvian bark, or quinine, the bark above all barks which, by a divine Providence, grows in Peru, the land of fevers."

But the king had not the strength to listen to him. He now lay burning with fever; a dark purple covered his cheek, and his eyes, which, but a few moments before, were dull and lustreless, now sparkled with fire. The king, overpowered by the disease, closed his eyes, and occasionally unconnected, senseless words escaped his dry, burning lips.

Fredersdorf now entered, and through the open door the anxious, inquiring faces of Pöllnitz, Bielfield, Jordan, and Kaiserling could be seen.

On tip-toe Ellart approached the private chamberlain.

"How is the king?" said he, hastily. "Is he in a condition to hear some important news?"

"Not now. Wait an hour, he will then be free from fever."

"We will wait," said Fredersdorf to the four courtiers who had entered the room, and were now standing around the royal bed.

"Is it bad news? If so, I advise you to wait until to-morrow."

"Well, I do not believe the king will think it bad," said Kaiserling, laughing.

"And I am convinced the king will be well pleased with our news," said Bielfield. "I think so, because the king is a sleeping hero waiting to be roused."

"If you speak so loud," whispered Pöllnitz, "it will be you who will wake this hero, and the thunder of his anger will fall upon you."

"Pöllnitz is right," said Jordan; "be quiet, and let us await his majesty's waking." And the group stood in silence around the couch, with eyes fixed upon the king. He at last awoke, and a smile played upon his lip as he perceived the six cavaliers.

"You stand there like mourners," said he; "and to look at you one would think you were undertakers!"

"Ah, sire, fever does not kill like apoplexy," said Jordan, approaching his friend and pressing his hand tenderly.

"Your majesty called us undertakers," said Pöllnitz, laughing. "As usual, the divine prophetic mind of our king is in the right. There is certainly a funeral odor about us."

"But God forbid that we should mourn," said Bielfield, 'we are much better prepared to sound the battle-song."

All this passed while the physician was feeling the king's pulse, and Fredersdorf was tenderly arranging his pillows. The king looked at him inquiringly. "Listen, Fredersdorf," said he, "what meaning have all these mysterious words and looks; why are you all so grave? Is one of my dogs dead? or are you only peevish because this abominable fever has cheated you of the rehearsal?"

"No, your majesty. The dogs are in excellent health."

"The king's pulse is perfectly quiet," said Ellart, "you can communicate your news to him." Baron Pöllnitz approached the king's couch.

"Sire, one hour ago a courier arrived who was the bearer of important information."

"Whence came he?" said the king, calmly.

"From your majesty's ambassador in Vienna, Count Borche."

"Ah!" said the king, "is the empress, our noble aunt, suffering?"

"The empress is perfectly well, but her husband, the emperor—

"Well, why do you not continue?" said the king impatiently?

"Would your majesty not wish some restorative first?" said Fredersdorf, but the king pushed him angrily away.

"I wish your phrase, Pöllnitz. What of the Emperor of Austria?"

"Sire, Emperor Charles the Sixth is no more, he died the twentieth of October."

"Truly," said Frederick, leaning back, "it was worth the trouble to make so much to do about such insignificant news. If the emperor is dead, Maria Theresa will be Empress of Germany, that is all. It does not concern us." He stopped and closed his eyes.

The physician again felt his pulse. "It is perfectly quiet,"

15

said he; "this prodigious news has not occasioned the slightest commotion or irregularity."

"You are right," said the king, looking up. "Neither is the death of the emperor Charles to make the slightest change in our plans, but to execute them I must be perfectly well. It must not be said that a miserable fever changed my intentions and condemned me to idleness; I must have no fever on the day the news of the emperor's death arrives, or the good people of Vienna will believe that I was made ill with fright. Give me that powder, Ellart, I will take it."

"But I told your majesty that I cannot, dare not give it to you, for I have not tried its effect yet."

"Then try it on me," said the king, positively. "Give me the powder."

It was in vain that Ellart called upon the cavaliers to support his opinion; in vain that they begged and implored the king not to take the powder, not to put his life in danger.

"My life is in God's hands," said the king, earnestly; "and God, who created me, created also this bark. I trust more in God's medicine than in that of man. Quick, give me the powder!" And as Ellart still hesitated, he continued in a stern voice: "I command you, as your king and master, to give it to me. On my head rests the responsibility."

"If your majesty commands I must obey, but I take these gentlemen to witness that I but do it on compulsion."

And amid the breathless silence of the room, the king took the medicine.

"Now your majesty must rest," said Ellart; "you must, by no means, return to Berlin; by my holy right of physician, I forbid it."

"And why should I return to Berlin;" said the king, laughingly. "Why should our harmless pleasure and amusements be given up? Are we not to act Voltaire's 'Death of Cæsar?' No, I will not return to Berlin. A trifle such as the emperor's death, should not create such great disturbances. We will remain here and renew our former happy days, and forget that we have any duty but our enjoyment. Now, gentlemen, leave me, I am well. You see, Ellart, I did well to take that medicine; I will dress. Fredersdorf remain here. Jordan, send me Secretary Eichel. I must dictate a few necessary letters, and then, gentlemen, we will meet in the music room, where I am to play a duet with Quanz. I invite you as audience."

The king dismissed his friends with a gracious smile, jested gayly with Fredersdorf, and then dictated three letters to his secretary. One was to Marshal von Schwerin, the other to the Prince of Anhalt Dessau, and the third to Ambassador Podrilse. The three held the same words, the same command, telling them to come immediately to Rheinsberg. He then entered the music room and never was Frederick so gay, so witty, and unconstrained; never did he play on his flute more beautifully than on the day he heard of the death of the Emperor of Germany. The following morning the three gentlemen arrived from Berlin and were at once admitted into the king's library. Frederick met them with a proud, happy smile; his eye beamed with an unusual light; his forehead was smooth and free from care; he seemed inspired.

"The Emperor of Germany is dead," said he, after the gentlemen were seated. "The emperor is dead; and I have sent for you to see what benefit we can derive from his death!"

"Oh, your majesty would not think of benefiting by a death which throws a royal house, nearly connected with you, into deep sorrow, and robs the reigning queen of Prussia of an uncle!" cried the old Prince of Dessau, solemnly.

"Oh, it is well known that you are an imperialist," said the king, laughing.

"No, your majesty, but a difficulty with Austria would be a great misfortune for us."

Frederick shrugged his shoulders, and turned to the other two.

"I also wish for your opinion, gentlemen," said he; "you are all men of experience, soldiers, and statesmen, and you must not refuse to advise one of my youth and inexperience."

With a quiet smile he listened to their wise, peaceful propositions.

"You then doubt my right to Silesia?" said he, after a pause. "You do not think I am justified in demanding this Silesia, which was dishonestly torn from my ancestors by the Hapsburger?"

"But your ancestors still kept the peace," said the Prince of Dessau; "they left Silesia in the undisturbed possession of the Austrians."

"Yes," said the king, in a firm voice,—"and when my ancestors, outwitted by the cunning intrigues of the Austrian court, accommodated themselves to this necessity,—when for rendered services they were rewarded with base ingratitude, with idle, unmeaning promises, then they called upon their descendants to revenge such injustice, such insults to their honor and rights. Frederick William, the great Elector, cried prophetically when the Austrian house deserted him and denied her sworn promises—'A revenger will rise from my ashes;' and my father, when he had witnessed to the full the ingratitude of the Austrian court, felt that there could be no peace between the houses of Austria and Brandenburg, and he intrusted to me the holy mission of punishing and humiliating this proud, conceited court; he pointed me out to his ministers, and said: 'There stands one who will revenge me!' You see that my ancestors call me, my grandfather and father chose me for their champion and revenger; they call upon me to perform that which they, prevented by circumstances, could not accomplish; the hour which my ancestors designated has arrived—the hour of retribution! The time has come when the old political system must undergo an entire change. The stone has broken loose which is to roll upon Nebuchadnezzar's image and crush it. It is time to open the eyes of the Austrians, and to show them that the little Marquis of Brandenburg, whose duty they said it was to hand the emperor after meals the napkin and finger-bowl, has become a king, who will not be humbled by the Austrians, and who acknowledges none but God as his master. Will you help me; will you stand by me in this work with your experience and your advice?"

"We will!" cried the three, with animation, borne away by the king's noble ardor. "Our life, our blood, belong to our king, our country."

Frederick laughingly shook hands with them. "I counted upon you," said he, "nor will Zithen and Vinterfeldt fail us; we will not go to battle hastily and unprepared. All was foreseen, all prepared, and we have now but to put in execution the plans that have for some time been agitating my brain. Here is the map for our campaign; here are the routes and the plan of attack. We shall at last stand before these Austrians in battle array; and as they dared say of my father, that his gun was ever cocked but the trigger never pulled, we will show them that we are ready to discharge, and thrust down the double eagle from its proud pinnacle. The combat is determined and unalterable; let us be silent and prudent, no one must discover our plans; we will surprise the Austrians. And now, gentlemen, examine these plans, and tell me if there are any changes to be made in them."

CHAPTER VII.

THE KING AND HIS FRIEND.

FOR several hours the king remained in earnest council with his advisers. As they left him he called Jordan, and advanced to meet him with both hands extended.

" Well, Jordan, rejoice with me; my days of illness are over, and there will be life and movement in this rusty and creaking machine of state. You have often called me a bold eagle, now we shall see if my wings have strength to bear me to great deeds, and if my claws are sharp enough to pluck out the feathers of the double eagle."

" So my suspicions are correct, and it is against Austria that my king will make his first warlike movement?"

" Yes, against Austria; against this proud adversary, who, with envious and jealous eyes, watches my every step; who is pleased to look upon Prussia as her vassal; whose emperor considered it beneath his dignity to extend his hand to my father, or offer him a seat; and now will I refuse the hand to Austria, and force her from her comfortable rest."

" For you also, my king, will the days of quiet be over; your holy and happy hours with poetry, philosophy, and the arts, must be given up. The favorite of Apollo will become the son of Mars; we who are left behind can only look after you, we can do nothing for you, not even offer our breasts as a shield against danger and death."

" Away with such thoughts," said Frederick, smiling; " death awaits us all, and if he finds me on the field of battle, my friends, my subjects, and history will not forget me. That is a comfort and a hope; and you, Jordan, you know that I believe in a great, exalted, and almighty Being, who governs the world. I believe in God, and I leave my fate confidently in His hands. The ball which strikes me comes from Him; and if I escape the battle-field, a murderous hand can reach me, even in my bed-chamber; and surely that would be a less honorable, less famous death. I must do something great, decisive, and worthy of renown, that my people may love me, and look up to me with confidence and trust. It is not enough to be a king by inheritance and birth, I must prove by my deeds that I merit it. Silesia offers me a splendid opportunity, and truly I think the circumstances afford me a solid and sure basis for fame."

"Alas! I see," sighed Jordan, that the love of your subjects, and the enthusiastic tenderness of your friends, is not sufficient for you; you would seek renown.

"Yes, you are right; this glittering phantom, Fame, is ever before my eyes. I know this is folly, but when once you have listened to her intoxicating whispers, you cannot cast her off. Speak not, then, of exposure, or care, or danger; these are as dust of the balance; I am amazed that this wild passion does not turn every man's head."

"Alas! your majesty, the thirst for fame has cost thousands of men their reasons and their lives. The field of battle is truly the golden book of heroes, but their names must be written therein in blood."

"It is true," said the king, thoughtfully, "a field of battle is a sad picture for a poet and a philosopher; but every man in this world must pursue his calling, and I will not do my work half way. I love war for the sake of fame. Pity me not, Jordan, because these days of illness and peace, and gayety are over; because I must go into the rough field, while you amuse yourself with Horace, study Pausanias, and laugh and make merry with Anacreon. I envy you not. Fame beckons me with her alluring glance. My youth, the fire of passion, the thirst for renown, and a mysterious and unconquerable power, tears me from this life of indolence. The glowing desire to see my name connected with great deeds in the journals and histories of the times, drives me out into the battle-field.* There will I earn the laurel-wreaths which kings do not find in their cradles, or upon their throne, but which as men, and as heroes, they must conquer for themselves."

"The laurel will deck the brow of my hero, my Frederick, in all time," said Jordan, with tears in his eyes. "Oh! I see before you a glorious future; it may be I shall have passed away—but where will my spirit be? When I stand near you and look upon you, I know that the spirit is immortal. The soul, noble and god-like, will be ever near you; so whether living or dead I am thine, to love you as my friend, to honor you as my sovereign, to admire you as a gifted genius, glowing with godly fire."

"Oh, speak not of death," said the king, "speak not of death; I have need of you, and it seems to me that true friendship must be strong enough even to conquer death! Yes, Jordan, we have need of each other, we belong to each other; and it would be cruel, indeed, to rob me of a treasure which we, poor kings, so rarely possess, a faithful and sincere friend. No, Jordan, you will be my Cicero to defend the justice of my cause, and I will be your Cæsar to carry out the cause happily and triumphantly."

Jordan was speechless; he shook his head sadly. The king observed him anxiously, and saw the deep, feverish purple spots, those roses of the grave, upon the hollow cheeks of his friend; he saw that he grew daily weaker; he heard the hot, quick breathing which came panting from his breast. A sad presentiment took possession of his heart, the smile vanished from his lips, he could not conceal his emotion, and walking to the window he leaned his hot brow upon the glass and shed tears which none but God should

* The king's own words.

see. "My God! my God! how poor is a prince. I have so few friends, and these will soon pass away. Suhm lies ill in Marschau, perhaps I shall never see him again. Jordan is near me, but I see death in his face and he will soon be torn from my side."

Jordan stood immovable and looked toward the king, who still leaned his head upon the window; he did not dare to disturb him, and yet he had important and sad news to announce. At last Jordan laid his hand upon his shoulder.

"Pardon, my king," said he, in trembling tones, "pardon that I dare to interrupt you; but a hero dare not give himself up to sad thoughts before the battle, and when he thinks of death he must greet him with laughter, for death is his ally and his adjutant; and even if his ally grasps his nearest and best beloved friend, the hero and the conqueror must yield him up as an offering to victory."

The king turned quickly toward the speaker. "You have death news to give me," said he curtly, leaning against the back of his chair. "You have death news for me, Jordan."

"Yes, news of death, my prince," said he, deeply moved; "fate will accustom your majesty to such trials, that your heart may not falter when your friends fall around you in the day of battle."

"It is, then a friend who is dead," said Frederick, turning pale.

"Yes, sire, your best beloved."

The king said nothing; sinking in the chair, and grasping the arms convulsively, he leaned his head back, and in a low voice asked, "Is it Suhm?"

"Yes, it is Suhm; he died in Marschau. Here is his last letter to your highness; his brother sent it to me, that I might hand it to your majesty."

The king uttered a cry of anguish, and clasped his hands

15*

before his pallid face. Great tears ran down his cheeks, with a hasty movement he shook them from his eyes, opened and read the letter. As he read it he sighed and sobbed aloud: "Suhm is dead! Suhm is dead! the friend who loved me so sincerely, even as I loved him. That noble man, who combined intellect, sincerity, and sensibility. My heart is in mourning for him; so long as a drop of blood flows in my veins I will remember him, and his family shall be mine. Ah, my heart bleeds, and the wound is deep."

The king, mastered by his grief, laid his head in his hand and wept aloud. Then, after a long pause, he raised himself; he was calm and stern. "Jordan," said he, firmly, "death hath no more power over me, never again can he wring my heart, he has laid an iron shield upon me, and when I go to battle I must be triumphant, my friend has been offered up as a victim. Jordan, Jordan, my wound bleeds, but I will bind it up, and no man shall see even the blood-stained cloth with which I cover it. I have overcome death, and now will I offer battle and conquer as become a hero, and a king. What cares the world that I suffer? The world shall know nothing of it; a mask before my face, and silence as to my agony. We will laugh and jest while we sorrow for our friend, and while we prepare to meet the enemy. We will *play* Cæsar and Antonius now; hereafter we may really imitate them. Come, Jordan, come, we will try 'The Death of Cesar.'"

CHAPTER VIII.

THE FAREWELL AUDIENCE OF MARQUIS VON BOTTER, THE AUSTRIAN AMBASSADOR.

THIS was to be a *fête* day in the royal palace of Berlin. The king intended giving a splendid dinner, after which the court would take coffee in the newly furnished rooms of the dowager queen, and a mask ball was prepared for the evening, to which the court, the nobility, and higher officials were invited.

The court mourning for the emperor was at an end, and every one was determined to enjoy the pleasures of the carnival. Never had the court led so gay, so luxurious a life. Even the good old citizens of Berlin seemed to appreciate this new administration, which brought so much money to the poorer classes, such heavy profits to tradesmen. They believed that this extravagant court brought them greater gains than an economical one, and were therefore contented with this new order of things.

The king had refurnished the palace with an unheard of splendor. In the apartment of the queen-mother there was a room in which all the ornaments and decorations were of massive gold. Even the French and English ambassadors were astonished at this "Golden Cabinet," and declared that such splendor and magnificence could not be found in the palaces of Paris or London. The people of Berlin, as we have said, were becoming proud of their court and their king, and they thought it quite natural that this young ruler, who was only twenty-eight years old, should interest himself very little in the affairs of State, and should give his time to pleasure and amusement.

The king had accomplished his desire. No one suspected

the deep seriousness that he concealed under this idle play. No one dreamed that this gay, smiling prince, on whose lips there was always a witty jest or *bon mot ;* who proposed a concert every evening, in which he himself took part; who surrounded himself with artists, poets, and gay cavaliers, with whom he passed many nights of wild mirth and gayety— no one dreamed that this harmless, ingenuous. young prince, was on the point of overthrowing the existing politics of the European states, and of giving an entirely new form to the whole of Germany.

The king had not raised his mask for a moment; he had matured his plans under the veil of inviolate secrecy. The moment of their accomplishment had now arrived; this evening, during the mask ball which had been prepared with such pomp and splendor, the king with his regiments would leave Berlin and proceed to Silesia. But even the troops did not know their destination. The journals had announced that the army would leave Berlin to go into new winter quarters, and this account was generally believed. Only a few confidants, and the generals who were to accompany the king, were acquainted with this secret. The king, after a final conference, in which he gave the last instructions and orders, said:

"Now, gentlemen, that we have arranged our business, we will think of our pleasure. I will see you this evening at the ball; we will dance once more with the ladies before we begin our war-dance."

As the generals left him, his servant entered to assist at his toilet. Pelissier, the French tailor, had prepared a new and magnificent costume for this evening, made in the latest Parisian style. The king desired to appear once more in great splendor before exchanging the saloon for the camp. Never had he bestowed such care upon his toilet; never had he remained so patiently under the hands of the barber; he even went to the large mirror when his toilet was completed, and carefully examined his appearance and costly dress.

"Well," he said, smiling, " if the Marquis von Botter is not deceived by this dandy that I see before me, it is not my fault. The good Austrian ambassador must be very cunning indeed, if he discovers a warrior in this perfumed fop. I think he will be able to tell my cousin, Maria Theresa, nothing more than that the King of Prussia knows how to dress himself, and is the model of fashion."

The king passed into the rooms of the queen-mother, where the court was assembled, and where he had granted a farewell audience to the Marquis von Botter, the ambassador of the youthful Empress of Austria. Frederick was right: the marquis had been deceived by the mask of harmless gayety and thoughtless happiness assumed by the king and court. He had been sent by the empress with private instructions to sound the intentions of the Prussian king, while his apparent business was to return her acknowledgments for the congratulations of the King of Prussia on her ascension to the throne.

The Marquis von Botter, as we have said, had been deceived by the gay and thoughtless manner of the king, and Manteuffel's warnings and advice had been thrown away.

The marquis had withdrawn with Manteuffel to one of the windows, to await the entrance of the king; the ladies and gentlemen of the court were scattered through the rooms of the queen-mother, who was playing cards with Queen Christina in the golden cabinet.

" I leave Berlin," said the marquis, " with the firm conviction that the king has the most peaceful intentions."

" As early as to-morrow your convictions will be somewhat shaken," replied Manteuffel, " for this night the king and his army depart for Silesia."

At this moment the king appeared at the door of the

golden cabinet. There was a sudden silence, and all bent low, bowing before the brilliant young monarch.

Frederick bowed graciously, but remained in the door way, glancing over the saloon; it appeared to afford him a certain pleasure to exhibit himself to the admiring gaze of those present. He stood a living picture of youth, beauty, and manliness.

" Only look at this richly-dressed, elegant young man," whispered Marquis von Botter; " look at his youthful countenance, beaming with pleasure and delight; at his hands, adorned with costly rings, so white and soft, that they would do honor to the most high-bred lady; at that slender foot, in its glittering shoe. Do you wish to convince me that this small foot will march to battle; that this delicate hand, which is only fitted to hold a smelling-bottle or a pen, will wield a sword? Oh! my dear count, you make me merry with your gloomy prophecies."

" Still I entreat you to believe me. As soon as your audience is over, hasten to your hotel, and return to Vienna with all possible speed; allow yourself no hour of sleep, no moment for refreshment, until you have induced your empress to send her army to Silesia. If you do not, if you despise my advice, the King of Prussia will reach Silesia before you are in Vienna, and the empress will receive this intelligence which you do not credit from the fleeing inhabitants of her province, which will have been conquered without a blow."

The deep earnestness of the count had in it something so impressive, so convincing, that the marquis felt his confidence somewhat shaken, and looked doubtfully at the young monarch, who was now smiling and conversing with some of the ladies.

But even in speaking the king had not lost sight of these two gentlemen who were leaning against the window, and

whose thoughts he read in their countenances. He now met
the eye of the marquis, and motioned to him to come forward.
The marquis immediately approached the king, who stood in
the centre of the saloon, surrounded by his generals.

Every eye was turned toward the glittering group, in
which the young king was prominent: for those to whom
the intentions of the king were known, this was an interesting piece of acting; while for the uninitiated, who had only
an uncertain suspicion of what was about to happen, this was
a favorable moment for observation.

The Austrian ambassador now stood before the king,
making a deep and ceremonious bow. The king returned
this salutation, and said:

"You have really come to take leave, marquis?"

"Sire, her majesty, my honored empress, recalls me, and
I must obey her commands, happy as I should be, if I were
privileged, to sun myself still longer in your noble presence."

"It is true, a little sunshine would be most beneficial to
you, marquis. You will have a cold journey."

"Ah! your majesty, the cold is an evil that could easily
be endured."

"There are, then, other evils which will harass you on
your journey?"

"Yes, sire, there is the fearful road through Silesia, that
lamentable Austrian province. Ah! your majesty, this is a
road of which, in your blessed land, you have no, idea, and
which is happily unknown in the other Austrian provinces.
This poor Silesia has given only care and sorrow to the
empress; but, perhaps, for that reason, she loves it so well,
and would so gladly assist it. But even Nature seems to
prevent the accomplishment of her noble intentions. Heavy
rains have destroyed the roads which had, with great
expense, been rendered passable, and I learn, to my horror,
that it is scarcely possible for a traveller to pass them without running the greatest danger."

" Well," said the king, quietly, " I imagine that nothing could happen to the traveller that could not be remedied by a bath and a change of dress."

" Excuse me, sire," cried the marquis, eagerly, " he would risk his health, yes, even his life, in crossing the deep marshes, covered with standing water, which are common in that country. Oh! those are to be envied who need not expose themselves to this danger."

The king was wearied with this crafty diplomatic play; he was tired of the piercing glances with which the ambassador examined his countenance. In the firm conviction of his success, and the noble pride of his open and truth-loving nature, it pleased him to allow the mask to fall, which had concealed his heroic and warlike intentions from the marquis. The moment of action had arrived; it was, therefore no longer necessary to wear the veil of secrecy.

" Well, sir," said the king, in a loud, firm voice, " if you feel so great a dread of this journey, I advise you to remain in Berlin. I will go in your place into Silesia, and inform my honored cousin, Maria Theresa, with the voice of my cannon, that the Silesian roads are too dangerous for an Austrian, but are most convenient for the King of Prussia to traverse on his way to Breslau."

" Your majesty intends marching to Breslau! " asked the horrified marquis.

" Yes, sir, to Breslau; and as you remarked, the roads are too dangerous for a single traveller, and I intend taking my army with me to protect my carriage?"

" Oh! " exclaimed the marquis, " your majesty intends making a descent on the lands of my exalted sovereign."

The king glanced proudly and scornfully at this daring man. An involuntary murmur arose among the courtiers; the hands of the generals sought their swords, as if they would challenge this presumptuous Austrian, who dared to reproach the King of Prussia.

The king quieted his generals with a slight motion of his hand, and turning again to the marquis, he said, composedly, "You express yourself falsely, marquis. I will make no descent upon the lands of the Empress of Austria; I will only reclaim what is mine—mine by acknowledged right, by inheritance, and by solemn contract. The records of this claim are in the state department of Austria, and the empress need only read these documents to convince herself of my right to the province of Silesia.

"Your majesty, by this undertaking, may, perhaps, ruin the house of Austria, but you will most certainly destroy your own."

"It depends upon the empress to accept or reject the propositions which I have made to her through my ambassador in Vienna."

The marquis glanced ironically at the king, and said, "Sire, your troops are fair to see; the Austrian army has not that glittering exterior, but they are veterans who have already stood fire."

"You think my troops are showy," he said, impetuously; "*eh bien*, I will convince you that they are equally brave."

Thus speaking, the king gave the Austrian ambassador a bow of dismissal. The audience was at an end. The ambassador made a ceremonious bow, and left the room, amid profound silence.

Scarcely had the door closed behind him before the noble countenance of the king had recovered its usual calm and lofty expression.

He said gayly: "*Mesdames et messieurs*, it is time to prepare for the mask ball; I have thrown aside my mask for a moment, but you, doubtless, think it time to assume yours. Farewell until then."

CHAPTER IX.

THE MASQUERADE.

THE saloons were brilliantly illuminated, and a train of gayly intermingled, fantastically attired figures were moving to and fro in the royal palace. It seemed as if the representatives of all nations had come together to greet the heroic young king. Greeks and Turks were there in gold-embroidered, bejewelled apparel. Odalisks, Spanish, Russian, and German peasant women in every variety of costume; glittering fairies, sorceresses, and fortune-telling gypsies; grave monks, ancient knights in silver armor, castle dames, and veiled nuns. It was a magnificent spectacle to behold, these splendidly decorated saloons, filled with so great a variety of elegant costumes; and had it not been for the lifeless, grinning, and distorted faces, one might have imagined himself transported to Elysium, where all nations and all races are united in unclouded bliss. But the cold, glittering masks which concealed the bright faces, sparkling with animation and pleasure, somewhat marred the effect of this spectacle, and recalled the enraptured spectator to the present, and to the stern reality.

Only in the last of these saloons was there an unmasked group. In this room sat the two queens, glittering with gems, for it was no longer necessary for Sophia Dorothea to conceal her jewels; without fear she could now appear before her court in her magnificent diamonds; and Elizabeth Christina, who well knew that her husband loved to see his queen appear in a magnificence befitting her dignity on festive occasions, had adorned herself with the exquisite jewelry which excited the admiration of the entire court, and which Baron Bielfield declared to be a perfect miracle of beauty. Next to the two queens and the princesses

Ulrica and Amelia, stood the king in his magnificent ball costume. Behind the royal family stood their suite, holding their masks in their hands, for all were required to uncover their faces on entering the room in which the royal family were seated.

The king and the queen were about to fulfil the promises they had made each other; Sophia Dorothea was about to receive Count Néal, while the king was to welcome the recently married Countess Rhedern to court.

The loud and ironical voice of the master of ceremonies, Baron Pöllnitz, had just announced to the royal family the arrival of Count and Gountess Rhedern and Count Néal, and they were now entering the saloon, the sanctuary which was only open to the favored and privileged, only to those of high birth, or those whose offices required them to be near the king's person. No one else could enter this saloon without special invitation.

The newly-made Countess Rhedern made her entrance on the arm of her husband. Her face was perfectly tranquil and grave; an expression of determination rested on her features, which, although no longer possessing the charm of youth and beauty, were still interesting. Her countenance was indicative of energy and decision. An expression of benevolence played around her large but well-formed mouth; and her dark eyes, which were not cast down, but rested quietly on the royal family, expressed so much spirit and intelligence, that it was evident she was no ordinary woman, but a firm and resolute one, who had courage to challenge fate, and, if necessary, to shape her own destiny.

But the proud and imperious Queen Sophia Dorothea felt disagreeably impressed by the earnest glances with which the countess regarded her. If she had approached her tremblingly, and with downcast eyes, crushed, as it were, by the weight of this unheard-of condescension on the part of royalty, the queen would have been inclined to pardon her want of birth, and to forget her nameless descent; but the quiet and unconstrained bearing of the newly created countess enraged her. Moreover, she felt offended by the elegant and costly toilet of the countess. The long silver-embroidered train, fastened to her shoulders with jewelled clasps, was of a rarer and more costly material than even the robe of the queen; the diadem, necklace, and jeweled bracelets could rival the parure of the queen, and the latter experienced almost a sensation of envy at the sight of the large fan which the countess held half open in her hand, and with which the queen had nothing that could compare. The fan was of real Chinese workmanship, and ornamented with incomparable carvings in ivory, and beautiful paintings.

The queen acknowledged the thrice-repeated courtesy of Countess Rhedern, with a slight inclination of the head only, while Queen Elizabeth Christina greeted her with a gracious smile.

The king, who noticed the cloud gathering on his mother's brow, and very well knew its cause, was amused to see the queen-mother, who had so warmly advocated the reception of Countess Rhedern at court, now receive her so coldly; and wishing to jest with his mother on the subject of this short-lived fancy, he greeted the countess very graciously, and turning to his mother, said:

"You have done well, madame, to invite this beautiful countess to court; she will be a great acquisition, a great ornament."

"A great ornament," repeated Sophia Dorothea, who now considered the quiet and unconstrained bearing of the countess as disrespectful to herself; and fixing her proud and scornful glances upon her as she contemptuously repeated the king's words, she said: "What a singular train you wear!"

"It is of Indian manufacture," said the countess, quietly; "my father is connected with several mercantile houses in Holland, and from one of these I obtained the curious cloth which has attracted your majesty's attention."

Sophia Dorothea reddened with shame and indignation. This woman had the audacity not only not to be ashamed of her past life, over which she should have drawn a veil, but she dared in this brilliant company, in the presence of two queens, to speak of her father's business relations—even while the queen magnanimously wished to forget, and veil the obscurity of her birth.

"Ah!" said the queen-mother, "you wear an article from your father's shop! Truly, a convenient and ingenious mode of advertising your father's goods; and hereafter when we regard Countess Rhedern, we will know what is her father's latest article of trade."

The smile which the queen perceived upon the lips of her suite was a sufficient reward for her cruel jest. The eyes of all were scornfully fixed upon the countess, whose husband stood at her side, pale and trembling, and with downcast eyes. But the young countess remained perfectly composed.

"Pardon me, your majesty," said she, in a full, clear voice, "for daring to contradict you, but my father's business is too well known to need any such advertisement."

"Well, then, in what does he deal?" said the queen, angrily.

"Your majesty," said the countess, bowing respectfully, "my father's dealings are characterized by wisdom, honor, generosity, and discretion."

The queen's eyes flashed; a shopkeeper's daughter had dared to justify herself before the queen, and to defy and scoff at her anger.

She arose proudly. She wished to annihilate this newly-created countess with her withering contempt. But the king, who perceived the signs of a coming storm upon his mother's brow, determined to prevent this outbreak. It wounded his noble and generous soul to see a poor, defenceless woman tormented in this manner. He was too noble-minded to take offence at the quiet and composed bearing of the countess, which had excited his mother's anger. In her display of spirit and intelligence, he forgot her lowly birth, and laying his hand gently upon his mother's shoulder he said, with a smile :

"Does not your majesty think that Countess Rhedern does honor to her birth? Her father deals in wisdom, honor, and generosity. Well, it seems to me that Countess Rhedern has inherited these noble qualities. My dear countess, I promise you my patronage, and will ever be a devoted customer of your house if you prove worthy of your father."

"That I can promise your majesty," said the countess, an expression of proud delight flitting over her countenance, and almost rendering it beautiful ; "and will your majesty have the kindness, at some future time," said she, taking her husband's arm, "to convince yourself that the house of Rhedern and Company, to which your majesty has so graciously promised his patronage, is in a condition to satisfy his requirements ?"

The queen-mother could hardly suppress a cry of anger and indignation. The countess had dared to give the king an invitation. She had committed a breach of etiquette which could only be accounted for by the most absolute ignorance, or the greatest impertinence, and one which the king would assuredly punish.

But Sophia Dorothea was mistaken. Bowing low, the king said, with that kindliness of manner which was peculiar to himself: "I will take the very first opportunity of paying your establishment a visit."

Sophia Dorothea was very near fainting; she could stand this scene no longer; and giving herself up entirely to her anger, she was guilty of the same fault which the countess had committed through ignorance. Forgetful of etiquette, she assumed a right which belonged to the reigning king and queen alone. Arising hastily from her seat, she said, impatiently:

"I think it is time we should join the dancers. Do you not find the music very beautiful and enticing? Let us go."

The king smilingly laid his hand on her arm. "You forget, madame, that there is another happy man who longs to bask in the sunshine of your countenance. You forget, madame, that Count Néal is to have the honor of an introduction."

The queen gave her son one of those proud, resigned, and reproachful looks which she had been in the habit of directing toward Frederick William during her wedded life. She felt conquered, humbled, and powerless.

The imperious expression fled from her brow, and found refuge in her eyes only. "And this, too!" murmured she, sinking back on her seat. She barely heard Count Néal's introduction. She acknowledged his respectful greeting with a slight inclination of the head, and remained silent.

The king, who to-day seemed to be in a conciliatory mood, again came to the rescue.

"Madame," said he, "Count Néal is indeed an enviable man; he has seen what we will probably never see. He has been in the lovely, luxurious, and dreamy South; he has seen the sun of India; he was governor of Surinam."

"Pardon me, your majesty," said the count, proudly; "I was not only governor, but vice-regent."

"Ah," said the king, "and what are the prerogatives of a vice-regent?"

"I was there esteemed as your majesty is here. The governor of Surinam is approached with the same submission, humility, and devotion, he enjoys the same homage as the King of Prussia."

"Ah, you are then an equal of the King of Prussia? Baron Pöllnitz, you have been guilty of a great oversight; you have forgotten to provide a seat for my brother, the King of Surinam. You must be indulgent this time, my dear brother, but at the next ball we will not forget that you are a vice-regent of Surinam, and woe to the baron if he does not then provide a chair!"

He then took his mother's arm, and signing to Prince Augustus William to follow him with the reigning queen, proceeded to the ball-room.

On arriving there he released his mother's arm and said: "If agreeable to you, we will lay aside etiquette for a short time and mingle with the dancers." And without awaiting an answer, the king bowed and hurried off into the adjoining room, followed by Pöllnitz. He there assumed a domino and mask.

The entire court followed the king's example. The prince, and even the reigning queen, took advantage of his permission.

The queen was deserted by her suite, and left almost entirely alone in this large saloon. Her marshal, Count Rhedern, his wife, and the page who held her train, were the only persons who remained. Sophia Dorothea heaved a deep sigh; she felt that she was no longer a queen, but a poor widow who had vacated the throne. Happily, Countess Rhedern, the wife of her marshal, was still there; upon her she could at least vent her rage.

"Madame," said she, looking angrily at the countess,

"your train is too long; you should have brought some of the lads from your father's store to carry this train for you, in order that it might be more minutely examined."

The countess bowed. "Your majesty must pardon me for not having done so, but my father's assistants are not at my disposal. But perhaps we can find a remedy if your majesty really thinks I need a train-bearer. I suggest that some of my father's principal debtors should fill this place. I believe these gentlemen would willingly carry my train if my father would grant them a respite. If your majesty agrees to this proposition, I shall at once select two of your noblest cavaliers for my train-bearers, and will then no longer put your brilliant court to shame."

The queen did not reply; she cast an angry glance at the quiet and composed countess, and then walked quietly toward the throne. around which the royal family had now assembled.

CHAPTER X.

THE MASKERS.

THE king, with the assistance of Pöllnitz, had now completed his toilet; he did not wish to be recognized, and his dress was similar to hundreds of others who were wandering through the rooms.

" Do you think I will be known ? "

" No, sire, it is not possible. Now have the goodness to push your mask slightly over your eyes; they might perhaps betray you."

" Well, these eyes will soon see some curious things. Did you ever stand upon a battle-field as a conqueror, surrounded by corpses, all your living enemies having fled before you?"

"Heaven in its mercy preserve me from such a sight! My enemies, sire, have never fled from me; they chase me and threaten me, and it is of God's great mercy that I have always escaped them."

"Who are these pursuing enemies of yours?"

"They are my creditors, your majesty, and you may well believe that they are more terrible to me than a battle-field of corpses. Unhappily, they still live, and the fiends torment me."

"Well, Pöllnitz, after I have seen my first battle-field, in the condition I have just described to you, and returned home victorious, I will assist you to kill off your rapacious enemies. Until then keep bravely on the defensive. Come, let us go, I have only half an hour left for pleasure."

The king opened the door of the cabinet, and, jesting merrily, he mingled with the crowd, while Pöllnitz remained near the door, and cast a searching glance around the room. Presently a mocking smile flitted over his face, and he said to himself: "There, there *are all three of them. There is the modestly dressed* nun who would not be recognized as Madame von Morien. There is the king of cards, Manteuffel, who is not yet aware that a quick eye has seen his hand, and his trumps are all in vain. There at last is Madame von Brandt, 'The Gypsy,' telling fortunes, and having no presentiment of the fate awaiting herself. A little scrap of paper carelessly lost and judiciously used by the lucky finder is quite sufficient to unmask three of the worldly wise."

"Well, baron," whispered the nun, "will you fulfil your promise?"

"Dear Madame von Morien," replied Pöllnitz, shrugging

his shoulders, "the king expressly commanded me not to betray him."

"Pöllnitz," said the nun, with a tearful voice, "have pity upon me; tell me the disguise of the king; you shall not only have my eternal gratitude—but look, I know you love diamonds; see this costly pin, which I will give for the news I crave."

"It is impossible for poor, weak human nature to resist you," said Pöllnitz, stretching out his hand eagerly for the pin; "diamonds have a convincing eloquence, and I must submit; the king has a blue domino embroidered with silver cord, a white feather is fastened in his hat with a ruby pin, and his shoe-buckles are of rubies and diamonds."

"Thank you," said the nun, handing the pin and mingling hastily with the crowd."

While Pöllnitz was fastening the pin in his bosom, the king of cards approached, and laid his hand on his shoulder.

"Well, baron, you see I am punctual; answer the questions of yesterday, and I will give you all the information necessary to secure you a rich and lovely wife."

"I accept the terms. You wish to know what route the king will take and the number of his troops : this paper contains the information you desire; I obtained it from a powerful friend, one of the confidential servants of the king. I had to pay a thousand crowns for it; you see I did not forget you."

"Well, here is a draft for four thousand crowns," said Manteuffel; "you see I did not forget your price."

"And now for the rich and lovely wife."

"Listen. In Nuremberg I am acquainted with a rich family, who have but one fair daughter; she will inherit a million. The family is not noble, but they wish to marry their daughter to a Prussian cavalier. I have proposed you, and you are accepted; you have only to go to Nuremberg and deliver these letters; you will be received as a son, and immediately after the wedding you will come into possession of a million."

"A million is not such a large sum after all," said Pöllnitz. "If I must marry a citizen in order to obtain a fortune I know a girl here who is young, lovely, and much in love with me, and I think she has not less than a million."

"Well, take the letters; you can consider the subject. *Au revoir*, my dear baron. Oh, I forgot one other small stipulation connected with your marriage with the Nuremberger: the family is Protestant, and will not accept a Catholic for their rich daughter; so you will have to become a Protestant."

"Well, that is a small affair. I was once a Protestant, and I think I was just as good as I am now."

Manteuffel laughed heartily, and withdrew.

Pöllnitz looked thoughtfully at the letters, and considered the question of the Nuremberg bride. "I believe Anna Pricker has at least a million, and old Pricker lies very ill from the shock of his wife's sudden death. If our plan succeeds, and Anna becomes a great singer, she will have powererful influence with the king, and it will be forgotten that she is a tailor's daughter. I believe I would rather have Anna than the Nuremberger. but I will keep the latter in reserve."

Pöllnitz had reached this point in his meditations, when the gypsy stood before him; she greeted him with roguish words, and he was again the thoughtless and giddy cavalier. Madame von Brandt, however, had but little time for jesting.

"You promised to give me information of the letter I lost at the last court festival," she said, anxiously.

"Yes, that very important letter, ruinously compromising two ladies and a nobleman. I suppose you would obtain the letter at any sacrifice?"

"Yes, at any sacrifice," said Madame von Brandt. "You

asked a hundred Louis d'ors for the letter; I have brought them with me; take them—now give me the letter."

The baron took the money and put it in his pocket.

" Well, the letter, let me have it quickly," said Madame von Brandt.

Pöllnitz hunted through his pockets anxiously. "My God!" he cried, " this letter has wings. I know I put it in my pocket, and it has disappeared; perhaps like yourself I lost it in the saloon ; I must hasten to seek it." He wished to go immediately, but Madame von Brandt held him back.

" Have the goodness to give me my money until you have found the letter," she cried, trembling with rage.

" Your money," cried Pöllnitz ; " you gave me no money. Why do you keep me ? allow me to go and seek this important letter." He tore himself from her and mingled with the crowd.

Madame von Brandt looked after him in speechless rage ; she leaned against the wall, to prevent herself from falling.

Pöllnitz laughed triumphantly. " This evening has brought me a thousand crowns, two hundred Louis d'ors, a splendid diamond pin, and the promise of a rich wife. I think I may be content. Through these intrigues I have enough to live on for months. I stand now high in the king's favor, and who knows, perhaps he may now give me a house, not the house in the Jäger Street—that is, alas, no longer vacant. I see the king—I must hasten to him." Suddenly he heard his name called, and turning he saw a lady in a black domino, the hood drawn over her head, and her face covered with an impenetrable veil.

" Baron Pöllnitz, a word with you, if you please," and slightly motioning with her hand, she passed before him. Pöllnitz followed her, curious to know his last petitioner. but the dark domino covered her completely. They had now reached a quiet window ; the lady turned and said :

"Baron Pöllnitz, you are said to be a noble and gallant cavalier, and I am sure you will not refuse a lady a favor."

"Command, me madame," said Pöllnitz, with his eterna smile. "I will do all in my power."

"Make known to me the costume of the king."

The baron stepped back in angry astonishment. "So, my beautiful mask, you call that a favor; I must betray his majesty to you. He has forbidden me positively to make known his costume to any one; you cannot desire me to be guilty of such a crime!"

"I implore you to tell me," cried the mask; "it is not from idle curiosity that I desire to know: I have an ardent but innocent desire to say a few words to the king before he leaves for the wars, from which he may never return."

In the excitement of deep feeling, the mask spoke in her natural voice, and there were certain tones which Pöllnitz thought he recognized; he must be certain, however, before speaking; he drew nearer, and gazing piercingly at the lady, he said: "You say, madame, that it is not in idle curiosity that you desire to know the costume of the king. How do I know that you do not entertain dangerous designs? how do I know but you are an enemy, corrupted by Austria, and wish to lead the king to his destruction?"

"The only security I can offer is the word of a noble lady who never told an untruth. God omnipotent, God omnipresent knows that my heart beats with admiration, reverence, and love for the king. I would rather die than bring him into danger."

"Will you swear that?"

"I swear!" cried the lady, raising her arm solemnly toward heaven.

Pöllnitz followed all her movements watchfully, and as the long sleeve of the domino fell back, he saw a bracelet of emeralds and diamonds, which he recognized; there was but

one lady at the Prussian court who possessed such a brace
let, and that was the reigning queen. Pöllnitz was too old
a courtier to betray the discovery he had made; he bowed
quietly to the lady, who, discovering her imprudence, lowered
her arm and drew her sleeve tightly over it.

"Madame," said the baron, "you have taken a solemn
oath and I am satisfied, I will grant your request, but, as I
gave my word of honor to tell no one the costume of his
majesty, I must show it to you. I am now going to seek
the king; I shall speak with no one but him; therefore the
domino before whom I bow and whom I address, will be the
king; follow me."

"I thank you," said the lady, drawing her domino closely
over her; "I shall remember this hour gratefully, and if it is
ever in my power to serve you, I shall do so."

"This is indeed a most fortunate evening! I have earned
money and diamonds and the favor of the queen, who up to
this time has looked upon me with cold dislike."

Pöllnitz approached the king and bowed low; the lady
stood behind, marking well the costume of his majesty.

"I have waited a long time for Pöllnitz," said the king.

"Sire, I had to wait for three masks; I have seen them
all—Madame von Morien, Madame von Brandt, and Baron
von Manteuffel. The baron remains true to his character; he
is in the costume of the king of cards."

"And Madame von Morien?" asked the king.

"She is here as a nun, and burns with desire to speak
with your majesty; and if you will step into the dark saloon,
I do not doubt the repentant nun will quickly follow you."

"Well, what is the costume of Madame von Brandt?"

"A gypsy, sire; a yellow skirt, with a red bodice embroidered in gold; a little hat studded with diamonds and a
beauty spot on the left temple; she wished me to give her

the letter I found, and I sold it to her for two hundred Louis d'ors."

"You had not the letter, however, and could not receive the money?"

"Pardon, your majesty, I took the Louis d'ors, and then discovered that I had lost the letter. I came to seek it."

The king laughed heartily, and said: "Pöllnitz, Pöllnitz, it is a blessed thing for the world that you are not married; your boys would be consummate rascals! Did you give Manteuffel the plan of the campaign and the number of the troops?"

"Yes, sire, I did; and the baron was so charmed that he made me a present of four thousand crowns! I took them, for appearance' sake; your majesty must decide what I must do with them."

"Keep the reward of your iniquity, baron. You have a superb talent for thieving, and I would prefer you should practise it on the Austrians to practising it on myself. Go now, and see that I find my uniform in the cabinet."

The king mingled again with the crowd, and was not recognized, but laughed and jested with them merrily as man to man.

CHAPTER XI.

REWARD AND PUNISHMENT.

SUDDENLY the king ceased his cheerful laughter and merry jests; he had for the moment forgotten that he had any thing to do but amuse himself; he had forgotten that he was here to judge and to punish. Frederick was standing by the once dearly loved Count Manteuffel, and as his eye fell upon him he was recalled to himself.

"Ah! I was looking for you," said the king, laying his hand upon the count's shoulder; "you were missing from my game, dear king of cards, but now that I have you, I shall win."

The count had too good an ear not to recognize the king's voice in spite of its disguise; but he was too nice a diplomatist to betray his discovery by word or look.

"What game do you wish to play with me, mask?" said he, following the king into an adjoining and unoccupied room.

"A new game, the game of war!" said the king, harshly.

"The game of war," repeated the count; "I have never heard of that game."

The king did not answer at once; he was walking hastily up and down the room.

"Count," said he, stopping before Manteuffel, "I am your friend. I wish to give you some good advice. Leave Berlin to-night, and never return to it!"

"Why do you advise this?" said the count, coolly.

"Because otherwise you are in danger of being imprisoned as a traitor and hung as a spy! Make no answer; attempt no defence. I am your friend, but I am also the friend of the king. I would guard you from a punishment, though a just one; and I would also guard him from embarrassment and vexation. The king does not know that you are an Austrian spy, in the pay of the imperial court. May he never know it! He once loved you; and his anger would be terrible if informed of your perfidy. Yes, Count Manteuffel, this prince was young, inexperienced and trusting; he believed in your love and gave you his heart. Let us spare his youth; let us spare him the humiliation of despising and punishing the man he once loved. Oh, my God! it is hard to trample a being contemptuously under foot whom you once pressed lovingly to your heart. The king is gentle and affectionate:

he is not yet sufficiently hardened to bear without pain the blows inflicted by a faithless friend. A day may come when the work of such friends, when your work, may be accomplished, when King Frederick will wear about his heart a coat-of-mail woven of distrust; but, as I said, that time has not come. Do not await it, count, for then the king would be inexorable toward you; he would look upon you only as a spy and a traitor! Hasten, then, with flying steps from Berlin."

"But how, if I remain and attempt to defend myself?" said the count, timidly.

"Do not attempt it; it would be in vain. For in the same moment that you attempted to excuse yourself, the king would hear of your cunning, your intrigues, your bribery, and your treachery; he would know that you corresponded with his cook; that Madame von Brandt kept a journal for you, which you sent to the Austrian court, and for which you paid her a settled sum; he would know that you watched his every word and step, and sold your information for Austrian gold! No, no, dare not approach the king. A justification is impossible. Leave here to-night, and never dare to tread again on Prussian soil! Remember I am your friend; as such I address you."

"You then advise me to go at once, without taking leave of the king?" said the count, who could not now conceal his embarrassment.

"I do! I command you," said the king; "I command you to leave this castle on the spot! silently, without a word or sign, as beseems a convicted criminal! I command you to leave Berlin to-night. It matters not to me where you go—to hell, if it suits your fancy."

The count obeyed silently, without a word; to the king he bowed and left the room.

The king gazed after him till he was lost in the crowd.

"And through such men as that we lose our trust and confidence in our race; such men harden our hearts," said he to himself. "Is that then true which has been said by sages of all times, that princes are condemned to live solitary and joyless lives; that they can never possess a friend disinterested and magnanimous enough to love them for themselves, and not for their power and glory? If so, why give our hearts to men? Let us love and cherish our dogs, who are true and honest, and love their masters, whether they are princes or beggars. Ah, there is Manteuffel's noble friend, that coquettish little gypsy; we will for once change the usual order of things: I will prophesy to her, instead of receiving her prophecies." The king approached and whispered: "Pöllnitz has found the precious letter, and is anxious to return it to you."

"Where is he?" said the gypsy, joyously.

"Follow me," said Frederick, leading her to the same room where he had dismissed Manteuffel. "Here we are, alone and unnoticed," said the king, "and we can gossip to our hearts' content."

Madame von Brandt laughed: "Two are needed for a gossip," said she; "and how do you know that I am in the humor for that? You led me here by speaking of a letter which Baron Pöllnitz was to give me, but I see neither Pöllnitz nor the letter!"

"Pöllnitz gave it to me to hand you; but before I give it up I will see if I have not already learned something of your art, and if I cannot prophesy as well as yourself. Give me your hand: I will tell your fortune."

Madame von Brandt silently held out her trembling hand; she had recognized the voice; she knew it was the king who stood by her side.

The king studied her hand without touching it. "I see wonderful things in this small hand. In this line it is written that you are a dangerous friend, a treacherous subject, and a cruel flirt."

"Can you believe this?" said she, with a forced laugh.

"I do not only believe it, I know it. It is written in bold, imperishable characters upon your hand and brow. Look! I see here, that from a foreign land, for treacherous service, you receive large sums of gold; here I see splendid diamonds, and there I read that twenty thousand crowns are promised you if you prevent a certain divorce. You tremble, and your hand shakes so I can scarcely read. Keep your hand steady, madame; I wish to read not only your past but your future life."

"I shall obey," whispered Madame von Brandt.

"Here I read of a dangerous letter, which fell, through your own carelessness, into the wrong hands. If the king should read that letter, your ruin would be unavoidable; he would punish you as a traitor; you would not only be banished from court, but confined in some strong fortress. When a subject conspires with the enemy during time of war, this is the universal punishment. Be cautious, be prudent, and the king will learn nothing of this, and you may be saved."

"What must I do to avert my ruin?" she said, breathlessly.

"Banish yourself, madame; make some excuse to withdraw immediately from Berlin; retire to your husband's estate, and there, in quiet and solitude, think over and repent your crimes. When like Mary Magdalene you have loved, and deceived, and betrayed, like her you must repent, and see if God is as trusting as man; if you can deceive Him with your tears as you once deceived us with your well-acted friendship. Go try repentance with God; here it is of no avail. This reformation, madame, must commence at once. You will leave Berlin to-morrow, and will not return till the king himself sends for you."

"I go!" said Madame von Brandt, weeping bitterly; "I go! but I carry death in my heart, not because I am banished, but because I deserve my punishment; because I have wounded the heart of my king, and my soul withers under his contempt."

"Mary Magdalene," said Frederick, "truly you have a wondrous talent for acting; a hint is enough for you, and you master your part at once. But, madame, it is useless to act before the king; he will neither credit your tears nor your repentance; he would remember your crimes and pronounce your sentence. Hasten, then, to your place of atonement. There you may turn saint, and curse the vain and giddy world. Here is your letter—farewell!"

The king hastened away, and Madame von Brandt, weeping from shame and humiliation, remained alone. The king passed rapidly through the crowded saloon and stepped on the balcony; he had seen the nun following him, and she came upon the balcony; he tore off his mask, and confronting the trembling woman, he said, in a harsh voice:

"What do you want with me?"

"Your love," cried the nun, sinking upon her knees and raising her hands imploringly to the king; "I want the love you once promised me—the love which is my earthly happiness and my salvation—your love, without which I must die; wanting which, I suffer the tortures of purgatory!"

"Then suffer," said the king, harshly; retreating a few steps—"go and suffer; endure the torments of purgatory, you deserve them; God will not deliver you, nor will I."

"Alas! alas! I hear this, and I live;" cried Madame von Morien, despairingly. "Oh, my king, take pity on me; think of the heavenly past; think of the intoxicating poison your words and looks poured into my veins, and do not scorn and punish me because I am brought almost to madness and death by your neglect. See what you have made of me! see how poor Leontine has changed!" She threw back her veil, and showed her pale and sorrowful countenance to the king.

He gazed at her sternly: "You have become old, madame," he said, coldly—"old enough to tread in the new path you have so wisely prepared for yourself. You who have so long been the votary of love, are now old enough and plain enough to become a model of virtue. Accept this order of virtue and modesty, promised you by the Empress of Austria. The king will not divorce his wife, and as this is supposed to be solely your work, the empress will not withhold the promised order."

"My God! he knows all, and he despises me!" cried Madame von Morien, passionately.

"Yes, he despises you," repeated the king; "he despises and he has no pity on you! Farewell!"

Without again looking toward the broken-hearted woman, he turned toward the dancing-saloon. Suddenly he felt a hand laid softly upon his shoulder; he turned and saw at his side a woman in black, and thickly veiled.

"One word, King Frederick," whispered the lady.

"Speak, what do you wish?" said the king, kindly.

"What do I wish?" said she, with a trembling voice; "I wish to see you; to hear your voice once more before you go to the battle-field, to danger, perhaps to death. I come to entreat you to be careful of your life! remember it is a precious jewel, for which you are not only answerable to God, but to millions of your subjects. Oh, my king, do not plunge wantonly into danger; preserve yourself for your country, your people, and your family; to all of whom you are indispensable."

The king shook his head, smilingly. "No one is indispensable. A man lost is like a stone thrown into the water; for a moment there is a slight eddy, the waters whirl, then all trace disappears, and the stream flows quietly and smoothly on. But not thus will I disappear. If I am destined to fall in this combat to which I am now hastening, my death shall be glorious, and my grave shall be known ; it must, at least, be crowned with laurels, as no one will consecrate it with the tribute of love and tears. A king, you know, is never loved, and no one weeps for his death ; the whole world is too busily engaged in welcoming his successor."

"Not so ; not so with you, my king ! you are deeply, fondly loved. I know a woman who lives but in your presence—a woman who would die of joy if she were loved by you ; she would die of despair if death should claim you ; you, her youthful hero, her ideal, her god ! For this woman's sake who worships you ; whose only joy you are ; who humbly lays her love at your feet, and only asks to die there ; for her sake I implore you to be careful of yourself ; do not plunge wantonly into danger, and thus rob Prussia of her king ; your queen of the husband whom she adores, and for whom she is ready at any hour to give her heart's blood."

The king clasped gently the folded hands of the veiled lady within his own ; he knew her but too well.

"Are you so well acquainted with the queen that you know all the secrets of her heart ? "

"Yes, I know the queen," whispered she ; "I am the only confidant of her sorrows. I only know how much she loves, how much she suffers."

"I pray you, then, go to the queen and bid her farewell for me. Tell her that the king honors no other woman as he honors her ; that he thinks she is exalted enough to be placed among the noble women of the olden times. He is convinced she would say to her warrior husband, as the Roman wives said to their fathers, husbands, and sons, when handing their shields, 'Return with them or upon them !' Tell

Elizabeth Christina that the King of Prussia will return from this combat with his hereditary foe as a conqueror, or as a corpse. He cares little for life, but much for honor; he must make his name glorious, perchance by the shedding of his blood. Tell Elizabeth Christina this, and tell her also that on the day of battle her friend and brother will think of her; not to spare himself, but to remember gratefully that, in that hour, a noble and pure woman is praying to God for him. And now adieu: I go to my soldiers—you to the queen."

He bowed respectfully, and hurried to the music-room. The queen followed him with tearful eyes, and then drawing her hood tightly over her face, she hurried through a secret door into her apartments. While the queen was weeping and praying in her room, the king was putting on his uniform, and commanding the officers to assemble in the court-yard.

Prince Augustus William was still tarrying in the dancing-saloon: he did not dance; no one knew he was there. He had shown himself for a few hours in a magnificent fancy suit, but unmasked; he then left the ball-room, saying he still had some few preparations to make for his journey. Soon, however, he returned in a common domino and closely masked; no one but Laura von Pannewitz was aware of his presence; they were now standing together in a window, whose heavy curtains hid them from view. It was a sad pleasure to look once more into each other's eyes, to feel the warm pressure of loving hands, to repeat those pure and holy vows which their trembling lips had so often spoken; every fond word fell like glorious music upon their young hearts. The moment of separation had come; the officers were assembled, and the solemn beating of drums was heard.

"I must leave you, my beloved, my darling," whispered the prince, pressing the weeping girl to his heart. Laura sobbed convulsively.

"Leave me, alas, perhaps never to return!"

"I shall return, my Laura," said he, with a forced smile. "I am no hero; I shall not fall upon the battle-field. I know this; I feel it. I feel also that if this was to be my fate, I should be spared many sorrowful and agonizing hours; how much better a quick, glorious death, than this slow torture, this daily death of wretchedness! Oh, Laura, I have presentiments, in which my whole future is covered with clouds and thick darkness, through which even your lovely form is not to be seen; I am alone, all alone!"

"You picture my own sufferings, my own fears," whispered Laura. "Alas! I forget the rapture of the present in the dim and gloomy future. Oh, my beloved, my heart does not beat with joy when I look at you; it overflows with despair. I am never to see you again, my prince; our fond farewell is to be our last! Oh, believe me, this sad presentiment is the voice of Fate, warning us to escape from this enchanting vision, with which we have lulled our souls to sleep. We have forgotten our duty, and we are warned that a cruel necessity will one day separate us!"

"Nothing shall separate us!" said the prince; "no earthly power shall come between us. The separation of to-day, which honor demands of me, shall be the last. When I return, I will remind you of your oath; I will claim your promise, which God heard and accepted. Our love is from God, and no stain rests upon it; God, therefore, will watch over it, and will not withhold His blessing; with His help, we will conquer all difficulties, and we can dispense with the approbation of the world."

Laura shook her head sadly: "I have not this happy confidence; and I have not the strength to bear this painful separation. At times when I have been praying fervently for help, it seems to me that God is standing by and strengthening me to obey the command of the dowager-queen and give my hand to Count Voss. But when I wish to speak the decisive word my lips are closed as with a band of iron; it seems to me that, could I open them, the only sound I should utter would be a cry so despairing as to drive me to madness."

The prince pressed her fondly to his heart: "Swear to me, Laura, that you will never be so faithless, so cowardly, as to yield to the threats of my mother," said he, passionately; "swear that you will be true to your oath; that oath by which you are mine—mine to all eternity; my wedded wife!"

"I swear it," said she, solemnly, fixing her eyes steadily upon his agitated countenance.

"They will take advantage of my absence to torture you. My mother will overwhelm you with reproaches, threats, and entreaties; but, if you love me, Laura, you will find strength to resist all this. As yet my mother does not know that it is I whom you love; I who worship you; she suspects that the king or the young Prince of Brunswick possesses your heart. But chance may betray our love, and then her anger would be terrible. She would lose no time in separating us; would stop at nothing. Then, Laura, be firm and faithful; believe no reports, no message, no letter; trust only in me and in my word. I will not write to you, for my letters might be intercepted. I will send no messenger to you; he might be bribed. If I fall in battle, and God grants me strength in dying, I will send you a last embrace and a last loving word, by some pitying friend. In that last hour our love will have nothing to fear from the world, the king, or my mother. You will always be in my thoughts, darling, and my spirit will be with you."

"And if you fall, God will have mercy on me and take me from this cruel world; it will be but a grave for me when no longer gladdened by your presence."

The prince kissed her fondly, and slipped a ring on her finger. "*That* is our engagement ring," said he. "Now you are mine; you wear my ring; this is the first link of that chain with which I will bind your whole life to mine! You are my prisoner; nothing can release you. But listen! what is that noise? The king has descended to the court; he will be looking for me. Farewell, my precious one; God and His holy angels guard you!"

He stepped slowly from behind the curtains and closed them carefully after him, so as to conceal Laura; he passed hastily through the rooms to his apartment, threw off the domino which concealed his uniform, and seizing his sword he hastened to the court. The king was surrounded by his generals and officers; all eyes were fixed upon him; he had silenced every objection. There was amongst them but one opinion and one will, the will and opinion of the king, whom all felt to be their master, not only by divine right, but by his mighty intellect and great soul. Frederick stood amongst them, his countenance beaming with inspiration, his eagle eye sparkling and glowing with the fire of thought, and a smile was on his lips which won all hearts. Behind him stood the Prince of Anhault Dessau, old Zeithen, General Vinterfeldt, and the adjutant-generals. Above them floated a magnificent banner, whose motto, "Pro gloria et patria," was woven in gold. Frederick raised his naked sword and greeted the waving colors; he spoke, and his full, rich voice filled the immense square:

"Gentlemen, I undertake this war with no other ally than your stout hearts; my cause is just; I dare ask God's help! Remember the renown our great ancestors gained on the battle-field of Ferbellin! Your future is in your own hands; distinction must be won by gallant and daring deeds. We are to attack soldiers who gained imperishable names under Prince Eugene. How great will be our glory if we

vanquish such warriors!   Farewell!   Go!   I follow without
delay!"

CHAPTER XII.

THE RETURN.

THE first campaign of the young King of Prussia had been
a bloodless one. Not one drop of blood had been shed. A
sentinel at the gate of Breslau had refused to allow the Prussian general to enter, and received for his daring a sounding
box on the ear, which sent him reeling backward. The general with his staff entered the conquered capital of Silesia, without further opposition. Breslau was the capital of a province which for more than a hundred years had not been
visited by any member of the royal house of Austria. The
heavy taxes imposed upon her were the only evidence that
she belonged to the Austrian dominions. Breslau did not
hesitate to receive this young and handsome king, who as he
marched into the city gave a kindly, gracious greeting to all;
who had a winning smile for all those richly-dressed ladies at
the windows; who had written with his own hand a procla-
mation in which he assured the Silesians that he came not as
an enemy, and that every inhabitant would be secured in
their rights, privileges, and freedom in their religion, worth,
and service. The ties which bound the beautiful province
of Silesia to Austria had long ago been shattered, and the
prophecy of the king had already been fulfilled—that prophecy
made in Krossen. As the king entered Krossen with his
army, the clock of the great church tower fell with a thundering noise, and carried with it a portion of the old church. A
superstitious fear fell upon the whole Prussian army; even

the old battle-stained warriors looked grim and thoughtful. The king alone smiled, and said:

"The fall of this clock signifies that the pride of the house of Austria will be humbled. Cæsar fell when landing in Africa, and exclaimed: 'I hold thee, Africa!'"

Those great men would not allow themselves to be influenced by evil omens. Quickly, indeed, was Frederick's prophecy fulfilled. The house of Austria was suddenly humbled, and the Prussian army was quietly in possession of one of her capitals. Frederick had been joyfully received, not only by the Protestants, who had so long suffered from the bitterest religious persecution, and to whom the king now promised absolute freedom of conscience and unconditional exercise of their religious worship, but by the Catholics, even the priests and Jesuits, who were completely fascinated by the intellect and amiability of Frederick. No man mourned for the Austrian yoke, and the Prussians became great favorites with the Silesians, particularly with the women, who, heart in hand, advanced to meet them; received the handsome and well-made soldiers as lovers, and hastened to have these tender ties made irrevocable by the blessing of the priest. Hundreds of marriages between the Prussians and the maidens of the land were solemnized during the six weeks Frederick remained in Silesia. These men, who, but a few weeks before, came as enemies and conquerors, were now adopted citizens, thus giving their king a double right to the possession of these provinces.

It soon became the *mode* for the Silesian girl to claim a Prussian lover, and the taller and larger the lover, the prouder and more happy was the lucky possessor. Baron Bielfeldt, who accompanied the king to Breslau, met in the street one day a beautiful *bourgeoise*, who was weeping bitterly and wringing her hands; Bielfeldt inquired the cause of her tears, and she replied naïvely:

" Alas! I am indeed an object of pity; eight days ago I
was betrothed to a Prussian grenadier, who measured five
feet and nine inches; I was very happy and very proud of
him. To-day one of the guard, who measured six feet and
two inches, proposed to me; and I weep now because so
majestic and handsome a giant is offered me, and I cannot
accept him."

The king won the women through his gallant soldiers;
the ladies of the aristocracy, through his own beauty, grace,
and eminent intellect. Frederick gave a ball to the aristocracy of Breslau, and all the most distinguished and noble
families, who had been before closely bound to the house of
Austria, eagerly accepted the invitation; they wished to behold the man who was a hero and a poet, a cavalier and a
warrior, a youth and a philosopher; who was young and
handsome, and full of life; who did not wrap himself in stiff,
ceremonious forms, and appeared in the presence of ladies to
forget that he was a king. He worshipped the ladies as a
cavalier, and when they accepted the invitation to dance,
considered it a flattering favor. While winning the hearts
of the women through his gallantry and beauty, he gained
the voices of men by the orders and titles which he scattered
broadcast through the province.

" I dreamed last night," said he to Pöllnitz, laughing,
" that I created princes, dukes, and barons in Breslau; help
me to make my dream a reality by naming to me some of
the most prominent families."

Pöllnitz selected the names, and Prince von Pless, Duke
Hockburg, and many others rose up proudly from this
creative process of the king.

Silesia belonged, at this moment, unconditionally to
Prussia. The king could now return to Berlin and devote
himself to study, to friendship, and his family. The first act
of that great drama called the Seven Years' War, was now

finished. The king should now, between the acts, give himself up to the arts and sciences, and strengthen himself for that deep tragedy of which he was resolved to be the hero. Berlin received her king with shouts of joy, and greeted him as a demigod. He was no longer, in the eyes of the imperious Austrians, the little Margrave of Brandenburg, who must hold the wash-basin for the emperor; he was a proud, self-sustaining king, no longer receiving commands from Austria, but giving laws to the proud daughter of the Cæsars.

The queen-mother and the young princesses met the king at the outer gates. The queen Elizabeth Christina, her eyes veiled with rapturous tears, received her husband tremblingly. Alas! he had for her only a silent greeting, a cold, ceremonious bow. But she saw him once more; she could lose her whole soul in those melting eyes, in which she was ever reading the most enchanting magical fairy tales. In these days of ceremony he could not refuse her a place by his side; to sit near him at table, and at the concerts with which the royal chapel and the newly-arrived Italian singers would celebrate the return of the king. Graun had composed a piece of music in honor of this occasion, and not only the Italian singer, Laura Farinelli, but a scholar of Graun and Quantz, a German singer, Anna Prickerin, would then be heard for the first time. This would be for Anna an eventful and decisive day; she stood on the brink of a new existence—an existence made glorious by renown, honor, and distinction.

It was nothing to her that her father lay agonizing upon his death-bed; it was nothing to her that her brother William had left his home three days before, and no one knew what had become of him. She asked no questions about father or brother; she sorrowed not for the mother lately dead and buried. She had but one thought, one desire, one aim—to be a celebrated singer, to obtain the hand of a man whom she neither loved nor esteemed, but who was a baron and an influential lord of the court. The object of Anna's life was to become the wife of the baron, not for love. She wished to hide her ignoble birth under the glitter of his proud name; 'it was better to be the wife of a poor baron than the daughter of a tailor, even though he should be the court tailor, and a millionnaire.

The king had been in Berlin but two days, and Pöllnitz had already made a visit to his beautiful Anna. Never had he been so demonstrative and so tender; never before had he been seriously occupied with the thought of making her his wife; never had he looked upon it as possible. The example of Count Rhedern gave him courage; what the king had granted to the daughter of the merchant, he could not refuse to the daughter of the court tailor, more particularly when the latter, by her own gifts and talents, had opened the doors of the palace for herself; when by the power of her siren voice she had made the barriers tremble and fall which separated the tailor's daughter from the court circle. If the lovely Anna became a celebrated singer, if she succeeded in winning the applause of the king, she would be ennobled; and no one could reproach the baron for making the beautiful prima donna his wife. If, therefore, she pleased the king, Pöllnitz was resolved to confess himself her knight, and to marry her as soon as possible—yes, as soon as possible, for his creditors followed him, persecuted him at every step, even threatened him with judgment and a prison. Pöllnitz reminded the king that he had promised, after his return from Silesia, to assist him. Frederick replied that he had not yet seen a battle-field, and was at the beginning and not the end of a war, for which he would require more gold than his treasuries contained; " wait patiently, also," he said, " for the promised day, for only then can I fulfil my promise." It was, therefore, a necessity with Pöllnitz to find some way of escape from this terrible labyrinth; and with an anxiously-beating heart he stood on the evening of the concert behind the king's chair, to watch every movement and every word, and above all to notice the effect produced by the voice of his Anna.

The king was uncommonly gay and gracious; these two days in his beloved Berlin, after the weeks of fatigue and weariness in Silesia, had filled his heart with gladness. He had given almost a lover's greeting to his books and his flute, and his library seemed to him a sanctified home; with joy he exchanged his sword for a pen, and instead of drawing plans of battle, he wrote verses or witty letters to Voltaire, whom he still honored, and in a certain sense admired, although the six days which Voltaire had spent in Rheinsberg, just before the Silesian campaign, had somewhat diminished his admiration for the French author. After Frederick's first meeting with Voltaire at the castle of Moyland, he said of him, "He is as eloquent as Cicero, as charming as Plinius, and as wise as Agrippa; he combines in himself all the virtues and all the talents of the three greatest men of the ancients." He now called the author of the "Henriade" a *fool;* it excited and troubled his spirit to see that this great author was mean and contemptible in character, cold and cunning in heart. He had loved Voltaire as a friend, and now he confessed with pain that Voltaire's friendship was a possession which must be cemented with gold, if you did not wish to lose it. The king who, a few months before, had compared him with Cicero, Plinius, and Agrippa, now said to Jordan, "The miser, Voltaire, has still an unsatisfied longing for gold, and asks still thirteen hundred dollars! Every one of the six days which he spent with me cost me five hundred and fifty dollars! I call that paying dear for a fool! Never before was a court fool so generously rewarded."

To-day Frederick was expecting a new enjoyment; to-day, for the first time, he was to hear the new Italian singer.

17

This court concert promised him, therefore, a special enjoyment, and he awaited it with youthful impatience.

At last, Graun gave the signal for the introduction; Frederick had no ear for this simple, beautiful, and touching music; and the masterly solo of Quantz upon the flute drew from him a single bravo; he thought only of the singers, and at last the chorus began.

The heart of Pöllnitz beat loud and quick as he glanced at Anna, who stood proud and grave, in costly French toilet, far removed from the Farinelli. Anna examined the court circles quietly, and looked as unembarrassed as if she had been long accustomed to such society.

The chorus was at an end, and Laura Farinelli had the first aria to sing. Anna Prickerin could have murdered her for this. The Italian, in the full consciousness of her power, returned Anna's scorn with a half-mocking, half-contemptuous smile; she then fixed her great, piercing eyes upon the music, and began to sing.

Anna could have cried aloud in her rage, for she saw that the king was well pleased; he nodded his head, and a gay smile overspread his features; she saw that the whole court circle made up enchanted faces immediately, and that even Pöllnitz assumed an entirely happy and enthusiastic mien. The Farinelli saw all this, and the royal applause stimulated her; her full, glorious voice floated and warbled in the artistic " Fioritures " and " Roulades," then dreamed itself away in soft, melodious tones; again it rose into the loftiest regions of sound, and was again almost lost in the simple, touching melodies of love.

"Delicious! superb!" said the king, aloud, as Farinelli concluded.

"Exalted! godlike!" cried Pöllnitz; and now, as the royal sign had been given, the whole court dared to follow the example, and to utter light and repressed murmurs of wonder and applause.

Anna felt that she turned pale; her feet trembled; she could have murdered the Italian with her own hands! this proud Farinelli, who at this moment looked toward her with a questioning and derisive glance; and her eyes seemed to say, " Will you yet dare to sing?"

But Anna had the proud courage to dare. She said to herself, " I shall triumph over her; her voice is as thin as a thread, and as sharp as a fine needle, while mine is full and powerful, and rolls like an organ; and as for her ' Fioritures,' I understand them as well as she."

With this conviction she took the notes in her hand, and waited for the moment when the " Ritornelle " should be ended; she returned with a quiet smile the anxious look which her teacher, Quantz, fixed upon her.

The " Ritornelle " was ended. Anna began her song; her voice swelled loudly and powerfully far above the orchestra, but the king was dull and immovable; he gave not the slightest token of applause. Anna saw this, and her voice, which had not trembled with fear, now trembled with rage; she was resolved to awake the astonishment of the king by the strength and power of her voice; she would compel him to applaud! She gathered together the whole strength of her voice and made so powerful an effort that her poor chest seemed about to burst asunder; a wild, discordant strain rose stunningly upon the air, and now she had indeed the triumph to see that the king laughed! Yes, the king laughed! but not with the same smile with which he greeted Farinelli, but in mockery and contempt. He turned to Pöllnitz, and said:

" What is the name of this woman who roars so horribly?"

Pöllnitz shrugged his shoulders; he had a kind of feeling as if that moment his creditors had seized him by the throat.

"Sire," whispered he, "I believe it is Anna Prickerin." The king laughed; yes, in spite of the "Fioritures" of the raging singer, who had seen Pöllnitz's shrug of the shoulders, and had vowed in the spirit to take a bloody vengeance.

Louder and louder the fair Anna shrieked, but the king did not applaud. She had now finished the last note of her aria, and breathlessly with loudly-beating heart she waited for the applause of the king. It came not! perfect stillness reigned; even Pöllnitz was speechless.

"Do you know, certainly, that this roaring woman is the daughter of our tailor?" said the king.

Pöllnitz answered, "Yes," with a bleeding heart.

"I have often heard that a tailor was called a goat, but his children are nevertheless not nightingales, and poor Pricker can sooner force a camel through the eye of his needle than make a songstress of his daughter. The Germans cannot sing, and it is an incomprehensible mistake of Graun to bring such a singer before us."

"She is a pupil of Quantz," said Pöllnitz, "and he has often assured me she would make a great singer."

"Ah, she is a pupil of Quantz," repeated the king, and his eye glanced around in search of him. Quantz, with an angry face, and his eyebrows drawn together, was seated at his desk. "Alas!" said Frederick, "when he makes such a face as that, he grumbles with me for two days, and is never pleased with my flute. I must seek to mollify him, therefore, and when this Mademsoiselle Prickerin sings again I will give a slight sign of applause."

But Anna Prickerin sang no more; angry scorn shot like a stream of fire through her veins, she felt suffocated; tears rushed to her eyes; every thing about her seemed to be wavering and unsteady; and as her listless, half-unconscious glances wandered around, she met the gay, triumphant eyes of the Farinelli fixed derisively upon her. Anna felt as if a sword had pierced her heart; she uttered a fearful cry, and sank unconscious to the floor.

"What cry was that?" said the king, "and what signifies this strange movement among the singers?"

"Sire, it appears that the Prickerin has fallen into a fainting-fit," said Pöllnitz.

The king thought this a good opportunity to pacify Quantz by showing an interest in his pupil. "That is indeed a most unhappy circumstance," said the king, aloud. "Hasten, Pöllnitz, to inquire in my name after the health of this gifted young singer. If she is still suffering, take one of my carriages and conduct her yourself to her home, and do not leave her till you can bring me satisfactory intelligence as to her recovery." So saying, the king cast a stolen glance toward the much-dreaded Quantz, whose brow had become somewhat clearer, and his expression less threatening. "We will, perhaps," whispered the king, "escape this time with one day's growling; I think I have softened him." Frederick seated himself, and gave the signal for the concert to proceed; he saw that, with the assistance of the baron, the unconscious songstress had been removed.

CHAPTER XIII.

THE DEATH OF THE OLD TIME.

THE music continued, while Pöllnitz, filled with secret dread, ordered a court carriage, according to the command of the king, and entered it with the still insensible songstress.

"The king does not know what a fearful commission he has given me," thought Pöllnitz, as he drove through the

streets with Anna Prickerin, and examined her countenance
with terror. "Should she now awake, she would overwhelm me with her rage. She is capable of scratching
out my eyes, or even of strangling me."

But his fear was groundless. Anna did not stir; she was
still unconscious, as the carriage stopped before the house of
her father. No one came to meet them, although Pöllnitz
ordered the servant to open the door, and the loud ringing
of the bell sounded throughout the house. No one appeared
as Pöllnitz, with the assistance of the servants, lifted the insensible Anna from the carriage and bore her into the house
to her own room. As the baron placed her carefully upon
the sofa, she made a slight movement and heaved a deep
sigh.

"Now the storm will break forth," thought Pöllnitz,
anxiously, and he ordered the servants to return to the carriage and await his return. He desired no witnesses of the
scene which he expected, and in which he had good reason
to believe that he would play but a pitiful *rôle*.

Anna Prickerin now opened her eyes; her first glance
fell upon Pöllnitz, who was bending over her with a tender
smile.

"What happiness, dearest," he whispered, "that you at
last open your eyes! I was dying with anxiety."

Anna did not answer at once; her eyes were directed
with a dreamy expression to the smiling countenance of
Pöllnitz, and while he recounted his own tender care, and
the gracious sympathy of the king, Anna appeared to be
slowly waking out of her dream. Now a ray of consciousness and recollection overspread her features, and throwing
up her arm with a rapid movement she administered a powerful blow on the cheek of her tender, smiling lover, who fell
back with his hand to his face, whimpering with pain.

"Why did you shrug your shoulders?" she said, her lips

trembling with anger, and, springing up from the sofa, she approached Pöllnitz with a threatening expression, who, expecting a second explosion, drew back. "Why did you shrug your shoulders?" repeated Anna.

"I am not aware that I did so, my Anna," stammered Pöllnitz.

She stamped impatiently on the floor. "I am not your Anna. You are a faithless, treacherous man, and I despise you; you are a coward, you have not the courage to defend the woman you have sworn to love and protect. When I ceased singing, why did you not applaud?"

"Dearest Anna," said Pöllnitz, "you are not acquainted with court etiquette; you do not know that at court it is only the king who expresses approval."

"You all broke out into a storm of applause as Farinelli finished singing."

"Because the king gave the sign."

Anna shrugged her shoulders contemptuously, and paced the floor with rapid steps. "You think that all my hopes, all my proud dreams for the future are destroyed," she murmured, with trembling lips, while the tears rolled slowly down her cheeks. "To think that the king and the whole court laughed while I sang, and that presumptuous Italian heard and saw it all—I shall die of this shame and disgrace. My future is annihilated, my hopes trodden under foot." She covered her face with her hands, and wept and sobbed aloud.

Pöllnitz had no pity for her sufferings, but he remembered his creditors, and this thought rekindled his extinguished tenderness. He approached her, and gently placed his arm around her neck. "Dearest," he murmured, "why do you weep, how can this little mischance make you so wretched? Do we not love each other? are you not still my best beloved, my beautiful, my adored Anna? Have you not sworn that you love me, and that you ask no greater happiness than to be united to me?"

Anna raised her head, that she might see this tender lover.

"It is true," proceeded Pöllnitz, "that you did not receive the applause this evening, which your glorious talent deserves; Farinella was in your way. The king has a prejudice against German singers; he says, 'The Germans can compose music, but they cannot sing.' That prejudice is a great advantage for the Italian. If you had borne an Italian name, the king would have been charmed with your wonderful voice; but you are a German, and he refuses you his approval. But what has been denied you here, you will easily obtain elsewhere. We will leave this cold, ungrateful Berlin, my beloved. You shall take an Italian name, and through my various connections I can make arrangements for you to sing at many courts. You will win fame and gold, and we will lead a blessed and happy life."

"I care nothing for the gold; I am rich, richer than I even dreamed. My father told me to-day that he possessed nearly seven hundred thousand dollars, and that he would disinherit my brother, who is now absent from Berlin. I will be his heiress, and very soon, for the physicians say he can only live a few days."

The eyes of the baron gleamed. "Has your father made his will? has he declared you his heiress?"

"He intended doing so to-day. He ordered the lawyers to come to him, and I believe they were here when I started to this miserable concert. It was not on account of the money, but for fame, that I desired to become a prima donna. But I renounce my intention; this evening has shown me many thorns where I thought to find only roses. I renounce honor and renown, and desire only to be happy, happy in your love and companionship."

"You are right; we will fly from this cold, faithless Berlin to happier regions. The world will know no happier couple than the Baron and Baroness von Pöllnitz."

Pöllnitz now felt no repugnance at the thought that the tailor's daughter had the presumptuous idea of becoming his wife. He forgave her low origin for the sake of her immense fortune, and thought it not a despicable lot to be the husband of the beautiful Anna Prickerin. He assured her of his love in impassioned words, and Anna listened with beaming eyes and a happy smile. Suddenly a loud weeping and crying, proceeding from the next room, interrupted this charming scene.

"My father, it is my father!" cried Anna, as she hastened to the door of the adjoining room, which, as we know, contained the ancestral portraits of the Prickers. Pöllnitz followed her. In this room, surrounded by his ancestors, the worthy tailor lay upon his death-bed. Pale and colorless as the portraits was the face of the poor man; but his eyes were gleaming with a wild, feverish glitter. As he perceived Anna in her splendid French costume, so wild and fearful a laugh burst from his lips, that even Pöllnitz trembled.

"Come to me," said the old man, with a stammering voice, as he motioned to his daughter to approach his couch. "You and your brother have broken my heart; you have given me daily a drop of poison, of which I have been slowly dying. Your brother left my house as the prodigal son, but he has not returned a penitent; he glories in his crime; he is proud of his shame. Here is a letter which I received from him to-day, in which he informs me that he has eloped with the daughter of my second murderer, this French Pelissier; and that he intends to become an actor, and thus drag through the dust the old and respectable name of his fathers. For this noble work he demands his mother's fortune. He shall have it—yes, he shall have it; it is five

17*

thousand dollars, but from me he receives nothing but my curse, and I pray to God that it may ring forever in his ears!'

The old man lay back exhausted, and groaned aloud. Anna stood with tearless eyes by the death-bed of her father, and thought only of the splendid future which each passing moment brought nearer. Pöllnitz had withdrawn to one of the windows, and was considering whether he should await the death of the old man or return immediately to the king.

Suddenly Pricker opened his eyes, and turned them with an angry and malicious expression toward his daughter.

"What a great lady you are!" he said, with a fearful grin; "dressed in the latest fashion, and a wonderful song-stress, who sings before the king and his court. Such a great lady must be ashamed that her father is a tailor. I appreciate that, and I am going to my grave, that I may not trouble my daughter. Yes, I am going, and nothing shall remind the proud songstress of me, neither my presence nor any of my possessions. A prima donna would not be the heiress of a tailor."

The old man broke out into a wild laugh, while Anna stared at him, and Pöllnitz came forward to hear and observe.

"I do not understand you, my father," said Anna, trembling and disturbed.

"You will soon understand me," stammered the old man, with a hoarse laugh. "When I am dead, and the lawyers come and read my will, which I gave them to-day, then you will know that I have left my fortune to the poor of the city, and not to this great songstress, who does not need it, as she has a million in her throat. My son an actor, my daughter a prima donna—it is well. I go joyfully to my grave, and thank God for my release. Ah! you shall remember your old father; you shall curse me, as I have cursed you; and as you will shed no tears at my death, it shall, at least, be a heavy blow to you. You are disinherited! both disinherited! the poor are my heirs, and you and your brother will receive nothing but the fortune of your mother, of which I, unfortunately, cannot deprive you."

"Father, father, this is not possible—this cannot be your determination!" cried Anna. "It is not possible for a father to be so cruel, so unnatural, as to disinherit his children!"

"Have you not acted cruelly and unnaturally to me?" asked the old man; "have you not tortured me? have you not murdered me, with a smile upon your lips, as you did your poor mother, who died of grief? No, no, no pity for unnatural children. You are disinherited!"

The old man fell back with a loud shriek upon his couch, and his features assumed that fixed expression which is death's herald.

"He is dying!" cried Anna, throwing herself beside her father; "he is dying, and he has disinherited me!"

"Yes, disinherited!" stammered the heavy tongue of the dying man.

Pöllnitz trembled at the fearful scene; he fled with hasty steps from this gloomy room, and only recovered his composure when once more seated in his carriage. After some moments of reflection, he said:

"I will ask the king for my release from his service, and I will become a Protestant, and hasten to Nuremberg, and marry the rich *patric* ."

CHAPTER XIV.

THE DISCOVERY.

THEY sat hand in hand in the quiet and fragrant conservatory; after a long separation they gazed once more in each other's eyes, doubting the reality of their happiness, and asking if it were not a dream, a delightful dream.

This was the first time since his return from Silesia that Prince Augustus William had seen his Laura alone; the first time he could tell her of his longing and his suffering; the first time she could whisper in his ear the sweet and holy confession of her love—a confession that none should hear but her lover and her God.

But there were four ears which heard every-thing; four eyes which saw all that took place in the myrtle arbor. Louise von Schwerin and her lover, the handsome Fritz Wendell, sat arm in arm in the grotto, and listened attentively to the conversation of the prince and his bride.

"How happy they are!" whispered Louise, with a sigh.

"Are we not also happy?" asked Fritz Wendell, tenderly, clasping his arm more firmly around her. "Is not our love as ardent, as passionate, and as pure as theirs?"

"And yet the world would shed tears of pity for them, while we would be mocked and laughed at," said Louise, sighing.

"It is true the love of the poor gardener for the beautiful Mademoiselle von Schwerin is only calculated to excite ridicule," murmured Fritz Wendell; "but that shall and will be changed; I shall soon begin the new career which I have planned for myself; my Louise need then no longer blush for her lover, and my adoration for her shall no longer be a cause of shame and humiliation. I have a means by which I can purchase rank and position, and I intend to employ this means."

"Pray tell me how; let me know your plans," said Louise.

He pointed with a cruel smile to the lovers in the myrtle arbor.

"This secret is my purchase money," said he, whisper

ing; "I shall betray them to the king, and he will give me rank and wealth for this disclosure; for upon this secret depends the future of Prussia. Let us, therefore, listen attentively to what they say, that—"

"No," said Louise, interrupting him with vivacity, "we will not listen. It is cruel and ignoble to desire to purchase our own happiness with the misery of others; it is—"

"For Heaven's sake be quiet and listen!" said Fritz Wendell, softly laying his hand on her angry lips.

The conversation of the lovers in the myrtle arbor had now taken another direction. Their eyes no long r sparkled with delight, but had lost their lustre, and an expression of deep sadness rested on their features.

"It is then really true," said Laura, mournfully; "you are affianced to the Princess of Brunswick?"

"It is true," said the prince, in a low voice. "There was no other means of securing and preserving our secret than to seem to yield to the king's command, and to consent to this alliance with a good grace. This cloak will shield our love until we can acknowledge it before the whole world; and that depends, my beloved, upon you alone. Think of the vows of eternal love and fidelity we have made to each other; remember that you have promised to be mine for all eternity, and to devote your whole life to me; remember that you wear my engagement ring on your finger, and are my bride."

"And yet you are affianced to another, and wear another engagement ring!"

"But this princess, to whom I have been affianced, knows that I do not love her. I have opened my heart to her; I told her that I loved you alone, and could never love another; that no woman but Laura von Pannewitz should ever be my wife; and she was generous enough to give her assistance and consent to be considered my bride until our union should no longer need this protection. And now, my dear Laura, I conjure you, by our love and the happiness of our lives, yield to my ardent entreaties and my fervent prayers; have the courage to defy the world and its preju dices. Follow me, my beloved; flee with me and consent to be my wife!"

The glances with which he regarded her were so loving, so imploring, that Laura could not find in her heart to offer decided resistance. Her own heart pleaded for him; and now when she might altogether lose him if she refused his request, now that he was affianced to another, she was filled with a torturing jealousy; she was now conscious that it would be easier to die than renounce her lover.

But she still had the strength to battle with her own weak heart, to desire to shut out the alluring voices which resounded in her own breast. Like Odysseus, she tried to be deaf to the sirens' voices which tempted her. But she still heard them, and although she had found strength to refuse her lover's prayers and entreaties to flee with him, yet she could not repel his passionate appeals to her to be his wife.

It was so sweet to listen to the music of his voice; such bliss to lean her head on his shoulder, to look up into his handsome countenance and to drink in the words of ardent and devoted love which fell from his lips; to know what he suffers is for your sake! It rests with you to give him happiness or despair. She knew not that the words which she drank in were coursing like fire through her own veins, destroying her resolution and turning her strength to ashes.

As he, at last, brought to despair by her silence and resistance, burst into tears, and accused her of cruelty and indifference, as she saw his noble countenance shadowed with pain and sorrow, she no longer found courage to offer resistance, and throwing herself into his arms, with a happy blush, she whispered:

"Take me; I am yours forever! I accept you as my master and husband. Your will shall be mine; what you command I will obey; where you call me there will I go; I will follow you to the ends of the earth, and nothing but death shall hereafter separate us!"

The prince pressed her closely and fervently to his heart, and kissed her pure brow.

"God bless you, my darling; God bless you for this resolution." His voice was now firm and full, and his countenance had assumed an expression of tranquillity and energy. He was no longer the sighing, despairing lover, but a determined man, who knew what his wishes were, and had the courage and energy to carry them into execution.

Fritz Wendell pressed Louise more closely to his side, and whispered:

"You say that Laura is an angel of virtue and modesty, and yet she has not the cruel courage to resist her lover; she yields to his entreaties, and is determined to flee with him. Will you be less kind and humane than this tender, modest Laura? Oh, Louise, you should also follow your tender, womanly heart; flee with me and become my wife. I will conceal you, and then go to those who would now reject my suit scornfully, and dictate terms to them."

"I will do as she does," whispered Louise, with glowing cheeks. "What Laura can do, I may also do; if she flies with her lover, I will fly with you; if she becomes his wife, I will be yours. But let us be quiet, and listen."

"And now, my Laura, listen attentively to every word I utter," said Prince Augustus William, gravely. "I have made all the necessary preparations, and in a week you will be my wife. There is a good and pious divine on one of my estates who is devoted to me. He has promised to perform the marriage ceremony. On leaving Berlin we will first flee to him, and our union will receive his blessing in the village church at night; a carriage will await us at the door which, with fresh relays of horses, will rapidly conduct us to the Prussian boundary. I have already obtained from my friend the English ambassador a passport, which will carry us safely to England under assumed names; once there, my uncle, the King of England, will not refuse his protection and assistance; and by his intercession we will be reconciled to the king my brother. When he sees that our union has been accomplished, he will give up all useless attempts to separate us."

"But he can and will punish you for this; you will thereby forfeit your right of succession to the throne, and for my sake you will be forced to renounce your proud and brilliant future."

"I shall not regret it," said the prince, smiling. "I do not long for a crown, and will not purchase this bauble of earthly magnificence at the expense of my happiness and my love. And perhaps I have not the strength, the talent, or the power of intellect to be a ruler. It suffices me to rule in your heart, and be a monarch in the kingdom of your love. If I can therefore purchase the uncontested possession of my beloved by renouncing all claims to the throne, I shall do so with joy and without the slightest regret."

"But I, poor, humble, weak girl that I am, how can I make good the loss you will sustain for my sake?" asked Laura.

"Your love will be more than a compensation. You must now lay aside all doubt and indecision. You know our plans for the future. On my part all the preliminary measures have been taken; you should also make whatever preparations are necessary. It is Hartwig, the curate of Orarien-burg, who is to marry us. Send the necessary apparel and whatever you most need to him, without a word or message. The curate has already been advised of their arrival, and will retain the trunks unopened. On next Tuesday, a week from to-day, the king will give a ball. For two days previous to this ball you will keep your room on the plea of sickness; this will be a sufficient excuse for your not accompanying the queen. I shall accept the invitation, but will not appear at the ball, and will await you at the castle gate of Monbijou. At eight o'clock the ball commences; at nine you will leave your room and the castle, at the gate of which I will receive you. At a short distance from the gate a carriage will be in readiness to convey us to Oranienburg, where we will stop before the village church. There we will find a preacher standing before the altar, ready to perform the ceremony, and when this is accomplished we will enter another carriage which will rapidly convey us to Hamburg, where we will find a ship, hired by the English ambassador, ready to take us to England. You see, dear Laura, that every thing has been well considered, and nothing can interfere with our plan, now that we understand each other. In a week, therefore, remember, Laura."

"In a week," she whispered. "I have no will but yours."

"Until then we will neither see nor speak with each other, that no thoughtless word may excite suspicion in the breasts of the spies who surround us. We must give each other no word, no message, no letter, or sign; but I will await you at the castle gate at nine o'clock on next Tuesday, and you will not let me wait in vain."

"No, you shall not wait in vain," whispered Laura, with a happy smile, hiding her blushing face on the breast of her lover.

"And you, will you let me wait in vain?" asked Fritz Wendell, raising Louise's head from his breast, and gazing on her glowing and dreamy countenance.

"No, I shall not let you wait in vain," said Louise von

Schwerin. "We will also have our carriage, only we will leave a little sooner than the prince and Laura. We will also drive to Oranienburg, and await the prince before the door of the church. We will tell him we knew his secret and did not betray him. We will acknowledge our love, Laura will intercede for us, and the preacher will have to perform the ceremony for two couples instead of one. We will then accompany the prince and his wife in their flight to England; from there the prince will obtain pardon of the king, and we the forgiveness of my family. Oh, this is a splendid, a magnificent plan!—a flight, a secret marriage at night, and a long journey. This will be quite like the charming romances which I am so fond of, and mine will be a fantastic and adventurous life. But what is that?" said she. "Did you hear nothing? It seems to me I heard a noise as of some one opening the outer door of the conservatory."

"Be still," murmured Fritz Wendell, "I heard it also; let us therefore be on our guard."

The prince and Laura had also heard this noise, and were listening in breathless terror, their glances fastened on the door. Perhaps it was only the wind which had moved the outer door; perhaps—but no, the door opened noiselessly, and a tall female figure cautiously entered the saloon.

"The queen!" whispered Laura, trembling.

"My mother!" murmured the prince, anxiously looking around for some means of escape. He now perceived the dark grotto, and pointing rapidly toward it, he whispered: "Quick, quick, conceal yourself there. I will remain and await my mother."

The stately figure of the queen could already be seen rapidly advancing through the flowers and shrubbery, and now her sparkling eye and proud and angry face were visible.

"Quick," whispered the prince, "conceal yourself, or we are lost!"

Laura slipped hastily behind the myrtle and laurel foliage and attained the asylum of the grotto, unobserved by the queen; she entered and leaned tremblingly against the inner wall. Blinded by the sudden darkness, she could see nothing, and she was almost benumbed with terror.

Suddenly she heard a low, whispering voice at her side: "Laura, dear Laura, fear nothing. We are true friends, who know your secret, and desire to assist you."

"Follow me, mademoiselle," whispered another voice; "confide in us as we confide in you. We know your secret; you shall learn ours. Give me your hand; I will conduct you from this place noiselessly and unobserved, and you can then return to the castle."

Laura hardly knew what she was doing. She was gently drawn forward, and saw at her side a smiling girlish face, and now she recognized the little maid of honor, Louise von Schwerin.

"Louise," said she, in a low voice, "what does all this mean?"

"Be still," she whispered; "follow him down the stairway. Farewell! I will remain and cover the retreat."

Louise now hastily concealed the opening through which Fritz Wendell and Laura had disappeared, and then slipped noiselessly back to the grotto, and concealed herself behind the shrubbery at its entrance, so that she could see and hear every thing that took place.

It was in truth Queen Sophia Dorothea, who had dismissed her attendants and come alone to the conservatory at this unusual hour.

This was the time at which the queen's maids of honor were not on service, and were at liberty to do as they pleased. The queen had been in the habit of reposing at this time, but to-day she could not find rest; annoyed at her sleeplessness, she had arisen, and in walking up and down had stepped to the window and looked dreamily down into the still and desolate garden. Then it was that she thought she saw a female figure passing hurriedly down the avenue. It must have been one of her maids of honor; and although the queen had not recognized her, she was convinced that it was none other than Laura von Pannewitz, and that she was now going to a rendezvous with her unknown lover, whom the queen had hitherto vainly endeavored to discover. The queen called her waiting-maids to her assistance, and putting on her furs and hood, she told them she felt a desire to take a solitary walk in the garden, and that none of her attendants should be called, with which she hurried into the garden, following the same path which the veiled lady had taken. She followed the foot-tracks in the snow to the conservatory, and entered without hesitation, determined to discover the secret of her maid of honor, and to punish her.

It was fortunate for the poor lovers that the increasing corpulence of the queen and her swollen right foot rendered her advance rather slow, so that when she at last reached the lower end of the conservatory she found no one there but her son Augustus William, whose embarrassed and constrained reception of herself convinced the queen that her appearance was not only a surprise, but also a disagreeable one. She therefore demanded of him with severity the cause of his unexpected and unusual visit to her conservatory; and when Augustus William smilingly replied—

"That he had awaited here the queen's awakening, in order that he might pay his visit—"

The queen asked abruptly: "And who, my son, helped to dispel the *ennui* of this tedious waiting?"

"No one, my dear mother," said the prince; but he did not dare to meet his mother's penetrating glance.

"No one?" repeated she; "but I heard you speaking on entering the conservatory."

"You know, your majesty, that I have inherited the habit of speaking aloud to myself from my father," replied the prince, with a constrained smile.

"The king my husband did not cease speaking when I made my appearance," exclaimed the queen, angrily; "he had no secrets to hide from me."

"The thoughts of my royal father were grand, and worthy of the sympathy of Queen Sophia Dorothea," said the prince, bowing low.

"God forbid that the thoughts of his son should be of another and less worthy character!" exclaimed the queen. "My sons should, at least, be too proud to soil their lips with an untruth; and if they have the courage to do wrong, they should also find courage to acknowledge it."

"I do not understand you, my dear mother;" and meeting her penetrating glance with quiet composure, he continued, "I am conscious of no wrong, and consequently have none to acknowledge."

"This is an assurance which deserves to be unmasked," exclaimed the queen, who could no longer suppress her anger. "You must know, prince, that I am not to be deceived by your seeming candor and youthful arrogance. I know that you were not alone, for I myself saw the lady coming here who kept you company while awaiting me, and I followed her to this house."

"Then it seems that your majesty has followed a *fata morgana*," said the prince, with a forced smile; "for, as you see, I am alone, and no one else is present in the conservatory."

But even while speaking, the prince glanced involuntarily toward the grotto which concealed his secret.

The Queen Sophia Dorothea caught this glance, and divined its meaning.

"There is no one in the saloon, and it now remains to examine the grotto," said she, stepping forward hastily.

The prince seized her hand, and endeavored to hold her back.

"I conjure you, mother, do not go too far in your suspicion and your examinations. Remember that your suspicion wounds me."

The queen gave him a proud, angry glance.

"I am here on my own property," said she, withdrawing her hand, "and no one shall oppose my will."

"Well, then, madame, follow your inclination," said the prince, with a resolute air; "I wished to spare you an annoyance. Let discord and sorrow come over us, if your majesty will have it so; and as you are inexorable, you will also find me firm and resolute. Examine the grotto, if you will."

He offered her his arm and conducted her to the grotto. Sophia Dorothea felt disarmed by her son's resolute bearing, and was almost convinced that she had done him injustice, and that no one was concealed in the grotto. With a benignant smile she had turned to her son, to say a few soothing words, when she heard a low rustle among the shrubbery, and saw something white flitting through the foliage.

"And you say, my son, that I was deceived by a *fata morgana*." exclaimed the queen, hurrying forward with outstretched arm. "Come, my young lady, and save us and yourself the shame of drawing you forcibly from your hiding-place."

The queen had not been mistaken. Something moved among the shrubbery, and now a female figure stepped forth and threw herself at the feet of the queen.

"Pardon, your majesty, pardon! I am innocent of any intention to intrude on your majesty's privacy. I had fallen asleep in this grotto, and awoke when it was too late to escape, as your majesty was already at the entrance of the conservatory. In this manner I have been an involuntary witness of your conversation. This is my whole fault."

The queen listened with astonishment, while the prince regarded with consternation the kneeling girl who had been found here in the place of his Laura.

"This is not the voice of Mademoiselle von Pannewitz," said the queen, as she passed out into the light, and commanded the kneeling figure to follow her, that she might see her face. The lady arose and stepped forward. "Louise von Schwerin!" exclaimed the queen and the prince at the same time, while the little maid of honor folded her hands imploringly, and said, with an expression of childish innocence:

"O your majesty, have compassion with me! Yesterday's ball made me so very tired; and as your majesty was sleeping, I thought I would come here and sleep a little too, although I had not forgotten that your majesty was not pleased to have us visit this conservatory alone."

Sophia Dorothea did not honor her with a glance; her eyes rested on her son with an expression of severity and scorn.

"Really, I had a better opinion of you," said she. "It is no great achievement to mislead a child, and one that is altogether unworthy of a royal prince."

"My mother," exclaimed the prince, indignantly, "you do not believe—"

"I believe what I see," said the queen, interrupting him. "Have done with your assurances of innocence, and bow to the truth, which has judged you in spite of your denial. And you, my young lady, will accompany me, and submit to my commands in silence, and without excuses. Come, and assume a cheerful and unconstrained air, if you please. I do not wish my court to hear of this scandal, and to read your guilt in your terrified countenance. I shall take care that you do not betray your guilt in words. Come."

The prince looked after them with an expression of confusion and astonishment. "Well, no matter how this riddle is solved," murmured he, after the queen had left the con--servatory with her maid of honor, "Laura is safe at all events, and in a week we will flee."

CHAPTER XV.

THE COUNTERMINE.

THREE days had slowly passed by, and Fritz Wendell waited in vain for a sign or message from his beloved. He groped his way every day through the subterranean alley to the grotto, and stood every night under her window, hoping in vain for a signal or soft whisper from her.

The windows were always curtained and motionless, and no one could give the unhappy gardener any news of the poor Louise von Schwerin, who was closely confined in her room, and confided to the special guard of a faithful chambermaid.

The queen told her ladies that Louise was suffering from an infectious disease; the queen's physician confirmed this opinion, and cautioned the ladies of the court against any communication with the poor invalid. No special command was therefore necessary to keep the maids of honor away from the prisoner; she was utterly neglected, and her old companions passed her door with flying steps. But the queen, as it appeared, did not fear this contagion; she was seen to enter the sick girl's room every day, and to remain a long time. The tender sympathy of the queen excited the

admiration of the whole court, and no one guessed what torturing anxiety oppressed the heart of the poor prisoner whenever the queen entered the room ; no one heard the stern,
hard, threatening words of Sophia ; no one supposed that she
came, not to nurse the sick girl, but to overwhelm her with
reproaches.

Louise withstood all the menaces and upbraidings of the
queen bravely ; she had the courage to appear unembarrassed,
and, except to reiterate her innocence, to remain perfectly
silent. She knew well that she could not betray Laura without compromising herself; she knew that if the queen discovered the mysterious flight of Laura, she would, at the
same time, be informed of her love affair with the poor gardener, and of their secret assignations. Louise feared that
she would be made laughable and ridiculous by this exposure, and this fear made her resolute and decided, and enabled
her to bear her weary imprisonment patiently. " I cannot
be held a prisoner forever," she said to herself. " If I confess
nothing, the queen must at last be convinced of my innocence, and set me at liberty."

But Fritz Wendell was less patient than his cunning
Louise. He could no longer support this torture ; and as the
fourth day brought no intelligence, and no trace of Louise,
he was determined to dare the worst, and, like Alexander, to
cut the gordian knot which he could not untie. With bold
decision, he entered the castle and demanded to speak with
the king, stating that he had important discoveries to make
known.

The king received him instantly, and at Fritz Wendell's
request dismissed his adjutants.

" Now we are without witnesses, speak," said the king.

" I know a secret, your majesty, which concerns the
honor and the future of the royal family ; and you will gra-

18

ciously pardon me when I say I will not sell this secret except for a great price."

The king's eyes rested upon the impudent face of Fritz Wendell with a dangerous expression. "Name your price," said he, "but think well. If your secret is not worth the price you demand, you may perhaps pay for it with your head, certainly with your liberty."

"My secret is of the greatest value, for it will save the dynasty of the Hohenzollerns," said Fritz Wendell, boldly; "but I will sell it to your majesty—I will disclose it only after you have graciously promised me my price."

"Before I do that, I must know your conditions," said the king, with difficulty subduing his rage.

"I demand for myself a major's commission, and the hand of Mademoiselle von Schwerin."

In the beginning the king looked at the bold speaker with angry amazement; soon, however, his glance became kind and pitiful. "I have to do with a madman," thought he; "I will be patient, and give way to his humor. I grant you your price," said he; "speak on."

So Fritz Wendell began. He made known the engagement of the prince; he explained the plan of flight; he was so clear, so exact in all his statements, that Frederick soon saw he was no maniac; that these were no pictures of a disordered brain, but a threatening, frightful reality.

When the gardener had closed, the king, his arms folded across his back, walked several times backward and forward through the room; then suddenly stopped before Fritz Wendell, and seemed, with his sharp glance, to probe the bottom of his soul.

"Can you write?" said the king.

"I can write German, French, English, and Latin," said he, proudly.

"Seat yourself there, and write what I shall dictate in

German. Does Mademoiselle von Schwerin know your hand?"

"Sire, she has received at least twenty letters from me."

"Then write now, as I shall dictate, the one-and-twentieth."

It was a short, laconic, but tender and impressive love-letter, which Frederick dictated. Fritz Wendell implored his beloved to keep her promise, and on the same day in which the prince would fly with Laura to escape with him to Oraienburg, to entreat the protection of the prince, and through his influence to induce the priest to perform the marriage ceremony; he fixed the time and hour of flight, and besought her to leave the castle punctually, and follow him, without fear, who would be found waiting for her at the castle gate.

"Now, sign it," said the king, "and fold it as you are accustomed to do. Give me the letter; I will see that it is delivered."

"And my price, majesty," said Fritz, for the first time trembling.

The king's clouded brow threatened a fearful storm. "You shall have the price which your treachery and your madness has earned," said Frederick, in that tone which made all who heard it tremble. "Yes, you shall have what you have earned, and what your daring insolence deserves. Were all these things true which you have related with so bold a brow, you would deserve to be hung; you would have committed a twofold crime!—have been the betrayer of a royal prince—have watched him like a base spy, and listened to his secrets, in order to sell them, and sought to secure your own happiness by the misery of two noble souls! You would have committed the shameful and unpardonable crime of misleading an innocent child, who, by birth, rank, and education, is eternally separated from you. Happily for you, all this romance is the birth of your sick fancy. I will not, therefore, punish you, but I will cure you, as fools and mad men are cured; I will send you to a madhouse until your senses are restored, and you confess that this wild story is the picture of your disordered brain—until you swear that these are bold lies with which you have abused my patience. The restored invalid will receive my forgiveness—the obstinate culprit, never!"

The king rang the bell, and said to his adjutants, "Take this man out, and deliver him to the nearest sentinels; command them to place him at once in the military hospital; he is to be secured in the wards prepared for madmen—no man shall speak with him; and if he utters any wild and senseless tales, I am to be informed of it."

"Oh, sire! pardon, pardon! Send me not into the insane asylum. I will retract all; I will believe that all this is false; that I have only dreamed—that—"

The king nodded to his adjutants, and they dragged the sobbing, praying gardener from the room, and gave him to the watch.

The king looked after him sadly. "And Providence makes use of such pitiful men to control the fate of nations," said he. "A miserable garden-boy and a shameless maid of honor are the chosen instruments to serve the dynasty of the Hohenzollerns, and to rob the prince royal of Prussia of his earthly happiness! Upon what weak, fine threads hang the majesty and worth of kings! Alas, how often wretched and powerless man looks out from under the purple! In spite of all my power and greatness—in spite of my army, the prince would have flown, and committed a crime, that perhaps God and his conscience might have pardoned, but his king never! Poor William, you will pay dearly for this short, sweet dream of love, and your heart and its illusions will be trodden under foot, even as mine have been. Yes, alas! it is scarcely nine years, and it seems to me I am a hundred years older—that heavy blocks of ice are encamped about my heart, and I know that, day by day, this ice will become harder. The world will do its part—this poor race of men, whom I would so gladly love, and whom I am learning daily to despise more and more!"

He walked slowly to and fro; his face was shadowed by melancholy. In a short time he assumed his wonted expression, and, raising his head, his eyes beamed with a noble fire.

"I will not be cruel! If I must destroy his happiness, it shall not be trodden under foot as common dust and ashes. Alas, alas! how did they deal with me? My friend was led to execution, and a poor innocent child was stripped and horsewhipped through the streets, because she dared to love the crown prince! No, no; Laura von Pannewitz shall not share the fate of Dorris Ritter. I must destroy the happiness of my brother, but I will not cover his love with shame!"

So saying, the king rang, and ordered his carriage to be brought round. He placed the letter, which he had dictated to Fritz Wendell, in his pocket, and drove rapidly to the queen-mother's palace.

Frederick had a long and secret interview with his mother. The ladies in the next room heard the loud and angry voice of the queen, but they could not distinguish her words. It seemed to them that she was weeping, not from sorrow or pain, but from rage and scorn, for now and then they heard words of menace, and her voice was harsh. At last, a servant was directed to summon Mademoiselle von Pannewitz to the presence of the queen.

He soon returned, stating that Mademoiselle Laura's room was empty, and that she had gone to Schönhausen to visit Queen Elizabeth Christine.

"I will follow her there myself," said the king, "and your majesty may rest assured that Queen Elizabeth will assist us to separate these unhappy lovers as gently as possible."

"Ah, you pity them still, my son?" said the queen, shrugging her shoulders.

"Yes, madame, I pity all those who are forced to sacrifice their noblest, purest feelings to princely rank. I pity them; but I cannot allow them to forget their duty."

Laura von Pannewitz had lived through sad and dreary days since her last interview with the prince. The enthusiasm and exaltation of her passion had soon been followed by repentance. The prince's eloquent words had lost the power of conviction, now that she was no more subject to the magic of his glance and his imposing beauty. He stood no longer before her, in the confidence of youth, to banish doubts and despair from her soul, and convince her of the justification of their love.

Laura was now fully conscious that she was about to commit a great crime—that, in the weakness of her love, she was about to rob the prince of his future, of his glory and power. She said to herself that it would be a greater and nobler proof of her love to offer up herself and her happiness to the prince, than to accept from him the sacrifice of his birthright. But in the midst of these reproaches and this repentance, she saw ever before her the sorrowful face of her beloved—she heard his dear voice imploring her to follow him—to be his.

Laura, in the anguish of her soul and the remorse of conscience, had flown for refuge to the gentle, noble Queen Elizabeth, who had promised her help and consolation when the day of her trial should come. She had hastened, therefore, to Schönhausen, sure of the tender sympathy of her royal friend.

As Laura's carriage entered the castle court, the carriage of the king drew up at the garden gate. He commanded the coachman to drive slowly away, and then stepped alone into the garden. He walked hastily through the park, and

drew near to the little side-door of the palace, which led
through lonely corridors and unoccupied rooms, to the
chamber of the queen. He knew that Elizabeth only used
this door when she wished to take her solitary walk in the
park. The king wished to escape the curious and wondering
observations of the attendants, and to surprise the queen and
Laura von Pannewitz. He stepped on quietly, and, without
being seen, reached the queen's rooms, convinced that he
would find them in the boudoir. He was about to raise the
portière which separated it from the ante-room, when he was
arrested by the voices of women; one piteous and full of
tears, the other sorrowful but comforting. The king let the
portière fall, and seated himself noiselessly near the door.

"Let us listen awhile," said the king; "the women are
always coquetting when in the presence of men. We will
listen to them when they think themselves alone. I will in
this way become acquainted with this dangerous Laura,
and learn better, than by a long interview, how I can influence her."

The king leaned his head upon his stick, and fixed his
piercing eyes upon the heavy velvet portière, behind which
two weak women were now perhaps deciding the fate of the
dynasty of Hohenzollern.

"Madame," said Laura, "the blossoms of our happiness
are already faded and withered, and our love is on the brink
of the grave."

"Poor Laura!" said the queen, with a weary smile, "it
needed no gift of prophecy to foretell that. No flowers
bloom around a throne; thorns only grow in that fatal soil!
Your young eyes were blinded by magic; you mistook these
thorns for blossoms. Alas! I have wounded my heart with
them, and I hope that it will bleed to death!"

"O queen, if you knew my doubts and my despair, you
would have pity with me; you could not be so cruel as to

command me to sacrifice my love and my happiness! My happiness is his, and my love is but the echo of his own. If it was only a question of trampling upon my own foolish wishes, I would not listen to the cry of my soul. But the prince loves me. Oh, madame, think how great and strong this love must be, when I have the courage to boast of it! Yes, he loves me; and when I forsake him, I will not suffer alone. He will also be wretched, and his tears and his despair will torture my heart. How can I deceive him? Oh, madame, I cannot bear that his lips should curse me!"

"Yield him up now," said the queen, "and a day will come when he will bless you for it; a day in which he will confess that your love was great, was holy, that you sacrificed yourself and all earthly happiness freely, in order to spare him the wretchedness of future days. He loves you now, dearly, fondly, but a day will come in which he will demand of you his future, his greatness, his royal crown, all of which he gave up for you. He will reproach you then for having accepted this great sacrifice, and he will never forgive you for your weakness in yielding to his wishes. Believe me, Laura, in the hearts of men there lives but one eternal passion, and that is ambition. Love to them is only the amusement of the passing hour, nothing more."

"Oh, madame, if that is so, would God that I might die; life is not worth the trouble of living!" cried Laura, weeping bitterly.

"Life, my poor child, is not a joy which we can set aside, but a duty which we must bear patiently. You cannot trample upon this duty; and if your grief is strong, so must your will be stronger."

"What shall I do? What name do you give the duty which I must take upon myself?" cried Laura, with trembling lips. "I put my fate in your hands. What shall I do!"

"You must overcome yourself; you must conquer your love ; you must follow the voice of conscience, which brought you to me for counsel."

"Oh, my queen, you know not what you ask! Your calm, pure heart knows nothing of love."

"You say that I know nothing of love?" cried the queen, passionately. "You know not that my life is one great anguish, a never-ceasing self-sacrifice! Yes, I am the victim of love—a sadder, more helpless, more torturing love than you, Laura, can ever know. I love, and am not beloved. What I now confess to you is known only to God, and I tell you in order to console you, and give you strength to accept your fate bravely. I suffer, I am wretched, although I am a queen! I love my husband; I love him with the absorbing passion of a young girl, with the anguish which the damned must feel when they stand at the gates of Paradise, and dare not enter in. My thoughts, my heart, my soul belong to him; but he is not mine. He stands with a cold heart near my glowing bosom, and while with rapture of love I would throw myself upon his breast, I must clasp my arms together and hold them still, and must seek and find an icy glance with which to answer his. Look you, there was a time when I believed it impossible to bear all this torture ; a time in which my youth struggled like Tantalus ; a time in which my pride revolted at this love, with its shame and humiliation ; in which I would have given my crown to buy the right to fly into some lonely desert, and give myself up to tears. The king demanded that I should remain at his side, not as his wife, but as his queen; ever near him, but forever separated from him ; unpitied and misunderstood ; envied by fools, and thought happy by the world! And, Laura, oh I loved him so dearly, that I found strength to bear even this torture, and he knows not that my heart is being hourly crushed at the foot of his throne. I draw the royal purple over my wounded bosom, and it sometimes seems to me that my heart's blood gives this ruddy color to my mantle. Now, Laura, do I know nothing of love? do I not understand the greatness of the sacrifice which I demand of you?"

The queen, her face bathed in tears, opened her arms, and Laura threw herself upon her bosom; their sighs and tears were mingled.

The king sat in the ante-room, with pale face and clouded eyes. He bowed his head, as if in adoration, and suddenly a glittering brilliant, bright as a star, and nobler and more precious than all the jewels of this sorrowful world, fell upon his pallid cheek. " Truly," said he to himself, " there is something great and exalted in a woman's nature. I bow down in humility before this great soul, but my heart, alas! cannot be forced to love. The dead cannot be awakened, and that which is shrouded and buried can never more be brought to life and light!"

"You have conquered, my queen," said Laura, after a long pause; "I will be worthy of your esteem and friendship. That day shall never come in which my lover shall reproach me with selfishness and weakness! 'I am ready to be offered up!' I will not listen to him; I will not flee with him; and while I know that he is waiting for me, I will cast myself in your arms, and beseech you to pray to God for me, that He would send Death, his messenger of love and mercy, to relieve me from my torments."

" Not so, my Laura," said the queen; "you must make no half offering; it is not enough to renounce your lover, you must build up between yourselves an everlasting wall of separation; you must make this separation eternal! You must marry, and thus set the prince a noble example of self-control."

" Marry!" cried Laura; "can you demand this of me? Marry without love! Alas, alas! The prince will charge me with inconstancy and treachery to him, and I must bear that in silence."

"But I will not be silent," said the queen, "I will tell him of your grief and of the greatness of your soul; and when he ceases, as he must do, to look upon you as his beloved, he will honor you as the protecting angel of his existence."

"You promise me that. You will say to him that I was not faithless—that I gave him up because I loved him more than I did myself; I seemed faithless only to secure his happiness!"

"I promise you that, Laura."

"Well, then, I bow my head under the yoke—I yield to my fate—I accept the hand which Count Voss offers me. I ask that you will go to the queen-mother and say I submit to her commands—I will become the wife of Count Voss!"

"And I will lead you to the queen and to the altar," said the king, raising the portière, and showing himself to the ladies, who stared at him in breathless silence. The king drew nearer to Laura, and bowing low, he said: "Truly my brother is to be pitied, that he is only a prince, and not a freeman; for a pitiful throne, he must give up the holiest and noblest possession, the pure heart of a fair woman, glowing with love for him! And yet men think that we, the princes of the world, are to be envied! They are dazzled by the crown, but they see not the thorns with which our brows are beset! You, Laura, will never envy us; but on that day when you see my brother in his royal mantle and his crown—when his subjects shout for joy and call him their king — then can you say to yourself, 'It was I who made him king — I anointed him with my tears!' and when his people honor and bless him, you can rejoice also in the thought, 'This is the fruit of the strength of my love!' Come, I will myself conduct you to my mother, and I will

say to her that I would consider myself happy to call you
sister." Turning to Queen Elizabeth, he said: "I will say to
my mother that Mademoiselle von Pannewitz has not yielded
to my power or my commands, but to the pursuasive eloquence of your majesty, whom the people of Prussia have
for years considered their protecting angel, and who from
this time onward must be regarded as the guardian spirit of
our royal house!"

He reached his hand to the queen, but she took it not.
Trembling fearfully, with the paleness of death in her face,
she pointed to the portière and said, "You were there—
you heard all!"

The king, his countenance beaming with respectful admiration, drew near the queen, and placing his arm around
her neck, he whispered, "Yes, I was there—I heard all.
I heard, and I know that I am a poor, blind man, to whom
a kingdom is offered, a treasure-house of love and all good
gifts, and I cannot, alas! cannot accept it!"

The queen uttered a loud cry, and her weary head drop-
ped upon his shoulder. The king gazed silently into the
pale and sorrowful face, and a ray of infinite pity beamed in
his eyes. "I have discovered to-day a noble secret—a secret
that God alone was worthy to know. From this day I consider myself as the high priest of the holiest of holies, and
I will guard this secret as my greatest treasure. I swear
this to you, and I seal my oath with this kiss pressed upon
your lips by one who will never again embrace a woman!"
He bowed low, and pressed a fervent kiss upon the lips
of the queen. Elizabeth, who had borne her misfortunes
bravely, had not the power to withstand the sweet joy of
this moment; she uttered a loud cry, and sank insensible to
the floor. When she awoke she was alone; the king had
called her maids—had conducted Laura von Pannewitz to the
carriage, and returned to Berlin. Elizabeth was again alone—

alone with her thoughts—with her sorrows and her love. But a holy fire was in her eyes, and raising them toward Heaven, she whispered: "I thank thee, O heavenly Father, for the happiness of this hour! I feel his kiss upon my lips! by that kiss they are consecrated! Never, never will they utter one murmuring word!" She arose and entered her cabinet, with a soft smile; she drew near to a table which stood by the window, and gazed at a beautiful landscape, and the crayons, etc., etc., which lay upon it. "He shall think of me, from time to time," whispered she. "For his sake, I will become an artist and a writer; I will be something more than a neglected queen. He shall see my books upon his table and my paintings on his wall. Will I not then compel him sometimes to think of me with pride?"

CHAPTER XVI.

THE SURPRISE.

THE day after the queen-mother's interview with the king, the court was surprised by the intelligence that the physician had mistaken the malady of Louise von Schwerin; that it was not scarlet fever, as had been supposed, but some simple eruption, from which she was now entirely .restored.

The little maiden appeared again amongst her companions, and there was no change in her appearance, except a slight pallor. No one was more amazed at her sudden recovery than Louise. With watchful suspicion, she remarked that the queen-mother had resumed her gracious and amiable manner toward her, and seemed entirely to

have forgotten the events of the last few days; her accusations and suspicions seemed quieted as if by a stroke
of magic. In the beginning, Louise believed that this was a
trap laid for her, she was therefore perpetually on her guard;
she did not enter the garden, and was well pleased that
Fritz Wendell had the prudence and forbearance never
to walk to and fro by her chamber, and never to place in her
window the beautiful flowers which she had been wont to
find there every morning. In a short time Louise became
convinced that she was not watched, that there were no
spies about her path; that she was, in fact, perfectly at
liberty to come and go as she pleased. She resumed her
thoughtless manner and childish dreamings, walked daily in
the garden, and took refuge in the green-house. Strange to
say, she never found her beautiful Fritz, never met his glowing, eloquent eyes, never caught even a distant view of his
handsome figure. This sudden disappearance of her lover
made her restless and unhappy, and kindled the flame of
love anew. Louise, who in the loneliness and neglect of her
few days of confinement, had become almost ashamed of her
affair with Fritz Wendell, and begun to repent of her foolish
love, now excited by the obstacles in her path, felt the
whole strength of her passion revive, and was assured of her
eternal constancy.

   " I will overcome all impediments," said this young girl,
"and nothing shall prevent me from playing my romance to
the end. Fritz Wendell loves me more passionately than
any duke or baron will ever love me; he has been made a
prisoner because of his love for me, and that is the reason I
see him no more. But I will save him ; I will set him at
liberty, and then I will flee with him, far, far away into the
wide, wide world where no one shall mock at our love."

   With such thoughts as these she returned from her anxious search in the garden. As she entered her room, she saw

upon her table a superb bouquet, just such a tribute as her loved Fritz had offered daily at her shrine before the queen's unfortunate discovery. With a loud cry of joy she rushed to the table, seized the flowers, and pressed them to her lips; she then sought in the heart of her bouquet for the little note which she had ever before found concealed there.

Truly this bouquet contained also a love-letter, a very tender, glowing love-letter, in which Fritz Wendel implored her to fly with him; to carry out their original plan, and flee with him to Oraienburg, where they would be married by the priest who had been won over by the Prince Augustus William. To-day, yes, this evening at nine o'clock, must the flight take place.

Louise did not hesitate an instant; she was resolved to follow the call of her beloved. A court ball was to take place this evening, and Louise von Schwerin must appear in the suite of the queen; she must find some plausible excuse and remain at home. As the hour for the queen's morning promenade approached, Louise became so suddenly ill that she was forced to ask one of the maids of honor to make her excuses, to return to her room, and lay herself upon the bed.

The queen came herself to inquire after her health, and manifested so much sympathy, so much pity, that Louise was fully assured, and accepted without suspicion the queen's proposal that she should give up the ball, and remain quietly in her room. Louise had now no obstacle to fear; she could make her preparations for flight without interruption.

The evening came. She heard the carriages rolling away with the queen and her suite. An indescribable anxiety oppressed this young girl. The hour of decision was at hand. She felt a maidenly trembling at the thought of her rash imprudence, but the hour was striking—the hour of romantic flight, the hour of meeting with her fond lover.

It seemed to her as if she saw the imploring eyes of Fritz ever before her—as if she heard his loving, persuasive voice. Forgetting all consideration and all modesty, she wrapped herself in her mantle, and drawing the hood tightly over her head, she hastened with flying feet through the corridors and down the steps to the front door of the palace. With a trembling heart she stepped into the street.

Unspeakable terror took possession of her. " What if he was not there ? What if this was a plot, a snare laid for her feet ? But no, no ! " She saw a tall and closely-muffled figure crossing the open square, and coming directly to her. She could not see his face, but it was surely him. Now he was near her. He whispered the signal word in a low, soft tone. With a quaking heart, she gave the answer.

The young man took her cold little hand, and hurried her forward to the corner of the square. There stood the carriage. The stranger lifted her in his arms, and carried her to the carriage, sprang in, and slammed the door. Forward ! The carriage seemed forced onward by the wings of the wind. In a few moments the city lay far behind them. In wild. haste they flew onward, ever onward. The young man, still closely muffled, sat near to Louise—her lover, soon to be her husband ! Neither spoke a word. They were near to each other, with quickly-beating hearts, but silent, still silent.

Louise found this conduct of her lover mysterious and painful. She understood not why he who had been so tender, so passionate, should remain so cold and still by her side. She felt that she must fly far, far away from this unsympathizing lover, who had no longer a word for her, no further assurances of love. Yes, he despised her because she had followed him, no longer thought her worthy of his tenderness. As this thought took possession of her, she gave a fearful shriek, and springing up from her seat, she seized the door, and tried to open it and jump out. The strong hand of her silent lover held her back.

"We have not yet arrived, mademoiselle," whispered he.

Louise felt a cold shudder pass over her. Fritz Wendell call her mademoiselle! and the voice sounded cold and strange. Anxiously, silently, she sank back in the carriage. Her searching glance was fixed upon her companion, but the night was dark. She could see nothing but the mysteriously muffled figure. She stretched her small hands toward him, as if praying for help. He seized them, and pressed them to his heart and lips, but he remained silent. He did not clasp her in his arms as heretofore; he whispered no tender, passionate assurances in her ear. The terror of death overcame Louise. She clasped her hands over her face, and wept aloud. He heard her piteous sobs, and was still silent, and did not seek to comfort her.

Onward went the flying wheels. The horses had been twice changed in order to reach the goal more quickly. Louise wept without ceasing. Exhausted by terror, she thought her death was near. Twice tortured by this ominous silence, she had dared to say a few low, sobbing words to her companion, but he made no reply.

At last the carriage stopped. "We have arrived," he whispered to Louise, sprang from the carriage, and lifted her out.

"Where are we?" she said, convinced that she had been brought to a prison, or some secret place of banishment.

"We are in Qraienburg, and there is the church where the preacher awaits us." He took her arm hastily, and led her into the church. The door was opened, and as Louise stepped upon the threshold, she felt her eyes blinded by the flood of light upon the altar. She saw the priest with his open book, and heard the solemn sounds of the organ. The young man led Louise forward, but not to the altar; he entered first into the sacristy. There also wax lights were burning, and on a table lay a myrtle wreath and a lace veil.

"This is your bridal wreath and veil," said the young man, who still kept the hood of his cloak drawn tightly over his face. He unfastened and removed Louise's mantle, and handed her the veil and wreath. Then he threw back his hood, and removed his cloak. Louise uttered a cry of amazement and horror. He who stood before her was not her lover, was not the gardener Fritz Wendell, but a strange young officer in full-dress uniform!

"Forgive me," said he, "that I have caused you so much suffering to-day, but the king commanded me to remain silent, and I did so. We are here in obedience to the king, and he commanded me to hand you this letter before our marriage. It was written by his own hand. Louise seized the royal letter hastily. It was laconic, but the few words it contained filled the heart of the little maiden with shame. The letter contained these lines:

"As you are resolved, without regard to circumstances, to marry, out of consideration for your family I will fulfil your wish. The handsome gardener-boy is not in a condition to become your husband, he being now confined in a mad-house. I have chosen for you a gallant young officer, of good family and respectable fortune, and I have commanded him to marry you. If he pleases you, the priest will immediately perform the marriage ceremony, and you will follow your husband into his garrison at Brandenburg. If you refuse him, the young officer, Von Cleist, has my command to place you again in the carriage, and take you to your mother. There you will have time to meditate upon your inconsiderate boldness. FREDERICK II."

Louise read the letter of the king again and again; she then fixed her eyes upon the young man who stood before her, and who gazed at her with a questioning and smiling face. She saw that he was handsome, young, and charming, and she confessed that this rich uniform was more attractive than the plain, dark coat of the gardener-boy Fritz Wendell. She felt that the eyes of the young cavalier were as glowing and as eloquent as those of her old love.

"Well," said he, laughing, "have you decided, mademoiselle? Do you consider me worthy to be the envied and blessed husband of the enchanting and lovely Louise von Schwerin, or will you cruelly banish me and rob me of this precious boon?"

She gazed down deep into his eyes and listened to his words breathlessly. His voice was so soft and persuasive, not harsh and rough like that of Fritz Wendell, it fell like music on her ear.

"Well," repeated the young Von Cleist, "will you be gracious, and accept me for your husband?"

"Would you still wish to marry me, even if the king had not commanded it?"

"I would marry you in spite of the king and the whole world," said Von Cleist. "Since I have seen you, I love you dearly."

Louisa reached him her hand.

"Well, then," she said, "let us fulfil the commands of the king. He commands us to marry. We will commence with that: afterwards we will see if we can love each other without a royal command."

The young captain kissed her hand, and placed the myrtle wreath upon her brow.

"Come, the priest is waiting, and I long to call you my bride."

He led the young girl of fourteen to the altar. The priest opened the holy book, and performed the marriage ceremony.

At the same hour, in the chapel of the king's palace, another wedding took place. Laura von Pannewitz and Count Voss stood before the altar. The king himself conducted Laura, and Queen Elizabeth gave her hand to Count Voss. The entire court had followed the bridal pair, and all were witnesses to this solemn contract. Only one was absent—the Prince Augustus William was not there.

While Laura von Pannewitz stood above in the palace chapel, swearing eternal constancy to Count Voss, the prince stood below at the castle gate, waiting for her descent. But the hour had long passed, and she came not. A dark fear and torturing anguish came over him.

Had the king discovered their plan? Was it he who held Laura back, or had she herself forgotten her promise? Was she unfaithful to her oath?

The time still flew, and she came not. Trembling with scorn, anguish, and doubt, he mounted the castle steps, determined to search through the saloons, and, at all risks, to draw near his beloved. Driven by the violence of his love, he had almost determined to carry her off by force.

Throwing off his mantle, he stepped into the ante-room. No man regarded him. Every eye was turned toward the great saloon. The prince entered. The whole court circle, which were generally scattered through the adjoining rooms, now forced themselves into this saloon—it glittered and shimmered with diamonds, orders, and gold and silver embroidery.

The prince saw nothing of all this. He saw only the tall, pallid girl who stood in the middle of the room with the sweeping bridal veil and the myrtle wreath in her hair.

Yes, it was her—Laura von Pannewitz—and near her stood the young, smiling Count Voss. What did all this mean? Why was his beloved so splendidly attired? Why was the royal family gathered around her? Why was the queen kissing even now his beautiful Laura, and handing her this splendid diamond diadem? Why did Count Voss press the king's hand, which was that moment graciously extended to him, to his lips?

Prince Augustus William understood nothing of all this. He felt as if bewildered by strange and fantastic dreams. With distended, glassy eyes he stared upon the newly wedded pair who were now receiving the congratulations of the court.

But the king's sharp glance had observed him, and rapidly forcing his way through the crowd of courtiers, he drew near to the prince. "A word with you, brother," said the king; "come, let us go into my cabinet." The prince followed him, bewildered—scarcely conscious. "And now, my brother," said the king, as the door closed behind him, "show yourself worthy of your kingly calling and of your ancestors; show that you deserve to be the ruler of a great people; show that you know how to govern yourself! Laura von Pannewitz can never be yours; she is the wife of Count Voss!" The prince uttered so piercing, so heart-rending a cry, that the king turned pale, and an unspeakable pity took possession of his soul. "Be brave, my poor brother; what you suffer, that have I also suffered, and almost every one who is called by Fate to fill an exalted position has the same anguish to endure. A prince has not the right to please himself—he belongs to the people and to the world's history, and to both these *he* must be ever secondary."

"It is not true, it is not possible!" stammered the prince. "Laura can never belong to another! she is mine! betrothed to me by the holiest of oaths, and she shall be mine in spite of you and of the whole world! I desire no crown, no princely title; I wish only Laura, only my Laura! I say it is not true that she is the wife of Count Voss!"

"It is true," whispered a soft, tearful, choking voice, just behind him. The prince turned hastily; the sad eye of Laura, full of unspeakable love, met his wild glance. Queen Elizabeth, according to an understanding with the king, had led the young Countess Voss into this apartment, and then returned with a light step to the adjoining room.

"I will grant to your unhappy love, my brother, one last evening glow," said the king. "Take a last, sad farewell of your declining sun; but forget not that when the sun has disappeared, we have still the stars to shine upon us, though, alas! they have no warmth and kindle no flowers into life." The king bowed, and followed his wife into the next room. The prince remained alone with Laura.

What was spoken and sworn in this last sad interview no man ever knew. In the beginning, the king, who remained in the next room, heard the raging voice of the prince uttering wild curses and bitter complaints; then his tones were softer and milder, and touchingly mournful. In half an hour the king entered the cabinet. The prince stood in the middle of the room, and Laura opposite to him. They gazed into each other's wan and stricken faces with steady, tearless eyes; their hands were clasped. "Farewell, my prince," said Laura, with a firm voice; "I depart *immediately* with my husband; we will never meet again!"

"Yes, we will meet again," said the prince, with a weary smile; "we will meet again in another and a better world: I will be there awaiting you, Laura!" They pressed each other's hands, then turned away.

Laura stepped into the room where Count Voss was expecting her. "Come, my husband," she said; "I am ready to follow you, and be assured I will make you a faithful and submissive wife."

"Brother," said Prince Augustus William, extending his hand to the king, "I struggle no more. I will conform myself to your wishes, and marry the Princess of Brunswick."

CHAPTER XVII.

THE RESIGNATION OF BARON PÖLLNITZ.

THE morning after the ball, Pöllnitz entered the cabinet of the king; he was confused and cast down, and that happened to him which had never before happened—he was speechless. The king's eyes rested upon him with an ironical and contemptuous expression.

" I believe you are about to confess your sins, Pöllnitz, and make me your father confessor. You have the pitiful physiognomy of a poor sinner."

"Sire, I would consent to be a sinner, but I am bitterly opposed to being a poor sinner."

" Ah! debts again; again in want!" cried the king. " I am weary of this everlasting litany, and I forbid you to come whining to me again with your never-ending necessities; the evil a man brings upon himself he must bear; the dangers which he involuntarily incurs, he must conquer himself."

" Will not your majesty have the goodness to assist me, to reach me a helping hand and raise me from the abyss into which my creditors have cast me?"

"God forbid that I should waste the gold upon a Pöllnitz which I need for my brave soldiers and for cannon!" said the king, earnestly.

"Then, sire," said Pöllnitz, in a low and hesitating tone, " I must beg you to give me my dismissal."

" Your dismissal! Have you discovered in the moon a foolish prince who will pay a larger sum for your miserable jests and malicious scandals and railings than the King of Prussia?"

"Not in the moon, sire, is such a mad individual to be found, but in a Dutch realm; however, I have found no such prince, but a beautiful young maiden, who will be only too happy to be the Baroness Pöllnitz, and pay the baron's debts."

"And this young girl is not sent to a mad-house?" said the king; "perhaps the house of the Baron von Pöllnitz is considered a house of correction, and she is sent there to be punished for her follies. Has the girl who is rich enough to pay the debts of a Pöllnitz no guardian?"

"Father and mother both live, sire; and both receive me joyfully as their son. My bride dwells in Nuremberg, and is the daughter of a distinguished patrician family."

"And she buys you," said the king, " because she considers you the most enchanting of all Nuremberger toys! As for your dismissal, I grant it to you with all my heart. Seat yourself and write as I shall dictate."

He looked toward the writing-table, and Pöllnitz, obeying his command, took his seat and arranged his pen and paper. The king, with his arms folded across his back, walked slowly up and down the room.

"Write! I will give you a dismissal, and also a certificate of character and conduct."

The king dictated to the trembling and secretly enraged baron the following words:

" We, Frederick II., make known, that Baron Pöllnitz, born in Berlin, and, so far as we believe, of an honorable family, page to our sainted grandfather, of blessed memory, also in the service of the Duke of Orleans, colonel in the Spanish service, cavalry captain in the army of the deceased Emperor, gentleman-in-waiting to the Pope, gentleman-in-waiting to the Duke of Brunswick, color-bearer in the ser-

vice of the Duke of Weimar, gentleman-in-waiting to our
sainted father, of ever-blessed memory; lastly, and at last,
master of ceremonies in our service;—said Baron Pöllnitz,
overwhelmed by this stream of military and courtly honors
which had been thrust upon him, and thereby weary of
the vanities of this wicked world; misled, also, by the evil
example of Monteulieu, who, a short time ago, left the court,
now entreats of us to grant him his dismissal, and an honorable testimony as to his good name and service. After
thoughtful consideration, we do not find it best to refuse
him the testimony he has asked for. As to the most important service which he rendered to the court by his foolish
jests and *inconsistencies*, and the pastimes and distractions
which he prepared for nine years for the amusement of our
ever-blessed father, we do not hesitate to declare that, during the whole time of his service at court, he was not a
street-robber nor a cut-purse, nor a poisoner; that he did
not rob young women or do them any violence; that he has
not roughly attacked the honor of any man, but, consistently with his birth and lineage, behaved like a man of gallantry; that he has consistently made use of the talents lent to
him by Heaven, and brought before the public, in a merry
and amusing way, that which is ridiculous and laughable
amongst men, no doubt with the same object which lies at
the bottom of all theatrical representations, that is, to improve the race. Said baron has also steadily followed the
counsel of Bacchus with regard to frugality and temperance,
and he has carried his Christian love so far, that he has left
wholly to the *peasants* that part of the Evangelists which
teaches that 'To give is more blessed than to receive.' He
knows all the anecdotes concerning our castles and pleasure
resorts, and has indelibly imprinted upon his memory a full
list of all our old furniture and silver; above all things, he
understands how to make himself indispensable and agree-

19

able to those who know the malignity of his spirit and his cold heart.

"As, however, in the most fruitful regions waste and desert spots are to be found, as the most beautiful bodies have their deformities, and the greatest painters are not without faults, so will we deal gently and considerately with the follies and sins of this much-talked-of baron; we grant him, therefore, though unwillingly, the desired dismissal. In addition to this, we abolish entirely this office so worthily filled by said baron, and wish to blot out the remembrance of it from the memory of man; holding that no other man can ever fill it satisfactorily. FREDERICK II."

www.ingramcontent.com/pod-product-compliance
Lightning Source LLC
Chambersburg PA
CBHW030946110726
47900CB00004B/1155